PENGUIN CANADA

THE VIOLENT FRIENDSHIP
OF ESTHER JOHNSON

TRUDY J. MORGAN-COLE lives in St. John's, Newfoundland. She published several works of young-adult fiction before writing *The Violent Friendship of Esther Johnson*, which won the H.R. (Bill) Percy Prize for Unpublished Novel in Atlantic Writing Competition in 2000. After working as a high-school teacher for many years, Trudy now teaches English and creative writing to adult learners. She is married to Jason Cole and has two children, Christopher and Emma.

The violent friendship of Esther Johnson

TRUDY J. MORGAN–COLE

PENGUIN
CANADA

PENGUIN CANADA

Published by the Penguin Group

Penguin Group (Canada), 90 Eglinton Avenue East, Suite 700, Toronto, Ontario, Canada
M4P 2Y3 (a division of Pearson Penguin Canada Inc.)

Penguin Group (USA) Inc., 375 Hudson Street, New York, New York 10014, U.S.A.
Penguin Books Ltd, 80 Strand, London WC2R 0RL, England
Penguin Ireland, 25 St Stephen's Green, Dublin 2, Ireland (a division of Penguin Books Ltd)
Penguin Group (Australia), 250 Camberwell Road, Camberwell, Victoria 3124, Australia
(a division of Pearson Australia Group Pty Ltd)
Penguin Books India Pvt Ltd, 11 Community Centre, Panchsheel Park, New Delhi – 110 017,
India
Penguin Group (NZ), cnr Airborne and Rosedale Roads, Albany, Auckland 1310, New Zealand
(a division of Pearson New Zealand Ltd)
Penguin Books (South Africa) (Pty) Ltd, 24 Sturdee Avenue, Rosebank, Johannesburg 2196,
South Africa

Penguin Books Ltd, Registered Offices: 80 Strand, London WC2R 0RL, England

First published 2006

1 2 3 4 5 6 7 8 9 10 (WEB)

*Publisher's note: This book is a work of fiction. Names, characters, places and incidents either
are the product of the author's imagination or are used fictitiously, and any
resemblance to actual persons living or dead, events, or locales is entirely coincidental.*

Manufactured in Canada.

LIBRARY AND ARCHIVES CANADA CATALOGUING IN PUBLICATION

Morgan-Cole, Trudy J.
The violent friendship of Esther Johnson / Trudy Morgan-Cole.

ISBN 0-14-301768-3

1. Johnson, Esther, 1681–1728—Fiction. 2. Swift, Jonathan, 1667–1745—Fiction. I. Title.
PS8626.O747V56 2006   C813'.6   C2005-904967-7

Visit the Penguin Group (Canada) website at **www.penguin.ca**

For the members of the Guild ...
my mentors, my community,
my extended family of writers,
with all my thanks

I know not what I am saying;
but believe me that violent friendship is much more lasting
and as much engaging as violent love.

JONATHAN SWIFT
writing to a mutual friend about
Esther Johnson shortly before her death

MOOR PARK, SURREY, ENGLAND
DECEMBER 28, 1694

I sett my pen to paper to write this Journal, which I intend to keep for the Improvement of my Mind. It is my intention to continue the Education which my good Tutor began in me, and yet I do fear that without his discerning Tutelage and his kindly Hand to guide Mee, I shall become shallow, and vain, and frivolous, which faults in Woman he ever condemned, and strove to train my Mind in such a way that I might grow to be studious, grave, and sober, not as other young women are, and such Virtues I do heartily wish to cultivate in myself. But alas! without his gentle guidance who so long has been my Help, how shall I have any hope of success? This Journal is the record of my struggle, and I keep it, to show no other ey's but his, should he return here to us, which I think not likely, but if he do, he shall see how I have endeavoured to please him and to follow his Instruction, while he is himself absent.

I see I have begunne this my Journal in most haphazard fashion, so that Mr Swift would chide me for it were he here. I should properly introduce myself as Esther Johnson, thirteen years of Age, living at Moor Park in Surrey. Moor Park is the home of Sir William Temple, a very great Man; my mother is his housekeeper. So you see I am no great lady, with little enough to boast of, save for the kindness of my Benefactors.

We are in the midst of the twelve merry days of Christmas, yet this day's merriment has been something clouded by the news Lord and Lady Onslow brought when they came tonight, that the Queen is ill. These tidings sore distress'd Lady Temple, who is the Queen's great Friend. I ought to saie that Lady Temple is Sir William's wife, our mistress here, though in truth it seems more Lady Giffard who is mistress. She is Sir William's sister, a very grand lady, and very learned. I should aspire to be like her in Learning, though not in Temper, I think. Lady Temple is far Sweeter, but she is often gone, being in London with Queen Mary. Only now the Queen is ill, and Lady Temple, I think, is not in good Health herselfe, and is worried for her friend the Queen.

But tonight we were merry indeed, in spite of the sad news. After a dinner of goose and chicken and meat pasties and roast pork finished with jellies, almonds and raisins, came mummers from the village and everyone, family, servants and all, met in the Great Hall to watch them play. And there was dancing, and Sir William and Lady Temple did lead the dance, and she look'd well, and all danced and sang and had good Cheer.

I had meant to write more about what happened today, before the dinner and the mummers, I mean. About Mrs Dingley in the brew house, and Jamie and the cottage, but I am tired; my eyes ache. I will write more tomorrow, but not so long or so Tedious.

Esther Johnson

Esther is reading through her journal. The old bound book, the first of several on the table before her, was a gift that year, her thirteenth Christmas. A gift from whom? Sir William, no doubt—who else could have, would have, given her an empty book? But its pages do not reach back as far as she wants to go tonight, back to her childhood, to the beginning of her life at Moor Park.

She opens the book on the desk, viewing the creased paper in the light of two tall wax candles, a surer and steadier glow than the sputtering rush lights she had used when she wrote those early entries. She remembers candle making at Moor Park: beeswax candles for the Great Hall, tallow for the kitchen, the workrooms, and the family bedrooms, and finally dipping rushes into the mutton fat to make the cheap candles considered good enough to light children and servants to bed—good enough for her, little Hetty, both servant and child.

Lady and mistress herself now, though not of a grand house like Moor Park, she sometime indulges in wax candles when she writes at night. She justifies the expense with the excuse of her eyes, though in fact she should not be writing after dark at all. Perhaps she should not even be writing. The headaches and blurred vision grow worse and worse. But that thought—a life without the written word—is too bleak to dwell on.

On the table before her is the untidy evidence of thirty years' scribbling: journal entries, letters, poems going back to that distant childhood world of Moor Park. How little she had written down in the journal at first—how cautious she had been! She had been thinking, perhaps, of Jonathan Swift returning someday, of showing him her journal, the life record of an educated young woman. She would have written down nothing she would not have wanted him to see.

She is not so careful anymore. She does not imagine showing her journal to anyone, least of all Jonathan Swift, while she lives. And when she dies? What matter, then, if anyone reads it? But no, perhaps she will burn it. If she were a famous man, it might be read, copied, published. But she is a woman, and no one need ever know what she thought.

On the desk beside her journals, set apart a little from them, is a letter in another hand, a letter she received only a few hours ago. One from a woman who never learned caution, who never rationed her words for fear of the eyes that might read them. That letter sent her on this mad midnight hunt through her own past, looking for some key, something to explain how things had turned out as they had.

She feels nothing but contempt for the letter's author, a woman utterly at the mercy of her own violent passions. Esther is a reasonable woman. She believes that reason has governed her life, all her loves, all her choices. But if that is so, why is she awake in the hours between midnight and dawn, driven to a distracted search through her own written past, all because of a few words on a page?

Perhaps, she thinks, she was not always this person, this calm and reasoned woman. She is peering back, trying to remember herself. The thought that she cannot recall who she is fills her with terror. Whom has she allowed herself to become, to be molded into?

She leafs ahead through the journal pages until a line leaps out: *I satt this Night besyde the body of Lady Temple, who pass'd to her Rest about Sunsett, and in that Room where her Corpse lay I did a deede I knowe I ought nott to have Done, yett I cannot find it in myself to Regret. How strange that picking up a bundle of old Papers should open the Doore to another World, another Life ...*

Here, for the first time, the young writer had let her caution slip, had allowed a hint of her tangled emotions onto the page. That night, perhaps for the first time, she had written without the imagined eyes of Jonathan Swift staring over her shoulder. Indeed, the night Lady Temple died she had hardly thought of him at all.

MOOR PARK
1694–1695

Queen Mary died the same night the mummers came to Moor Park, though days passed before the Temple household learned the news. Lady Temple took to her bed at once, her already fragile constitution crushed by her friend's death. Esther, poised on the edge of her fourteenth birthday, was from Christmas onward a member of a household that seemed to wait with held breath by its lady's bedside. Lady Temple had never been the true mistress of Moor Park—that had ever been

Lady Giffard's role, while Lady Temple, so often away at Court, had been loved by all the household—perhaps loved the more because she kept her distance. Esther took her turn along with her mother, Bridget, and Mrs. Dingley and Jane Swift to bring tea and broth and various ill-tasting drenches to the invalid. Her room was darkened: she lay, a small figure in a large bed, dwarfed by the draperies around and above her. Esther knew from the Sir Peter Lely portrait of her in the Long Gallery that Lady Temple had been beautiful when she was young, but years ago she had survived the smallpox and her skin now was pockmarked as well as wrinkled. She lay with her iron-grey hair combed out and spread all across the pillow, a startling sight to Esther who had never seen the mistress without her hair carefully powdered and piled behind a stiff frontage. When Esther tiptoed to her bedside, Lady Temple's eyelids fluttered, then lifted to reveal dark eyes, huge in her gaunt face.

"She'll not live out the month, the physician assures me of that," Lady Giffard was saying to Mrs. Dingley when Esther went back down to the housekeeper's room. "I feel as if I am caring for two invalids, not one, for Papa is prostrate with grief." Lady Giffard always called her brother Papa. "He loves her to distraction—always has. Ah, Hetty, did she drink the tea? Good, very good. The doctor says it will ease her pain and help her to sleep. Now, run to the kitchen with this list and give it to your mother or Mrs. Mose—it is for tomorrow's dinner, though I hardly think there will be dinner in the hall. Papa will want to continue taking his meals in his rooms, no doubt, and I will have mine brought to Lady Temple's chamber."

It was like that for a month—the house busy with the doctors coming and going, special meals and draughts and physicks being prepared, special food to be sent in, and even, at the beginning of February, a trip by Esther and her mother to the clothier's in Farnham to purchase several bolts of black stuff.

"Isn't it dreadful?" Esther asked her mother as they rode back from Farnham past rolling fields that were already showing green again, under bare branches that soon would unfurl into bud. "How would Lady Temple feel if she knew we were buying cloth for mourning clothes?"

Bridget Johnson, her hands on the reins and her eyes on the road, clicked her tongue. "Lady Temple knows nothing of it, nor ever will. It's Lady Giffard who rules the roost, and she's nothing if not practical."

And then, when Death came, it was almost unnoticed. Esther did not know what she had been expecting—a great bell to toll? a darkness to fall across the house?—but when Mrs. Dingley came into the housekeeper's room during supper and said, "Lady Temple died at five o'clock," she felt curiously let down and was at once ashamed of that feeling. She could not help thinking that this death, so long expected, was in some ways like the long-ago death of her father—the loss of someone who had never really been there.

"Sit down, Dingley, you look wretched," said Esther's mother, pulling back a chair at the table. Mr. and Mrs. Mose and Thomas Swift were eating with them; Jane Swift was at the cottage eating with her sister-in-law, Lucy, who was in the last days of her confinement. Dingley sank gratefully into the chair.

"This last three days, I doubt I've slept above an hour together," she said, downing the glass of small beer Mr. Mose poured for her. "Lady Giffard and I have taken it in turns to sit up with her, and there's always something wants doing. And Sir William—poor man—he came down today, and sat there for hours, just holding her hand and staring at her. But he left at four, and she lived another hour past that. Lady Giffard was with her at the last. Her ladyship's gone now to lie down for an hour—I told her she must, but there's so much to be done …"

"And well I know it," said Esther's mother, pushing back her chair. "I must send Nell down to the village for the seamstresses, and we'll to work tonight on the mourning clothes, for I'm sure her ladyship will want everyone in mourning by tomorrow."

"Has she been laid out yet? Has the carpenter got her coffin finished?" asked Mr. Mose, rising from the table. "Come, Parson, we men must see what arrangements are being made about the funeral. Will Sir William be able to talk to us at all, do you think?"

And he and Thomas Swift were gone too, and Mrs. Mose stood up and started to clear the table, saying, "Mrs. Dingley, do you know anything at all of the funeral dinner? When it's to be, or what Lady Giffard will want, or how many? I'll send down to the farm tonight for some hogs and order them to slaughter a cow, just to be sure …"

Esther, too, was clearing away the supper dishes as the others went about their work. Only Rebecca Dingley was left sitting, looking as if she had no strength to stand. Her dull brown wispy hair was all escaping in loose strands from the pins under her cap, and her usually pleasant round face wore a vacant expression. Her eyelids drooped. Esther felt a sudden rush of tenderness for poor Dingley.

"Becca, you must take your own advice. You need a rest as much as Lady Giffard does, I'm sure. Why don't you go lie down?"

Dingley's eyes opened. "As if I could! Don't you know, Hetty, someone's got to sit up with the corpse? Sir William is in there with her now—he wanted to be left alone with the body—but he'll need to go rest in a few moments and someone will have to sit up the night with her. Lady Giffard is worn out and everyone else is so busy—I don't see who it can be if not me."

"I will do it," said Esther quickly, before she could form too clear a picture in her head of dead Lady Temple in her dark room. "I haven't anything special to do; I'll sit by her."

"What? A child like you? It's not to be thought of."

"I'm not a child, Becca, I'm fourteen years old. It won't fright me to sit beside poor Lady Temple's body. Get you to bed."

Dingley took very little persuading. So it was Esther, not she, who went up an hour later to Lady Temple's bedchamber and tapped lightly on the door. Sir William's voice sounded as though he were at the bottom of a well rather than behind an oak door. "Come in."

The room was no longer as dark as it had been. Someone—Dingley, perhaps?—had lit wax candles all around, in the sconces on the walls, on the table beside the bed, and on the dressing table across the room. Lady Temple, in the middle of the bed, looked just as she had looked for days, though the candles gave her ashen face a lovely glow and made her look, Esther thought, a bit like a picture of some very old lady saint. Lady Giffard and Dingley must have already done the laying-out, for the great eyes were closed, the grey hair combed, and the thin hands folded above the coverlet. Sir William sat beside her; his waistcoat was unbuttoned, his white hair askew: He had been sitting with his head in his hands, and at his feet was a bundle of papers tied with ribbon.

"I've come, sir, to sit by the … by her ladyship, sir, so you … I don't mean to disturb. If you wish to be alone with her, I'll wait—"

"No, no—come in. I cannot stay …" He looked about, as if he were not sure he remembered where he was. "Sit down,

Mrs. Johnson, thank you, I'm most grateful." He gestured to a chair on the other side of the bed. Esther sat down, uneasy. He did not recognize her—thought she was her mother, whom she scarcely resembled. Was he so disordered in his grief that he was going to stop knowing who people were, like madmen and very old people? He rose slowly and bent to pick up the papers that had lain at his feet, then reached out for her unsteadily, grasped her shoulder. He might have been only steadying himself, but there was an intimacy in the gesture quite unlike the many times he had patted her hair and embraced her as a little girl. He was about to say something. His eyes fixed on hers, blurred, focused—she found herself afraid of what he might say—and then something changed in his face, and he said, "I am sorry—Miss Hetty, it's you, is it not?" He paused a moment; she could hear his breath. Then he said, "This is a sober duty for one so young."

"This is a sober time, sir," she said, rather pleased with having found such a good answer so quickly.

He nodded and looked down at the papers in his hand. "I was reading these—her letters. She wrote them to me when she was young—before we married. You never knew her when she was ... young, and so full of life, before we lost our babies, and ... I wish you children could have known her as she was then." He stood up, clutching the little bundle of papers, and started for the door, stopped to button his waistcoat, fumbled after the first two buttons, and started out again, nodding and groping ahead of him like a blind man.

He left the papers on the dressing table, Esther realized a moment later; probably he had laid them down when he tried to button his coat. They sat there in an untidy pile, and although she thought at first of gathering them up and running after

Sir William, she did not. He wished Esther had known Lady Temple when she was younger. And there was Lady Temple, her younger self, in that pile of papers. It was a great temptation to go over and pick them up. But she would not, of course. Even if it were not a betrayal of trust, it would be too eerie to sit beside a dead woman, reading letters she had written in her youth—like trying to conjure her spirit, and Esther did not want to wake any uneasy shades.

She was already regretting the ease with which she had made her offer to Dingley. It was well enough, down in the house-keeper's room among company, to talk of sitting by a dead woman all through the night. It was quite different to be here, with all the candles, and Sir William acting so strangely, and Lady Temple lying on the bed but no sound of shallow, raspy breathing to fill the room any longer. Esther was not so very pious, but piety was meant for moments like this: she picked up Lady Temple's prayer book from the table and read some prayers aloud, and sat for a while with her fingers running over the pink roses embroidered on the cover of the book, trying hard to feel that God was there, come to take Lady Temple to heaven.

Strange that it should be so hard to imagine God at a time when it was so easy to imagine every other kind of shade and spirit. The walls of Lady Temple's bedchamber were hung with vast tapestries, their colours vivid in daylight but barely visible now. Unlike the ones downstairs in the public rooms, these tapestries had not been bought but had all been stitched by Lady Temple and Lady Giffard themselves: they depicted hunting scenes that seemed cheerful and pastoral when viewed in daytime. Now it was too easy to imagine when a breeze stirred the tapestry that one of the shadow picture trees was moving in its own phantom breeze, to see a dark embroidered figure move out from the blackness between those trees, to hear the far-off trill of the hunting horns. As a child, first come to Moor Park, Esther had looked at the splendid paintings and sculptures and tapestries and dreamed they might come to life, talking and moving about on their own. The idea suddenly seemed possible again, but no longer pleasant. She was sure she heard the baying of the hounds.

She looked away, but figures were worked everywhere: in the wall hangings, the bed hangings, the carpets. A looking glass hung over the dressing table and reflected back another roomful of candles and shadows; Esther moved across the room to close it and was sorry she had. The doors covering the glass were covered in the raised work that had been popular when Lady Temple was a girl, so that the little figures lifted off their silk background and seemed almost alive. Esther stood unable to move, her fingers tracing the tiny heads and bodies: the embroidery told the tale of Jephthah's daughter in Scriptures. There she was, her embroidered hair streaming behind her, racing with joy toward the father who had vowed to sacrifice her in the flames—

No more of this—this would make her run mad. How many hours could she stay here looking at everything but the corpse, imagining the very pictures on the walls were moving about? And the prayer book made things better, not worse … *Ashes to ashes, dust to dust … In the midst of life, we are in death …* She needed a diversion, and Sir William would never know if she read the letters. Perhaps, she tried unsuccessfully to convince herself, perhaps he had left them here with that very thought in mind. She knew he had had no thought in his mind at all—he was distracted and had forgotten; and he certainly would not want his housekeeper's daughter prying into his old love letters.

But the letters were here, and they were the only things in the room that did not seem haunted.

She turned away from the dressing table and then back to it, making the candles flicker with her passing, and she picked up the letters. Sir William and Lady Temple, she knew, had had a famous romance—they had courted for nearly seven years before both families had agreed to the match. The letters, tied around with faded ribbon, looked very old—as indeed they were. *Forty years ago,* Esther thought, and untied the bundle. She picked up the first one to read.

The handwriting was unfamiliar, the light dim, and the paper cramped and crowded, since Lady Temple—young Dorothy Osborne, as she was then—had turned her paper sideways when she finished each page and filled up the margins with writing too. Still, by the second or third letter Esther could not have been startled from her reading if the corpse beside her had sat up and spoken. The letters were alive—far more alive than Lady Temple had been even before her death, more alive than Sir William. A young woman in her twenties sat just on the other side of each page, hidden from view but speaking in a voice so vigorous that it was almost audible. Dorothy Osborne had been melancholy and suffered from the spleen in her girlhood as she had in her later life, and complained plenty about the various physicks she took for it, but there was a strength and humour in her written words that belied her protestations of unhappiness. When Sir William (whose letters were absent) must have warned her to take care of her poor health, she replied,

The truth is I cannot deny but that I have bin very carelesse of myself but alas who would have bin other? I never thought my life a thing worth my care whilst nobody was concern'd

in't but my self, now I shall looke upon't as something that
you would not loose, and therefore shall indeavour to keep it
for you. But then you must retourne my kindenesse with the
same care of a life that's much dearer to me.

For all the stories Esther had heard of the Temples' romance, she had never been able to picture them young and passionately in love, but now she saw in Dorothy's own hand the plea, *O, if you do not send me long letters then you are the Cruellest person that can bee. If you love me you will and if you do not I shall never love myeselfe.* His love for her was *all that I propose of happinesse to myeself in the world.*

The course of their love had not run easily; Esther discovered in the letters what she had already heard in family stories, that both Temples and Osbornes were ambitious to make better marriages for their children. Though Dorothy Osborne had apparently loved to read romances, and was ever recommending them or sending copies to her beloved, she did not fancy herself living a romance: there was no talk in her letters of dying for love. Rather, she said,

Nothing can alter the resolution I have taken of settling mye
whole stock of happinesse upon the affection of a person that
is dear to mee ..., and I shall not blush to tell you, that you
have made the whole world besides so indifferent to mee,
that if I cannot bee yours They may dispose mee how they
please.

It was a jarring practicality to realize that the heroine of the romance was quite willing to be married off to someone else if she could not have her prince, though she did not care who and had no intention of being happy with another. In another place, when again it seemed unlikely they could ever marry, she wrote: *I was borne to bee very happy or very miserable, I know not which, but I am certaine that as long as I am anything I shall be your most faithfull friend and Servant, Dorothy Osborne.*

Esther looked up at those words. She was well past the halfway point in the letters and, she thought, in her night watch as well, for the candles were burning low. Lady Temple lay as still as ever on the bed, and for the first time Esther felt a profound sense of loss that the old woman was gone, gone forever, that she could never wake her and say, "Lady Temple, which was it? Were you very happy, or very miserable? Or neither?" It was, Esther thought, the best thing to hope for out of life—that there would be no dull middling way but either great joy or great tragedy. Which had Lady Temple had? When she was young Dorothy, writing these letters, surely she had thought that if she married William Temple she would be very happy, and very miserable if not. But had it happened that way? They seemed to have loved each other, but then all their children had died, and all in all it seemed as though they had been sometimes happy and sometimes miserable, like most folk, with no great extremes. If only, if only there was some way to keep that bright candle of passion burning ever, not to let it gutter down into married middle age, and then old age and finally this, this silence on a bed in a dark room. Esther's throat tightened, and tears blurred her eyes as she went back to the letters.

She read on, to the ending just before their marriage—the happy ending, with everything resolved and the lovers united. But it was not the real ending, was it? The real ending was here, in this room, and every fairy tale and romance that ended with a happy marriage was only hiding the true ending that waited ahead. Grey light came to the room, and Esther sat, the letters on her lap, wishing she had left them untouched, wishing she had read them while Lady Temple yet lived, wishing she had known that Lady Temple, or any old person, had ever had such thoughts and feelings as these. *If I had known,* Esther thought, *I could have asked* ... ah, but what? There was the rub; she did not know what she could have asked.

A knock came on the door; Esther said, "Come in," mechanically. Her mother stood outside, and it took a moment to remember who she was, when and where one was.

"Are you well, Hetty?" Bridget was more solicitous than was her wont, and very apologetic for having left her daughter alone there all night, but there had been so much work for everyone to do that *none* had got a wink of sleep. "You go to my room, now, and lie down—all's well in order, and you've done your duty," said Bridget.

Esther heard all this as though it came from very far away. She nodded at her mother, tied the letters back into their bundle on the dressing table, stood up, and left the room, shutting the door behind her. In after years she was to recall the shutting of that door and put to the moment words she had not thought at the time: that she was closing the door on her childhood.

DUBLIN
1723

She has not thought of that night, of Dorothy Osborne's letters and her own candlelit vigil, for years. The moment leaps from the page to her memory as vividly as if this were that same death chamber. Esther looks at her own bed and sees herself on the pillows, hair spread out around her, peaceful as old Lady Temple. *Not yet,* she thinks. *A few more years, please.* Lady Temple was sixty-seven; Esther is forty-two.

She had reached out blindly that night, for a choice—the heights and depths of passion, the life of great misery or great joy, over the mild, cautious middle way. Looking through the papers before her, she wonders now where the weight of evidence lies? Esther sees no bundle of cherished love letters tied with a faded ribbon. She sees, instead, her journals, letters from friends and correspondents in England and Ireland, the manuscript of Swift's latest pamphlet with the fair copy she is transcribing for him, a small pile of letters from Jonathan Swift to herself. This is what she has—notes from Swift in London, filled with complicated puns and literary gossip, assuring her that he has bought her a pair of spectacles and delivered a parcel to her mother. If some young girl—Jenny, perhaps—were to sit by this bed and watch over dead Esther, read through these letters and journals, would she find any hint of that long-ago choice? Could she guess that young Esther Johnson had once dreamed of a life of violent passion, of glory and despair?

It was not a choice Jonathan Swift would have approved. Her tutor's name appears rarely in this first year of journal pages: he was not then living at Moor Park, having returned to Ireland on another of his endless attempts to forge a career for himself. His presence, in those first journals, is that of a distant guardian spirit, the mentor to whom young Esther addressed her lofty goals and aspirations. Yet her own handwriting, looking back at her from the page, resembles his; even then, at thirteen, she had begun to copy his hand. By now one can scarcely tell her writing and his apart: friends who receive letters from them both often remark on the likeness.

She picks up the journal again, but it does not go back far enough. She wants to go further back, to see through the eyes of Esther as a child, newly come to Moor Park, to her first meeting with Jonathan Swift. But in those days she kept no journal, and only memory can take her there.

Part One

MOOR PARK
1689–1699

MOOR PARK, SURREY, ENGLAND
1689–1690

Esther was called Hetty then, eight years old and small for her age. She sat at the bottom of the great carved staircase in the big house called Moor Park, and wondered if she was going to be ill again, because the whole of the Great Hall seemed to be spinning gently around her. But perhaps it was only that everything was so huge, so strange and new, that her life had been so suddenly uprooted and changed.

Only her mother was familiar, yet she too was changed by the move to Moor Park. A fortnight earlier, Mother had been kneeling on the bedroom floor in their rooms above the shop in Richmond, folding her own clothes and Hetty's into a square leatherbound trunk, its black bindings gone rusty with age. The room was dim because Hetty was only just better of her fever and could not bear the sunlight. She sat cross-legged on the bed she shared with her sister, Nancy, rolling stockings as her mother folded drawers and vests.

"But why cannot Nancy come with us?" Hetty repeated. "Why must she go to London?"

Mother's lips tightened; she stood up to shake out her one good petticoat and folded it briskly. "Nancy will be well cared for by Cousin Maria's family in London—and so will Neddy. And you will be with me at Moor Park, and very lucky to be so. You will have advantages you could never have here—learning the work of a great house, living among the gentry. You must be grateful that Sir William allows me to bring you." She tucked a red curl under her cap, then reached forward and did the same with a twist of her daughter's black hair.

Mother's everyday petticoat went in next; she was wearing her other one. "Shall I ever see Nancy again?" asked Hetty. She ought to have included Neddy in the question, but he was only ten months old and more of a nuisance than anything.

"Not for a long time, most like. Pass me those stockings." Mother began stuffing stockings into the toes of Hetty's boots. And no more was said of Nancy and Neddy's new home in London.

And soon, nothing was said of the old home in Richmond—the slope-roofed attic room where Nancy and Hetty had slept on one side of the curtain and Mother with Neddy on the other, the shop below with its mingling of smells, its barrels of tea and sugar and spices and all the other mysterious things that came off Papa's ship. Hetty sat on the bottom of the great staircase at Moor Park and tried to remember the sights and smells of the Richmond house and shop and found them already vanishing, crowded to the back of her mind. If she lay on her back now—and no one came to shoo her away to the back stairs—she could see the oak panels with their intricate carving, soaring all the way up to the third storey. The carved eagle on the bottom newel post seemed poised in mid-flight, ready to swoop down and catch her up in its claws as if she were a mouse; it was made so that you could feel every feather if you reached up to touch it. She did not go near the lion on the second-storey post: its terrible teeth were too real. On either side of the black-and-gold lacquer cabinet from mysterious Japan were two stern portraits of Sir William's ancestors wearing old-fashioned but grand clothes, and on the table by the door was a marble head of a man. Liza called it a "bust," though it was certainly a head; she also said it was of a god.

And here now was Liza, come to drag her out into the garden. Liza was so little, younger even than Nancy, that Hetty was often tempted to tell her to run away and play by herself, but of course that could not be done and she went meekly out with Liza to the garden, to sit on the edge of the Diana fountain and float leaf boats on water that danced in the October sunshine. From the fountain she gazed up at the stately bulk of Moor Park, shaded from them by a long double row of elms, towering over its gardens and the two little girls playing there.

"My boat went down, Hetty! Make me another boat!" Hetty dragged her attention away from the manor house and toward Miss Liza Temple, the granddaughter of that house, whose chubby fingers tried vainly to stick a spear of grass back onto a raft made of an inch or two of tree bark. Hetty took it from her, explaining as she reassembled the toy boat.

"We shall need another leaf for a sail," she said, and Liza willingly hopped down and ran to pluck one. Hetty had done the same less than two years ago when Jim Saunders, the innkeeper's son in Richmond, had shown her how to make a boat. She put the sail on and launched the little boat on the smooth water of the fountain, sped on its way with a puff of breath from Liza's round cheeks.

"That's splendid, Hetty!" They watched as the little craft drifted toward the bubbly water in the centre of the fountain, at the base of the pillar where the lady called Diana eternally bent her marble bow toward the elm trees. Hetty much preferred this Diana to the one in the Great Hall, who had her bow and arrows slung over her back and a poor dead rabbit dangling by the ears from her hand. She looked powerful and strong with her bow, but it would be much nicer if she was just shooting at the butts instead of at rabbits.

Liza was not very good company. She was four years old, and sometimes Hetty felt more like her nursemaid than her friend. She was certainly poor compensation for Nancy and for her friends back in Richmond—Jim and Harry Saunders, and Mabel Gilbert, the blacksmith's daughter. But Liza was a lady. And Hetty's mother had told her to be especially nice to Liza because Liza's father was dead.

Hetty had wanted to point out that no one had ever had to be especially nice to *her* because her father was dead. But it would have been impertinent to speak so to Mother, and besides that, she sensed that the loss of Papa had not been a tragedy of the same kind as the loss of Liza's father. Though Mama had worn black dresses for a while after the news came that Papa's ship had been lost, and made Hetty and Nancy wear them too, life in the shop and the rooms above had not changed greatly with his death. He had been so rarely at home. His last visit had been ages ago, months before Neddy was born, even, and he was already drowned before his youngest son came into the world. Hetty remembered her father: a bristly beard and a rough coat that smelt of fish, salt, and tobacco.

Liza was dressed head to toe in mourning black except for the white of her coif and cravat, and a mask of fine green linen that was supposed to be keeping the sun off her face but that lay discarded on the ground at her feet. Inside the house somewhere, Liza's mama was no doubt dabbing her eyes with a scented handkerchief and saying sad low things in French to Liza's French *grandmaman*, Madame du Plessis, while the other grandmother, Lady Temple, would be up in her room with the blinds drawn, talking to no one. Liza's grandfather, Sir William, would be reading in the library and shaking his head sadly; they were all in mourning, quite a long way in. Hetty had decided during her short weeks at Moor Park that Sir William's sister, Lady Giffard, was the only member of the family who was not sad: she seemed to be a great angry whirlwind that managed the house and scolded children and servants, but Hetty had not been able to judge yet if her anger was because of the tragedy or if she was like this always.

Despite the mourning, Hetty thought it might be nice to go find Liza's mother, who spoke French. Hetty wanted to learn French; she thought it would be very useful as well as cultured. Liza knew it of course because her mother and grandmother were French, but all ladies learned French anyway. And Liza was a lady, or would be when she grew up. Hetty was very interested in ladies: she had never had much opportunity to observe any at close range before, and suddenly here she was at Moor Park, surrounded by them.

Any passerby would know at once which of the girls was the little lady and which the young servant girl by the sheen of Liza's dark silks and the sheerness of her holland linens. The passerby, too, might have thought the age difference between them less than it was, for Liza with her thick honey-gold curls and rounded pink cheeks was both tall and big for her four years, and Hetty knew herself to be thin, short, and so sallow-skinned that with her dark hair and eyes her papa had sometimes called her "the little gypsy."

"Ooh! It's gone over!" Liza's small round hand plunged into the water to retrieve her boat and brought it up dripping and triumphant.

"You've gone and wetted your gown," said Hetty in her most grown-up voice. If they were going to use her as a nursemaid, she might as well act the part. But Liza looked completely unrepentant: clearly Hetty had not got her scolding voice quite right.

Her own fingers trailed in the deliciously cool water. In Richmond, a few times, she and Nancy and Mabel Gilbert had followed the boys to the shallows of the river and, shedding their overskirts and stockings, had tied petticoats between their legs to go wading. Jim Saunders, as brown and slender as a trout, had dived off the bridge into the deep water as Hetty watched the smooth arc of his body. She had begged Jim to teach her to swim, but he said no, 'twasn't fittin' for no maid. Her mother thought the same, for she chided Hetty when the girls arrived home, fresh and sundried with their noses beginning to freckle. Hetty, as eldest, got all the blame, though Nancy had wanted to go just as badly.

Now Hetty looked longingly at the canals of Moor Park and the river farther down; she imagined balancing on the edge of Diana's fountain and plunging headfirst into the pool—how deep was it?—petticoat and all. Fancy what her mother would say then. Or, worse yet, fancy running into Lady Giffard at such a moment!

"What's funny?" Liza asked.

"Nothing—only … I was thinking what Lady Giffard would say if we went bathing in the pool."

Liza laughed too at the thought of how soundly they would be reprimanded: less, perhaps, if they were boys, Hetty thought, but even boys (had there been any at Moor Park) would be scolded for such escapades in a house like this. She splashed her hand down into the water, hard, so that the droplets flew up and sprinkled herself and Liza. Liza's little round mouth formed an O, and then she scooped up a handful of water and splashed it in Hetty's face.

In moments the water was flying in earnest: the starched lace around Liza's coif and her crisp muslin cravat were damp and wilted, and since Liza, being younger, was more careless, Hetty suspected her own garments were in even worse repair. Liza was laughing and squealing so hard that she was almost breathless.

A voice from the terrace above cut into their giggling and shrieking. "Miss Elizabeth! Miss Hetty! Come in out of the sun!"

Hetty scrambled down and reached up to lift Liza down. Hand in hand, they raced away from the fountain but slowed their steps as they came in sight of the great house and walked up to the terrace with proper small steps.

The harsh voice belonged to red-faced Mrs. Dingley, a plump, fussy young woman who was some sort of relative to the family and lady-in-waiting to Lady Giffard. Hetty couldn't see why that meant Dingley had to fuss and worry over where the girls went and what they did, but such was life at Moor Park—someone was always looking over her shoulder.

Dingley was easier to deal with than Lady Giffard, but she did not miss the splashes of water. "Shame on you, Hetty. What foolishness have you been getting Miss Liza up to? It'll be no thanks to you if she is dosed with a cold! And you should have more care for your own health—you that have lately been so sick! Do you want to worry your poor mother into her grave?" Dingley's mild chastising followed them around the house to the servants' door and down the passageway. "You'll both have to change at once—

go to your mother, Hetty, and see that the two of you get Miss Liza into dry clothes before you take her to her mama."

Stepping through the side door into the servants' hall was like stepping into another house altogether. Upstairs there were never enough people to fill the huge rooms, where you moved through marble, oak, and tapestry in an ocean current of silence. Downstairs was a warren of narrow hallways with stone floors where the walls rang with the clatter of pans in the kitchen, a burst of laughter from two footmen in the wine cellar, and the high chattering voices of the maids. Sally and Jane and Nan, who upstairs glided like smooth black-and-white shadows, gossiped and complained like a roost of hens as soon as they got downstairs. Two of them stood in the hall outside Hetty's mother's room, their heads bent together.

"That's the first time she's given me the edge of her tongue, and it'll be the last," Jane was vowing. "I'll not cross her again. I'd be glad to see poor old Edwards back, for all his roving hands." The other girl silenced her with a finger to her lips, and they both passed down the hall in silence, bobbing their heads to Mrs. Dingley, their voices rising again as soon as they turned the corner.

"That was your *mother* she talked of!" Liza whispered. "She oughtn't to be allowed!"

Hetty lifted her chin, torn between hurt and pride. Foolish girls—it would serve them right to have their nasty old butler back again! But to Liza she said, "'Tis all one to Mama. She's as good a housekeeper as she was a shopkeeper, and the maids don't like that—our Sal at home was forever whining about Mama's tongue."

"Your maid was named Sally too? We have a Sally at Sheen," Liza said, wide-eyed.

"Maids are usually called Sally," said Hetty.

They hushed as they entered the room where Mrs. Johnson was sitting at the table, making up a list. In the weeks since they had come to Moor Park, Hetty's mother seemed always to be making lists, or making preserves, or scolding the maids in the kitchen. Now she looked up irritably at her daughter's arrival, but when she saw Liza trailing behind, she stopped short of whatever she had been about to say.

"Mrs. Dingley told us to come in and put on dry clothes," said Hetty.

"And why might you need dry clothes?"

"Because ours got wet playing by the fountain," Hetty recited.

Mrs. Johnson took charge of the situation. In short order both girls were changed, then conducted to the Little Parlour, where Liza's mother, young Mrs. Temple, and her grandmother, old Madame du Plessis, sat. Both were dressed in black and talking softly in French as they embroidered. Liza's two-year-old sister, Dotty, sat on the floor playing with a rag doll, and Dotty's nursemaid sat quietly in the corner on a rush-bottomed chair, sewing flounces on a small petticoat.

"*Bonjour, ma petite,*" Liza's mother said, as though it took a great effort even for her to open her mouth to speak. She went on in French, and Hetty lost the thread of what she was saying.

Liza turned back to her. "You can sit with us and do your work," she translated.

"Fine," said Hetty without much enthusiasm, and sat down beside Liza on the settee. Liza's mother handed them each an embroidery hoop and a skein of wool. The picture Hetty had been working was a wreath of red roses and green leaves, and she was growing tired of it. Before coming to Moor Park she had known only the simplest sewing stitches, but shortly after her arrival Dingley had sat her down and taught her the cross-stitch and the stem stitch, and set her to work on a sampler that included fruits, flowers, fishes, the alphabet, a verse: "When this you see, Remember me," and the legend "Esther Johnson Eight Yeares of Age, 1689." The sampler finished, Hetty had begun work on this pattern of roses, which was meant to be a prayer-book cover for Lady Temple. At first it had been wonderful. She loved learning fancy-work, and Dingley had promised that when the prayer-book cover was done she would teach Hetty the tent stitch, and after that she could learn fancier stitches and work with silks. Hetty had spent hours sitting beside Dingley, or here with Liza's family in the Little Parlour, tracing out the picture with her needle, running her fingers over the pretty nubbed surface of the roses. But it took so long! She was likely to be doing the cross-stitch for ever and never to learn anything new, and she was now so tired of these particular roses and the pale green of the leaves surrounding them that she thought she could gladly fling hoop and all out through the open window. Imagine the sensation that would create! The one consolation was that as she and Liza sat here and worked silently, she could listen to Madame du Plessis and Mrs. Temple talk in French and perhaps learn more that way.

There were men's voices in the corridor outside, which was a novelty, as almost everyone at Moor Park was a woman. One of the voices was Sir William's; he was talking to a younger man. Sir William, Liza's grandfather, was a nice man, but he was always so sad. Since Hetty had come to Moor Park, she had never once seen him smile.

He came into the room now, his black coat filling the doorway so that at first Hetty couldn't see the other man. "Good day, ladies," he said with a graceful bow, which was echoed by a much less graceful bow from the man behind him. "I was seeking my sister, but I see she is not with you."

"I have not seen Lady Giffard since dinner," said young Mrs. Temple in her lovely French-accented voice.

"Then let me say only a word to my favourite girls, and Mr. Swift and I will be away," said Sir William, crossing to where Dotty played on the rug. He swept her up on the floor and mussed up her curls, talking to her in baby talk until she giggled and drooled. Then he handed her to her nurse and came over to the settee and looked intently at what Liza and Hetty were doing.

"Busy with your needles, young ladies?" he said, with a hand on each head. Hetty didn't especially like having her head patted as though she were Liza's or Dotty's age, but she was hoping there might be a sweetmeat in it for her. Sir William was really very kind; he gave her sweets whenever he gave them to Liza and often talked quite nicely to her. This time, however, there was no sweetmeat, only praise. "You both are doing lovely work—how very decorative, like your own pretty selves. Liza, so skilful for one so young! And you, Hetty, are making great strides. I can see that."

"Ah yes—great strides at the usual worthy pursuits taught to young ladies," came another voice, younger and harsher. There was something in that voice Hetty couldn't put a name to, but she knew very well that the man was mocking her, and her work.

She looked up from her needle to stare full at him, and he returned her glare. Mr. Swift, Sir William's new secretary, was a young man of middle height, with a coat and waistcoat of cheap material and his wig slightly askew. His eyes bulged a little: the rest of his face was neither very handsome nor very ugly, but it looked somehow awkward, as if he didn't know quite what to do with his nose and mouth.

Sir William seemed shocked at his secretary's bluntness and quickly ushered Mr. Swift out of the room. As they left she heard Sir William say, "I am sure if you would like to under-take instructing the young ladies in Greek and Latin, or any more abstract subjects, I should have no objection, but they, perhaps, might object." His polite chuckle echoed down the hall. Mrs. Temple turned to her mother, rolled her eyes, and said something fast in French, and then everyone went back to her work as if Mr. Swift had never been in the room.

Hetty supposed she was the only one who was angry—Liza was too young to understand, anyway. But who was he, and how dared he look at them like that and speak so slightingly? She was used to being ignored; children often were, but any adult who did trouble to speak to her always praised her for being diligent at her needle, or quiet, or good-tempered. She would have liked to run after him and shout that she was *not* merely doing needle-work, she was learning French, and if he wanted to teach her Greek and Latin he would be amazed at how quickly she learned. How dared anyone so ill clad and awkward be so smug and sure of himself?

But of course she said nothing and bent over her work, stab-bing the roses with as much fervour as if they had been so many little scarlet Mr. Swifts.

And yet he became her tutor: Sir William set Swift the task of tutoring Liza, and Hetty was, as always, allowed to join her. The lessons quickly became more Hetty's than Liza's: she was older and brighter and a far more interesting pupil for a young man who had no interest in teaching little girls their horn books, and before many weeks passed she ventured to tell him that she wanted to learn Latin and Greek.

He laughed. "Latin and Greek! You ridiculous little goose—what does the housekeeper's daughter want with Latin and Greek?"

Hetty flushed. They were in the Little Parlour, she sitting on a chair by the spinet and Mr. Swift standing by the fireplace. Liza had just gone to her mother, and Mr. Swift looked as if he, too, was eager to be somewhere more interesting. But her request had arrested his attention, and now she had to think what to say next.

"I should like to learn Latin, and French as well if I can, because I wish to travel in foreign lands someday," she explained.

"Travel, would you, impudent rogue?" he said, his smile breaking out again. He looked almost more like a boy than a man when he laughed: she supposed that he was young for a grown-up. She had already considered the possibility that he might marry Mama and become her stepfather, which would be interesting, but he was clearly too young for Mama; perhaps he might marry Mrs. Dingley. "You'll find quick enough that Latin will do you little good," he said, "nobody speaks it nowadays, not for hundreds and hundreds of years, except clergymen and scholars. I don't suppose you're thinking of becoming a scholar?"

Hetty turned the question over, tried to find a picture for the word *scholar*. An old man in a long black robe? "No … I don't believe girls *can* be scholars, can they? What I would like to be, is a lady—like Lady Temple or Lady Giffard. But not really like Lady Temple, for all she does is weep and sigh, and sit alone in her chamber with the blinds drawn, they say."

"She has had a heavy loss to bear."

"I know—Liza's father was the only child she had left. Isn't it a great tragedy?" She sat forward, clasping her hands round her knees. "She and Sir William had nine children, and they are *all* dead! All as babies, except for Liza's father, and Diana. Have you seen Diana's portrait? It hangs in the Great Hall. Sometimes Lady Temple can't bear to look at Liza because she looks so much as Diana did at her age. But Liza's father was the saddest loss of all, because"—she lowered her voice and glanced toward the door—"they say he took his own life."

Mr. Swift raised his eyebrows. Surely he had heard this information before? "Hush, little baggage, where do you hear such gossip? Hanging about the kitchen, no doubt?"

"For the most part. There is a good deal to hear in the kitchen, you know."

Their conversation ground to a halt. She was terribly afraid he would go. This was the longest talk she remembered having with anybody since coming to Moor Park. He talked to her almost as though she were grown up: better than Sir William, really, because she was fairly sure Mr. Swift was *not* fond of children as a rule, and should never have paid half so much attention to Liza.

"Perhaps when I go abroad," she said now, "I shall start with Ireland. You are from Ireland, are you not, Mr. Swift?"

She had meant to go on amusing him, but his smile fled. "Yes, I am from Ireland," he said.

"What sort of a country is Ireland?"

"What sort?" He looked almost angry at the question, and strode across the room. "It is a terrible country, a poor country, a backward country. A country where no man stands any chance of getting ahead or making anything of himself, a miserable and stinking country. Miss Hetty, if you do go abroad, I strongly recommend that you *not* begin your travels in Ireland. Not only is it geographically improbable to continue on to Europe from there, it is a country best avoided altogether."

And with that, he turned and left the room.

Then there were no more lessons for several weeks, for Hetty fell ill just before Christmas-tide. When she recovered, she began to have visitors. She was sitting up in her mother's bed in the housekeeper's room, her mantua wrapped about her shoulders, when she heard Mr. Swift's voice outside the door, talking and laughing with her mother and Dingley. Dingley had just been down to visit, brought her sweetmeats, and taught her a new card game called whisk, so all in all she was having a very satisfactory convalescence. A visit from Mr. Swift would be an unexpected bonus. Mrs. Johnson opened the door for him, then followed him in and sat down on the foot of her daughter's bed as Mr. Swift took the stool beside it.

"So, saucy wretch, you have been getting sick and worrying everyone to distraction, have you?" he began.

"Has everyone been worried about me?" Hetty asked, quite pleased at the idea.

"Most terribly: Sir William asks every day after your condition. With Liza and Dotty gone, and you ill, he finds the house quite empty of children and wishes you back again."

"Yes, Mama told me Liza and her family had gone back to Sheen after New Year's. Isn't it terrible? I missed Christmas, and New Year's, and Twelfth Night and everything. But Mother said Christmas was all very solemn, with no mummers or dancing, because everyone is still in mourning, so I don't quite so much mind missing it. And now Liza is gone and I shan't have anyone to practise my French on. I don't suppose you could tutor me in French as well, could you, Mr. Swift?"

He smiled. "I am afraid, dear Miss Hetty, my French would be little good to you, for I am not much skilled in that language."

Mrs. Johnson, who had listened to this exchange with interest, said, "Are you my daughter's tutor, Mr. Swift, and I not told of it?" Hetty was glad she smiled when she said it, for she was afraid Mr. Swift might have taken offence.

But he merely said, "Your daughter, Mrs. Johnson, professes interest in a classical education. She wishes me to teach her Latin and Greek."

Hetty had often seen the little glance and smile grown-ups gave one another when they were laughing at children and thought the children didn't understand. Her mother and Mr. Swift exchanged it now, and her mother said, "I thought I'd done well by her, teaching her to read and write. Don't let her be a hindrance to you, Mr. Swift—I know you have your own work to do."

"Indeed," said Swift, "but there is little enough of that. I sometimes feel Sir William has no great need for a secretary and is only making up excuses to keep me busy. I think I will run mad if I am not better occupied, and being Miss Hetty's tutor would serve to keep me busy as well as anything." He turned back to Hetty. "But we cannot start reading Latin today, for I doubt your eyes will be strong enough to bear the strain."

"Oh, they are!" Hetty protested, but as she had expected her mother cut her short.

"Not yet," she said, "but in a week or so, perhaps, if she continues to improve."

"I am very sorry you have been sick, Miss Hetty. What has your trouble been?"

Hetty rolled her eyes. "Shortness of breath, and headaches, and sore eyes, and a sore throat, and chills," she recited.

"I do sympathize. As it happens, I have not been well myself."

"Have you not?" Hetty's mother asked. "What do you suffer from, Mr. Swift?"

"Some odd attacks of dizziness, and a ringing in my ears, and biliousness. I was very sick in the autumn from eating apples that were hardly ripe, and I have suffered attacks ever since."

"I do sympathize," echoed Hetty, liking the grand sound of the words. "I hope you are better soon." After a pause, she said, "You might tell me a little about the Greeks and Romans, as I can't begin reading about them yet."

"Very well. Have you heard of Homer?"

The butcher's son at Richmond had been called Homer, but Hetty was tolerably sure this was not the Homer intended. "No," she admitted after a long hesitation.

"Homer was an ancient Greek who wrote two great poems about heroes and adventures in the ancient world," Swift began, and launched into a tale that kept her spellbound for the better part of an hour. It had the additional benefit of being restful to her eyes, since she kept them closed and saw the glories of Troy behind her closed lids, called to vivid life by the young secretary's words.

When he was finished, she opened her eyes and drew a long sigh. Her mother, she saw, had left the room. "That was lovely—thank you very kindly. Will you come and tell me stories again, or read to me?"

He stood up and bowed. "It would be my very great pleasure."

"Or perhaps we could play cards sometime. Dingley has been teaching me whisk—would you like to play with me now?"

"I am afraid my time does not permit, but when I come again, we shall certainly play whisk."

"Only … you had better bring a sweetmeat with you."

"What?" He looked shocked, pretend shocked, she could see. "Do you order me to bring you presents, Miss Impudence?"

"Oh, I'm sorry, I didn't mean that at all. I meant bring a sweet because we must have something to wager, and I have hardly any money, just some sweets Sir William sent me." Sir William had also given her a gold piece at her last birthday, but she was hardly likely to wager that.

"And you certain enough of winning to insist that I bring something I can lose? Very well, little Helen of Troy, I shall bring sweets when I come again."

"Helen's a nice name, isn't it?" she said, gazing at the drawn curtains over the window.

"Very lovely. Why, are you thinking of changing yours? Hetty's a fine name, I think."

"I don't like it at all!" she burst out. "It sounds like ... like a maid, or something. It's not a real lady's name."

"What is your real name—Hester?"

"Yes—Hester or Esther, it's the same name really. I prefer Esther—it sounds more dignified."

"I suppose you could tell the others you wanted to be called Esther."

"Impossible: I said something of the sort to Mrs. Dingley, and she said I was putting on airs. But if she's content to have people calling her Dingley all her life, how can she possibly understand why I would want to be called Esther? Esther was a queen in the Bible, you know."

Mr. Swift nodded. "Indeed she was—brave Queen Esther."

"Was she brave? What did she do?"

"Have you not read your Scripture, then?"

"No—only the Lord's Prayer and a few Psalms."

"Perhaps after you master Greek and Latin, we can begin on Hebrew, and you can read about Queen Esther in the original language."

She knew he was jesting then, but she made a very serious face to make him laugh. "I think Greek and Latin will be *quite* enough for me, thank you."

Latin was enough and more than enough, she thought

months later, as she sat in the library puzzling over Latin verbs and phrases in Lily. Latin was day after day, page after page of that tedious grammar book, till it looked as if it might be endless years before she ever got to actually read a line of Virgil or Homer. But Mr. Swift had told her that Lily was the book all boys were given to work through when they were sent to school, the one he himself had studied as a boy, and she was determined not to give up. A girl, of course, could never be as clever as a boy, but perhaps by diligent application to *Lily's Grammar,* she could please Mr. Swift enough to make up for the fact that he had only a girl to teach.

But outside the window the green of Sir William's beloved gardens sang beneath the blue of a spring sky, and Esther squirmed in her seat, finding it hard to concentrate. Mr. Swift was not even there to tutor her; he had gone away for a while and she was trying to carry on alone. Liza was not at Moor Park to share lessons with her: Esther's best friend at the moment, and the only person she wanted to see, was the gardener's grandson, Jamie Plumridge. He was just Esther's age; his sister, Nora, was a year or two older, and Esther sometimes played with her too, but lately Nora's mother was keeping her too busy to play much. Two days ago Esther and Jamie had stowed away in the back of a cart and ridden all the way to Farnham, walked about the town all afternoon, and then had to walk back, making up stories Esther could tell to explain being gone so long. Latin was poor competition for such adventures.

At last she threw down her pen and books, grabbed her cloak, and headed down the back stairs as quietly as possible. If her mother or Dingley saw her she would be snared in a tangle of kitchen work or needlework that would be even harder to escape than Latin. She didn't breathe easily till she was out in the garden under the yew trees, finding her way through the intricate network of paths down to the wilderness.

Old Plumridge was there, pruning some of the new rose-bushes Sir William was so proud of. Half the time the old gentleman was down here himself, advising Plumridge on the proper care of this plant or that, but today no one was around but the gardener himself.

"Hello, Plumridge, is Jamie about?"

"Hello, Miss Hetty. No, I believe he's down at the cottage, splitting wood for his mother."

"Thank you, I'll go down there."

She loved the Plumridges' cottage; it reminded her of her own home in Richmond and was a pleasant retreat when Moor Park felt too vast and grand. She found Jamie, as his grandfather had said, splitting firewood out behind the cottage, and she perched on a stump nearby to watch.

"You done work?" Jamie asked between axe blows.

"I've done enough," Esther replied, shifting her weight a little on the stump. When Jamie asked about her work he meant her work about the house, helping her mother. She had never told him about Latin and Greek. Jamie knew his letters; he could write his name and read a little. He would be gardener after his grand-father someday, and he had all the book learning he needed.

Jamie grinned. "You've got it easy in the big house—you can sneak off and nobody watching you." He nodded toward the cottage door. "Ma's got me here in the yard and Nora in the house, and neither one of us likely to get away till the work's all done. But I'm near finished here." He heaved the axe again and shat-tered another junk of wood.

"Ma, I'm done!" Jamie put his head inside the cottage door to yell, and Esther jumped off the stump.

She wanted to be away at once, but Mrs. Plumridge called, "Tell Miss Hetty to come in and say hello."

Inside, her eyes adjusted to the dim light. Jamie's older sister, Nora, stood at the table, dipping eggs in sugar water to preserve them, nestling them gently in a bowl of straw when they were done. Esther knew the chore well—it was one of her jobs in the big kitchen.

Mrs. Plumridge took two cakes from a pan on the hearth. A hen scratched nearby in the dirt; Mrs. Plumridge shooed it away with her foot. She handed one cake each to Esther and Jamie. "Don't be getting into any mischief, now," she said by way of benediction. "Jamie, see Miss Hetty doesn't come to any harm, and be back before dark."

As she made for the door behind Jamie, Esther felt Mrs. Plumridge's sharp eyes on her back. "How old would you be now, Miss Hetty?" she asked.

"Nine, ma'am."

"Ah." Esther took advantage of a pause after the "Ah" to scoot out the door. She could hear the edge of disapproval in Mrs. Plumridge's voice. At nine she was still a child—but barely. Nora was only eleven, and she was bound to the house and her duties all day now, though just last fall she had been free to run and play.

The same tone that had been in Mrs. Plumridge's voice was in Lady Giffard's when she looked across at Esther's mother and said, "Bridget, it's time that girl of yours began to learn the work of the house. Send her to the kitchen in the mornings; Mrs. Mose will have plenty for her to do." Esther ran barefoot through the prickly spring grass as if she could outrun the walls conspiring to close in about her.

DUBLIN
1723

Around her now the walls are closing, too—or is she being fanciful? She is young to imagine her life ending, but she has been so sick for so long that she cannot remember how it feels to be free of pain. The woman who wrote this letter before her is younger still than Esther, but she is dying—proclaims herself dying. Or is she dying only because she says she is, because she has given in, admitted the fact?

All her life Esther has believed her fate is largely in her own hands, to weave as she will. She was born into a world where others were expected to make her choices and shape her future, but her move to Moor Park had shown her early that life could take unexpected twists and turns, could offer undreamed-of choices. No one ever told her that she was allowed to take her pick from among those choices; in fact, her mother and Dingley and Lady Giffard would have insisted she had no business at all to go through life as through a crowded market stall, choosing what she liked and leaving behind the rest. Yet in her heart she had believed that, had treated her life in just that way. She remembers the array of possible futures spread out before her in girlhood, how she walked among them, sampling and tasting and dreaming, not yet ready to choose.

The life she has now is not one she ever imagined, or could have imagined, in those days: the life she now lives was made possible by a gift she had not then dreamed of receiving. Yet it is a life she has chosen, and her will to choose, to order her destiny, must have begun in that very early time. She has prided herself on choosing her life, not being carried along like a leaf in a stream.

Esther looks again at the journal pages, but her mind is still further back, back in the years before she took up journal writing. She is thinking of the first book she ever owned for herself—a gift, of course, from Jonathan Swift.

MOOR PARK
1694

Esther turned thirteen on the thirteenth of March: an auspicious occasion, Mr. Swift said. Her birthday supper was one of those celebrations that blurred the line between the upper servants and the members of the family: she and her mother, Dingley and Mr. Swift, sat down in the Painted Parlour with Sir William and Lady Giffard.

It was a lovely supper, with boiled chicken and boiled duck, cold roast goose and ham. Esther was coaxed to play on the spinet, and was not badly pleased with her performance. Then Mr. Swift, at Sir William's urging, stood to propose a toast to her. He held his glass aloft and said that for a young lady to reach the age of thirteen years in this pestilent, dangerous age was miracle enough, "but for her to have achieved that age as our Esther has, with grace, charm, and a clever mind, is a fine accomplishment indeed. May she go on to live a life worthy of its beginning." Everyone clapped and cheered and drank her health: she had never felt so adored and important.

Her gift from Sir William, Lady Temple, and Lady Giffard was fine indeed: a gown and petticoat, the finest she'd ever had, and all new: the gown of blue cambric and the petticoat of poplin, lavishly embroidered in red and blue with four layers of flounces. She wanted to try it on, to parade around in it, but modesty prevented that: she could not make such a show of herself, even on her birthday. She took the gown back with great care to the housekeeper's room that night and folded it carefully off by itself in a corner of the trunk, not touching any other clothes, and pictured herself walking into the village church with it on Sunday morning.

Yet even the gown wasn't the best present. Mr. Swift's gift was the very finest, the best thing she had ever received: he gave her a book. She began reading it that very night, after her mother had sent her to bed but had not yet come in herself. The rush-light candle beside the box bed she shared with her mother flickered a dim, greasy light, and by it Esther painstakingly picked out the first words. *In a certain corner of La Mancha, the name of which I do not choose to remember, there lately lived one of those country gentlemen, who adorn their halls with a rusty lance and worm-eaten target, and ride forth on the skeleton of a horse, to course with a sort of starved greyhound.*

Don Quixote was a long book, but she was caught up in the tale of the poor foolish man who wanted to be a gallant knight of old, and she found a little time day after day to curl up in a corner and follow the adventures of Quixote and Sancho Panza and Rosinante, and sometimes to laugh aloud at Quixote's folly. At the same time Mr. Swift started her reading Terence in Latin and recommended more English poetry for her to read: he showed her the poems of a man called Cowley and began her on *Paradise Lost,* by Milton, which was slow going. After all this it was a pleasure to steal moments with *Don Quixote.* It took her the better part of the spring to get it read, and not until she had finished it and she and Mr. Swift were again on one of their brisk walks on a clear windy day did she answer his oft-repeated question about how she had enjoyed it.

"I did not want to say before," she explained, "until I had done reading it. Because my opinion might have changed, when I read the ending. Do you understand?"

He nodded gravely. "Yes, I quite agree. The ending can make all the difference to one's opinion of a book. Did the ending of *Don Quixote* satisfy you?"

"Quite, yes. It was a splendid book. I especially liked the parts about Dulcinea, and about the windmills that Quixote thought were giants."

"And what lesson did you draw from the tale of the windmills?" he asked, pulling his coat more closely around him. Though the air was cool, the rolling landscape all around was green and vibrant. This spring their walks took them farther afield than the Moor Park gardens: they walked the roads around the manor and its tenant farms, exulting in the brilliant greens and golds of the Surrey countryside. One day they had almost reached Farnham when rain caught them, and been lucky enough to be picked up by Sir William's coachman on the way back. Right now they were not so far from the house: they were going past the home farm and the air was pungent with manure. Two dairymaids came up the path carrying buckets of milk from the farm to the dairy: one was Nora Plumridge, lately taken on at the Moor Park dairy. Esther waved and called hallo to both of them before considering the question about the windmills.

"There were two lessons, I believe," she said when the dairymaids had gone by. "One is that we ought not to be fools and make trouble for ourselves where there is none by creating imaginary enemies." That was the sensible meaning, the one she thought he would approve of; the other was closer to what she really thought, but harder to put into words.

"Very good—and the second?" he prompted.

"That we should ... that it is not good to be content with a dull, middling sort of life, and that we can find adventure anywhere if only we look for it," she said after a moment's hesitation. Mr. Swift received her opinion in silence, and she felt a knot tighten in her stomach. Would he chide her for such bold views?

"Have you not been taught that everyone, high and low, ought to be content with his station in life and not look for anything better? Is it not doing so that causes poor Quixote all his troubles?" he asked at length.

Esther nodded. It was a lesson drilled into her from earliest childhood. "I suppose I am wrong, sir," she said quietly. "It may be that I did not understand the book very well."

He sighed, then turned the radiance of his smile on her. It lit up his ungainly face and made him look almost handsome. "In that case, I too misunderstood it. For while I believe it in the main to say we are foolish to pattern our lives after romances and dreams that can never be, I cannot believe we are quite meant to abandon dreams altogether."

"Else you would not dream of being a great writer," said Esther.

He laughed aloud. "Yes, my poems are my windmills, no doubt! I can supply more than enough wind to keep them spinning about." He picked her up by the waist, swung her about till she squealed, and set her on the stone wall that bordered the canal so that her eyes were nearly level with his. "So our little poppet has not been dozing behind her needlework all those evenings Sir William has let her sit in the Great Parlour, has she now, la?"

"No indeed!" she assured him. He talked to her sometimes like that, in baby talk as if she were a little girl, though he had never done that when she was eight years old. The next minute he would be wanting her to talk and reason like a young scholar.

She had a particular reason for wishing to turn the talk toward Mr. Swift's poems, even if she knew she might be in for a scolding if she did so. Among the women of the house—Lady Giffard, her mother, and Mrs. Dingley—there was great speculation about Mr. Swift. His sister, Jane, who had spent a little while in service to Lady Giffard, sent news that he was engaged to a young lady down in Leicester, where his mother lived.

Dingley took every opportunity, over the next weeks, of slipping sly hints into the conversation—hints Mr. Swift never seemed to pick up on. Esther found it hard to believe she had once cherished hopes of a romance between Swift and Dingley. Who could be a less likely heroine of romance than Rebecca Dingley? She liked the idea of Mr. Swift having a mysterious sweetheart, someone far away and beautiful, and was disappointed that all Dingley's hinting yielded no confessions.

"I know what the trouble is, Becca," Mrs. Johnson said one night as she, Esther, Dingley, and Lady Giffard were playing a game of whisk in her ladyship's chamber. They gossiped less in front of Lady Giffard, of course, but she had been made privy to the story of Mr. Swift's liaison and seemed not to mind them talking of it. "You have it all wrong—that's the reason Mr. Swift won't rise to the bait. I have it on good authority that Betty is a tale of the distant past—he fancied her long ago, before he first came here, and is married now to an innkeeper. The latest is named Margaret Something-or-other; she is the one he was taken up with on his last visit to Leicester."

"Ah, so your news is fresher than mine," said Dingley. "Well, I shall talk of Meg, not of Betty, next time, and see if I find any warmer response."

"You would do better to look to your cards, Dingley," said Lady Giffard, "if you are my partner. We are very nearly beaten by these Johnsons. Just move that firescreen, if you would—my face is beginning to flush. And then come help me win this round."

Dingley shifted the embroidered screen to shield her mistress's face from the fire, but she was not able to be so obliging in the matter of winning. Esther and her mother won that game, and Lady Giffard congratulated Esther on being a grand little card player. "Though you would do well to remember, Hetty, that card playing is a frivolous amusement, and a wise woman will not occupy much of her time with it, but will give herself to honest work instead." It seemed Lady Giffard was incapable of passing even the most innocuous comment without attaching a moral to it. Since she was an avid card player herself, this moral seemed particularly unfair.

Now Esther wondered if she dared press Mr. Swift on the subject of the mysterious Meg. Perhaps he had written her a love poem. He wrote a great many poems, sometimes reading them aloud to the household in the evenings, but they were all on serious, important subjects, and sometimes Esther had been caught falling asleep before he had quite finished. Lately, there had been fewer evenings of poetry altogether. Mr. Swift was often in a bad mood and spent many evenings shut up in the library working or out walking alone. Sir William had sent him to London with an important commission, a message to carry to the king. Mr. Swift had not been successful, and since his return his bad mood seemed to infect every conversation he had. Darting a wary glance at his face, Esther concluded this would not be a good time to tease him about affairs of the heart.

Esther's days were too full for many walks with Mr. Swift, or much speculation about his affairs. She spent most mornings following either her mother or Mrs. Mose around the house and kitchens, taking a turn at doing a kitchen maid's work or changing the linens with the chambermaids, helping her mother write lists and buy food at the market in Farnham. Afternoons, Mr. Swift tutored her. When Liza was at Moor Park, the two girls had lessons together, and Esther was included in Liza's music, drawing, and dancing lessons. Sometimes she felt quite weary as she flew through her crowded days, but she had learned to beware of the feeling. Tiredness was followed by headaches, and dizziness, and coughing, and before long she would have to take to her bed.

As spring warmed into summer, Esther fell ill again—this time no little matter of a day or two abed. She lay in the box bed in the small cottage now set aside for her and her mother, drifting in and out of a twilight world in which blinds were drawn, doors opened and closed quietly, and people talked beside her bed in whispers. Once she had a vague sense that a man stood beside her bed holding something that glittered: a knife. She heard the word *bleed* and felt a sharp, swift pain in her arm. Another time—she was sure it was night, though the darkness never wavered—she opened her eyes and saw her mother. Then she knew she must still have been dreaming, for her mother was weeping, and Bridget Johnson never cried.

Finally she began to rally, and almost the first sensation she was aware of was surprise from those around her. Her mother, with no sign of tears now, felt Esther's forehead and said, "Your fever has gone down, I'm nearly sure."

Dingley came in one day with a bowl of beef broth for her.

"My, but it's good to see you well again, Miss Hetty. Look, there's even colour coming back in your poor pale cheeks. I never did think—"

"Never did think what, Dingley?" Esther asked, sitting up as Dingley fluffed the pillow behind her head. "Did everyone think I was going to die?"

"Die? No, never," said Mrs. Dingley, with a shock that was clearly pretense. "Oh, the doctor shook his head and looked most grave, but surely, Miss Hetty, those of us who knew you believed you were made of stronger stuff. Why, Mr. Swift even said, I heard him say myself over dinner one day not a fortnight ago, to your mother, he said, 'Never fear, Mrs. Johnson, so bright a star as our Esther will not be easily put out.'"

That brought to her face the first smile in long weeks, not only for the evidence of Mr. Swift's concern for her but for the little pun in it, that Dingley might have missed. How often had he pointed out to her the evening star, Venus, and told her that "Esther" was the name in Persian for that same star.

"Thank you, Mrs. Dingley," she said after a moment and another few mouthfuls of broth.

"What, for the broth? Oh, thank Mrs. Mose, she's forever thinking of the invalids—for did you know, Sir William has been ill too? Oh, there's been a great upheaval, so much so that some days folk hardly remembered little Hetty was ill as well—but it was all to your good, for it meant the doctor was here and able to look in on you."

"Sir William ill?" Her mother had said nothing of this, and she had always seemed most fond of the old man. "Is he better yet?"

"Not yet, though they say he takes a turn for the better. He is old and not able to recover so fast as you."

The next day a letter was brought to the cottage for her, from Mr. Swift. She unfolded it with rare delight: this was the first thing he had ever written to her alone.

*The doings at the great house are great indeed, as Sir William
is barely able to sit up again after his fever, and those of us
not nursing the sick are bearing twice the burthen. And in
all this uproar lies poor Hetty, the naughty poppet, still as a
mouse and uncomplaining though no one pays her hardly
any heed. Poor pretty thing! but soon you shall be among us
again, gallantly losing your money at whisk and ombre, and
struggling with the Greek alphabet. For now all your struggle
shall be to get well, and think no thoughts but pleasant ones,
even of the foolish rogue who signs himself,*

Your faithful servant,
J. Swift

Though Esther's recovery seemed slow to her, it was far
quicker than that of Sir William, and before the old man had
left his bed, she was again at Moor Park learning Greek while
Mr. Swift wrote an ode on the illness and recovery of Sir William.

"It is splendid," declared Esther when she was allowed to read
it, some days before its unveiling to the family. She and Mr. Swift
sat at the big desk in the library, amid a torrent of papers, pens
and books. "He will surely like it. But I am put out."

"Why?"

"Because where is your ode on the illness and recovery of
Miss Esther Johnson? I should like to see that same event celebrated in verse!"

Mr. Swift laughed heartily. "So, just as the Muse chides me in
this poem for being slow to write about Sir William, you will
chide me too? Does Hetty imagine herself my muse?"

His tone was jesting still, but his eyes had a serious look that
she could not fathom; for some reason she was quick to say, "No,
not that. Not your muse."

As quickly as it had come, the sober look was gone. "You are right, I have been remiss in my duties as court poet of Moor Park. Very well then, I must scribble down some verses on Miss Hetty, or Miss Esther if you prefer—no, neither will do for a poem."

"Must you find the name of a goddess to give me?"

"If not a goddess, a good classical name at least," he said, frowning.

"Like Dorothea and Dorinda for Lady Temple and Lady Giffard?" she asked, looking again at his new poem on the desk before her. A smile quirked the edges of her mouth. "Dorothea is not so far off, for Lady Temple's name is Dorothy, but Dorinda for Martha Giffard? You are too kind to her."

"Impudent baggage! Don't go slandering our benefactress, or we shall both be out in the cold begging our bread. It's a convention for poets to give classical names to their ladies when they celebrate them in verse."

"Like Quixote and Dulcinea!" Esther could not resist pointing out.

"Well, if you say I am Quixote, I will not deny the charge. And perhaps Dorinda is no more a goddess than Dulcinea was, but such things should not be said aloud."

"Never by me!" Esther assured him, putting her chin in her hands while her elbows rested on the polished surface of the great desk. "Why is it, Mr. Swift, that we have a dozen poems from you on great men and politics and religion and learning but never an ode to a goddess of your own? Do you write no love poems, like Mr. Cowley's to his mistress?" The question was daring, and as close as she could sail to asking straight out about the lady in Leicestershire.

"I am no master of that sort of poetry," Mr. Swift said stiffly.

"Your poems are quite the opposite, aren't they? In your Athenian poem you spoke so harshly of women. You wrote about 'Pride and Cruelty' and …'the vain sex.'" Something had curled like a fist inside her when he read those words aloud. She had rather hoped he didn't quite mean them.

He looked out the window, not meeting her eyes. "Yes, I remember. Well, Miss Esther, I am often disgusted by the folly of men, myself included, but it ranks as nothing beside the folly of women—their silliness, frivolity, falsity, and vanity."

"Then we shall expect no love poems from your pen?"

She had expected a glib reply, but a cloud passed over his features, and Esther saw she had asked something difficult for him to answer. "There is always, of course, a great difference between one particular woman, and women in the mass, just as there is with men. And also, the poet elevates his mistress when he writes of her, and writes not of the real flesh-and-blood woman with her powdered hair and the lice crawling underneath her frontage, but of a marble goddess." He let his voice trail away, then seemed to snap back to attention and look directly at her, as if remembering whom he was speaking to: only little Hetty, after all.

She wished her words unsaid: the whole exchange left her with an odd image of dark wine spilled and spreading across a white cloth. Something uncorked that should have been left closed, something spoiled that would never quite come clean. Quickly, she said, "This brings us no closer to finding a name for you to use in *my* poem."

Swift's eyes lit up again and met hers. "I've a good mind to call you Hecate."

"Queen of the witches? Oh, thank you very much."

"Here—I have it—" He scribbled on a scrap of paper and slid it across the desk to her.

"Verses on the late illness and recovery of Stella? Stella?" she repeated.

"Latin for—"

"'Star,'" I know. And Esther is for Venus, the evening star—very nice. Stella," she said again, trying on the name. She had never been overfond of the nickname Hetty, but she had grown to like Esther since Mr. Swift had opened her eyes to the world of Hebrew queens and Persian stars. Stella was a fine-sounding name, but seeing it on paper made her feel less like herself.

"Here, I'll begin," he said, snatching the paper back from her. As he wrote, he read aloud:

> *While licking her embroid'ry thread*
> *Did Stella start to feel her head.*
> *"Alas!" she cried, in accents dire*
> *"Again my eyes begin to tire!"*

"Enough of that!" Esther shrilled, leaping up to tear the paper away. "I'll not have my illness made a mockery, not when you have done such a fine solemn job with Sir William's. Give that here!" Laughing, she tussled with him over the paper and finally succeeded in ripping it from his hands.

"Ah! Now how to please the poor pretty maid!" said Swift, laughing as hard as she was. He put on his childish baby-talk lisp again. "First oo wants a poem, la, and then, mercy! oo shrieks and scowls at the poor poet! Take pity, Miss Hetty, on a poor foolish rogue!"

Mr. Swift's good mood was restored, and the awkward conversation about women and goddesses forgotten for the moment. He ate supper that night with Esther and her mother in their cottage; they were joined by Dingley and made a foursome at ombre.

Esther sat in the most comfortable chair with a quilt folded over her lap and Dingley's new lapdog curled asleep across her knees. She studied her cards and ran her fingers through the little dog's soft white hair and scratched its neck under the stiff orange ribbon—all the fashion for lapdogs, in honour of King William of Orange. The dog submitted to her caresses for a moment, then turned and ran back to Mrs. Dingley on four short, furiously pumping legs. "Dingley is ever so fond of dogs," Esther said to Mr. Swift. "She says she has always wanted one. Do you like them?"

"Not especially," he said, "though they are often cleaner and better tempered than the animals that keep them."

"Ah, are you weary of humanity again? You had better go and live in a hut in the woods, like a hermit."

"It's not a hut Mr. Swift wants," Esther's mother said, eyeing her own cards sharply. "Odd, isn't it, that a man who hates people so much should want to be always at court surrounded by them?"

"Court life is vanity and foolishness," Mr. Swift said, "but a man needs an occupation. What I have here with Sir William is not an occupation—not, I mean, a career for a man to spend his life at. Why should I spend my best years transcribing a great man's memoirs when I could be the great man myself, and living out the material for my own memoirs?"

"Which I will transcribe for you," Esther promised.

"I shall depend on it. Sir William still thinks I should take holy orders and go into the Church, but he makes no promise that he will help me find a living if I do. I think I have more of a leaning for Court. If only my mission to London had met with success … I mean to be someone in this world, not to be Sir William Temple's lapdog!"

Dingley's brow furrowed at his tone, but Bridget laughed. "You'd do well, indeed, to be treated as well as this lapdog!" She reached forward to scratch the ears of the dog now curled up asleep on Mrs. Dingley's ample lap.

❧

The following Sunday Esther felt well enough to go to church again: she had stayed home on Sundays during her illness and recovery. She put on her birthday gown and was surprised to note the changes: before her illness it had fitted her like a glove, but now it was too short, and loose in the waist, and a little tight across the bust. Still she was glad to be wearing it again, happy to let its bright splendour out of the trunk where it had lain so long.

That afternoon, the gown back in its trunk, Esther wrote a letter to Liza, read some poems by Mr. Cowley, and found herself bored. It was a rainy day, chill and grey, and she had no desire to take a walk. She went upstairs to the library, thinking of choosing a new book. At first she thought the room was empty, but then she saw the small fireplace at the end of the room and a figure kneeling in front of it.

She paused, wondering what his mood might be today—it grew harder and harder to judge. Finally she said, "Good day, Mr. Swift."

When he looked up she knew it had been a mistake to speak. His face was shuttered, entirely without warmth, and there was something burning in his eyes, a wild anger that almost scared her. "Good day, Miss Esther. Are you not going to ask what I am doing?"

"Lighting the fire, I suppose?"

"And with what, Miss Esther? I feed the flames with my scribblings, giving my verses to the fire." As he spoke he placed a piece of paper in the grate: the flames gobbled it. "Not my new work, not the things I struggle over and burn, but the things I have already written—an ode to the great Sir William Temple, an ode to the king, an ode to—"

"Why?" Esther could not keep herself from bursting out. "Your poems are … they are lovely! Everyone thought they were wonderful!"

"Wonderful?" He looked down at one of the crumpled papers in his hand. *"Ode to Sir William Temple: Shall I believe a Spirit so divine / Was cast in the same Mold with mine?"* He laughed a harsh, unpleasant bark. "These are vile, Esther, vile and puerile. These are the scribblings of a schoolboy who has long since outgrown his desk and found no place for himself in a man's world. No doubt you do like them—that is perhaps exactly what they are good for—to amuse pampered ladies who like to pretend they know something of literature."

Tears sprang to her eyes as fast as words to her lips. "Is that what I am? Is that what … is that what you have made me?"

He straightened up. "I have made you, little Hetty? Yes, I suppose I have—filled your head with a form of knowledge, like a parrot taught to repeat its owner's curses. Given you one more accomplishment to lay beside needlework and card playing and gossip and vanity—a passing acquaintance with literature, by which you presume yourself fit to judge the works of men!" He had, she saw now, been feeding his papers almost gently to the flames: now he crumpled the remaining ones, threw them in, and strode away.

Esther stood alone in the library, watching the flames, her stomach suddenly bilious. The beginning of another headache pounded behind her eyes, and her fists were clenched. Anger, she thought—no, rage. She had never been so furious in her life.

She turned and ran from the room, down the hall, down the great curved staircase, through the Great Hall and parlours, down into the servants' rooms, to the housekeeper's room. Her mother was not there. No one was there, and Esther was glad. To whom could she have spoken this impotent fury? How could she be angry at Mr. Swift, when so much of what he had spoken was truth? How angry at herself, when she had had no choice about being born what she was?

She went to the trunk, yanked open the lid, and tore out her new petticoat. She threw it on the floor, planted her foot on it, and began ripping away the flounces. The coat was well made, and it took a huge effort to rip out the stitches, and she was glad for the effort, glad for the tearing sound and the gaps that appeared in the fabric, though even as she tore it she knew, and tried to quell the knowledge, that she would try to mend the gown and have a wretched time doing so. She tore and tore till all four flounces were strewn around her, and sat on the floor in the middle of her ruined petticoat, longing to cry.

DUBLIN
1723

The candles are burning lower; she is back to the first journal page. Esther rubs the coarse fabric of her gown between her fingers, remembering those bright and gaudy flounces as they ripped free of their seams. Not long after that birthday, that argument, that petticoat, Jonathan Swift left Moor Park, swearing it was for the last time and he was done forever with Sir William Temple and any hope of help from that great man. He was gone back to Ireland, to take holy orders and begin a career in the Church.

If these were his memories, if he were telling the story of Esther's youth, the story would pause now; she would cease to exist, only to take up her life again when next he saw her. Sometimes, though it angers her, she remembers her own past that way, as a darkened room into which he came, carrying a lamp, illuminating furniture and features for as long as he stayed. It takes effort to remember who she was, what happened to her in those years after he went away. But here the journal begins, and she picks it up now, hoping that written words can fill the void that memory alone cannot.

She is looking for herself, but it is like looking at her face in a cracked and clouded mirror, trying to piece together a whole from so many distorted fragments. Here and there a line, a phrase, brings to life a whole world of memory: *We are in the midst of the twelve merry days of Christmas,* she had written on the first page. Esther stares at the rounded childish hand, trying to see the hand that held the pen, the white arm and shoulder, the dark ringlets beneath the cap, the eyes of the girl who stood in the Great Hall and laughed and clapped to see the mummers play.

MOOR PARK
1694

No season of the year brought as much work for the servants as Christmas-tide. Lady Giffard had decreed that Esther had to learn all the work of the house "so that you might someday have a position as good as your mother's." Esther liked the idea of being housekeeper and having a great ring of keys at her waist, though in truth she would have preferred to work under a different mistress than Lady Giffard.

Lady Temple—home from London for the holidays—would be the right sort of lady to be housekeeper for, Esther thought. Lady Temple wanted the servants out of her way, but she reciprocated by keeping out of their way. She did not come down to the housekeeper's room with endless lists, nor did she submit every detail of everyone's day to minute scrutiny. Lady Temple was doing well if she recalled Esther's name when they passed on the stairs; Lady Giffard knew exactly what pattern Esther was embroidering for the new parlour chair covers, and how much progress she had made before laying it aside in favour of a book of poetry.

Their differing methods of household management led, usually, to some strain between the two ladies of the house, but at present Lady Giffard was clearly in the ascendancy, perhaps because it was Christmas and that season required a strong hand at the helm. Or perhaps the difference was due to Lady Temple's own mood, which was unusually melancholic, even for her. She was again in poor health, and spent a great deal of time in her bedchamber.

Meanwhile, Esther kept her goal of being housekeeper clearly in mind through the long workdays of making candles and soap, helping the maids with one of the three great washes of the year, taking apart the box beds to wash them with vinegar and water, and writing as fast as she could while her mother and Lady Giffard tallied the household supplies and made lists of what needed to be bought before Christmas guests arrived.

On the morning of the third day of Christmas she was in the kitchen, where a huge pig turned slowly on the roasting jack in the fireplace; she was pressing Mrs. Mose's carefully rolled pastry into dozens of pie plates so that Betty could fill them with meat and gravy. Then Mrs. Mose called, "Miss Hetty, run and get Jack or Robin to turn the crank!" The weights that turned the spit had reached the bottom of the chain and would have to be cranked up again so the pork could go on roasting. Esther fetched Jack for the task, then went back to her pastry.

By late forenoon she was in the brewery, watching the great copper pot on the fire while Mrs. Mose worked at bottling the latest batch of small beer. When the pot was about to boil, Esther was to call Mrs. Mose so they could make the mash. The roaring fire was unbearable when she did this task in summer; on a cold December day it was exactly what was needed to take the chill out of the brew house.

Esther sat on a stool with her feet stretched toward the fire, thinking about her Christmas gift from Sir William, a large bound book with blank pages. "For copying out your poems, my dear," he had said with an indulgent smile, which made Esther's cheeks flush. No one had paid any attention to her poetry since Mr. Swift had gone away, and for a long time she had not written any, for the things he had said on the afternoon when he burned his own poems still stung. Esther wondered at times if she had any right to scribble poetry at all, or if she were only being a foolish and vain woman. Of late, though, the urge to put her thoughts on paper had been irresistible. Without Mr. Swift to talk to, she felt lost: no one else in the house would have been interested in her ideas and opinions. To be sure, he and she had made up their quarrel, after a fashion, before he left: he had not apologized, but had been civil and pleasant enough to her when he said his goodbyes. But after the distance that had grown between them, she could not imagine writing letters to him far away in Ireland, so she needed to find some other outlet. Poetry could only go so far; Esther wondered if she might use the blank book for a journal of sorts, a place to record what she was reading, learning, and thinking.

She was still sitting there, half mesmerized by the dancing flames and the heat they gave off, when Becca Dingley blew into the brew house on a gust of chilly air.

"Ah, is this where you are? Miss Elizabeth has come with her mother and sister, and was looking high and low to see where Hetty might be found."

"Well, she will have to see me at dinner, for I'm too busy being the housekeeper's daughter this afternoon to be her playmate," said Esther.

"Busy! My dear girl, let me tell you about busy—her ladyship has Jane and me set to going through every sheet in the house and laying aside the ones that need mending, and I'll assure you there's precious few that don't. What we're going to do tonight when Lord and Lady Onslow come, I do not know, unless they bring their own sheets with them."

Esther rolled her eyes. "They bring enough servants to weave and sew their own sheets once they get here. I don't know what they need such a retinue for; Mama's at her wits' end knowing where to sleep them all."

"Ah, but 'twill be worth it all if they bring that footman of theirs, that fellow Hal," said Dingley with a smile. She had wasted considerable time the previous summer trying to attract Hal's notice when he was entirely taken up with Betty in the kitchen. But now Betty was engaged to be married to Jack.

"You've no chance, Bec, not with Jane Swift here." Jane, having served Lady Temple in London for a time, was now back in residence at Moor Park, as was her cousin Thomas Swift, who had replaced Jonathan as Sir William's chaplain and secretary. Esther privately agreed with Lady Giffard's observation that the Swifts seemed to have no other occupation in life but to serve the Temples.

"Aye, Swift, she's well named, for I never saw anyone quicker to get her claws into a man. But I don't think she's the sort Hal would fancy," said Dingley, casting a knowledgeable eye at the pot. "That's not going to boil yet, not for a good while. Don't you mind it, though, being stuck down here instead of visiting upstairs with the young ladies?"

Esther glanced back at the fire. "Not very much."

Dingley folded her arms in front of her and leaned against the wall, nodding in the direction of the still room. "Well, if you do mind, you'd best not let Mrs. Mose see it, for I've heard herself and some of the servants say Sir William is giving you ideas above your station, treating you the same as Miss Elizabeth, letting you have dancing lessons with her and all that tutoring with Mr. Swift. I don't say it myself, now—I know you're as hard a worker as anyone in the house. I'm only telling you what I've heard said."

"Ideas above my station?" Something twisted and changed inside Esther; a feeling she had never examined till that moment suddenly turned against her. She remembered being a child and enjoying the fact that she was equally at home above and below stairs; she had loved the heady exaltation of being privy to the secrets of the kitchen maids in the morning, then sitting on Sir William's footstool to be read to in the evening. She had had the freedom of the Plumridges' cottage and Mr. Swift's library, and she had been everyone's pet. Now she was nearly fourteen and nobody's pet, and words rushed out in a flood. "My station? What is my station, Mrs. Dingley? Have you any idea? Because I swear I haven't! What am I meant to be in this house? Everything and nothing, it seems."

Dingley, for once, did not throw a torrent of words into the silence but let it be, while she pulled up another stool and sat down across from Esther, watching her with a steady-eyed expression that was rare for her. "Well," she said at last. "Well."

"Well?" said Esther.

"Well-a-day, I never thought I'd hear my own words coming out of someone else's mouth. I never did think … But I should have known, Hetty, for who else would feel the same as I do?"

"You?" Esther felt a bit stupid, but she had never imagined any connection between Rebecca Dingley and herself.

"Yes, I! Do you know what I am, Hetty? Sir William's own first cousin, that's what I am. You know that, don't you? My blood is as good as his—but my branch of the family has the ill luck to have no fortune. So here am I, old Rebecca, the poor cousin, no fortune, no dowry, no great beauty to make up for that lack—dumped here on the Temples' doorstep like so much old baggage." Esther knew Dingley was speaking as she had herself a moment ago—letting loose a gush of feelings that had never been said aloud before.

"You spoke a moment ago of seeing Miss Elizabeth at dinner. Do you not mind, Hetty, not knowing from one day to the next whether you'll be dining in the hall with the family, or at the second table, or down in the servants' hall? Shunted about from upstairs to downstairs depending on which lady is at home—for Lady Temple may be sweet as pie, but you notice she don't like the upper servants dining in the hall, if she can help it—or depending on how fine the guests are? Doesn't it bother you one bit?"

"Why … no … I mean, it never did …" Esther began. A great many things had not bothered her until this moment. Then she added, "But my case is different from yours, Becca, and I think yours is far worse. I know I am but the housekeeper's daughter, and it's only by privilege that I'm able to dine in the hall or play with Miss Liza or take lessons with Mr. Swift—only because Sir William has always treated me and my mother so much more kindly than a housekeeper is generally treated. I wonder why that is?" she added.

Dingley gave her a sharp glance. "You wonder, do you? Have you no idea?"

"Why, no. Do you?"

Becca Dingley pulled her mouth down and her eyebrows up, seemed about to speak, then shook her head. "No, I've not a clue," she said after a moment. "Happen he's fond of you, for you've been here since you were a child, and Sir William dotes on children."

"But I was talking of you, not of me," Esther said. "I know my place, or what it ought to be—but yours should be so much better! Why should your father's lack of a fortune make a difference whether you sit in the hall or below stairs? You are a member of the family—the real family, by blood, not just one of the household. 'Tis no wonder if you're angry, Becca!" She had never called Dingley by her first name before: as a child she had said Mrs. Dingley, and now she called the older woman by her last name as Lady Giffard and most of the rest of the house did. But in this conversation, it seemed impossible to call her anything other than Becca.

Dingley shrugged. The fire seemed to have gone out of her suddenly; perhaps she was the sort of person who could not stay angry or sad or elated for long. "Ah well, it rankles me, I'll confess, but there's worse fates for a poor spinster than to be Lady Giffard's maid, for all she's a sharp-tongued old termigant.

Though I'll have to look to my position in a year or so, for I think you'll take it from me."

"I? Lady Giffard's maid?"

"She's said she'd like to have you, when you're old enough."

Lady's maid. There was another goal to tuck away, alongside housekeeper—perhaps a step on the upward ladder. "I don't know if I should like that," said Esther.

"She's not so hard to serve as you might think," Dingley said, standing up. "Ah, it's done me good, to talk of all this, Hetty, for there's no one else I'd say such things to. But I hope I've not gone putting discontented thoughts in your head, making you to be bitter."

"Bitter?" Esther laughed, looking around the brew-house shelves. "There are enough bitters about here, Becca, without adding any of mine." She was proud of her little pun; Mr. Swift would have liked it, but Dingley only smiled as Esther continued, "No, I think—"

"Look to the water!" Dingley shouted, and Esther turned to see that the pot was boiling furiously, water hissing out of it onto the coals below.

"Oh no! It will be no good for the mash now! We'll have to start another pot again, and that will take forever! Mrs. Mose! Mrs. Mose!"

The cook appeared in the doorway, her mouth set in a hard line. "How careless, Hetty! Mrs. Dingley, you might have been watching it rather than here nattering, distracting Miss Hetty. Lady Giffard won't be pleased at all—there's no time to start another pot on the boil now."

Dingley squinted out the door of the brew house. "Oh, I see her ladyship coming down from the house now. Well, I've a great need to go to the privy suddenly; perhaps she won't chase me in there." And with a quick rustle of petticoats she was gone.

Esther, silently chiding herself for not thinking of the privy ruse first, decided that if she could leave quickly enough she would need no excuse at all. Her head was still spinning from her talk with Becca; she wanted more than anything to get away quietly and think through it all. It was just the sort of thing one might want to put down in a journal—perhaps she would begin that very night. For the moment, what she wanted least of anything was to endure a scolding from Lady Giffard.

She whisked out the door and down the path that led away from the house, into the gardens. She slipped through a hedge and was soon out of Lady Giffard's sight. It had been a long time since she'd run away like a child to avoid a scolding or a chore, and she remembered the guilty pleasure of truancy. Perhaps she'd play truant all day and never go back to the house till dinner—a daring thought, on the third day of Christmas with company on the way. Also an unlikely one, she realized with a shiver, since she'd brought no cloak with her.

"You must be cold, Miss Hetty," a voice echoed her thoughts, and she glanced around to see Jamie Plumridge, an axe over his shoulder.

"I am," she admitted, "but I'm in no hurry to return to the house, for I've gone and spoiled the small beer, and Lady Giffard will want to give me the edge of her tongue."

"Ah, no wonder you'd want to stay away! That's the great thing about working out of doors at Moor Park—it's one area where her ladyship doesn't reign, so I never have anything to do with her. I've just been clearing some dead wood and chopping it for firewood, but it's hard to go wrong with that job, unless I cut down one of his lordship's prize rose trees."

"And you haven't done that, I hope."

"No, I don't think so—though some of those dead yew trees had an awful plague of thorns on them, now you mention it."

They laughed together. Esther had seen little of Jamie this year, both being so busy about their work, and she was surprised to see that he had grown several inches taller than she and that with his broad shoulders and added inches he was a very handsome young man indeed. His voice had changed too—deeper, a man's voice. Suddenly it was easy to reply when Jamie said, "Come for a little walk with me, then, till her ladyship forgets you and finds someone else to rate."

It seemed natural to fall into step beside him, even to slip her arm through his when patches of ice made the paths slippery under her boots. He reached out once to steady her, and she felt the warm place on her back where his hand had touched. They went by his cottage, where Jamie went in and borrowed Nora's cloak for her, and then continued down through the farm, talking about all the work there was to do over Christmas, both inside and out. Esther, who had assumed the gardeners did nothing all winter, was interested in Jamie's conversation, and they were in among the tenant cottages when she thought to ask, "Where are you taking me?"

"To my friend Stephen's house—we're all going mummering tonight, and you can come watch us get ready. 'Tis a great laugh."

"Oh, that would be such fun!" Esther had always loved the Christmas-tide visits of the mummers to the great house and wished she could go mummering too. She might not be able to go so far as that, but she could at least see the mummers getting dressed in their ridiculous costumes. If they came to Moor Park tonight, she'd have no trouble guessing who was who.

Just as they were about to turn aside into a cottage, Jamie turned to her and pulled her hood up over her head, letting his hand brush briefly against her cheek. He looked thoughtfully at her, then said in a half whisper, "No, no one will know who you are."

Esther opened her mouth to ask why it mattered, then shut it again as he unlatched the door to the cottage and pulled her through behind him.

It had been years since she had been accustomed to visit Jamie and his sister, Nora, in their cottage; the only tenant cottage she had been in, all the years since, was the one close to Moor Park where she and her mother had sometimes stayed, and where now Thomas Swift lived with his wife, Lucy. That cottage seemed small, cramped, and dark to her, used as she was to Moor Park, but she realized that it was likely the best on the grounds. The room she now entered was so dark that at first she could see nothing till her eyes adjusted. She could hear and smell, though, enough to know that the room was full of people. Smoke from the fireplace tickled her nose and stung her eyes, but she was grateful that it muted the smell of sweat from the dozen or more young people crowded into the room.

She put up a hand to push back her hood, remembered Jamie's last comment, and stopped. She could see enough to examine faces in the dim light; many she knew by sight. Stephen, whose house this was, was a young farm worker, and there was his wife, big with a baby, and there were two boys who worked in the stables; they often saddled the horses when she and Liza went riding. There was Nora with another of the dairymaids, a giggling girl called Annie.

Esther didn't know the others. She didn't know the young man, about eighteen or so, standing in the centre of the room preening like a peacock while a short red-haired girl stood in front of him, painting up his face with a chunk of coal. Over his work clothes the young man wore a woman's petticoat, too wide and too short for him, and a grimy apron in eye-catching blue.

"That's it, make a right woman of him, go on!" cried Annie the dairymaid.

"There's no work to that—he's half a woman already," said one of the stableboys. As the bystanders laughed, the fellow in the petticoat turned away from his makeup artist and lunged at the stableboy.

"Ah, look what you made me do—you've ruined it!" cried the girl as she dropped the coal.

The two boys wrestled briefly, and an older man pushed his way to the centre of the room. "That's all right, my love—make a beautiful young girl out of me instead," he said, thrusting his grizzled face forward.

"Lord, I'd be doing more than God himself, to make anything beautiful out of you, Nick," said the girl, and again the room rocked with laughter. Esther laughed too, letting go, moving into the moment and the fun. She knew old Nick Sparkes; he had worked on the farm for ages. Now he was demanding a gown for himself as well.

"The best I could do for you is a sheet!" shouted one of the women, wrapping a frayed flaxen sheet about Nick's head. "Cut two holes for his eyes—that'll do him fine."

Someone else came forward with a knife and Nick shouted, "Mind you take it off me face first—I won't greet the New Year a blind man!"

In the corner, three men and a girl squeezed onto the room's only bench began to clap and sing.

Come, bring, with a noise,
My merry, merry boys,
The Christmas Log to the firing
While my good Dame she
Bids ye all be free,
And drink to your heart's desiring.

Soon the whole room was clapping and singing along as the young man in the petticoat, whose name was Earl, came back to have his makeup finished. Esther joined in too, raising her voice loudly, although she noticed a few people nearby glancing at her curiously. Well, Jamie could make up some explanation about her, if he felt the need to.

Drink now the strong beer,
Cut the white loaf here,
The while the meat is a-shredding;
For the rare mince pie,
And the plums stand by
To fill the paste that's a-kneading.

The mention of the mince pie, the white bread, and especially the beer gave Esther a quick stab of guilt, but it was buried under another burst of laughter as Annie darted over and grabbed Jamie's hand. The dairymaid shot a quick look at Esther, frowned, then looked back at Jamie. "Come, Jamie, 'tis your turn now. I've got a lovely petticoat for you. You'll make such a fair maid that Sir William himself will want you for his chambermaid!"

"Yes, and watch out he don't have a hand up your skirts when your back's turned!" another woman's voice hollered from the back of the room.

There were a few hoots and whistles, and Esther looked at the ground. In the dim light, surely no one would see her blush—but really, to talk of Sir William that way! That good old man, who was like a grandfather to everyone on the estate—she would never have imagined anyone making bawdy jests about him. She wished she were closer to the door—despite the cold outside, the room was dreadfully hot and she needed a breath of air.

Meanwhile, Jamie was struggling into an ample petticoat, assisted by Annie and the girl with the chunk of coal, who had already begun to highlight his brows and cheeks. Annie stepped back and put a finger to her chin. "Now, see how pretty he looks! But what is he missing?" With a little shriek, she ran to a trunk in the corner of the room, pushed off the boy sitting on it, and drew out a pair of woollen stockings. Rolling them up as she went, she hurried back to Jamie, pulled down the bosom of the gown, and thrust them inside.

"Now, there's a pretty pair!" someone called, and Jamie put his hands up under his makeshift breasts to push them up high in the air. Annie screamed with delight and grabbed the two breasts, one in each hand, and squeezed hard while the crowd whooped. "Now, don't let her away with that, young fellow! Give as good as you get!" cried old Nick. Jamie laughed, but when a few more voices took up the chorus he reached out to Annie, who squirmed and wriggled but put up very little real protest, and quickly thrust his hand into and out of the front of her gown.

Shouts, cheers, and applause greeted his boldness, and someone quickly struck up another round of a carol. Annie ran back beside Nora, who was shaking her head at her younger brother. If Nora's eyes had not met Jamie's just then, the moment might have passed, but she looked at Jamie at the same moment he suddenly remembered Esther, and turned, his face clouded and confused, to look at her. Nora followed his gaze, and even above the singing and laughter Esther could hear Nora's sharp gasp.

Esther pulled the hood—Nora's own hood, she remembered—over her face, but it was too late. Nora's strong voice rang out. "Jamie! Shame on you! What was you thinking, to bring Miss Hetty here—and then to carry on in such a way before her!"

Not everyone heard Nora's exact words, but everyone caught her tone, and even as Esther turned away from a dozen peering eyes she heard three or four voices repeat, "Miss Hetty ... from the house ... the housekeeper's daughter ... Mrs. Bridget's young girl ... her that goes about with Miss Elizabeth ..."

The carol died; the laughter died; Esther saw Jamie's face and knew that their moment of escape back to childhood had died too. Old Nick was at her side in a moment, pulling back her hood, suddenly a sober and proper old man.

"Miss Hetty, you must excuse all this rough crowd—they're nothing but youngsters; they know no better. If they'da knowed 'twas you, a young lady like yourself"—he was pushing her out the door as he spoke, elbowing the door shut with himself and Esther standing out on the step "—why, we would have never ... but everyone's right foolish during the Twelve Days. They're not a bad lot, really. Now let me walk you back up to the house. Did you come down with young Jamie? He's a foolish lad—he knows no better. Come on now, let Nick take you back home."

Esther wished she could explain, wished she could ask why it mattered so, wished she knew who exactly she was meant to be at any given moment. Nick was chattering away about quite inconsequential things, as if he were trying to erase those moments in the cottage from her memory. And then, recalling the jest about Sir William, she realized he was trying to do exactly that. With that realization, her fear that Nick might tattle on her slipped away. This visit would be forgotten. It was for everyone's best.

She was barely through the door before her mother caught her—by the ear. "You wicked slut! What a day, of all days, you would choose to disappear. Off with your head in a book, I suppose. Do you know the tongue-lashing I've had from Lady Giffard over you? If you know what's good for you you'll get into the kitchen and start scrubbing platters. Make sure Mrs. Mose sees you working, and her ladyship doesn't see you at all, until tonight."

"Scrubbing platters!" Esther bit off her protest as her mother steered her firmly to the kitchen door. Yet there was something soothing, after all, about doing the lowliest kitchen maid's job, she found as she scoured one plate after another. She could lose herself in the steady strokes of her washrag, concentrate only on the hard work and not think, not replay the scene in the cottage. She pretended scrubbing was her only life, her only reality, and it worked for a little.

But too soon she was summoned out of the kitchen and back into a life of oddities, for her mother ordered her to change her dress and go up to the Little Parlour where Miss Elizabeth was asking to see her. "And be sure you take your work with you," Bridget said, flinging hoop, embroidery, and needle in Esther's direction. "'Tis no time for idle fingers with all we have to do."

So there was Esther, an hour before dinner, sitting with Liza in the Little Parlour, listening to her chatter about her dancing master and her painting lessons and the long stay her mother had planned at Moor Park after Christmas. "So I shall ask Grandpapa to hire me an art teacher and bring back the dancing master so I can go on with my lessons, and you'll have them too—won't that be great fun? Oh, and Maman says I may dine with the family today, and not up in the nursery with Dotty, so shall I ask if you may, also? We can sit at the second table with Mrs. Dingley. I'll tell Maman you and Mrs. Dingley will watch over me—won't that be splendid?"

Esther felt terribly weary; she allowed herself to be buoyed along on Liza's enthusiasm, carried like a leaf on the stream, just as earlier that day she had allowed Jamie to lead her off to Stephen's cottage. She sat at the second table during dinner, along with Becca Dingley and Thomas Swift and a few others, watching the grand guests at Sir William's table, tasting the very dishes she'd helped to prepare that morning, drinking the small beer that was the last of the old batch—had Mrs. Mose had time to brew another?

Esther ate; Esther watched; Esther thought. And then the dinner was cleared (by Betty and Sally; Esther had freed them for other work by scrubbing the platters today), the chairs and tables pushed back, the hired musicians who had been playing in the background struck up dance tunes, and everyone began forming sets for the country dances.

The hall was filling up; for the Christmas festivities the servants, even the lowest stableboys and scullery maids were welcome in the great hall to feast and dance. Bridget was here, and Mr. and Mrs. Mose, and the maids and footmen. Esther was pulled into a set; her partner was Thomas Swift, and as she danced up and down and met and parted, her mind still hung on to the turmoil of her day, of all the Esthers she had been and all she had seen and done. Yes, when she was a child it had been great sport to be upstairs and down, seeing and doing every-thing—*But I am a woman now, or nearly,* she thought, *and I must choose, must decide who I am and what I am to be, or someone else will decide for me.* Surely no girl had ever been presented with such an array of possible lives as she. How would she know? Who would she be?

Then the music changed, and partners changed again, and she was dancing with Sir William, who was very merry while they waited at the bottom of the dance together and asked her if she had been reading any nice poetry lately. Perhaps she could read to him some evening. "My eyes are not what they were," he said, before music whisked them into action again.

With the third dance Esther finally lost her sober mood and let the music and movement carry her away, as it always did when she danced. For the fourth dance she found herself partnered with Lord Onslow, to whom Sir William had introduced her, and although he said not a single word to her, it was still quite breathtaking to be dancing with a lord; he was very fast and skilful, and she had to watch her feet to keep up with him.

The musicians took a rest as the dancers drifted toward food and drink. Just then a pounding at the door interrupted the talk, and a babble of shouting rose from outside. "'Tis the mummers!" cried Dingley, and a dozen voices took up the cry as twenty or more outlandishly dressed mummers trooped into the great hall, their workboots muddy and heavy on the marble floor.

And Esther, who always loved the mummers' visits during the Twelve Days, was cold again as the garishly dressed crowd struck up a carol—*"Come, bring, with a noise, My merry, merry boys / The Christmas Log to the firing."* Yes, Jamie was there, in the petticoat and apron, false bosom and all. Everyone was clapping and singing along; the mummers began to dance.

They had a fiddler, a good deal less skilled than the hired musicians, but his tunes were irresistible, and soon the family and servants were dancing again. Now, with people of their own sort in the hall, the maids and footmen were much bolder than they had been before. Sally, the kitchen maid, was courting a lad who worked on the home farm, and as the mummers did their stomping dance and rowdy chorus, she flew from one man to the next, poking at their masks and crying, "Earl, be that you? Be you Earl?"

Earl, thought Esther. The young man preening in the centre of the room, putting on a woman's gown. She did not laugh with the others as Sally searched loudly for her sweetheart, until one rough voice cried, "I be he, miss!" and a mask was pushed back to reveal the leathery face of old Nick Sparkes, who gripped Sally around the waist and claimed a kiss while she wriggled and squealed.

Then Esther did laugh, but only a little. She looked outside the circle, to see Sir William with Dotty on his lap, beaming at the noisy intruders and liberties they were taking, and laughing with Lord Onslow. Her mother, Bridget, was insisting to Lord Onslow's secretary that she did not want to dance, then allowing herself to be led into a set; nearby, Jane Swift danced with Hal the handsome footman; Dingley stood alone, watching Bridget and Jane with their partners. And then, as everyone formed new sets for a new dance and the mummers mingled with the Moor Park people, Esther found herself across from Jamie Plumridge, who had a pillowcase over his head with holes for eyes. She knew quite well it was he and met his eyes through the mask. She could read several things in those eyes alone: apology, hope, a smile. He started toward her, hesitated, held out his hand.

Esther looked away; she turned away. Away from Jamie's eyes, from the mummers' loud voices and heavy boots. She heard a girl's voice—it was Annie, the dairymaid—saying, "Dance with me, Jamie," and saw Annie take Jamie's outstretched hand. And Hal the footman was coming toward Esther with his hands out, and she took them, and danced with him, and shut her eyes as the fiddler played.

DUBLIN
1723

Esther picks up the journal again. *I sett my pen to paper to write this Journal, which I intend to keep for the Improvement of my Mind.* Those were the first words she had written in her book, penned that same night—the mummers had gone, the guests were in their beds, and Esther was below stairs in the housekeeper's room, sitting at a table across from her mother's box bed, writing by a rush light while her mother was in the kitchen with Mrs. Mose, making sure all was ready for morning. Bridget would have come in a few moments later, fluffed the pillows, told Esther her eyes would be ruined writing in the dark and she was wasting the candle, come to bed. And to bed Esther must have gone, closing her eyes to shut in the visions of that strange day.

She leafs through the early pages, those entries she wrote in the weeks and months after Lady Temple died. That strange nighttime vigil by Lady Temple's body had changed Esther, even more, perhaps, than the day the mummers came. Perhaps neither event caused the change—a girl turning from thirteen to fourteen was turning from child to woman. It was a time of change.

She was melancholic for a long while after Lady Temple's death—she recalls being irritated at Liza, who grieved loudly and stormily for her dead grandmother. *She knowes nothing of her Grandmother, who she truly was or what manner of life she lived,*

Esther had written, *and I cannot tell her, for I must never tell anyone that I read the Letters.* She went often to Sir William's study, and read to him, feeling closer to the old man than she ever had, though she could not tell him why. He did not want her to read gardening books or philosophy or history, as he had done before: he wanted her to read the old romances his wife had given him as courting presents. Reading them tied Esther even more closely to the long-dead world of the letters.

Young Dorothy Osborne had suffered often from melancholy and spleen and took drenches of orange-flower water to cure herself. *I wonder if Lady Giffard keeps any among her simples?* Esther had written in her journal. Had she gone as far as to ask her ladyship for some? Surely not—that would have required explanation and no doubt a lecture on how diligent application to one's work was an excellent cure for the spleen. Lady Giffard had had little sympathy with ailments of the mind and spirit. Esther has tried orange-flower water in the years since but has not found it helpful. Diligent application to work is, indeed, a better tonic. The older she grows, the more things she agrees with Lady Giffard about.

MOOR PARK
MARCH 13, 1695

Today is my Birthday. I am Fourteen yeares old. I feel I might be Forty rather than Fourteen, so heavily does my Life weigh upon me. Liza (that is, Miss Elizabeth Temple) is here Yett, and gave me a lovely work'd Pincushion that she had work'd herselfe, which is most Kind, yet I wish she might go back againe soon to Sheen, for she irritates me with her constant Chatter. She is but Ten yeares old, and knowes nothing of Life.

Mye only other companion in my solitude is Mrs Dingley, who is as Unsatisfactory in her waye, as Liza is in Hers, for though Mrs Dingley is a good Kind woman, and when I am feeling Merry (which is nott often) we have great sport together mocking and making jests at mye Mother, and Jane Swift, and even at Lady Giffard, still Mrs Dingley is no Scholar, and is a very Simple soul, though a good one.

I have attempted to continue mye studies, but with no one about to tutor me, nor anyone even with Whome to discuss what I read, it is very difficult. This day I set myself some lines of Virgil to translate, and these being done went and talk'd French half an hour with old Madame du Plessis. This in the forenoon, then in the afternoon I wrought with my needle, then satt with Liza for a painting lesson. We were to copy a bowl of Oranges, and I painted so poorly, I had a mind to tear my Paper in two, and throw it in the Grate, but I composed myselfe and remember'd that such a display of Choler is unseemly in one of my Sex and Station, and a poor Example for Liza, so I kept still and said nothing. If I maye nott Destroy the painting, I must give it to Dingley for a present, for I loathe the sight of those oranges.

MOOR PARK
JUNE 1, 1695

I am in the greatest of excitement, and can scarce contain myselfe. Today while Liza and I work'd in the Little Parlour, she ask'd whether I might be willing to enter her Mother's service, and goe back with them to Sheen when they retourn. For in the summer, they maye go to France, and I might accompany them.

I had thought only of staying heere at Moor Park, to enter Lady Giffard's service as she has saied I should, but now I can think of noe other Thought than going to France with Liza and Dotty and their Mother. I have soe long desir'd to Travel, but had begunne to think it might never Be, but nowe my dearest Dream may come True.

I have spoke of this to no one yett, not to mye mother or to Lady Giffard, though if it comes to pass I shall need leave of them both, and I doe nott know what they might say. I think mye Mother will be glad to see me with a chance of such a good Position, and I hope Lady Giffard will too, though she is so Contrary I know nott what she will saye.

But first Liza must speake to her Mother, and see if she will be Satisfied to employe me. I satt at dinner today in the servants' hall (for guests were dining upstairs in the hall, the Duke and Duchess from Petworth) and contain'd my Secret within me, as if I had trapp'd a Moth in my hands and could feel its trembling against mye Fingers. I have been so Weary of this world, of mye life heere at Moor Park, and nowe this new Hope has come, and lighten'd everything. The very Spoons seem'd to Shine against the tablecloth, and Dingley's chatter in my ear sounded like the music of bells, and even Jane Swift was bearable.

In the meantime I continue with my Occupation of Learning to serve Lady Giffard. I spend each morning with Dingley learning about her lady-ship's clothes and wigs and all her doings, for there is a great deal to Do. Lady Giffard also has me to write some of her letters for Her, which I am better at than Dingley is.

I was right glad this Afternoon, for Sir William sent for me to read to him, which he has nott done but twice since his Wife's death, and then he had me read Romances such as she gave to Him in their Youth. Today he ask'd me to read Plato, and it cheer'd me to think he was againe able to give his Minde to sterner Matter. And I think mye minde too, has growne stronger, for it did me good to dwell on Philosophie. Then he ask'd me to read some passages of his owne Writing, to say what I thought on't, and I was much flatter'd by this.

I think he misses Mr Swift, M. Jonathan Swift, I meane, for he sayes Thomas was never half so goode a secretary, and now that he has his living at Puttenham, he is even lesse heere. Sir William has had a letter of Mr Jonathan, to saye what we knew already from Jane, that he has a living at a parish called Kilroot, but when I read over the letter it did not seeme he lik'd it very well, and it is just as Jane saies, that I am sure he still would wish to retourne to England, and just *as I am dreaming of leaving it! But it is the will of God where we goe, and I must submit myselfe ever to His will.*

MOOR PARK
JULY 15, 1695

Yesterday Dingley and I accompanied Lady Giffard to Petworth, and staid there the night, retourning only this morning. I have heard so much of this house where the Duke and Duchess of Somerset live, for Dingley has beene there many times, but I never before saw it, for this is mye first time out as Lady Giffard's lady-in-waiting, and I found it to be a far pleasanter experience than I might have dream'd.

The duke of Petworth is a most Haughty man, and his servants saie that Everyone is made to Stand in his presence, even his owne Wife and children. The duchess is a Famous beauty with an even more famous Past, for she was Married as a young girl, and when she was but Fourteene her Lover, a German count, murder'd her husband! It was thrilling indeede to be in the Home of such grand People.

There was a great party of gentry from all the country round, and seventeen ladies and gentlemen sat down to dinner at three o'clock, and at the second table sat Dingley and I with the upper servants from Petworth and those whoe had come with the guests, and a merry party it was. A young man was there, one Jonathan Frye, who is the Duke of Somerset's valet. He was a fayre, well-made fellow of some twenty-four or twenty-five years old, and Dingley railed at me all the evening through that he was in love and was casting looks of Love upon me, at which I but Laughed, but then she made a jest that anger'd me, for she saied that a man need only have the Christian name Jonathan to win my heart. And this made me blush with anger, to hear my good tutor's name link'd with my owne in so Low a Connexion. But I soon master'd my Choler, and told her That either one Jonathan or the other would be a fitter match for Her than for me, for I am young yet, and meane to marry no old man, and then it was her turn to be Cross.

So we had a merry time save for Dingley's folly, and after dinner we plaied faro, that I have not plaied as much as whisk, for we play whisk all the time at home, and soe before supper I had lost all the money I had brought with me, which thanks be to God was nott soe muche. For dinner we had a great feast of beef and mutton, and the same cold for supper, the which Dingley and I ate in the servants' hall, far larger and grander than ours at Moor Park.

Dingley and I were given a bed in a room down the corridor from the house-keeper's room. This morning I attended Lady Giffard, and helped her to dress and packed her clothes for our retourne to Moor Park. And while we were thus alone, she prais'd me, and said, to my surprise, that she had been watching me, and that I comported myselfe well in company, and that I made a better lady's maid and companion than Dingley, for tho' Dingley be older, and her birth far above mine, yett, Lady Giffard saies, I am quick to learn, and good in conversation, and have sought to better myself by good education. And all this gave me great cause for pleasure, and I doubt not an excess of Pride, but some sorrow too, for that I have growne so fond of Dingley tho' she does anger me at times, yet she is my friend, and I would not heare myselfe prais'd, at the cost of Blame to my poor Becca.

In truth I am glad to please Lady Giffard, stern though she is, for now that I am so much in her Company my Admiration for her is the greater. She has Suffered greatly, poor soul, for she was widow'd only a fortnight after her wedding day, and vow'd herself afterward never more to marry, but to dedicate herselfe entirely to her Brother, for whome she has a passing great Love. She is a very learned woman, for she has learn'd of her brother, soe that she may help him in all his Work and his Writing.

And I thought as she talk'd, of how very noble a Love this was, and how Blessed is Sir William, for in his life he has been greatly lov'd by two noble Women, his wife and his sister, and I thought much on which kind of Love I should rather have, if either were to be granted to me. For it would be a wonderful thing to have a great Passion, as Sir William and Lady Temple had for one another in their Youth, and to marry the person one so esteem'd, yet tho' they were well matched and happy enough, I suppose, still I do not think that great

Adoration can last life long. And when I listened to Lady Giffard talk, I heartily wish'd I had such a Brother as Sir William, that I might devote myself to keeping his House and helping him with his Worke, and I should rather have that, I believe, than any great Romance or Passion. I think often, now, about what sort of life might suite me, whether to marry a poor man and have a little household of my owne, or to remaine in service and enjoy the comforts of a Great House, perhaps even one so great as Petworth. The governess there, Alice, told me I might well Aspire to such a place as hers, with my learning and mye needleworke.

But of all this I saied nothing to Lady Giffard, save to thank her, and say that I praied I might learn to serve her better. And she saied that I should have better opportunities, and that she would take me to London when next she went there to staye. And in truth, this thought of going to London thrilled me full as much as Liza's plan to take me to France, of which I have heard nothing for some Time now. I know nott which I would rather doe, so long as I maye travel, and see more of the world, than I have done.

MOOR PARK
MARCH 25, 1696

The wind howls outside the walls; it is a wild night of storm and not at all as the daye had promis'd it would be. And indeede I feel some Kinship with the Night, for mye heart is wild within my Breast and not at all as it ought to be, when all I have heard is that my old friend and Tutor, Mr Swift, is coming againe to Moor Park. Jane Swift told us tonight that Sir William had taken him back into his service, and that he has left Ireland, and is now at Leicestershire and soon to retourne here.

It is more than two years since I saw him, and in those two yeares have been weeks on end when I scarce thought of him till someone chanc'd to recall his name to my Memory. Yet now that he is to retourne, I feel as if it is the most momentous Occourence, and yet I knowe not why.

Perhaps it may be that there was such harsh words said between us ere we parted, that tho' in some wise we made it up, yett I feel the Friendship and Esteem we once had must be forever gone, and if he were here, and nott my Friend, I doe not think I could bear it. Or it may yet be that I have changed and growne so, since last we mett, that I wonder will he approve the changes in me, or think that I have grown to be Vain and Foolish despite all his training, and my owne Strictest efforts.

Or is it this, which writing I know I shall never show to any living soul, that I know myselfe now to be a woman grown, and as Others view me in such a light, I wonder ... No, I cannot write what I meane, cannot find words to say it. It is a wicked Thought, and never would be in my head at all if Dingley were not so saucy, to say what she should not. For she has, I have learn'd, very fine Fantasies of myselfe and Mr Swift, to which I reply by telling her that I once thought the same of Herself, but that I was a Child at the time, and may be excus'd my fancies. Hers are but folly, and such could never be nor would I wish it. But, like the Evil One tempting Eve in the Garden, she has planted the thought, and now I cannot think of Mr Swift without the thing coming to Mind, to wonder if he would find me fair.

DUBLIN
1723

Half a smile pulls at Esther's mouth as she reads those last lines. *All Becca's fault, then,* she thinks. What an idea to put into the head of a fifteen-year-old girl—to make her pin her fancies, her affections, on an older man whose station in life was far above hers. And yet, looked at another way, it was—had always been— the logical choice. What better destiny for young Hetty, educated above her station, than to marry Sir William's ambitious young secretary?

And so it began: a lifetime of suggestion, of innuendo, of possibility that couldn't rightly be called either hope or fear. Looking back at her own description of Petworth, Esther saw that her feet had been set in those days on a straight and sensible road. She was a lady's maid, and a good one: remaining unmarried, as her mother and Lady Giffard advised, she would have been well set to take a position as a governess in a great household, or perhaps to rise to housekeeper at Moor Park after her mother's time. A clear and straightforward life, one she might have enjoyed and been good at.

But then came that other possibility, like a fly buzzing just behind her ear—the idea that her future might be linked, in some way, to that of Jonathan Swift. Becca had imagined, in her prosaic way, that that would mean marriage. It had not, in fact, meant anything so simple, yet Becca had been right, for all that. Esther Johnson's path had become twined with that of Jonathan Swift, and nothing since had been straightforward or simple.

Love? No, she had not fallen in love with him, she was sure of that. At fifteen a girl is ready for love, ready to have her heart stolen and even broken. But Mr. Swift had had no interest in hearts, or even in bodies, she was sure. Not for the first time, Esther tried to imagine herself as seen through his eyes—herself at fifteen, on the day he returned to Moor Park.

MOOR PARK
1696

He arrived in the rain, on a dull day when Esther sat reading aloud to Lady Giffard while her ladyship and Dingley worked on a tapestry—a pastoral scene, with nymphs and shepherds—to replace the rotting wall hangings in the Little Parlour. Sheets of rain sluiced against the window, providing a steady background to the translation of Plutarch's *Lives* that Lady Giffard had requested.

One of the chambermaids entered the room and curtsyed to Lady Giffard. "Beg pardon, ma'am, but Sir William sent to tell you that Mr. Swift has arrived, and that he would like the upper servants to take dinner with you both in the hall this afternoon."

Lady Giffard nodded shortly. "Very well. Go tell Mrs. Johnson and Mrs. Mose. Read on, Hetty."

Esther, who had lost her place in the life of Alexander, turned quickly back to the book, but not before catching the glance Dingley shot her. Her heart beat harder, and she knew her cheeks were flushed. A curse on Dingley, with all her foolish gossip! Mr. Swift, Esther reminded herself, knew her as a precocious little girl—one he had scolded roundly at their last encounter. He would probably pay her no attention at all now that he had returned. He was a successful young clergyman with a secure living in Ireland, taking his first steps on that upward ladder he so wanted to climb. The housekeeper's daughter, too old now to amuse him with her childish attempts at Greek and Latin, would hardly merit his attention.

Yet she paused before the mirror in Lady Giffard's room before they all went down to dinner. Beneath her white cap she saw two long dark ringlets hanging to her shoulders, framing a small face with wide dark eyes. *No great beauty,* she reminded herself, and followed Lady Giffard down to the hall.

Mr. Swift was there already, seated with Sir William. They rose as the women came in, and Mr. Swift made a graceful bow to Lady Giffard. She accepted his hand with something less than her usual disdain, and said, "Welcome back to Moor Park, Mr. Swift."

He passed on, then, to greet Dingley and Bridget, and came at last to Esther. He looked so different, older and more sure of himself. His shoulders were broader, and he looked altogether more solid and serious. His dress was far more sophisticated and stylish than it had been before he went away. His wig was curled in the newest style, with the slightest suggestion of horns on either side of his head, and his coat was cut just above the knee. He took her hand, bowed over it, and said, "Good day, Miss Esther."

Esther flushed a little: she remembered now that he was the only one at Moor Park who always used her proper name. She was still Hetty or Miss Hetty to most people in the house: a few of the newer servants, who knew her as Lady Giffard's maid, called her Mrs. Hetty. The name *Esther*, on Jonathan Swift's lips, was a gift, for with it he offered her not only dignity but friendship returned. She was sure he remembered nothing of their last quarrel—and why should he? It was a small matter in the career of an ambitious young man, no matter how large it might loom in a girl's memory.

Mr. Swift talked little at dinner until Sir William drew him out by asking him about his writing, and he began to discuss with great energy a pamphlet he was working on—a complex allegory about three brothers who represented the Church of Rome, the Church of England, and the dissenters. Earlier, when he had talked about his parish in Ireland, he had sounded dull and dutiful: now his eyes sparkled and his hands danced in the air. His book sounded very witty, quite different from the poems he had burned in the library fireplace so long ago, and Esther was caught up in his description of it. She was quite unprepared when he turned to her and said, "While I am acting as Sir William's secretary, I shall need a secretary of my own, to transcribe my rough copies of my work. Are you still willing to honour the promise you made so long ago, Miss Esther?"

"To be your secretary? Oh yes!" Esther said. "I have kept up my studies, Mr. Swift, and would be glad to aid you. Although, of course, I am in Lady Giffard's employ now," she added belatedly, "and my first duty is to serve her."

"Hetty writes a fine hand," Sir William said. "She might assist you in your work on my papers as well, Swift—if my sister can spare her for a few hours a day."

Lady Giffard held her cup out for the footman to refill it. "Dingley will serve as well as Hetty to sit with me at needlework, though I will have to do without a book to listen to—Dingley can't read decently at all, can you, Dingley? Of course, Papa, your work must come first, and if Hetty can help Mr. Swift at all, I shall release her gladly."

And with those few sentences, all their old roles were changed, and the pieces lined up for a new game. Much as Esther enjoyed her work as a lady's maid, she was far more excited by the chance to be Mr. Swift's assistant. To help him with Sir William's memoirs was an honour—to help him make fair copies of his own work was exhilarating. If she could be to him even a little of the kind of helper Lady Giffard had been to Sir William—well, it was the very thing she had dreamed of, and far more real than all Dingley's fantasies of romance.

Not that Dingley's fantasies ceased once the real Mr. Swift was on the scene. Her tongue rattled on into the night as Esther lay beside her in bed. "Imagine Mr. Swift, with all his railing about women's vanity—to show up looking the very height of fashion! I almost expected to see red heels on his shoes."

Esther laughed in spite of herself, remembering the new wig and the cut of his coat. "That would be too much altogether—

but no doubt now that he is out in the world he is more concerned about the impression he makes."

"And what is that but vanity, to be concerned about the impression you make?" Dingley said. "Still, he's much handsomer than when he went away, isn't he?"

"I wouldn't know, I was only a little girl when he was here before," Esther said, turning away and pulling the blanket over her shoulders.

"Ah, but you're not a little girl now, and I'll wager he sees that."

"For shame, Dingley. If anyone heard your chatter, they'd be sure indeed that *one* woman in this house was in love with Mr. Swift—but they'd hardly think it was me."

That quieted Dingley for the night, but not for long. A few evenings later, Mr. Swift joined Esther, Dingley, and Bridget for a card game in the housekeeper's room. He was in high spirits, jesting with Bridget and with Dingley. "Look how she takes the snuff! What a great pinch of it!" he said as Dingley reached for her snuffbox again. "Mrs. Johnson, you'll have to ration her, or enter 'Mrs. Dingley's snuff' as an entirely new item in the household budget."

"Oh, and I'm sure you've no bad habits," Dingley countered.

"Indeed not, I am a paragon of sober and upright living. You can ask anyone in Ireland."

"Only because Ireland is such a dull country, you found no temptation to sin there," Esther's mother suggested.

Esther herself kept quiet, and as a result won that game. Her luck was not so good in the next, and Mr. Swift turned his raillery in her direction. "How much money have you lost at cards since I went away, Miss Esther? Have you gambled away all the gold pieces Sir William gave you?"

"Indeed I have not, sir! I gamble with other people's money, never my own!"

"A wise card player indeed, though I find it hard to believe." He smiled at her as he laid down a card.

"Oh, our Hetty has grown in wisdom and stature since you went away," Dingley said, reaching out to squeeze her arm and entirely ignoring the look Esther shot her. "Truly now, Mr. Swift, what do you think of her? Hasn't she grown to be a fine young woman?"

Esther ducked her head, but Mr. Swift looked at her thoughtfully, his lower lip thrust out, as if he were a farmer appraising a cow at the market. "Her face and form have filled out quite nicely," he judged, "only she is, perhaps, a little too fat."

"How dare you!" Esther gasped in mock horror. She was secretly rather pleased, because all through her childhood she had been called too skinny. "But," she pointed out to Dingley later, "those are hardly the words of a suitor, are they? So perhaps now you can stop this foolishness, and let Mr. Swift and me get on with being friends and fellow labourers."

Dingley sniffed. "Friends, indeed," she said, but held her tongue for once.

Later that night, in the faint glow of a rush light, Esther wrote the whole scene in a few hasty lines in her journal. As she looked at them on the page, she remembered that she had first started keeping a journal when Mr. Swift went away, hoping that the habit of reflecting soberly on each day's lessons might replace his teaching and guidance. She had even thought, back then, that she might show it to him someday so that he might approve the course her education had taken in his absence.

How quickly the journal had grown to be … well, something quite different. She could never show it to him now; it was full of such vanity and folly. And yet she could not lay it aside, either. Her tutor had returned, more the friend and less the tutor, and she found that just as the journal could not take his place, neither could he take the place of her journal. She must go on writing here, putting down on paper the things she would never tell Mr. Swift or anyone else, continuing her education in something other than Latin or Greek.

MOOR PARK AND LONDON
1697–1698

"What a fine, stout girl you've grown, Hetty!"

It was hard to know how best to respond to one of Jane Swift's compliments. Jane sat with her feet to the fire in Esther's mother's room, stitching away at a pillowcase and looking for all the world as if she'd been planted and grown there. Everything about Jane was small, sharp, and pointed: her nose, her chin, her breasts, her feet, and certainly her mind. Bridget was nowhere to be seen: the other chair was occupied by Dingley, plump and round faced, with her soft hair flying out in wisps from under her cap.

"Yes, she's filled out grand, wouldn't you say?" Dingley reached out an arm, hooked it around Esther's waist, and drew the girl to her side, throwing her a little off balance. "She took another fit of illness in August—but see how she thrives since then." Dingley slapped Esther's bottom as though the girl's figure was something for which she herself could take credit.

"Becca, *please*," Esther moaned, which brought a high-pitched laugh from Jane. "You should be pleased, girl, 'tis only Bec and me here praising how plump you've grown. I'll wager there's many a young footman hereabouts has noticed you've grown a real bosom at last!"

Esther struggled to swallow the hot rage rising in her throat and reddening her cheeks. The only thing she really wished to do was choke Jane, and that would hardly be decorous behaviour. "I have no interest in the opinions of footmen," she said with all the dignity she could muster.

"Ah, set your sights higher, have you?" said Jane with a very broad wink at Dingley. "No harm in that, my girl. Sit down, rest yourself. You're not so busy as all that, are you?"

A fine thing, thought Esther, *to see how she makes free of my mother's room!* But she said only, "I came to look for my mother. Lady Giffard has orders for her. Do either of you know where she is?"

"Down in the still room," Jane said. "Sure you won't sit with us? 'Twould be a shame if you'd grown into such a fine-looking girl only to get ideas above your station."

Above her station. How many more times, Esther wondered, would she have that phrase flung at her in her lifetime? And from such as Jane Swift? She shot a glance at Dingley: here, at least, she and Bec ought to be of one mind. For that matter, if there were any fairness, Jane ought to be an ally too, for her status was as murky as theirs. But Bec only laughed along with Jane as Esther turned and went out to the still room.

Lady Giffard had Esther, Dingley and Jane all in her rooms to supper and for cards afterwards: when her ladyship expressed a desire for an early bedtime the party moved downstairs to the housekeeper's room, where Bridget made up the fourth. Esther came a little late, having helped her mistress prepare for bed, to find that the tone of talk and laughter had predictably become several degrees coarser.

"And I told him, sir, it hardly becomes a man of your position, to be caught with your hand in a maid's bosom!" Jane finished a story triumphantly as Esther came in. Bridget glanced up at her daughter with a frown but must have decided Esther was old enough now to hear such talk, for she said nothing.

"Tush! You never!" said Dingley, dealing the cards. "'Tis no wonder you lost your place there! Did he not chide you for being saucy?"

"Saucy? It was no more than right for me to say so, be he gentleman or no," shot back Jane. "Paying my wages don't entitle him to have a hand down my gown! If he'd kept up he'd have seen what happens to a man who uses Jane Swift so! As if I were a common trollop, a scullery maid! A poor woman has nothing but her virtue to protect, and he'd no intention of making me his mistress or any such thing. What kind of match could I hope to make after he'd finished with me?"

A moment passed between the three older women: Jane caught Bridget's eye; they held each other's gaze a moment, neither looking away, while Dingley shifted her glance nervously from one to the other and licked her lips. Esther had no idea what was being unsaid, but she suddenly felt protective of her mother and eager to wound Jane.

"Why, Jane, have you great hope of making a match—still?" Esther asked pointedly, and was rewarded with a narrow-eyed glance from Jane. Dingley and Bridget snickered.

"Yes, Hetty girl, I've not given up hope entirely, though I'm barely on the right side of thirty yet. Your mother and Bec and I, we're all still looking for our chance, though no doubt we'd be better off pinning all our hopes on you. Perhaps you'll marry rich, and your fortune will keep us all."

"Hush! Don't go filling the child's head with nonsense!" Bridget said, laying down her cards with a snap.

"What, marriage?" Dingley protested after a moment's silence. "'Tis a sensible thing to be thinking of at her age, for she's a woman grown now, and with as pretty a face as Hetty's, there'll be offers soon enough."

Bridget eyed her daughter across the table. "No foolish thoughts of marrying a rich man for you, my girl. If you marry, you'll marry poor and live poor, and you're better off not to think of it at all. With a constitution like yours, childbed might well be the death of you. Steer clear of men—that's my advice."

"And I shall take your advice, Mother—at least until I am old enough to choose wisely," said Esther primly, darting a glance at Dingley and one at Jane. The barbs went home; there was no more talk of her marriage. And a good thing too, for with Dingley's insistence on what a fine girl she'd grown into, Esther was in mortal fear that Dingley would proudly announce to Jane that Esther had just started her monthly flux. Bridget herself had done little more than tell Esther where to find the rags, but Jane and Dingley were forever talking and complaining of it, moaning about their aches and recommending infusions that might ease their pain. She had heard so much of it before it came that she thought it easily the single most important thing in a woman's life, yet it was odd that Lady Giffard never spoke of it, though she still had it— Esther knew because of the laundry. It was a thing for common women to talk of, not for ladies. She tried unsuccessfully to imagine the duchess of Somerset discussing, or indeed experiencing, her flux.

To ward off any such discussion, Esther pleaded a sore head and took herself off to bed. She now slept with Dingley in the little chamber off Lady Giffard's room, a place Jane greatly coveted when she was at Moor Park. But as Lady Giffard said privately to Esther, Jane Swift was really superfluous now: she fancied herself lady's maid, but there was no need for another woman in that position. What they needed were more kitchenmaids and chambermaids, a topic that was uppermost on Lady Giffard's mind the next morning when Esther's mother arrived in her rooms to discuss the day's duties.

Esther was dressing Lady Giffard's hair: it had just received one of its infrequent washings during which, with the aid of a comb, a pan of warm water, and a soap-and-egg mixture, Esther had tried to remove months' accretions of powder, grease, dirt, and lice. Now she was combing it out, gently so as not to hurt her mistress, who was swaddled in robes and blankets while a fire burned briskly in the hearth and her feet rested on a warming pan to avoid chill. Bridget, standing next to Lady Giffard, was rattling through the list of things Mrs. Mose needed in Farnham. As an afterthought, she added, "And there's Bessie—I suppose I must have a talk with her."

"There is no question, Bridget, that girl must go." Lady Giffard's voice was crisp as a newly starched apron. She flinched a little as Esther worked the comb through a tangle. "I have given her every opportunity, but what good is a chambermaid who won't work?"

"I heard her myself tell Sir William that she had never washed up a room in her life, nor never expected to," Bridget agreed; Esther could see the quirk in her mother's cheek that meant Bridget was trying hard to suppress a smile. Bridget had never liked the girl Bessie; she thought she put on airs above her station, but it was Lady Giffard who had insisted Bessie came well recommended, from a good family in Farnham, and had been determined to give her every opportunity. Bridget had held her tongue—she was good at doing that, in the presence of her betters, though not to her inferiors—and now she had her reward: Bessie was being turned out, with Lady Giffard convinced it was all her own idea.

"The impudence of the chit!" the lady of the house was still storming after Bridget left. "Telling me she thought herself a gentlewoman! I told her quite plain, 'I have Hetty, and I have Dingley, and I hardly have need of *three* gentlewomen to attend me! What I do have need of is a good chambermaid. Lord and Lady Onslow are coming in less than a fortnight, and the condition of the guest rooms is deplorable.' There, that's fine, Hetty," she added, glancing in the mirror. "Go down to your mother's rooms and tell her that we need an extra girl to scrub down the floors in the Green Chamber."

"Easy for her to say," said Bridget when Esther delivered the message. "Little does she know the problems of finding good help. We've got Sally gone and married now, and Betty, and there's no one in the kitchen with enough brains in her head to make a chambermaid, so I shall have to look outside again, and listen to Nan and Nellie complain that they're being passed over." She stood up too, the keys at her waist jingling. "Hetty, run to the kitchen and tell Mrs. Mose I need Nellie for a few hours. She'll have to do the work of a chambermaid for today, at least."

Esther went down the hallway to the kitchen. The stones beneath her feet rang with the impact of her boot heels as she strode past, and Nellie, who was peeling potatoes in the kitchen, looked up sullenly when she entered. "Good day, Mrs. Hetty, ma'am," she said. Nellie was not a good servant; she did not take naturally to deference, and she resented having to be respectful to a girl four years her junior, just because that girl was Lady Giffard's lady-in-waiting.

But Esther, who always tried to be kind to servants, said only, "Good day, Nellie. Do you know where I may find Mrs. Mose?"

Pride was a sin Esther struggled against in her prayers and on the pages of her journal, but how could she not be proud to have such a good position at her age? She was immensely privileged to have been granted a life of freedom from scrubbing and dusting and making beds—tasks that might so easily have been hers, had things been a little different. Some girls worked their way up through the levels of household service to become, finally, ladies' maids if they were qualified, but anyone who could step right into the position was fortunate indeed, and Esther's only defence against pride was to continually thank God for that good fortune—and, in her heart, Lady Giffard, who had had a less divine but more direct hand in it.

She was well content with life at Moor Park in the autumn and winter of her sixteenth year. To be sure, she had not yet achieved her dreams of travel, having been no farther than Petworth and Clandon Park and other nearby manors with Lady Giffard; the family had removed to London at the end of last winter, and Esther was supposed to have accompanied them, but she had taken ill just before the departure date and been left behind to recover. But the war with France was over at last, with great celebrations and fireworks in London, which had started young Mrs. Temple and her family talking about a trip to France next year, and Liza still talked of Esther accompanying them. This winter there would be another visit to London, and in the meantime there was Christmas, with visits and visitors, and family evenings of card playing and reading aloud, and her work in the library with Mr. Swift on the great mountain of writing Sir William had managed to produce in his long and busy life. It was there that she managed to escape after dinner, with apologies to her mentor as she slipped into the desk across from his.

"I am sorry, I had thought I could come this morning," she explained, "but her ladyship needed me. Some great matter of choosing fabric for a new gown for Christmas—she trusts my taste over Becca's, it would seem."

"Wise lady, our mistress," said Swift. "Poor Hetty! Queen Esther the Indispensable, still being all things to all people at Moor Park. Ah! Wait till she comes into her fortune, and can be a lady of leisure, sipping chocolate at eleven in the morning and having no nasty French letters to translate.

"Come, Esther, see what you think of this. I do not believe I have caught the sense of it, after all, though I've been slaving over it all morning." He pushed a piece of paper across the desk to her, the top part written in French, the bottom in English.

"I ought to have paid more attention to my French, all that time you were teaching me Latin and Greek," said Esther, screwing up her nose. "I think this is—no, wait, I see what you mean. There is a problem here, though if you can't solve it, I hardly think I could. Do you wish me to take it to Sir William and see if he can recall what he might have meant?"

"Meant by words he penned in another tongue thirty years ago? I hardly think so," said Swift with a quick smile. "Unless this is one of his better days."

"He was very amiable at dinner; I ate with him and Lady Giffard," Esther said. Poor old Sir William was really old now, having never really regained his spirit after his wife's death. Sometimes his mind wandered, though usually he was still quite sharp, and his moods were unreliable too; he could become cross without a moment's notice. Just last week he had been terribly angry at her and Swift for misplacing some vitally important chapter of his memoir—a chapter both were quite certain they had never seen. Their denials proved no use, and when at last the missing chapter was discovered in his own desk drawer, no apology followed; he had quite forgotten accusing them. "It's a race to see which will finish first," Swift said at the time, "Sir William's memoirs or Sir William's memory." But, though Esther hated to imagine the old man ever dying, she knew that the memoirs, which were a huge task, would probably last many years longer than the man who had written them. She tried to push the knowledge as far back as possible: making jests about Sir William's memory and moods was one thing, but imagining Moor Park— or the world—without him was quite another.

She and Swift worked on for a companionable hour, occasion-ally exchanging comments on the work they had done. She was editing and copying a chapter of the manuscript, and when she was done, she handed it to Swift for his approval.

"It looks well enough," he said when he had read it. "Did you enjoy it?"

She grinned. "You know well enough I did not! Page after tedious page of politics, politics, politics! I enjoy quite well the places where he writes of his travels, or the essays on literature or on gardening, but I think you should be left to do all the political works, for you enjoy it and I despise it!"

"Ah well, politics is men's business anyway. Perhaps you are right, and a lovely female head such as yours need not be troubled with it."

"I suppose politics will take you away from us again soon?" said Esther, walking away from the desk and stretching her arms.

"To London at the end of the month, with messages to the king," said Swift with immense satisfaction. He too stood up, and came to stand behind her, looking out the window at the leafless elms in the garden below. "But back again in time for Christmas."

"Indeed you must be!" Esther said. "For what would Christmas and New Year's be without our poet of Moor Park?"

"Oh, someday I shall go off to London for good and leave you to make the verses, Esther. No, don't deny it, no shaking of the pretty locks, la, for I sees you and I knows your secrets, and all your little scribblings, so oo mustn't try to hide it." He had lapsed into baby talk again, as he still sometimes did, and although it irked her a little if she was already full of spleen, today she was in a cheerful mood and laughed at him. He was the only person who did know that from time to time she wrote poetry: nothing great, of course, nothing that would ever be published, only little verses that she tried to make pretty, the sort of thing young women quite commonly wrote.

She had written two quite long poems over the summer: one was about Moor Park, describing its beauties, and the other was about Virtue. Mr. Swift had praised them both and given her suggestions for their improvement, but she was not quite happy with either. She felt that some cataclysm in her life was needed to produce better poetry; the best thing would be if she could fall in love. Without love there did not seem to be so much to write about, not for a woman, anyway, if she avoided politics as a subject. But love had not yet happened to her. Dingley still railed her about having a fancy for Jonathan Frye at Petworth, and—more scandalously—about marrying Mr. Swift someday, but neither of those inspired her to the heights of romance as she had glimpsed them on that long-ago night when she had read Lady Temple's love letters. A man who combined the qualities of both—as young and handsome as Mr. Frye, as clever and wise as Mr. Swift—would she fall in love with such a paragon, if he existed? Certainly he would be a man well worth marrying—if she were to marry at all—but there was something more, some elusive other thing required for romance, that she felt she could never find by simply pulling together all the best qualities of all the admirable men she knew.

But there was world and time enough yet to find love, if that was her destiny, Esther concluded. Not, perhaps, at Moor Park, where she saw few new faces from one week to the next, especially as Sir William's health deteriorated and they received fewer and fewer visitors. But perhaps in London, where the household was going after a too-quiet Christmas season—who knew what London might hold?

Esther was so eager for the trip that she had her trunk packed a fortnight in advance, which was inconvenient as she had to keep taking things out of it to wear. Her mother went ahead to London before the family, for the London housekeeper had given notice. Two weeks later Sir William and Lady Giffard followed, accompanied by Esther, Dingley, and Sir William's valet, Mr. Robinson, a dour unsmiling young man who had recently joined the household. Esther had been trying to interest Dingley in Mr. Robinson as a possible suitor and kept up the raillery in low tones all throughout the jouncing ride to London in the coach, and during the two nights that she and Dingley shared a bed in inns on the way, but no spark of attraction seemed to fly between Dingley and Robinson despite their sudden proximity.

On the third day Esther was obliged to give it up, for they were approaching London, and her eyes were glued to the tiny window of the coach, watching as the rolling farmlands and neat villages she had been accustomed to all her life gave way to the sprawling suburbs of the great city. Houses crowded closer and closer together so that when the coach stopped at an inn, Esther thought they were in the heart of London. But no, they were still a long way from the city itself, despite the noise and crowding of the inn, and they had to wait there for their own carriage from Temple House to come out and bring them into the city.

The carriage was more comfortable by far than the coach had been, but this last stage of the ride was torment for Esther, who so longed to be out in the streets she could barely glimpse, seeing London at last.

Noise hit like a solid wall when at last she stepped down from the carriage. Riders on horseback and carts and carriages of all descriptions clattered through the street, but far more numerous were the people on foot, children shouting, women's voices shrilling after them, the singsong chant of men hawking their wares. All this she heard before she saw it, for the carriage was inside the gates of Temple House, and not until she turned away from the house and toward the busy thoroughfare of Dover Street did she see the passing throng making all the noise.

She blinked. Not only the sudden assault of light after dimness but also something in the air was making her eyes sting. The very air smelled different. She drew in a deep breath of London, then coughed.

"Hetty!" Lady Giffard's voice was sharp above the din, and Esther turned quickly to help her mistress out of the carriage and arrange her cloak over her shoulders. Jack was handing down trunks to a bevy of strange menservants who had suddenly appeared before the house.

Lady Giffard sailed up the steps of Temple House like a frigate under the wind, leaving Esther and Dingley in her wake to steer Sir William, who was more unsteady than usual after the long ride. The servants disappeared round the side of the house with the trunks, and too soon the enticing street noises were shut out by the great doors of Temple House, and an impeccable footman was saying, "My lord, my lady," and bowing low as he led them through a hall gleaming in marble and plaster and up a staircase. Esther was surprised—were they being shown up to the bedchambers at once?—but at the top of the stairs was another hall, and beyond that a blue parlour hung with tapestries. When, sometime later, she and Dingley were shown up to a small bedchamber adjoining Lady Giffard's rooms, they had to climb two more flights of stairs. The house seemed to have nearly as many and as large rooms as Moor Park, but they were all stacked on top of one another.

"Well," said Dingley as she unlaced her stays, "this trip to London will be a better one for me than most." She hauled a voluminous nightgown over her head.

"Why better?" asked Esther.

"Young Mrs. Temple and Miss Elizabeth are here, so there will be more outings and more entertainments, and you are here, so I will have to be included in all the fun."

"Whatever do you mean?" Esther could see why the presence of Liza and her mother would make the party livelier than it would be if Lady Giffard and Sir William alone were there, but she did not at all understand how her own presence made such a difference.

"When I come up as her ladyship's companion, she often as not leaves me behind when she goes out, or takes me only on the dullest of visits," Dingley explained. "But she told your mother and me before we left Moor Park that she means to take you out into society and have you meet people. And as I'm her relation, even she can't be barefaced enough to treat you better than me, so we shall both be treated as ladies—not just *her* ladies, but ladies in our own right."

Esther thought through this possibility. Lady Giffard had been most insistent on having new gowns and petticoats made for both Esther and Dingley, quite the nicest Esther had ever had. "Where will she take us?"

"Well, not to the Court ball—we're not fine enough for that—but to the theatre, and on visits, and to dinners and balls from time to time, I imagine," said Dingley, settling herself into bed with a little grunt of contentment. Esther turned back the covers and slipped in beside her. The flaxen sheets felt clean and smooth and wonderful against her skin, and her tired bones relaxed into the mattress. She had been shaken and tossed about the coach for two long days, and the beds in the inns had been dirty and lumpy—one probably infested with fleas, the other certainly so, as she remembered watching one suck on Dingley's plump forearm and slapping it away.

Dingley had been asleep then, as she was now. As always when they shared a bed, Esther reflected how quickly the other woman lapsed into unconsciousness, while Esther always stared wide-eyed at the bed hangings for a good half-hour—nearly an hour tonight, what with such words as *theatre, balls,* and *court* rolling through her head. Would it be better, after all, to be as simple and placid as Dingley, untroubled by doubts and questions about her place in the world?

As it turned out, she was to see the shops and markets before she saw any theatres or balls. Lady Giffard's primary purpose in coming to London was always to shop, and while Esther's mother was sent on the more prosaic errands to purchase linens, plate, and supplies for Moor Park, Esther and Dingley were invited along to confer with her ladyship on the purchase of fabrics and the process of having them made up into gowns.

Liza and her mother were also included in this expedition, which made it considerably more interesting. Esther had never really liked the haughty young Mrs. Temple, but she certainly admired that lady's sense of style and her taste in gowns. "And I am to have three new gowns as well," Liza confided as she climbed into the carriage beside Esther. "You must help me choose. I want everything in silk, and someone will have to persuade Maman that I am grown-up enough. You would think, now that I am betrothed, that she would stop treating me like a child." Esther caught Dingley's eye. They had a wager on how long it would take Liza to work her betrothal into the conversation. Last night she had only got ten minutes into conversation before it somehow came up.

She's such a child still, she thought with a sudden rush of tenderness. Liza carried herself like a little lady, and she had always been tall and well formed for her years, but she was still only thirteen. Though she was fully as tall as Esther now, the curve of her cheek still held a child's plumpness, and her bosom was only a hint beneath the tight-laced robings of her gown. She was playing at being a woman now, with this new toy of being betrothed, but Esther could hardly imagine Liza actually grown and married and mistress of a house.

Yet someday she would be mistress of Sheen and Moor Park too, in a coup that had delighted everyone in the family, for she was going to marry her cousin, Jack Temple, who was the heir to all his uncle William's property. If Liza had been a boy it would all have been hers, but now she was marrying the man who would inherit it all, and everyone saw the rightness of that. Esther had wondered how Liza saw it—if she liked Cousin Jack, if she felt her own sensibilities were being put aside in the interests of property—but she saw that she need not have worried. Liza, Esther thought, might have been betrothed to the very tsar of Muscovy himself and would have been quite charmed, despite his barbaric country and his uncouth habits, so long as she was able to toss the magic word *betrothal* into every conversation.

It was the tsar all the ladies were talking about now, trading stories of the fabulous creature who was even now visiting England for the first time. "Do you think we'll see him while he's in London?" Liza asked.

"If you do, you will certainly not miss him!" said Lady Giffard. "They say he is head and shoulders above normal men, as tall as a giant!"

"And his eyes bulge, and he twitches and has fits all the time," Dingley added.

"And that his manners are scarcely civilized, and he eats with his fingers!" put in young Mrs. Temple.

"*I* heard that no one has seen him, except the king, for he can't bear being looked at, and flies into a rage if he thinks anyone is staring at him," said Liza. "So we may never see him at all."

"Your mama and grandfather and aunt will see him," Dingley said to Liza, "for he's sure to go to the Court ball for the Princess Anne's birthday, isn't he?" She looked to Lady Giffard for confirmation.

"I think it very likely," said Lady Giffard. "Surely all the nobility will expect to meet him there."

"Oh, I wish I could go! Am I not old enough to go, Maman?" Liza began the predictable fuss. Esther wondered how old one had to get to realize that the plea "I am old enough to do such-and-such" sounded more childish than anything else. Surely she had stopped using it herself before she was Liza's age.

Then the carriage stopped, and she had no more time to speculate either about the tsar's foibles or Liza's, for they were stepping down into the street. Everything she had noticed yesterday in Dover Street seemed doubly true today—the noise, the crowds, the stink in the air—now that they were in London itself, inside the very walls of the City. At an array of market stalls all up and down the street, merchants hawked their wares, and a bewildering variety of patrons stopped to look at what was on display.

"Hetty! Come look at the combs! Oh, Maman, may I buy one?" Liza headed off already to a stall where ivory combs were on display, towing Esther along behind her. Next to the combs, another stall sold lengths of lace in every conceivable colour and pattern, and on the other side the merchant was selling fans, which Mrs. Temple was picking up and eyeing critically.

To Esther, the items on display were not nearly as fascinating as the people buying and selling them. Right next to Liza's white hand with its rosy nails was a clawlike red hand that belonged to a skinny old woman who pawed through the pretty combs eagerly, although she looked as though one of them might cost more than she earned in a year. She smelled overwhelmingly of fish—or was that the buxom woman on the other side, with her baby clutched to her breast? She was ignoring the combs but fingering the cheaper varieties of lace. A tug at Esther's skirt made her look down. A thin, dark-faced child who might have been a boy or a girl, with ragged dark hair and enormous eyes, held out a dirty hand. "Penny, miss?" the child piped.

How awful! A little child with so little to eat that she had to beg in the street! Esther had heard of beggars in London, but it was shocking to actually see one. Her fingers fumbled at the purse at her waist, but before she could find a penny the dark-eyed child was sent spinning off into the crowd with a kick from the plump woman at the next stall. "Gerrout, don't be bothering the laidy with yer filthy self!" she spat, and Esther looked up in surprise to meet the woman's face. Her expression of righteous rage was replaced at once by one of deference. "Don't mind the likes of her, ma'am, London's crawling with 'em. Just up from the country, are you?"

A firm hand on Esther's elbow made her wonder if another, more confident, beggar was approaching her, but she turned to find Lady Giffard instead. "Do be careful, Hetty—not just of beggars, but of pickpockets. The town is full of them, and anytime one is in a crowd one is in danger, especially if one looks well-to-do." Her other hand latched on to Liza's shoulder. "Come now, girls, we are going to the dressmaker's. You can spend more time in the markets this afternoon."

Esther was out constantly, accompanying Lady Giffard on her calls in the morning, shopping in the afternoons, walking in the evenings along Dover Street or in St. James's Park. When the family went to the theatre, Esther and Dingley were included in the party. Esther agonized all morning over which of her new London gowns to wear and was so excited that she could scarcely swallow her dinner. At three o'clock they left in the carriage for the Theatre Royal in Drury Lane. Esther stared out the window at the passing streets, so crowded, so alive with colour despite the grey air. The street sounds drifted in. London! She had waited all her life for this, and now, this crowning moment—a visit to the theatre! She thought of the things Mr. Swift had said about theatres—how crowded and foul-smelling and stupid they were. But all of London was crowded and foul-smelling, and no doubt a good many of the people were stupid, and Esther adored it all.

When they stepped from the carriage they were swallowed by a mob. "Watch for pickpockets," hissed Lady Giffard. Esther caught Dingley's eye and giggled: Lady Giffard's warning had been repeated so often that it had become a joke, but none of them had yet lost a penny. Esther was cautious none the less, for of all the places Lady Giffard had given this warning since their arrival in the city, Drury Lane seemed by far the most likely place to encounter a cutpurse. Dirty children, barefoot in spite of the raw cold, ran and reeled heedlessly, bumping against Esther. She pulled her cloak tightly around her and kept her hands tucked away.

"Buy an orange, miss?" The shrill voice rang above the cries of the crowd, and Esther looked into the eyes of a red-haired girl about her own age, shivering in a thin low-cut gown and clutching a huge basket of jewel-bright oranges. Having looked, she felt she could hardly refuse, though the girl turned away at once to another customer. Esther searched her purse for a coin and bought two oranges, handing one to Dingley. In the delay, the rest of her party had got ahead, and she had to push through the crowd to catch up to them. She felt a tug as someone stepped on her cloak and heard the cloth tear. *That'll want mending now,* she thought with a sigh.

Inside, Sir William led them to a box. Though the opera didn't start till four, the place was filling already: there was a crowd in the gallery and an even larger crowd in the pit, and several of the other boxes were full. Just as they got settled the duke and duchess of Somerset arrived, the duchess's red hair glowing as brilliantly as one of the oranges. Her gown was blue and gold over a petticoat embroidered all in gold. They stopped to greet Sir William's party, and Esther curtsyed very low, mindful of what she had heard about the duke's great haughtiness.

"Can't you imagine what it must be like to be married to someone as proud as the duke?" Esther whispered to Dingley as the Somersets moved on to their own box. "Do you think he makes her stand when they're alone—just the two of them?"

Dingley laughed. "I can think of a few occasions on which he'd rather have her lying down!"

"Don't be so coarse, Dingley, she's a duchess."

"She's a duchess with four brats. I'm sure she got them the same way the scullery maids get theirs."

Esther stared at the flame-haired duchess settling into her seat. "How *could* she have had a lover when she was only fourteen, Becca? Isn't that … awfully young?"

"She'd been married twice. I suppose she knew what men were for."

"But imagine someone being so passionately in love with her that he'd kill her husband? Her lover was a count, you know, from the Continent—I wonder why she didn't run away with him? I would have done, I think, if someone had loved me that much."

"Do be still, Hetty, you're prating of things you know nothing of. Leave the poor duchess be, and thank God you were born a simple girl without such things to think of."

"What are you chattering about?" Liza asked, poking her head between Esther's and Dingley's. Esther looked at Liza's round face beneath her elaborate blond curls. The duchess had hardly been older than Liza when a count had fallen in love with her. Esther, at seventeen, felt as if she were getting off to a very slow start.

"We're talking of nothing," she said, "only looking at the people. Everyone seems to come to the theatre. Look at that crowd in the galleries—why, they look like the beggars in the park, some of them. How could they afford to go to an opera—or why would they wish to?"

"Likely enough some of them are beggars," said Dingley, who had been to London before. "There are beggars and pickpockets inside the theatre as well as out, you know."

"But it's very cheap in the galleries," Liza pointed out. "Servants go there sometimes while their masters and mistresses are in the pit or up in the boxes. Everyone loves the shows."

"I would have preferred a comedy to an opera," said Esther, staring at a woman who was suckling her infant in the second gallery.

"Lady Giffard and Sir William don't approve of all the comedies," Dingley said. "Look! In the royal box!"

"Is it the king?" Esther asked, torn away from the spectacle below.

"No, but it's the Princess Anne and Mrs. Churchill, her greatest friend."

"Can you see what they are wearing?" Esther's eyes swam suddenly with the effort of taking in all the new surroundings. She hoped fervently that she would not be subject to a headache or weak eyes during the performance, or any more fits of coughing.

The show on stage began at last, and it was spectacular, but only slightly more so than the show all around them in the audience. In the pit, young men in brilliant coats and elaborate wigs preened and strutted around, pulling girls down onto their laps and kissing them without paying the slightest attention to what was happening on stage. At one of the intervals, Dingley nudged Esther again. "See that man who's come into the box next to the princess's?" she said.

"Yes—oh, my." Everyone in boxes, pit and galleries seemed to be darting glances at the ungainly giant who, along with a crowd of other men, occupied the box. "Is it …?"

"I believe it is, the Russian tsar," said Lady Giffard, who was gaping as shamelessly as anyone.

"They do say he loves the theatre, though normally he shuns crowds," said Sir William.

"Well! I'm glad to have seen him at last! What an incredible man!" exclaimed her ladyship. "How tall do they say he is?"

"Nearly seven feet, my dear," Sir William said.

The Russian tsar! Esther, leaning back in her chair and peeling her orange, was swept by a wave of longing to know what Muscovy was like. Were there theatres in Russia, with orange girls and pickpockets outside them? How marvellous to see the man who ruled this strange land. He had a pleasant face, with full lips and a tiny moustache, but his eyes did look oddly wide and staring. He wore a uniform with a great many medals, and he talked and laughed loudly with the people in his box. But when the music started again and the soloist stepped out on stage, he gave her his undivided attention.

"That is Mrs. Cross playing the part of Eromena," Liza said, pointing to the singer, who had a great pile of powdered curls and a large heaving bosom that was displayed to great advantage for the occupants of the boxes. "They say she has become the tsar's mistress."

Mistress. The word, like *lover,* was dropped into everyday conversation all the time, yet it had a force that drew Esther's eyes from the singer on the stage to the tsar in his box. Despite his foreign face—or perhaps because of it—Esther could easily see why the opera singer might want this giant-king for a lover. His large hands rested on the rail of the box, tapping in time to the music, and Esther had a sudden unbidden vision of those hands on the lacings of Mrs. Cross's gown, exposing that great bosom, of the tsar and the singer locked in an embrace. Her face flushed and she dropped her orange.

Mrs. Cross had a powerful voice, and the soprano notes washed over the audience, almost drowning out the hubbub of voices below in the pit. Esther lost herself in enjoyment of the theatre. She hoped she would have a chance to come again.

But before that happened, she had an even more ardent wish fulfilled. Lady Giffard, Sir William, and Mrs. Temple were invited to a ball being given by the duchess of Ormonde at her house in St. James's Square, and Lady Giffard had announced that Dingley and Esther would accompany them.

A ball! Even the very nicest of the new London gowns would not suffice, but Mrs. Temple sprang to her assistance with the gift of one of hers, which was quite splendid and only a year old. It was daringly low cut, with a gold-embroidered stomacher and a bodice and overskirt of purple silk, lined with gold, the overskirt caught up in loops to better display the lining as well as the splendidly flounced petticoat in white and gold. Poor Dingley got only one of Lady Giffard's gowns, not nearly so fashionable. There were quite a lot of fittings and measurings during the week as the seamstress made the gowns over for their new owners, and endless debate about hairdressing. After several experiments with each other's hair, Esther and Dingley finally chose styles that met young Mrs. Temple's approval. Esther decided to wear hers piled high behind a frontage in the colours of her gown, with two dark ringlets hanging down over her almost bare shoulders. "And patches," Mrs. Temple said on the morning of the great event, as Esther stood before the mirror. "You must have a couple of patches—they are the very height of fashion."

"Oh no!" How often had she heard Mr. Swift and even Sir William mocking the vanity of ladies who covered their faces with patches? The fashion had started with women trying to cover up their pox scars, although now even those who had never had the pox wore them. Silly and vain, but still ... young Mrs. Temple wore them herself, and despite some disapproving looks from Lady Giffard it was finally decided that patches would be appropriate.

When it was finally time to dress for the ball, Esther and Dingley got Lady Giffard and Mrs. Temple ready and then helped each other to dress and do their hair. It was Esther who was sitting at the dressing table, with her hair pinned up behind the frontage and a heart-shaped patch just being applied to her cheek, when Liza burst in. The younger girl had been suspiciously absent all morning: she looked as though she had been crying, with her cheeks flushed and her eyes glittering.

"So! Everyone is ready for the ball!" she said brightly, as she stepped into the room. Her gaze swept over Dingley and Esther at the dressing table, over Lady Giffard and Mrs. Temple sitting, already dressed, in their chairs by the fire.

"Yes, Elizabeth, everyone is very nearly ready," her mother said in a tone of exaggerated patience so that Esther knew at once what this was about.

"And you have not relented, Maman? I could be ready so quickly—and my dress is all laid out. Hetty could help me with it. Grandmother? May I not go, after all? I am sure I would not be the youngest one there."

"I am quite sure you would be," her grandmother said, "and it would be very dull for you, an evening surrounded by older people."

"*Dull? A ball?*" Liza shrilled. She looked at Esther, then back at her mother. "I should have a lovely time, and I would not be out of my place as some might, by trying to rise above my station!"

"*Elizabeth!*"

"But it's true, Grandmother. Why would you bring Dingley and Hetty to a ball and not me? They aren't even proper ladies, and I am Sir William Temple's granddaughter! And betrothed to Mr. John Temple as well! Dingley's only a ... a poor relation, and as for Hetty—why, she's the housekeeper's daughter! How can you even think of taking her out in society?"

And leaving me behind. That was the unspoken coda; it rang in the room and Esther clung to those words, knowing it was only Liza's jealousy at being left out that had made her say such cruel things. Cruel, but true. Liza was marched out of the room sobbing, with her mother's hand twisting firmly at her ear, but her words could not be banished so effectively. Esther looked at her own reflection in the glass. Would everyone see and know her for an imposter? She almost felt like refusing to go. But that would cause more upset, and she could see from Lady Giffard's haggard face that there must be no more upset.

At the Ormonde house, which was larger and grander than Temple House and might almost be called a palace, Esther curt-syed deeply before the duchess. The woman's sharp, glittering eyes seemed to bore right through her, and she wished she had never allowed young Mrs. Temple to persuade her about the patches. It was silly and artificial and vain. Her hand moved to touch her cheek, and she had to restrain herself.

When the introductions were over she was free to look around. The great hall was crowded with ladies and gentlemen, all talking and laughing in little groups. The cloying scent of dozens of different perfumes and powders mingled in the air, and Esther, alarmed, felt her chest tighten a little. Oh, not on this night of all nights, let her not have trouble breathing! She forced herself to breathe slowly and deeply, and although she could still feel a little wheeze she was sure she would be all right.

A string quartet played in one corner. The music was pretty, though it could hardly be heard. Dingley grabbed Esther's elbow. "Fellows aplenty here, aren't there?" she whispered. Esther turned to look at her friend and felt her heart go over with a little turn of pity. Poor Dingley. After all her care with her toilette, she still had a little of the look of an unmade bed about her. Her hair was already escaping, her cheeks were flushed, and her gown was slipping down a little. Not that that would matter here, thought Esther, looking around at some of the younger ladies. Their gowns barely covered their bosoms at all. And the men—not just the young ones but dignified gentlemen as old as Sir William— could hardly drag their eyes away from the chests of the ladies they were talking to.

"Come, let's find the gaming tables," Dingley said, but instead of leading the way she steered Esther ahead of her through the crowd.

"Won't there be dancing?" Esther asked. Playing cards was something one did all the time at home, but at a London ball she had imagined herself dancing.

"Oh, yes, for those that want it," said Dingley, grabbing Esther's elbow in a way that made it quite clear that she wasn't one of those. It was disappointing, but Esther allowed Dingley to take the lead. After all, she had been to London before and might have a better idea what would be expected. Perhaps ladies-in-waiting, poor relations who were only brought along out of their mistresses' kindness, were not allowed to dance. Esther thought

of Liza's words and wondered if everyone could tell that she and
Dingley were not really ladies. Would their gowns give them
away? True followers of fashion would spot last year's styles in a
moment.

The room they entered, Esther would have been willing to
wager, was called the Green Room, all hung with green tapestries
and the floor laid with a green Persian carpet. Here were the
gaming tables, and already people were gathering around them.

"See here—whisk," said Dingley. Two very well-dressed
middle-aged ladies were standing by the whisk table; they looked
with disappointment and perhaps a little disdain at Esther and
Dingley. No doubt they had been hoping to attract two gentlemen. "Are you playing here?" Dingley asked.

"No," the blonder of the two answered quickly, "we are joining
some friends for faro. Pray take our places, and perhaps you will
find two more to make up a table."

Esther slid into a chair and picked up the cards listlessly.
Sitting at a table, playing cards with Dingley. This was hardly
how she had imagined her adventures in London.

"Becca, everyone young and interesting is dancing! Why must
you be such an old maid? We'll never meet anyone if we sit here
and play cards—there's no one here but old people," Esther
hissed, scanning the room quickly.

"Nonsense, look at those four young men over there," Dingley
said, nodding at a nearby table as she picked up the deck and
shuffled the cards with a practised hand.

"They are probably the worst kind of confirmed gamblers,"
Esther said, "and that is who we shall meet, no doubt, if we stay
here."

"Hush now," Dingley said placidly, "If you've a sour look on
your face, perhaps those two nice officers won't care to join us."

"Hah!" said Esther humourlessly—and looked up to see two strapping redcoats in full dress uniform, one quite young, the other a little more portly and closer to middle age. "The young one is mine," she whispered, before turning a pleasant smile on the two men, who were bowing and asking if they might join the ladies for a game of whisk.

The elder of the two soldiers turned out to be acquainted with Dingley, having met her at the home of one of Lady Giffard's friends on a previous visit to London. Dingley introduced him to Esther as Lieutenant Matthew Briggs; the younger man was Ensign Geoffrey Howe. Ensign Howe, on closer inspection, confirmed Esther's initial impression of him as young and good-looking. His wig was impeccable, curled into high peaks on either side of his head, his eyes were large and dark beneath dark eyebrows, and his hands, as he took up the cards that Dingley dealt, were long and slender and strong. Esther found herself staring at his mouth as he spoke, at the full lips and very fine set of teeth. She smiled broadly when he made a jest, the better to display her own teeth, which were also very good. Poor Dingley had quite a few missing, and often tried to talk behind her fan or her hand.

Esther considered herself a good card player, and she and Dingley usually played well together, but the effort of keeping up polite conversation with two strange men, one of them hand-some, wore down her concentration.

"And this is your first visit to London, Mrs. Johnson?" asked Geoffrey Howe, turning a dazzling smile upon her. "How do you find the delights of our capital city?"

Esther bit back the flood of superlatives that sprang to her lips and searched frantically for something to say that would make her sound witty and not too terribly provincial. "I find London suits me quite well," she said quickly, "though everything stinks—the air, the gutters, the river and even the people—yet everything sparkles, too."

"How apt! D'you hear that, Briggs—everything stinks, yet everything sparkles! This young lady has given as neat a description of London as anyone I've met yet."

Thank heaven no one could see or hear how her heart raced! But she'd fantasized for years about playing the game of flirtation with a handsome young man in just such a setting, and she hoped she was doing rather better at it than she was at whisk.

She and Dingley won back some of their money on the next game, after which Lieutenant Briggs went to get more wine for them. But the game after that they lost again.

"Mrs. Dingley, I do believe we are out of our depth in this company," she said as pleasantly as she could.

"Perhaps the ladies would care to dance instead?" Ensign Howe said, smiling from Esther to Dingley and then raising an eyebrow at Lieutenant Briggs.

"What do you say, Mrs. Dingley?" Briggs said. "Care to try your fortunes on the dance floor?"

Dingley, blandly insensible to the wild glances of entreaty from Esther, merely laughed as she reshuffled the cards. "No, I imagine I'd do worse there than here. I don't care overmuch for dancing."

Esther ground her teeth and clenched her fists under the table. Dingley was simply *bent* on ruining this ball for her.

"And you, Mrs. Johnson? Are you also reluctant to dance?" asked Ensign Howe.

Now it was Esther's turn to ignore the looks Dingley shot her. "I am very fond of dancing, Ensign Howe," she said.

"Then by all means, let us dance." He stood up, smiled with a pleasure that seemed completely unfeigned, and held out his arm to her. "Please excuse us," he said to Dingley and Briggs. "No doubt you will quickly find two other players to fill our places."

"Then shall we play as partners?" Esther heard Lieutenant Briggs ask Dingley as she and Ensign Howe sailed out of the gaming room. His arm felt solid, warm and muscular under the rough fabric of his uniform coat. She felt light-headed as well as lighthearted—oddly detached from the brightly clad, laughing, chattering men and women all about her. She could only hope she would be light of foot as well.

As she and her partner joined the line of couples waiting for the dance to start, she reviewed every dancing lesson she had had with Liza all those years ago. The memory of herself and Liza, two bright little girls so eager to learn to dance, stung a little. Liza had been her friend then—had seen no differences between them. No, that was silly. Liza had always seen the differences; it was Esther who ignored them, who moved above her station. She lifted her chin a fraction higher as the music started and the top couple danced down between the lines. Geoffrey Howe caught her eye across the dance and smiled again. Esther would disgrace no one—least of all herself—by being at this ball tonight.

Her feet were indeed light, and when the time came for her and Ensign Howe to take their place in the dance, she executed the steps flawlessly, though because of her concentration they spoke little until they were waiting at the bottom of the line. They danced three dances together, the last one a galliard that left them both breathless and laughing. The other couple in their set had been unsure of the steps, got all fouled up at the end of the dance, and bowed out with profuse apologies.

"It might have been worse," Ensign Howe said to Esther. "It might have been our fault."

She laughed. He was witty, and pleasant, and a delight to be with. As to whether he was very wise, or kind, or judicious, ballroom conversation did not seem very well designed to test those qualities. He might be anything, but he was certainly handsome and charming, and he seemed devoted to her despite the many other attractive young women in the room. What more could one ask of a dancing partner?

"Come, I must have another glass of wine, and so must you," he said, whisking her off to a table at the end of the room where footmen presided over glasses of wine and small dainty pasties. He brought her one of each, and said, "Would you like to walk in the gallery, Mrs. Johnson? There are some very fine paintings here."

"Yes, I should love that," she said, her heart beginning to pound again furiously as he led her away from the crowd. Surely he had to be interested if he was trying to get her alone. Or was she just being vain and silly? She had never been out in such company before, and it was hard to know whether a man was simply being polite, or showing interest—or showing improper interest.

The long gallery was lined with impressive portraits, like every other gallery Esther had seen in her life. There were some very fine ones of past kings and queens, including a splendid painting of King Henry VIII that dominated the gallery.

"Doesn't he look genial and kindly?" Ensign Howe said. "Hardly the monster who beheaded so many wives."

"Well, he beheaded only two," Esther pointed out. "And besides, I think this painting was done earlier, while he was still married to Queen Katherine of Aragon, so he probably hadn't beheaded anyone by that time." She could have bitten off her tongue—surely she sounded as though she was boasting of her knowledge, and he was bound to think her impertinent.

"So, you are well versed in both art and history, are you?" he said. Was there a sneer behind the words? Oh, it was so hard to know! She looked at him, helplessly silent. "I am hardly an expert," she managed at last, and was rewarded with a smile.

Then, quite unexpectedly, he leaned closer. "You are quite beautiful, Esther Johnson," he said. "You say London suits you well, but I think you suit London even better. You are the prettiest sight I've seen in this City in many a long day." His face came closer and closer. He was going to kiss her. She still had her wineglass in one hand and her pasty in the other and could do nothing with her hands, but he seemed to have got a free hand, which he stroked along the side of her face. His hand moved over one of the foolish patches. Did he think they were vain, or pretty? His face came closer still. There were voices outside, but no one was in the gallery. She prayed no one would come in for another moment at least. His lips were parted a little, and she parted her own. What exactly would it feel like?

Then his lips were upon hers, moving a little as though sucking at something, but it wasn't unpleasant. She felt flushed all over, not only her face and neck but her bosom and all the rest of her that was hidden underneath her gown. She was concentrating so on the movement of his lips that she didn't notice at once that his fingers were brushing the top of her breast above the edge of the stomacher. By the time she realized he was doing it, he had stopped. The kiss was over. He moved away. She looked down at her breast as if expecting to see the white imprint of his fingers on skin that felt red-hot. Looking up, she saw that his gaze had followed hers. He too was blushing, which made her like him more.

"Forgive me, I ... d-did not mean to take liberties," he said with a hint of a stammer.

She breathed deeply, without the slightest wheezing. "Come, I think we had best return to the dance." He still looked uneasy, so as she took his hand to go back into the ballroom, she gave him her most brilliant smile. She wanted to dance—she felt very much like dancing. Indeed, she felt she might well be able to fly.

They remained together the next several dances, changing partners as required so that Esther met several new men, all of whom were very pleasant and polite to her. No one, she was sure, could tell she was the housekeeper's daughter or think she had no right to be here. Geoffrey Howe caught her eye and smiled when they passed in the dance, and at the end of every complicated set of steps they were together again, facing each other across the lines of the dance.

After a while they returned to the gaming room, where Dingley and Briggs had won a lot of other people's money and were in very high spirits. Dingley looked Esther up and down shrewdly, and Esther thought of the imaginary fingerprints on her breast. If anyone could see them, Dingley would.

But Dingley was at least able to hold her tongue until it was time for them to leave. Geoffrey Howe had kissed Esther's hand and helped her on with her cloak and said he hoped they would meet again before he had to leave London in a few weeks, and she said that that would be very nice. Dingley could hardly wait till they were seated in the carriage to begin her questioning. Lady Giffard and Mrs. Temple were deep in conversation—though Esther had noticed Lady Giffard giving her an appraising glance while Geoffrey Howe said his farewells—and Sir William was dozing.

"You had better tell me everything, every detail," Dingley whispered in her ear.

"Wait till bedtime," said Esther.

"If you'll tell me then."

"Why, do you tell me every detail of your romances?"

"If I had any, I surely would."

They both stifled their laughter. Esther still did not know how she would answer Dingley's questions, or the inevitable ones from her mother that would follow. How could she answer? She had gone to a ball, danced with a soldier, drunk three glasses of wine, lost all her money at cards and been kissed. Who could have had a better time?

London was a whirlwind, and for the next several weeks Esther was caught up in it. There was a constraint between herself and Liza now. The younger girl had never apologized for her words on the afternoon of the ball; no doubt she thought to apologize would be beneath her. She was friendly again, and Esther, after some angry entries in her journal, decided to accept Liza's friendliness—but not her friendship. That was done with forever.

In the meantime, the rift would not spoil her visit to London— she was determined on that. There were more shopping expeditions in the Strand, afternoon calls, walks in St. James's Park, two more trips to the theatre, and three more evening parties, though none as grand as the duke of Ormonde's ball.

One call was less fine and more awkward than the rest: Esther went along with her mother one afternoon to a small house on the east side of the City, the house where her sister and brother were being raised by relatives. Bridget went there on each of the few occasions when she got up to London: it would be Esther's first time in nearly ten years seeing Nancy and Ned.

"But you will see them much more often now," her mother said as the Temple House carriage rolled through the streets, "for

Anne—she likes to be called Anne now, not Nancy any longer—will be coming to live in Farnham, with my friend Mrs. Filby. The Filbys think Anne might be a good match for Mr. Filby's younger brother, though I won't give my consent till I know the man myself. And I am thinking of bringing Neddy to Farnham too, as soon as he is old enough to put to school there."

The idea of her siblings living near Moor Park seemed strange to Esther—they had been dim memories for so long. She remembered that she and Nancy had had great fun together as children, but when she sat in Cousin Maria's drawing room and met the solemn, quiet girl of fifteen who now called herself Anne, she saw nothing familiar. Anne had red-gold hair, a few shades lighter than their mother's, under a white cap; her colouring was very fair, and she scarcely spoke above a whisper. Only Neddy, a fair-haired boy of about ten, made the visit lively with his chatter and his teasing for a sweetmeat. On the way home, Esther remembered how keenly she had missed her sister's company when she first went to Moor Park as a child. Now they were grown up, and strangers to each other. Would that change, if Anne moved to Farnham?

What troubled her about the visit was that Anne had seemed to treat her with a sort of frightened deference, as though Esther's station in life was far above her own. It was another of the sad things that seemed to come with having no clear place in life. Her old friend Liza thought she was getting above herself, and her own sister treated her like a strange and distant lady. Was there no end to this confusion?

Esther saw Geoffrey Howe twice more before he had to leave to join his regiment in Ireland. Once he appeared at the theatre when they were there and sat in the pit with some other soldiers; she was only able to catch his eye a few times and wave. On the other occasion, he was again with Lieutenant Briggs and was calling at the home of Sir Henry Sidney while Sir William and Lady Giffard, with Dingley and Esther in tow, were visiting there. Esther and Ensign Howe sat quietly on the fringes of the discussion, with little freedom to say much to each other, but at least he was properly introduced to Sir William and Lady Giffard. Unfortunately he was leaving soon, he told her, and might not see her again. "But if ever I am in Surrey—"

"You must visit at Moor Park. I am sure you would be very welcome," she said, dropping her head as he kissed her hand. She still did not really know how much she liked him. She would have to have a proper conversation with him to find out, and that looked unlikely to happen anytime soon. But she very much wished he would kiss her again. She recalled vividly the touch of his lips and the feeling of blushing all over her body. It would be a lovely feeling to have again.

Sir William noticed the exchanges between the two and made a point of teasing Esther about her admirer at every opportunity. Indeed, every time a young man struck up a conversation with her on any social occasion, Sir William, Dingley, Mrs. Temple, and sometimes even Liza were quick to draw attention to it. Lady Giffard was quieter; she watched but said little.

Lady Giffard planned to return to Moor Park at the end of April or early in May. Rob, one of the Moor Park grooms who had come up to London with them, was sent back to the country with a wagonload of supplies they had purchased in town and numerous verbal messages for those who remained behind— primarily Mr. Swift, and Mr. and Mrs. Mose. When Rob returned, he brought letters and packages: one letter was addressed to "The Ladies of London," and placed in Esther's hands. It was from Mr. Swift, and she read it aloud to her mother and Dingley in the housekeeper's room.

"*I received your kind letter from Robert by word of mouth, and think it a vast condescension in you to think of us in all your greatness: now we shall hear nothing from you for five months but 'We Courtiers ...*' What a mad ape he is!" she said, skipping down the page. "Listen to this: *Mr Mose and I desire you will remember our love to the king, and let us know how he looks ... Robert says the tsar is there, and is fallen in love with you, and designs to carry you to Muscovy; pray provide yourself with muffs and sable tippets, &c.*" She had not thought a great deal about Mr. Swift during her whirlwind time in London, except to judge the city and its entertainments by his exacting standards, but reading his words on paper again reminded her of his humour and how he loved to jest, and she decided he might not disapprove of London life as much as she'd thought. After all, he always enjoyed it when he came up to town himself. And it was nice to think that he'd written to *her,* out of everyone in the household.

And then, as if thinking of Swifts brought them to life, Jane Swift arrived in her usual unannounced fashion. She was not looking for either work or hospitality this time: since leaving Moor Park several months before she had been in Dublin, and was now staying with a friend in London. Jane was eager to boast about the fact that she was now engaged to be married to a Mr. Fenton in Dublin. *She's as bad as Liza,* Esther thought. *Perhaps it's not childishness at all, but something some people never outgrow.*

"So it looks as though Mother will soon have the worry of both her children off her hands," Jane said, "for I'm to marry Mr. Fenton next year, and my brother has it pretty well all fixed up with Miss Waring—you've heard of her, no doubt?" Jane's eyes darted from one of the women to the other: it was clear she was hoping she was the first to deliver this news. "No? Oh, my, I was talking to Miss Waring's brother, Mr. Ned Waring, just the other day, and he agreed that we'd soon be related. She's a clergyman's daughter in Ireland; Jonathan courted her all the time he was over there and asked her to marry him before he came back to England, but she refused. But they've been writing ever since, and apparently they have an understanding now. Jonathan is still waiting, of course, for a permanent place so he can offer a wife some security, but it's only a matter of time now, I've been told."

It was Bridget who turned the talk to other things, and Jonathan's engagement was mentioned no more, though Jane's was thoroughly rehashed. When she had gone, after dinner, Dingley urged Esther out for another walk in St. James's Park. She could hardly wait to pounce upon this new intelligence.

"Well, that is a pretty piece of news to carry back to Moor Park! And him so dead silent about it, never giving a hint!" Dingley's voice was intolerably loud; surely everyone in the park must have been staring. "What do you make of it, Hetty? Do you think it can be true?"

"I'm sure I don't know what you're talking of, Becca."

"Why, what Jane said, of course, that Mr. Swift was as good as engaged to this Miss Waring. What do you make of that? And not a word of it from him."

Esther found her tongue quite suddenly. "Why should he say a word of it? You've just proven ably enough that anyone would have to be a perfect fool to confide anything of a private nature to you. Gossip is your meat and drink!" No hint of laughter blunted the edge of her words, and when she saw Dingley's dimpled grin collapse into a pout, she felt both better and worse.

She turned away from Dingley and toward the river. When she was a child, her mother and Dingley had teased Swift over one girl and another—always there seemed to be a girl somewhere, usually far away—and she remembered that she had been delighted to join in the raillery, but pleased, too, when the romance was discovered to be nothing serious. Surely no lady could ever be lovely enough, clever enough, perfect enough for Mr. Swift.

Well, thought Esther, viciously kicking a stone ahead of her in the path, *I was a child then. I am a woman now.* Hardly a blinding revelation, but she was afraid to carry the thought any further. Aloud she said, "You see what nonsense this makes of all your silly talk about Mr. Swift and me. I know you've said as much to Jane, and she was proud enough to be able to tell me he'd made a better match. I told you it was folly—now do you believe me?"

Dingley's mouth formed an O that quivered at the edges as if she were struggling to say something, but in the face of her friend's fierceness she apparently chose silence as the wiser course. Following Esther's lead, both women turned back toward Dover Street and Temple House.

An hour later, alone at the table in her room, Esther opened her journal and dipped her pen. In the park she had thought she could hardly wait to let all her feelings come gushing out in a great flood of words, but now that she was alone here with her pen it seemed there were not so many words, after all. Finally she began to write, very slowly, the things she knew, or thought, were true. And what formed on her paper was nothing in the style of a letter or an essay, as her journals usually were, but something more like a list she might keep for her mother, an inventory of some forgotten trunk or closet at Moor Park.

She wrote:

I doe esteem and honour Mr Jonathan Swift above any other man of my acquaintance.

For a long time that was all that was on the paper, then she added:

I have no wish to be married.

Mye mother saies that I am too Frail for bearing children and ought to stay unmarried.

I would like to be either very happy or very miserable, I knowe nott which.

I wish I were Mr Swift's sister, and could help him as Lady Giffard does Sir William.

I doe nott believe Mr Swift could ever be in love with me.

I wish to travel, and see the World.

When Ensign Geoffrey Howe kissed me, I enjoied it verry much.

I wish someone might fall in Love with me.

Upon hearing of Mr Swift's engagement to Miss Waring, I felt

She read over her list again, seeing where its flaw lay. If this truly were a household inventory, she might write: *11 pair fine holland sheets, 16 pair flaxen sheets, 23 pair coarse sheets,* add it up and find the sum: *50 pair sheets.* But these disjointed statements could produce no sum: no final statement could make sense of them all. They were all she knew, and they added up to nothing.

She put her head in her hands and closed her eyes. Another of her headaches was coming on, and she wrote no more.

MOOR PARK
1698

"It was quite an adventure, was it not?" The voice that broke into her reverie was Lady Giffard's, and Esther roused herself with an effort. They were in the coach, travelling back toward Moor Park after the long weeks in the city. "Begging your pardon, ma'am?"

"Your first time in London. Don't fear, it won't be your last. Only the beginning of many wonderful things—of the world opening up all around you." Lady Giffard's voice had its usual didactic tone, implying that if Esther failed to notice the wonderful things opening all around, her ladyship would point them out and quiz her on them afterwards. But there was unmistakable kindness in her tone, also, and a hint of nostalgia. that made Esther ask, "Do you still recall your first visit to London, my lady?"

Lady Giffard nodded. "Vividly. I was much younger than you are, of course—perhaps eleven years old or so, and many, many years ago, long before the fire, London was not half the spendid city it is today. That was in the time of the first King Charles, you understand, before the Civil War, even." She gazed out the window at the village they were passing through. "How very long ago it seems … and how much everything has changed. I envy you, Esther, being at the beginning of your life instead of its end. I should not mind having another lifetime to live again."

What would you do differently? Would you marry again? Live with your brother and keep his house as you did in this lifetime? Such questions were, of course, impossible to put to one's mistress, but Esther was seized again with a desire she remembered from the long-ago night when she had sat up beside Lady Temple's corpse. If only one could ask old people the questions one really needed the answers to … if one could only be certain what the questions were!

"I hope you are not beginning to get silly ideas about young men, Hetty," Lady Giffard said abruptly.

"I have no ideas at all about young men, my lady," said Esther carefully, curious where this might be leading.

"And 'tis best you keep it that way. I will tell you truthfully, Hetty, that when my husband died I wept bitterly, but in later years I have not been sorry to be a widow. Marriage gives an intelligent woman few opportunities to develop her mind, and little independence. And the rigours of the marriage bed and childbirth—ah well, they are not for every woman. You may perhaps consider yourself blessed if you escape them."

"Yes, my lady. Thank you, my lady." Esther looked out the window, wondering now what she herself would answer, if forced to give an honest reply. She had a great many thoughts about young men, and a great many about her own future. For months, she had been turning over possibilities in her mind, seeing herself now as a housekeeper like her mother, now as governess to a clutch of well-behaved children in a great house, now as mistress of a little house of her own. Marriage? She thought of Ensign Howe's kiss, and admitted privately that marriage might have some appeal. But there was a great deal more to it than a stolen kiss from a redcoat at a fancy ball. She liked to dream of a great romance—of a love that would make her, like Lady Temple, either very happy or very miserable, or of a lover who desired her unto death, like the duchess of Somerset's German count. But what she had seen of marriage seemed to accord very little with such ideals of romance. How pathetic it would be to be like Dingley or Jane, pinning all her hopes on a man's fancy!

Carefully now, for every word must be weighed. "I think your counsel very wise, Lady Giffard. I have no great inclination to marry. I have been very happy in your service at Moor Park, and I should be happy to stay on in such a good home."

And then they were home, and everything about the home-coming was so normal, so everyday, so joyous, that melancholy thoughts were banished, and Mr. Swift swept her down from the coach and bowed over her hand with a great flourish, saying, "Allow me to present my most humble greetings to the toast of London, the conqueror of so many hearts, the would-be tsarina of Russia, Mrs. Hetty Johnson herself!" And immediately the possibility that he might be engaged to some woman in faraway Ireland seemed remote and ridiculous, and it was easy to laugh and say, "Ah, but I turned down the tsar, and told him that all the glories of Muscovy could never compare to Moor Park in Maytime, and his court jester could never be so amusing as ours!"

"Court jester? I was court poet when you went away—has my status slipped since then?" Swift parried as he beckoned Rob over to take Esther's trunk.

She looked up at the splendid brick facade of Moor Park. "Oh, it is grand to be home!" she exclaimed. "The town house is lovely, but wedged in among so many other houses it looks cramped and crowded—and how sweet the air is here! I'd almost forgotten how to breathe!"

It was a beautiful spring that warmed into a golden summer. If Swift were pining for the mysterious Miss Waring, he showed no sign of it, but seemed to be more at Esther's side than ever before, asking her opinion quite seriously about his work on

Sir William's memoirs and also about his own writing: he was still working on his great allegory, which now bore the title *A Tale of a Tub*.

"Politics and religion: do you ever write about anything more interesting?" Esther said as they walked under the elms one day in August. Swift was puzzling aloud about *A Tale of a Tub* and seemed not to hear her. It didn't matter: she hadn't expected a response. He was a man, and politics was his passion, and it was pleasant enough to hear him ramble on about his writing and know that he trusted her as critic and confidante.

Sun splashed down through the leafy ceiling above them; the day was warm and brilliant, and every colour in the gardens seemed three shades more vivid than it had the day before. Such summer days were rare enough to make it worth looking closely at everything, memorizing each pattern of light and shade, which Esther did while Swift talked. Suddenly he broke off.

"You are not attending to me at all, are you?" She jumped at his tone, and started guiltily, then saw his smile. "Never mind, you are forgiven; I was hardly attending to myself. What foolish creatures we humans are, to talk so loftily of our own ideas and philosophies when all around us is a garden and an afternoon that makes nonsense of philosophy. Come!" He held out his hand to her, and after a moment's hesitation she took it, wondering if he still imagined her to be eight years old. His hand felt as large and strong as it had then, but a warmth she had never imagined as a child flooded her body at his touch, and she was reminded of Geoffrey Howe's kiss. If only, she thought, if only Mr. Swift could be a handsome young soldier rather than a short, portly middle-aged scholar—yet still possess all his own qualities!

"Esther, do you still dream of travelling the world? Could any place be lovelier than Moor Park, no matter how far we roamed?" Swift was looking about him with delight.

"No place could. Write a poem about it," she urged. "It will make a nice change from politics."

He laughed. "No, I never could. Something as simple and unspoiled as an ode to a summer day at Moor Park—that I could never write. Not unless it had some twist, some dark side to it. No, I had better leave such pretty versifying to you. And you did not answer my question—about travelling the world."

No, she had not answered that; she had not been sure what answer he wanted to hear, and so had to risk trying to find the truth, aloud. "Part of me wants to … to see London again, to visit Holland and France and all the great capitals of Europe— perhaps even Muscovy, if Tsar Peter will come back for me! But with another part of me, all I want is a beautiful place to call home, where everything is perfectly familiar and exactly as I like it. As it is at Moor Park," she added.

"Many people have both," Swift pointed out. "The advantages of travel, and a home to return to. Think of Sir William, who saw so much of the world, yet wants his heart to be buried by the sundial in this very garden."

"Only fortunate people have both," said Esther. "Wealthy people!"

He looked at her very intently all of a sudden, and stopped walking. "Fortunate Esther—seventeen, and beautiful, and wise, and with a head full of dreams. If I could order the universe— well, there are a great many things I would do differently, but the first I would do is give you the means to fulfill all your dreams— the home you desire, and the means to travel as widely as you chose."

His gaze was very intense, with those blue eyes that seemed almost to burst out of his face; she dropped her eyes and pulled away her hand to pick a stray leaf off her gown. All her confusion came rushing back at once, but she made her voice light and jesting as she said, "Thank you—you are most kind, Mr. Swift, sir." She added a tiny curtsy.

But he did not laugh. "Esther, could you not ... I think you ought to call me Jonathan. You are my dearest friend in all the world, you know, and it seems wrong that you should be so formal with me."

You are my dearest friend in all the world. She felt she had been waiting ten years for him to say those words; her heart surged and her cheeks flushed. But again, her words must say something different from what her heart said: she said, "But, sir, you are my elder by ... a great many years, and very much above me in station and birth, and besides, you have been my teacher since I was a child. I could not ... it would not be proper."

"Could you not? Would it not be?" He was still fixing her with that uncomfortable stare. "In private, at least? Call me one name for the ears of Moor Park, for their sense of propriety, but when you and I are alone, can we not forget formality?" She said nothing: every humming insect and each breath of wind in the trees was amplified tenfold. "It means ... a great deal to me, Esther, more than you can know—to have a friend with whom I can truly be myself, to whom I can tell the truth."

For the first time since his unwonted seriousness began she looked him full in the face, and saw there that, no matter what artifices he might practise as a rule, here he was honest.

"Very well—Jonathan. If you will allow me some time to accustom myself to the name, for it sounds strange to hear myself say it."

"As much time as you need, little sauce box!" The mood was broken, he was laughing again, and suddenly he took a most unexpected object—a small knife—out of the pocket of his waistcoat, and turned to the elm tree they had been standing under. Esther peered round him to see: he was carving a motto into the trunk. In spite of his stoutness and the faint beginnings of a double chin—for he was, after all, nearly thirty—he looked, for a moment, like a schoolboy.

"What does it say?" she demanded.

"Read it yourself; I didn't teach you Latin for nothing. But wait a moment; it's a long one."

She waited while he finished carving his Latin motto, then read it aloud. "*Factura nepotibus umbram:* a shade ... for generations to come?" she translated.

"Roughly, yes. My wish for the elm trees of Moor Park—that future generations may be as happy under them as we are today."

"Oh, I wish nothing need ever change!" It was her first unguarded statement of the afternoon, and it burst out of her almost without volition as they emerged from the shade trees and into the full sunlight of the formal garden.

"Ah, but that's a foolish wish, Esther."

"No—is it? I don't think so. Today, everything is perfect—look at it all." She waved her arm in a broad circle at the house, the gardens, the sunlight. "Why can't it stay always like this?" The litany chimed on in her mind, but she did not continue aloud: *Someday—perhaps soon—Sir William will die, and then Lady Giffard, the household will be broken up, you will go off to London, to court, to seek your fortune, you will marry Miss Waring, and someday you and I will grow old, and I ... I only want this day to last forever, the day you told me I was your dearest friend.*

But it would have been futile as well as forward to go on, for he was already shaking his head. "All life lives by change, Esther. Think of a pool that does not constantly receive new water from a stream, and pour out the old. What happens? Stagnation, corruption, stink. Or the fruit trees here, if the fruit was never picked or fell? Corruption again, decay, rot. All that does not change becomes rotten and putrid and finally chokes with its own stink."

"Hark at you!" she said, cutting him off. "A gorgeous summer day, and you must talk of corruption and stink? I thought your enjoyment of the season was too good to last—as you say, there must be a dark vein in it somewhere."

"For me—always. I cannot see the light without the darkness, or the beauty without corruption. But keep reminding me, Esther—keep pointing out the beautiful to me. I should not want to forget it altogether." Again he was very solemn, and his mood changed as quickly as before when he said, "At any rate, if this day lasted forever you would never see the world, or go again to London, or meet any more handsome young soldiers."

"I've no idea what you're talking of," she protested, but she looked at him closely, wondering why he might have brought up the subject they all teased her about. Could he be jealous? Or warning her of something? There was so much about a man's mind that it was simply impossible to know. What would he do if suddenly she said, And what of you and Miss Waring? Is that another change we must look forward to? But of course she did not say it. It would be bold. Besides, he had told her she was the friend to whom he could be truthful, and she was not sure she wanted to hear the truth about Miss Waring.

"You must be careful, now that you're grown, of the men you meet, and keep a discreet distance," he said in a voice that sounded very much like a tutor and very little like a dearest friend. "You are a wise and virtuous girl, and I should hate to hear of you getting a reputation for careless coquettry. Nor should you get yourself embroiled in a situation that might lead to an unsuitable marriage. You ought not to marry a military man, I think," he went on, another smile flickering across his features, "they say it's a difficult life for a woman. Nor a tradesman either; I could not see you living above the shop."

"Never!" she agreed heartily. "But what if I do not wish to marry at all?"

"I think that might be wisest," he agreed. "Or if you must marry, perhaps a clergyman would make a respectable husband. You've seen our cousins Lucy and Thomas in their domestic nest—do you think you could be happy, married to a clergyman?"

For a moment the proposition presented itself to her simply as a practical question. "I think it is possible," she said. "Clergyman are usually learned and respectable, and socialize with the gentry, and their wives are known for doing good works, which I think I could do well at." She was picturing the home of Thomas and Lucy Swift and imagining herself installed there, when the full import of his words hit her. For of course—though she often forgot it—Mr. Swift—no, Jonathan—was a clergyman. She looked at him, but he was examining the new rosebushes the gardener had planted that spring, and whether his interest was feigned or genuine, she could not tell.

Call me Jonathan … You are my dearest friend … Could you be happy, married to a clergyman? This time she could see the sum quite clearly, adding up on the page before her. If only he would say one more thing, it would be quite clear—at least, the question would be clear, and she would be free to consider the answer. But he said nothing else about marriage at all, but called

her attention to the roses, and led the conversation into questions of gardening without any apparent strain, leaving Esther's
head all in a whirl.

When they returned to the house, her only thought was to get
away to a room by herself, and finally, in the Painted Parlour, she
hid herself behind her needlework and tried to go through every
moment of the strange afternoon, step by step in her mind. He
had asked her to call him by his first name. He had told her she
was his dearest friend. He had told her she ought to marry a clergyman. Surely she had come as close as any girl could to having
marriage proposed to her, without the actual words being said?

Either the actual words were waiting for another, better
time—or she had misunderstood everything horribly, and really
knew nothing about men. But she could hardly ask anyone, her
mother or Lady Giffard or poor old Becca, how the matter
seemed to them. It would seem much too forward, as if she were
being presumptuous.

But surely, she thought, there could be no truth now to the
story of Miss Waring!

MOOR PARK
1699

"Graciously look upon our afflictions, O Lord."

"Pitifully behold the sorrows of our hearts," the congregation
replied in unison.

The sorrows of our hearts. Esther mouthed the words and
thought not of sorrow, not even of Sir William's immortal soul,
which was being committed to God, but of what might become
of her now. She wondered what Mother and Dingley would do;

she saw the mingled anger and anguish on Jonathan Swift's face and knew he was thinking about the preferment Sir William had so often promised and never helped him find. She looked at the bowed heads all around her, family and friends and servants, and wagered silently that every one of them, or at least every one of the Moor Park household, thought more of their own futures than of the dead man. Sir William had been a great man, and a good one, though tiresome in his last illness, but to his family and household he had represented, above all, security.

Certainly when they gathered a few days later in the library for a more worldly ceremony, the reading of the will, she knew that everyone there was eager to know what provision Sir William had made for him or her—and ashamed of that eagerness. They ringed the room in their black clothes: Lady Giffard in the chair of honour, close to the fire and next to the lawyer, young cousin Jack on the other side with his parents, and Liza close to him. Liza's mother, sister, and French grandmother sat a little farther away, and in an outer ring of chairs sat the upper servants: Dingley, Esther herself and her mother, Swift, Leonard Robinson, Mr. and Mrs. Mose, her old playmate Jamie Plumridge the gardener, newly married to Annie from the dairy. The lower servants stood around the room, eyes cast down, but Esther saw a few of them darting glances at young Jack Temple. What kind of master would he be? Would he keep them on, or let them go?

There were no surprises in the major bequests: Moor Park and Sheen were both left to Jack, as was most of Sir William's fortune. Lady Giffard received enough to make her comfortable, along with being made executrix of his papers and given the right to live at Moor Park for the rest of her life. There were bequests for the other relatives, and a lot of tedious details about Liza's inheritance and her marriage to Jack, and then the minor bequests to the servants and retainers began. Bridget was to have twenty pounds and a half year's wages and Dingley twenty pounds a year; Swift was given a hundred pounds and the right to continue editing the memoirs, and Robinson and Mr. Mose each got twenty pounds. Esther was sure there would be a legacy for her, not as handsome as her mother's or Dingley's perhaps, but maybe ten pounds, which would be a tidy sum to start her off on any of her possible plans in life.

"... And to Esther Johnson, servant to my sister Giffard, a leasehold property in County Wicklow, in Ireland ..."

A property? Esther wished the lawyer would slow down, go back and explain. He was telling more about the property, but not what she wanted to know. How much would a property like that be worth? What was she meant to do with it? When she looked away from the lawyer, her throat tightened. Every eye in the room was upon her, and very few of them looked friendly. Everyone was angry with her, she saw at once. Her heart pounded. How much was the property worth? What was this supposed to mean?

Nobody answered her questions until the reading of the will was all over. She sat alone while endless discussions between Jack Temple, Lady Giffard, and the lawyer about the administration of the properties droned on. Nobody came over to speak to her— until finally Liza did. Liza, fourteen now and in her glory as the future mistress of the house, looked suddenly quite grown up.

"Well, what good fortune for you, Esther. Of course, Grandpapa was always so fond of you."

She turned away without waiting for a reply. *Why should she resent me?* Esther thought. By any standards, Liza and Jack would inherit enough that they need be jealous of no one.

They were all up now, and milling around the room, talking and making plans for the future. Esther still stood alone. At last

Bridget came over and put a hand on her daughter's arm. Her mother was not angry, but a frown wrinkled her high forehead. Confusion? Concern?

"It's … very good fortune, Esther," she said, echoing Liza. "I'm not sure, but I think the property will be quite valuable."

"How valuable?" Esther said. "And why should he single me out to own a valuable property? Sir William knew I wouldn't know a thing about what to do with it."

"I am sure Mr. Swift will help you," Bridget said, the odd expression not leaving her face. "I think that is what he intended."

Mr. Swift! Esther looked around the room for Jonathan, but when she caught his eye he looked away. If anyone had a reason to be angry he did, for he had been left only a pittance and an unfinished job to complete—nothing that would secure his future as he had hoped. But at last he came over to her. He offered no congratulations; she had expected none.

"I don't even know its worth," she said at last, "much less why he left it to me."

"It is worth about a thousand pounds altogether, though the best thing would be for you to draw a modest annual income from it," he said, his voice carefully neutral. "I would be glad to take care of the paperwork for you, be your steward, if you would. Sir William discussed the bequest with me and expected me to help you manage it." She looked up at him, trying to read something in his eyes. But neither eyes nor tone told her anything, save that he was not happy with Sir William's will. "As for why he left it to you—he was always fond of you, Esther, and wished you to have some measure of independence. That is all, I think."

Independence. She had not thought of the bequest in that light before. A thousand pounds! She wondered how much it might produce annually, and then realized she had no idea how many pounds a year it would take to live independently. She earned ten pounds a year as Lady Giffard's maid—but that was in a household where all her food and clothing were provided. What if she had a house of her own? Would a thousand pounds allow her to keep it? To travel? And what ... whatever could she do with herself, if she was not in service?

She wanted desperately to talk it over with someone who did not seem irritated by the generosity of the bequest, but her next opportunity was little better. She was in Lady Giffard's chambers that evening with Dingley, who was barely speaking to her, and her mother, who was also very quiet. The three older women had been talking about Moor Park while Esther remained quiet, listening, hoping for a hint about her own future.

"I shall stay on here, just as Papa intended," said Lady Giffard, "for I do not believe Jack means to make this his residence at present. Apparently he plans to live at Sheen as soon as he and Elizabeth are married. And of course, Bridget and dear Rebecca, I shall expect you to continue in my service as long as you wish to."

Nobody said Esther's name, but everyone turned to look at her, and she looked back in silent entreaty. Why was she being excluded?

Finally Lady Giffard broke the silence. "Your position is somewhat different, Hetty," she said. "It is obvious from the size of your legacy that my brother did not intend you to continue in service."

"But I—it is what I had always intended to do," Esther blurted. "I know no other life!"

"Then you shall have to learn another. I know you had intended on becoming a lady's maid or a governess, but nobody will expect to take into their household a servant with her own fortune—a fortune worth a thousand pounds or more."

It was hard to bite back her words and questions. "Lady Giffard, begging your pardon, I don't even know what a thousand pounds is worth, or what I might be expected to do with it. How … where … how shall I live?"

"It's an odd amount for a legacy," Bridget said, when Lady Giffard did not answer at once. "What Lady Giffard says is right, Hetty, you cannot expect to stay in service with a fortune such as that. But I do not think it will be enough for you to live very comfortably as an independent woman."

"Surely not," said Lady Giffard. "Why, the rent on a little cottage alone would eat up most of what you would earn in a year."

"Can he have expected you to go live on the property?" Dingley said, drawn into the speculation despite her obvious (and, Esther thought, quite well-founded) jealousy. "Imagine, living over in Ireland! County Wicklow! Where is that?"

"I am sure Papa proposed no such plan," said Lady Giffard. "The income from the property is too great for Hetty to continue as a servant, yet too little to allow her to live independently. It is good for only one thing."

Bridget nodded, and after a moment Dingley did too. They all understood something that was obscure to Esther. It was her mother who finally spelled it out. "For a girl of your birth, Hetty, what Sir William has given you makes a very handsome dowry."

"A dowry," Esther repeated.

"Yes," said Lady Giffard, who had advised Esther against marrying. "It seems clear that my brother intended the legacy to enable you to make a good marriage. And there can be little doubt about whom he intended you to marry."

This time Esther said nothing. It was not safe even to echo Lady Giffard's words.

"You must see his plan, Hetty," her ladyship continued. "It is not for me to say I approve or disapprove, but Sir William left you enough property for a good dowry, and asked Mr. Swift to help you in administering it. He always approved of the friendship between the two of you, and I believe this makes it clear that his plan was for you to marry."

The idea that she might marry Mr. Swift had been a jest between herself and Dingley and a secret possibility in her own heart—one she was not quite sure she liked—but to hear it stated so baldly by Lady Giffard was appalling. Could Sir William have really planned such a thing without consulting the two people most involved? Or—Mr. Swift had said Sir William had discussed Esther's legacy with him. Was that all he had discussed? If Jonathan had agreed to look after her by marrying her, why had he never asked her? And why had he looked so angry this morning when the will was read?

Esther's head throbbed and she stood up unsteadily. "Lady Giffard, may I be excused please? I wish to go to bed," she said, and left the room at her ladyship's nod, trying to ignore the three pairs of eyes that watched her every move.

She was lying in bed an hour later, very far from sleep, when the door opened. She expected Dingley: they shared the room, little more than a closet, off Lady Giffard's chambers.

The figure moved in slowly, with a rustle of skirts, carrying only a rushlight inside a jar. "Hetty? Are you awake?" It was not Dingley but Bridget.

Esther did not reply. Her mother set the rush light down on the table and pulled up a stool next to the box bed. "There's something I must tell you," she said. Strange, Esther thought, that she hadn't waited to hear any reply. Perhaps she cared only about saying what she had come to say and not whether Esther heard.

Perhaps she could see her daughter's wide-open eyes staring at her. But that was unlikely. The sputtering light barely illuminated the dark room. Esther could see only the tip of her mother's nose and chin touched by light, and the edge of her white coif. All the rest of her face, like the mourning gown beneath, was black with shadow.

"People are wondering, Hetty, why Sir William would leave such a valuable property to his housekeeper's daughter. No matter how fond he was of you, it looks odd. Lady Giffard has her own ideas, that he meant you to marry Mr. Swift—there may be something in that, I don't know. But there's another reason folk will think of at once. They'll not say it to your face or mine, but tongues will wag, no doubt." She lapsed into silence, perhaps waiting for Esther to say something. Esther had no idea what her mother might be talking of. But she was not going to make it easier for her by asking questions.

"Hetty, there are many people in Farnham, and more than a few here at Moor Park, who believe that Sir William was … was your father."

"My father?" Esther had to speak at last, if only to repeat her mother's nonsensical words. Her father had died at sea when she was seven. How could Sir William …? It took half a moment to understand. She searched her mother's face, but it was still shrouded in darkness. She had to rely on the voice, tight and angry now, words bitten off short.

"There's been gossip enough since he brought you and me to live at Moor Park with him. And folk say you look nothing like your father or me, or your brother or sister. You're the image of my poor mother, but who about here would know that?"

She waited again, but Esther said nothing. Bridget drew a long breath. "I'd thought all the talk had died down long since, but then this legacy—it's not that I'm ungrateful to Sir William for seeing you so well cared for, but … to slander my good name, and your father's—to dredge all that old gossip up again …" Another awkward silence. "At any rate, Hetty, I only thought you should know what folk will be saying. Better you hear it from me than from Becca Dingley." She stood up, picked up her light, and went to the door. She paused a moment, looking at her daughter.

Is she waiting for me to ask if it's true? Esther wondered. She might go mad wondering if she did not say the words aloud. But why should she ask? Should she not be freely told—if Bridget were so determined upon honesty at last—that the story was only gossip, and a lie? Did her mother's silence mean the opposite?

There were no clues in the darkness, and Esther asked no question, and Bridget turned and left without another word. Esther knew her mother had needed her to say something— something to ease the awkwardness. But neither woman would say what the other needed to hear. The years of careful constraint between them had brought them to this—this incomplete revelation that Esther knew would not be spoken of again. Any hope Esther had of learning who her father was had ended when Bridget left the room.

What did you want from me? Esther cried out silently. *Absolution? But I cannot absolve you, Mother, without knowing what your sin was.*

Tears came then—tears for Sir William, for Bridget, for herself—and Esther cried herself to sleep.

⁂

In the days ahead there was plenty of talk of change at Moor Park, but no one spoke of the questions that were pounding in

Esther's head. Had Sir William really been her father? Had he intended her to marry Jonathan Swift? And what was to become of her?

The business of Sir William was too confusing altogether. She thought back over her memories of him. He certainly had been often peevish and quarrelsome in recent years: Mr. Swift had written at New Year's a set of "resolutions" headed "When I Come to Be Old," in which he had resolved *Not to tell the same story over and over to the same People ... Not to boast of my former beauty, or Strength, or favor with Ladyes ... Not to keep Young company unless they really desire it ..."* He had read it in the housekeeper's room to much laughter, but Esther had felt guilty about laughing. Poor Sir William—surely he couldn't help becoming old, and would not have chosen it if he could. She tried hard to remember his better days, the kindness he had always shown her, though now she could not think of that kindness without wondering at its motive.

But Sir William was a problem of the past, albeit a vexing one. Esther's most pressing problems concerned her future. Lady Giffard said that until something was settled about her future, Esther was welcome to stay at Moor Park for as long as she wished. Dingley, who could not hold a grudge for long, sank her teeth into the idea of Esther marrying Mr. Swift like a cat into a mouse. For a few weeks Esther heard her future spoken of incessantly, but not, unfortunately, by one who could be expected to have any real influence. She grew tired of Dingley's speculations. Why did not Mr. Swift say something?

She had gone over her own feelings in the matter, in the pages of her journal, until she was well nigh sick of them. She had long liked and admired Mr. Swift—she never called him Jonathan in her journal—and while she did not feel the sort of love she had once dreamed of, she had seen nothing to convince her that such passion really existed. Perhaps for the young Lady Temple or the tempestuous Elizabeth Percy, duchess of Somerset—but for Esther Johnson? She remembered the feeling of Geoffrey Howe's kiss and wondered if a kiss from Mr. Swift would feel the same. He was certainly not as young or as handsome—yet she remembered vividly the day he had called her his dearest friend and talked of her marrying a clergyman. She had been something more than flattered, then. She had finally decided that the whole business of being in love was much too difficult to untangle.

But marriage ... that was a different matter. She had never been overly fond of the idea, yet the thought of trying to live independently on her new fortune, without the security of a place in some great house, was lonely and frightening. Marriage might be a better choice, after all, despite the danger of childbirth. She could not, in truth, be Mr. Swift's sister and help him with his work as Lady Giffard had done for Sir William, but could not a wife play something of the same role?

Marriage to anyone, she saw now, would take away certain exciting possibilities, but might offer her many other consolations. Marriage to Mr. Swift would be better than marriage to some unknown stranger, for she knew he was good and kind and wise despite his faults. If Sir William had wanted it, that was different from Dingley's jests and her own daydreams. Sir William, even if he had been only her benefactor and not her father, had certainly had every right to arrange a marriage for her. If only he had arranged it, with Mr. Swift's consent, while he was still alive, she would have had no quarrel.

But this! The uncertainty, the legacy, Lady Giffard's broad hints and obvious disapproval, Dingley's comments, her mother's cryptic confession, and worst of all, Mr. Swift's complete silence on the subject—all were combining to give her a headache that sometimes abated but never fully went away. And then Swift announced he was going to London.

It was not Esther he told first, but Lady Giffard; it was only by chance that Esther happened to be sewing in her own closet two rooms away from her ladyship's sitting room when Mr. Swift came in to say what he had decided to do. She did not intend to eavesdrop, but their voices carried very clearly through the open doorways, and neither knew she was there.

"I hope, Mr. Swift, this does not mean you intend to neglect the duties my brother left for you here," said Lady Giffard.

"If you mean the manuscripts, I shall take some of them to London to continue working on, and Hetty can work on some of the others here, with your guidance. In London I shall be in a position to look for a publisher."

"And to look for your own fortune."

"Indeed, why should I deny it? Lady Giffard, I am nearly thirty years of age, no longer a young man, and Sir William is dead and cannot keep me dependent on him any longer. I am ambitious. You have always known that; so did your brother. I do not know why he chose to reward my years of service with only a hundred pounds, but if I must make my own way without any help from him, that I shall do."

"You know very well that he intended you to have more than a hundred pounds. To all practical purposes, he left you a thousand pounds," said Lady Giffard. Esther dropped her needle and wondered if it could be heard in the silence that filled the sitting room.

"My dear Lady Giffard, if you knew anything of men, you would know that the help a young man wishes from an older one is help in starting his career, and then to be allowed to choose a

wife for himself! Like any other man in my position, I wish to
have a place in the world and some security of my own, and then
invite a wife to share it—*if* I so desire!"

"Yes—I hear there is a young lady in Belfast who can attest
to your determination to remain unmarried till you can
support a wife."

"You hear, my lady? Perhaps, like many another spinster, you
would understand a man's mind better if you paid less attention
to women's gossip and tales."

There was no mistaking the heavy closing of the door. Esther
sat trembling in her closet, hoping Lady Giffard would soon
leave her chambers too, else Esther might be trapped in there all
day long, and her eavesdropping discovered. She was shocked
that Mr. Swift could speak with such bald anger to Lady
Giffard—and such devastating knowledge of what would hurt
her, for she hated above all things to be called a spinster when she
had been, however briefly, a wife—but Esther was hurt, too, by
his apparent slight against her. Was it Esther herself that he did
not wish to marry, or was it only that he did not wish someone
else to choose his wife? He had spoken of taking a wife when he
was established in his career, but those words could apply as
well to Miss Waring of Belfast as to Esther. And she had been
fool enough to consider the matter as though he had already
proposed! Well, she had spoken of her folly to no one but her
journal, and no one else should ever know of it.

But Swift's farewell, when he said goodbye to her, confused her
again. "I shall write often," he said, "for you must not think our
friendship is at an end. You must go on working on Sir William's
papers, and we will correspond often about our joint work.
When I know my fate, I shall visit you here at Moor Park—never
fear. If I do not find a place at Court or in London, perhaps I am

fated to return to Ireland. You are a property owner in Ireland now—perhaps someday you will want to visit there. Until then, think well of me, my Esther."

She had no more to say to that than, "I wish you well, Jonathan." He clasped her hand tightly, then turned to make some parting jest to Dingley about buying her a new snuffbox and ribbons for her lapdogs when he was in London. And he left, with Esther no wiser about her future than she had been on the day of Sir William's funeral.

Part Two

IRELAND
1701–1723

DUBLIN
1701

"I wish I was dead! Dear God, take me now, let me die now, don't let me suffer like this any longer ..."

"Hush, Becca, what nonsense!" Esther laid another damp cloth on her companion's forehead. Becca Dingley's hair, sweat soaked, clung to cheeks as white as new bedsheets. She moaned and clutched Esther's hand. Esther, already framing reassurances, sighed and kept her peace. What was the use of telling Becca she wouldn't die, that no one—as far as Esther knew—ever died from seasickness? She was even a little glad her friend was so ill; nursing Becca kept her mind off her own queasiness. They'd both been violently ill the first day, but Esther had more quickly got used to the heaving swells of the Irish Sea and the constant swaying of decks beneath her feet. Still, for two ladies who had never set foot off dry land in their lives, it was, to say the least, an unsettling experience.

The air in the cabin was rank, for Becca was not the only passenger to suffer from sickness on what even the crew admitted was an unusually stormy crossing. Twenty people slept here below, and chamberpots were overflowing. And these were the passengers who had been able to pay well for their fare! Esther shuddered to think what conditions might be like in the crowded hold where the poorer class of travellers were stowed.

She wished she could leave Becca for a moment and go out on deck—not to see the rolling waves or feel the bracing sea air, for she'd had enough of both those to last a lifetime—but to see if the coastline of Ireland were drawing any nearer. They had been told in Chester, when they finally arrived there and when a packet-boat finally came to take them to Dublin, that the crossing might take two days, but other travellers had shared dire tales of storm-tossed crossings that had lasted for weeks. At the time Esther, with her yearning for travel and utter inexperience of the sea, hadn't much cared how long the voyage took or how rough it was—it would all be part of this amazing adventure that was taking her and Becca to a new land. Now, she cared nothing for travel, adventure, or new countries. She had not yet gone as far as Becca in wishing for death. Her wishes were simple: she wanted to get off the ship and onto solid ground and never set foot on a boat again.

"Ooohhhh … the pail …" Becca groaned, and Esther slid the metal bucket up to the edge of the bunk and averted her eyes as Becca retched.

Damn Mr. Swift, she thought, and as quickly chided herself for both profanity and ingratitude. But really, how could he have been thoughtless enough to send them off on this journey—they were the only two unaccompanied ladies on the ship—weeks ahead of his own planned return to Ireland? *And why*, thought Esther, *was I fool enough to agree to it? Properly he should have travelled with us, and if that were impossible he should have brought us over after he'd gone back himself, so he could meet us in Dublin.* As it was, they were travelling to Ireland on Mr. Swift's money and on his advice but with no other support from the man Becca insisted on calling "your Intended." Esther didn't doubt that moving to Ireland was the best plan for them—somewhere inside, under layers of nausea and fear, she could even still imagine looking forward to it—but the whole thing had been carried out in an ill-advised manner. Mr. Swift had simply told them to get a coach to Chester and the ferry from there to Dublin, and to look up his sister, Jane, at Bride Street in Dublin until they found lodgings of their own. A coach trip across half of England, a ferry ride across the sea, and the task of finding lodgings in a foreign city—all these were to be Esther's responsibility, for Mr. Swift's business would keep him in England for weeks yet. It had seemed relatively simple when they talked about it back in Farnham; now Esther thought she must have been mad to go along with it.

Now here they were, five days on the water; Becca wanted to die, and Esther wanted to live—well away from the sea. And there were no shouts of "Land ho!" from anyone on board the cursed ship.

But even the worst of horrors had to come to an end, and land drew near late that afternoon. Esther had hoped for a morning landfall: the idea of arriving alone in Ireland after dark had little appeal. She left Becca still huddled and moaning below and went up on deck to catch her first glimpse of her first foreign country. The skies had cleared and a magnificent red and gold sunset painted the clouds as the packet-boat sailed up the mouth of a broad river. Esther looked around for some hint of what sort of city Dublin might be, but saw only a few drab cottages lying well back from the shore. Surely they would travel farther upriver before docking.

But to her surprise, the ship soon dropped anchor and passengers were conducted down over the side into a much smaller boat that would take them to the barren shore. Esther hurried below to rouse Becca, who was too miserable even to have noticed that the rocking motion of the sea had ceased.

"Come, Becca, collect your bags, we're docking. They're putting us off in boats to take us to shore." Esther scurried around the cabin making sure all her goods were with her.

Becca struggled to unsteady feet. "We're in Dublin?" she asked.

"Not Dublin—I can hardly say what it looks like. It must be outside the city."

"But how will we get into Dublin?"

"There must be a coach from here."

The journey down over the side of the ship and into the smaller boat, and across a little stretch of water to the dock, was short but unpleasant. The other passengers, many of whom spoke Irish, did not seem at all put off by the bleakness of the spot where they had been set down, but Esther, looking around in vain for some sort of an inn where she and Becca might rest and find out about the coach to Dublin, felt cold and alone at the sight of the forlorn huddle of shacks in the deepening twilight.

When their three trunks were unloaded from the packet-boat and set down, Becca immediately collapsed upon one of them. The other passengers were disappearing. Going over to a middle-aged English couple who had shared their cabin during the crossing, Esther asked, "What place is this? How does one get to the city from here?"

As the man opened his mouth to answer, she was gripped by a wild fear that he would say, This *is* the city—that there was nothing more to Dublin than this. What kind of place had Mr. Swift sent them to? But the man said, "This is Ring's End, on the River Liffey. The ships go no farther than this because the water is too shallow. You can hire a Ring's End car from here." He pointed to the edge of the little cluster of cottages, where Esther could dimly make out horses and carriages of a sort.

Of a sort. The Ring's End car was like no other conveyance Esther had ever seen. She stared at it, unbelieving, as the driver quoted the price to her and she told him about their trunks, hoping the distance to Dublin was not far. The one-horse cart was nothing more than two wheels with a pair of planks suspended between them. She and Dingley might be able to squeeze on along with the driver; there would certainly be no room for their trunks and no comfort of any kind.

"You can send your trunks on with another driver—just pay him another threepence," the man said in a thick accent she could hardly decipher. She was aware that he was sizing her up with interest: probably he met few twenty-year-old girls travelling without a male chaperon. Thank goodness for the spinsterish solidity of Mrs. Dingley! Esther went back to retrieve her subdued friend. Leaving their precious belongings in the care of one of these drivers hardly seemed safe, but there was no alternative. Certainly Ring's End offered no accommodations for the night. They had to go on to Dublin and trust their bags would follow after.

The ride was more uncomfortable than she could have predicted. Esther was squeezed on the seat between the driver, who kept up a non-stop flow of unintelligible talk, and Becca, who moaned every time the cart hit a rut—which was frequently. Was the road to Dublin really so rugged, or was it simply that this cart offered no protection either from the road beneath or the elements around them? Esther shivered in the cold night air and wrapped her cloak around her. It was completely dark out now, and she saw no welcoming homely lights in the dark shapes of buildings they passed.

Mr. Swift had had so many good reasons why they should move to Ireland—most of them having to do with money. With the property Sir William had willed her two years ago and some other money he had left her, Esther had a fortune worth about fifteen hundred pounds—a staggering sum when you said it all at once, but able to produce a very meagre annual income, as she had discovered in the few months she and Becca Dingley had tried independent living in Farnham. Becca's income was even smaller. But in Ireland, Swift told them, money earned a great deal more interest, and living was much cheaper. And now that he had found a position for himself in Ireland, as Lord Berkeley's secretary and vicar of Laracor, why, what would prevent his two dearest ladies from coming there to live as well?

Those were his reasons—the ones he'd explained as he sat in their little parlour in Farnham, in a rented house Esther knew she could never begin to think of as a home. She agreed, but her agreement had very little to do with money. It had more to do with the old urge to see the world, and her great weariness with the bit of world she was now living in.

Moor Park was no longer home. For nearly two years after Sir William's death, she had gone on living there with Lady Giffard and the rest of the household, still fulfilling her old role as lady-in-waiting, although she knew this was not meant to be a permanent arrangement. It was an uneasy time. The strangeness she had felt since Sir William's death had never receded. She had no real sense of what she was meant to do with her life. Mr. Swift—Jonathan—kept in constant touch with her and visited often, but he never spoke of the marriage that everyone else assumed was a foregone conclusion. Relations between Esther and her mother were strained, too. Esther had not been able to broach the subject of Sir William being her father again, but she never ceased to think of it. It lay between them like a sword.

And then everyone got swept up in the grand plans for Liza's marriage to Jack Temple, and Lady Giffard announced that she would remove to Sheen after the wedding and let the newlyweds live at Moor Park. The old friendship between Liza and Esther was gone forever, and nothing comfortable had replaced it. They did not know how to treat each other, and certainly the long-ago offer of a position for Esther in Liza's household had never been repeated. Esther knew that the home of the sixteen-year-old bride was no place for her.

But she did not follow Lady Giffard and her mother to Sheen—in fact, she was not invited. Both older women seemed at a loss what to do about Esther, so she made up her own mind—she would stay in Farnham. Dingley wanted to stay with her, so they had set up house together. They had stayed for three months, till Mr. Swift's latest visit, when he did, at long last, make a proposal. Not a proposal of marriage to Esther, but a proposal that both ladies should move to his new home city of Dublin.

What was a girl to make of that?

"Gracious me! What is this, a road or a cowpath?!" said Becca, rousing Esther from her thoughts as the cart jerked violently to the right.

Esther felt the seat sliding away beneath her and threw her arm about the driver, who immediately put his around her and said, "That's right miss, you just hold on to me, and you'll be all right."

"I'm paying you to keep your hands on the reins, not on me," Esther replied.

There was no hope of locating Jane Swift's—now Jane Fenton's—house in Bride Street at this time of night, so Esther directed the driver to take them to a respectable inn in that neighbourhood. She knew it was very likely that she and the driver would have different ideas of what was respectable—indeed, Ireland and England might turn out to have quite incompatible standards on that score—but it was too late to worry about that. They were exhausted, the hour was late, and Becca, whose head had sagged forward onto her chest and who had begun to snore, might soon wake and become less docile. Any decision would be harder to make with two people thinking about it instead of one, so Esther took advantage of the opportunity to decide single-handedly. When the Ring's End cart pulled into the yard of an inn called the Cock and Bull, she told him it would do very well and asked him to arrange for their trunks to be delivered there as soon as possible.

The Cock and Bull was not a very nice inn by English standards, certainly not by Moor Park standards, but Esther and Becca barely noticed. Neither could eat or wanted to, and the straw mattress they shared in an upstairs room had hardly enough fleas to keep them awake an hour. Sleep was welcome: rest not only for the body, for the mind.

And of course the morrow was better—mornings, especially those tinged with a watery sunlight, were always less dreary. Though the inn did not look better by the light of day, Mrs. Dingley did—the colour had returned to her round cheeks, and she was lively enough to chide Esther for choosing such a poor lodging.

"I hadn't a great deal of choice," said Esther over breakfast, "and you were no help, moaning and whingeing like a great cow in calf. We don't plan to live here; as soon as our trunks come we'll be off to find Jane's house and settle there for a few days. Till we can get a place of our own."

Becca looked around at their fellow customers in distaste. They were mostly working men, with loud Irish voices and dark dirty faces. "I hope it's not in this neighbourhood," she said.

One trunk actually arrived not long after breakfast, with promises that another was to follow, though the driver—a different fellow from last night—looked vague when Esther reminded him that she had paid for three trunks, not two, to be transported. That was worrisome, but after waiting a little while in vain for another delivery, they decided it was best to set out and find Bride Street and collect their things from the inn later.

Dublin's streets were much like London's, except that they were, if possible, narrower and dirtier, and besides the crowds of peddlers and prostitutes and pickpockets, there were more beggars than in London—especially children. Too many children with dark pleading eyes under tangled dirty hair—Esther's store of pennies was quite gone by the time they found Bride Street, while Becca chided her soft-heartedness and quietly passed out her own pennies on the other side.

They had not written to Jane to announce their arrival— Mr. Swift had assured them he had already done so, and she would be happy to have them. Esther, who was never delighted to see Jane, doubted Jane would be so happy to see her, but Jane and Becca were cronies and anyway, it was only for a little while. "I wonder what this Mr. Fenton will be like?" she mused aloud.

"None too choosy, I'd say," said Becca, and Esther reflected she'd better not count on the friendliness between Becca and Jane lasting too long.

Indeed, as soon as they stepped inside the modest town house of Mrs. Jane Fenton, it was clear that their visit was not going to be a long one. Jane did not go out of her way to welcome them. She asked how long they thought they might stay in Dublin.

"Your brother said ... that is, we had planned ... I thought if we found it suitable, we might settle here permanently," said Esther, perched on the very edge of the settee in Jane's parlour and wishing she had a cup of coffee, if only to occupy her hands. They had been offered nothing.

Jane snorted. "Suitable? Permanent? Well, this place is no Moor Park, as you can see." She waved her thin hand in a gesture that might have been meant to indicate her narrow house, or all of Dublin. "It won't be what you *ladies* have been used to, that's for certain." She placed a mocking stress on the word *ladies*. "I'll wager you'll be back in Farnham before summer."

"Little you know of it!" Becca spluttered. "Do you think we was living in a palace in Farnham, once Lady Liza moved into Moor Park? I won't be going back to serve under that little chit, I can tell you, and as for Sheen—"

"All that's as it may be," Esther interrupted, swallowing rage instead of coffee, "but for now, we plan to make our home in Dublin. Jonathan said you would be glad to put us up and help us find a place to stay." She threw out the casual "Jonathan" deliberately, difficult though it was to say, hoping to discomfit Jane. But her shot misfired.

"Oooohh, *Jonathan*? Is that the way of it? Well, that makes it all a good deal clearer—though not *your* position, Bec. I suppose you're a sort of chaperone—in which case you'd best not burn your bridges, for a chaperone's not needed once the wedding's done." Greeted by the silence that was the only possible reply, she smiled once, briefly, at the flushed cheeks of her two guests, and said, "You're welcome here, naturally. I've already asked some friends about lodgings for you—though I don't know, of course, what you can afford."

"If you can give us the names of some people whose rooms we can visit, I am sure we can discuss the price with them," Esther replied quickly, before Becca could give a full account of their joint finances.

After a welcome like that, there would have been little temptation to tarry long with Jane, but matters in Bride Street quickly got worse. Jane thawed a little and did invite them to dinner, over which meal she dropped her nastiness to Becca and engaged her in lively conversation of the type they both liked best—gossip about people they both knew back in England. She sent her manservant to bring the trunks from the Cock and Bull, where only two trunks had arrived and the driver who delivered them had failed to return. The three women were doing needlework in the parlour in a fair semblance of happy cameraderie when the front door banged open and Esther saw Jane stiffen with a white-faced look of fear she had never seen on that feisty lady. The master of the house was home.

Dingley and Esther got themselves up to the spare room as soon as possible after their first glimpse of Mr. Fenton, who was roaring drunk. "Poor Jane," Dingley said, opening one of the trunks to check its contents. "She's no saint, but I don't envy her that husband." Shouts, banging doors, and stamping feet echoed up through the house.

With little regret they began hunting for lodgings the following morning. Reality quickly shaped their ideas of what sort of house they would like to live in, and when Jane recommended an address in William Street that was reasonably priced, they were happy to inspect it, though their cab driver warned them it was an awful ways out. "Out by Minchen's Fields, with hardly any houses around."

It was an apt description. The house for rent was one of only a handful on a straggling street. "Cheer up, Becca, it will be like country living," Esther said as they toured the empty rooms. "I don't think I could bear to live right in the city as Jane does, with other houses and shops and crowds all around."

"I could," said Becca.

But Esther's images of city life were coloured by Temple House in London, with its spacious grounds well back from the street. She had never imagined living in the narrowness and darkness of a house like the Fentons', though she well knew it was Mr. Fenton's drunken temper that gave the house a good deal of its air of squalour—not the squalour of the truly poor, but of her own class of people, which, Esther was slowly beginning to realize, she had not lived among since childhood.

They took the house in William Street, over Becca's dire warnings. It was nearly affordable, and Esther was determined they should live within their means. The third trunk never did arrive, but they moved in with the two they had and set about at once buying furniture for the bare three-storey house. Esther's resolve to be frugal did not stand up long against the lure of owning a few beautiful things that would turn the rented house into a home.

"It's grand, but can we afford it?" Becca said, not for the first time, as they stood in their parlour looking at new carpet that had just been unrolled.

"Truth to tell, I hardly care," said Esther, stepping onto the new carpet, exulting in its softness and the way its bright colours hid the bare floorboards. "We *must* have good furniture, Becca— we can't live like paupers. *You* may be satisfied to live like a poor relation all your life, but we are independent women now and I won't put up with threadbare carpets and hand-me-down furniture." It bothered her that Becca cared so little for appearances: it was as if she had never really minded being the poor cousin, the unpaid servant. "Mr. Swift promised to help us if we need money—and as it is his whim that brought us here, perhaps he should pay for it."

"I don't like the sound of that," muttered Becca. "Now, two women are coming today for the cook's position—do you want to talk to them, or shall I, or shall we do it together?"

Esther dragged her attention away from the carpet. "Together, I suppose," she said, though she knew that in practice Becca would do most of the questioning. Privately Esther thought of herself as the lady of the house—it was mostly her fortune that was paying for it, after all—and she sensed that Becca thought of their arrangement in the same terms. She had to be very careful never to condescend to dear Becca—but still, Esther had made most of the decisions up till now. When it came to hiring staff, she was more than happy to turn the task over to Becca. She, Esther, might be a housekeeper's daughter, but Rebecca Dingley was a housekeeper by nature. If she ended up doing most of the domestic tasks in this ménage they were setting up, Esther was more than willing to grant them to her.

The truth was, the whole enterprise was beginning to pall. Esther stood alone in the parlour when Becca had gone, looking at their few furnishings in that narrow room. She remembered Moor Park with a longing that was almost physical—its soaring vaulted ceilings and spacious halls. This cramped city house, a series of boxes stacked on top of one another—it could never be a home in the way Moor Park had been. But she was mistress here—or joint mistress, with Becca—and that pleasure almost balanced the sting of loss. Almost. It was exhausting, prowling the shops, bickering with shopkeepers and delivery men and workmen and would-be servants, having to constantly think and decide about every detail down to where their dinner would come from. She sank down onto one of the two needleworked chairs that had arrived yesterday and stared out the window at the unlovely vista of William Street. There were no houses on the other side. They were virtually isolated here—and not just because of their address.

❧

Three weeks had passed, and they knew no one in Dublin but each other. No letter had arrived from Mr. Swift, no one had called on them, no one had spoken to them on the three Sundays they had attended St. Patrick's Cathedral, and Jane appeared to have washed her hands of them as soon as they had left her doorstep. A sudden thought of the missing third trunk unleashed the tears Esther had been struggling to hold back— she could not even remember exactly what had been in it, but no doubt every day would bring some fresh loss—and she laid her head down on her arms and wept. An hour ago, walking on the new carpet, the new experience had seemed like such fun. Now she could only cry and wonder what they were doing here.

She had no idea how long she indulged her tears, nor how long after that she sat staring through the window. She was flooded with memories of Moor Park—but even the memories were sullied now. It was not her home and never would be again. Liza was mistress there—the thought of her childhood friend, turned into the haughty young woman with the distant ice-blue eyes, threatened to start tears again—and what was left of the Moor Park family, Mother and Lady Giffard, were at Sheen. Esther felt an unaccustomed longing for her mother. She knew she and Bridget were not close as mother and daughter ought to be, and that Bridget would cluck her tongue and chide her for her sentiment, but in her absence it was easy to imagine a comforting, loving mother who would make everything well, if only she were here.

Esther thought of the scattered shreds of her family—Mother now at Sheen, Anne married and living in Farnham, and ... Neddy. Part of the reason Esther had stayed in Farnham when Lady Giffard moved to Sheen was the thought of her brother and sister—for Neddy was then at school in Farnham—and the hope that she might at last come to know them a little better. Well, she had spent time enough with Anne—time enough to see that married life in a little cottage was not the idyll some people painted it as, for Anne and her husband were ever quarrelling and fretting about money, and how they would feed the baby that was on the way. Esther had just begun getting to know her little brother again when Neddy, a thin fair-haired boy starting to grow long-legged and tall, had taken a sudden fever and died. And now, for no good reason, Esther Johnson had put the Irish Sea between herself and the only family she had left. She began to cry again.

Slow footsteps and a hand on her shoulder broke into her gloom. "You didn't come to talk to the cooks," Becca said.

"No—I'm sorry—" said Esther, wiping a hand over her wet face.

"No, hush, never mind now," said Becca, crouching on the floor beside her, taking one of Esther's hands between her plump warm ones. "Don't you fret about that, Hetty. I'll take care of all that, the servants and all. I've engaged a lovely woman. Her name's Sally, Sally West, and the best of it is, she can start tonight. And she's going out now, to the market, and she'll cook dinner for us when she comes back, our first proper meal cooked by our own cook, in our own house. Won't that be lovely?"

She spoke with a soothing, cooing voice as to a fractious child, and Esther could not be offended, for that very voice, and Becca's gentle touch, brought smiles from her tears. "We haven't even any proper dishes," she sniffled.

"I doubt we'll be entertaining company with our best plate anytime soon."

"Becca, will we ever have friends here?"

"Of course, of course we will. Mr. Swift will come back soon and introduce us to all his friends, and we'll have a lovely dinner here—and by that time, you'll see, we'll have dishes and all."

"Perhaps we ought to go buy some now," Esther suggested. And her morning of tears ended with an afternoon of browsing through the shops, and settling on a lovely china plate, and arranging for its delivery, and not thinking at all about how to pay for it. They came home to mutton pies by Mrs. Sally West, laid before them on the table in such steaming, gleaming splendour that Esther was grateful to both Becca and the cook and felt a little of the burden of independence slide off her shoulders.

Mrs. Dingley hired a young girl named Margaret as a daily maid-of-all-work, and a manservant named Jack who also came by day, for there was not really room for anyone but Mrs. Sally to live in. And Esther continued to spend her small hoard of money on pretty things for the house, so that gradually it began to look comfortable and familiar.

On their fourth Sunday at St. Patrick's, a sprightly looking little woman somewhere between Esther's age and Becca's came up and asked them were they Mrs. Esther Johnson and Mrs. Rebecca Dingley. "I am Dorothy Walls, wife of Archdeacon Walls," she said, "a great friend of Mr. Jonathan Swift, who wrote us to tell of two ladies who were coming from England to make their home in Dublin. We are so very glad to meet you." But even as she said "very glad" her eyes swept over Becca quickly and lingered on Esther, taking in every detail from petticoat to bosom to cap. Her thoughts about Mr. Swift's pretty young friend could not have been more blatant had she spoken them aloud. Esther thought of Jane's cutting words: "Well, *that* makes it all a good deal clearer."

Esther drew herself up to her full height, wishing it was greater, and put out her hand. "We are very pleased to meet you, Mrs. Walls, for my friend Mrs. Dingley and I have not yet many acquaintances in Dublin. We came over, as you say, on the advice of Mr. Swift, who has been a kind friend and adviser to our family since I was a child. The late Sir William Temple left me property in Ireland, and Mr. Swift suggested it would be wise to live in this country. I have always wished to travel, and Dublin is so very different from England that everything in it is proving an education."

Esther was very pleased with her little speech, which she thought a model of propriety. Mrs. Walls's eyebrows lifted and her head inclined a fraction, as if letting Esther know she had passed some test.

An invitation to dinner later in the week followed, and Esther and Becca combed the contents of the two trunks for finery to wear. Dinner at Archdeacon Walls's home was half a pleasure and half an ordeal—it was lovely to be someone's guest, in a pleasant if not grand home, and be introduced to a round of new acquaintances whose names Becca and Esther quizzed each other on for days afterwards, hoping to fix them in memory. But most of those new acquaintances gave Esther the same searching glance Mrs. Walls had, and apparently drew the same conclusion—that she had to be Mr. Swift's intended bride, and that for her to come virtually unescorted to Dublin without having married him first suggested that she might be something worse.

One face she saw at the Wallses' dinner party was entirely without censure, and a pleasant one in its own right, and she found that when she went to bed that night it was still before her eyes. It belonged to a young clergyman called William Tisdall. He had been at the dinner with his mother, with whom he lived, and his loud laughter, tall handsome frame, and bright brown eyes had singled him out. Later in the evening, when they were properly introduced, he made no comments about Mr. Swift at all, and the appraising glance he gave Esther was full of appreciation, not of condemnation. He asked about the home they had left behind in Surrey, and about their sea crossing, and sympathized about the lost trunk. "The Irish cart driver," he said, "is not a creature to whom one would normally think of entrusting one's dearest earthly possessions, but sadly one often has no choice. I hope nothing of great value was lost?"

"Oh, everything!" Esther assured him, laughing. "You would not think we would have been so foolish as to pack everything useful in one of three trunks, but now that one is missing, it seems every lost or forgotten object for the next ten years will be said to have been in the missing trunk."

Reverend Tisdall's laughter was deep and warm, and made her feel more at home than anything else had in Dublin so far.

The cool weather that had greeted their arrival had warmed into days that, if not exactly like an English June, seemed at least to belong to the same season. A letter from Mr. Swift, warning of his arrival later in the summer, was delivered on such a brilliantly sunny day that Esther received it without any trace of the anger she had felt toward the sender for weeks, and wrote a very pleasant reply saying how happily settled they were in Dublin, and how wonderful it would be to see him again.

The next day was the first of July, and Esther and Becca set out along with most of the population of Dublin to College Green, between Trinity College and Dublin Castle, where the new statue of King William was being unveiled. The sun beat hotly down and the crowds milled so close that Becca warned Esther to watch for pickpockets. "You sound like Lady Giffard," Esther joked, but she kept a hand on her purse nonetheless.

The statue was a splendid one, of the king on horseback, "Though I don't think the face is very like him," Becca said. "Do you remember the time he came to Moor Park, Hetty, or were you too little?"

"I was a little girl, but I remember," said Esther. "He was very splendid, even without robes and crowns, and he and Sir William walked about the terrace and talked all day. I remember the Queen better—she was so much younger than he was, and pretty, and she seemed so sad."

"Poor lady, rest her soul," Becca said.

The boom of guns being fired shattered the summer air, and the crowds cheered, though when various dignitaries got up to give speeches the people chattered so loudly that no one could be heard. But the announcement that free wine and cakes would be served caught people's attention and sent them milling toward the refreshments. Nearby, two gaily dressed men played on a pipe and a drum, pausing from time to time to pass a hat for pennies, and the merry thrumming music made Esther want to dance. Dublin was a lovely city after all, and she was glad she had come.

"Have you been to the theatre in Smock-Alley?" Mr. Tisdall asked the next time they met, playing ombre at the home of Alderman Stoyte.

"No, but we have often thought of going," Esther said quickly. "I love the theatre—we went sometimes in London. But we have been warned it is a rough place for two women alone."

"Then you must not go alone," said Mr. Tisdall, "but I would gladly escort you and Mrs. Dingley if you wished to see a play. Shadwell's *The Libertine* is playing next week—an old play, of course, but one often revived, and I have never seen it, have you? Perhaps we could make up a party?"

"Splendid," said Esther, "I should love that. Mrs. Dingley?"

"Oh, I do love a play," said Becca, "and we'd better hurry and go before Mr. Swift comes back, for you know how he disapproves of plays and will never take us to see one."

"Mr. Swift does not own us, and I am sure we will be capable of arranging our own amusements with or without him," Esther said, folding her hands in her lap and darting a glance at Mr. Tisdall.

On the promised day, a carriage came round to William Street bearing Mr. Tisdall and his mother, along with the Stoytes, who were to make up the theatre party. The Smock-Alley Theatre was not so grand as Drury Lane in London, Esther thought, but on a smaller scale it was much the same—the crowds, the beggars, the orange girls, the view from their box of pit and gallery, the tumblers and jugglers on stage who entertained the audience before the play began.

When the curtain rose on *The Libertine*, Esther did her best to pay attention. Mr. Tisdall in the next seat was a distraction: was it his large, handsome presence or simply his murmured comments that made it hard for her to concentrate? She could feel his breath warm on her face as he said, "I hope this will not prove too shocking for you ladies." The three libertines, Don John, Don Carlos, and Don Antonio appeared on stage and began boasting of the many rapes and murders they had committed. "The principal characters are terribly wicked men, but it is a very moral play, in which they receive proper retribution in the end."

"Like every Don Juan, he is, I suppose, dragged off to hell in the final act?" Esther whispered.

"Along with his companions, I believe."

Mr. Tisdall was nervous too, she saw, studying his profile in the dim light. He wanted very much to please her, that was clear, and he whispered nervous apologies as the play continued and Don John mercilessly murdered the menfolk and ravished their ladies. Esther assured him she was not disturbed. It might have been intended to be a serious moral play, but she found a good deal of it very funny, and laughed aloud when Don John's six wives arrived and began quarrelling over him.

At the interval she looked around, studying the other boxes, wondering who the famous and important people of Dublin were. She remembered her very first trip to the theatre, and the fantastic spectacle of Tsar Peter in the box, and the opera singer who had been his mistress. Esther looked back at William Tisdall, and found him looking at her. He smiled and offered an orange.

Near the end of the fourth act, after the libertines had ravished a company of happy shepherdesses, the ghost of Don John's father made his second appearance. As he intoned, "Tremble, you impious wretches, and repent," a scream rang out from the audience. The ghost tried to go on—"Behold, the powers of Hell wait for you!" but a second scream quickly erupted, and all eyes turned to the gallery.

A horrible noise of splintering wood was almost drowned out by a rising chorus of shouts and cries. "Clear the gallery!" several voices took up. The action on stage stopped, and even the actors stared. People in the pit were screaming, running toward the stage or out of the theatre, as a huge beam from the gallery fell free and plummeted onto the heads of those below. The patrons trapped in the gallery, the poorest of the playgoers, screamed too, but there was nowhere for them to run, for the stairs, already clogged with bodies, were impassible. People were jumping from the collapsing gallery; others were falling; more beams and a huge section of the gallery floor were dropping away. The fortunate occupants of the boxes sat frozen with horror, watching the display.

Mr. Tisdall put an arm around Esther's shoulders, and she huddled close to him. On his other side, his mother began a fit of hysterics, shrieking, "We shall all be killed!" and William put his other arm about her.

We are the only ones who won't be killed, thought Esther, transfixed. With a horrible screech, the entire balcony, shorn of its supports, caved into the pit, carrying dozens of screaming bodies with it. There was utter chaos below as people scrambled free of the rubble or worked to pull others loose from beneath it.

It was close to an hour before the theatre was cleared and all the patrons stood in the lane outside, comforting one another. Mrs. Tisdall was still not breathing normally, and Becca, always open to suggestion, had joined her in her hysteria and had to be soothed by Esther. But the box holders had been lucky. More than a dozen of the people in pit and gallery were dead, and scores of others were wounded.

When the hysterical ladies had calmed down, the crowds had thinned, and the excitement abated, the party found their carriage and headed home. "I *am* sorry, Mrs. Johnson and Mrs. Dingley, to have invited you to the theatre on such an unfortunate day," said Mr. Tisdall. He looked as worried as if he expected them to blame him personally for the gallery's collapse.

Esther knew they had never been in any real danger, despite the histrionics of Becca and Mrs. Tisdall, yet she felt a rush of gratitude—if Mr. Tisdall had not quite saved them from death, he had certainly taken good care of them. He stood in the crowded alley, as handsome as Don John, as splendid as the tsar of Muscovy—no libertine or madman but a hero, a saviour. Esther remembered vividly the warm pressure of his arm across her shoulder. She put on a brilliant smile.

"Nonsense, Mr. Tisdall. Of course I feel sorry for the poor people who were killed or injured, but really, what more historic day could we have chosen to go to Smock-Alley? We may never have seen Don John and his companions dragged down to hell, but surely their descent could not have been more spectacular than the one we witnessed! I will certainly not forget this visit to the theatre."

DUBLIN
SEPTEMBER 25, 1701

This week Mr Swift is retourn'd from England, to the great rejoycing of all his Dublin friends. There was a dinner given in his Honour at Dr Stearne's home, and some twenty of us were gathered there to welcome him, tho' as for Becca and myselfe, we had already seen him, for he came to call on us here at William Street. But at the Dinner there were many speeches in his Honour, and I found out what he had nott told me in so great Detail, that he was much acclaimed in London for a pamphlet he wrote there, and has become a great Friend to all the Whig party, and is now a very Important man indeede. Which I cannot help being happy for,

for well doe I remember that from his earliest days, such was ever his wish, to go to London and move among the great.

But now he has come home to us here in Ireland. See how easily I say "Home" of Ireland, but my Heart does not saie it so easy as mye Pen. Moor Park will ever be my onely home, tho' I doe not knowe if I shall ever see it again. But Dublin is more Congeenial to me now, than it was when I came here first in the Summer, and Becca has got to be very comfortable in our home and with our circle of Acquaintance, and so have I. We goe about to the Stoytes, and the Wallses, and to Mr Tisdall's home, eating dinner and playing cards, and they are all most Agreeable people.

One thing troubles me, that I cannot think whoe to turn to, for no one could help us but Mr Swift—or Jonathan as he bids me call him when alone, but as I can never truly doe in mye Heart—and yet, tho' he could help Us out of this Difficulty, I shame to tell him, whoe is always so wise and so careful, and whoe always urged such caution on me. For the truth is, living in Ireland is much more expensive than what we had been told, or perhaps it is just that Living is expensive anywhere, and having spent all my Childhood yeares in service, I am not Accustomed to that harsh fact. But Dingley and I are greatly in Debt, or I should say, I am, for the greater store of the fortune is Mine, and I have run up most of the debts, buying furniture, and books, and plate and glass for our House, though I am Proud to say I have spent but Little on Clothes, which Mr Swift would surely despise, for how he urges Women to eschew Vanity, and putting on of gay apparel.

My apparel is very little gay at the moment, my three best petticoats almost threadbare, and I run through the same Cycle of Gowns over and over till all our friends must think me quite bare—with whatever else they think of me! For no one saies it now, but I know they still all think of my Curious position, and expect it to be Resolved now that Mr Swift has come.

Becca expects the same, and has begun to drop Hints, as to whether she shall be sent back to England, when I wed Mr Swift. And I assure her, that I will never send her away, and she shall be part of my household always, yet even as I say it the words sound like a jest or a game, for I cannot now Imagine myselfe married to Mr Swift.

The plain truth is I think it unlikely Mr Swift will ever broach the subject of marriage, should I tarry in Ireland for twenty yeares, for he is not inclin'd to that State. And this finds me reliev'd, but yet a little angry, that he should put me in such a Position, where every Tongue speculates, and gossips and slanders me, and he should not clear my name. No, I do not wish to marry, but wish instead that all things could continue as they are, with Mr Swift and I dear friends, only that two things should be remov'd: gossip, and my debts.

DUBLIN
FEBRUARY 15, 1702

Yesterday I had a very unwelcome visitor delivering, as I afterwards said to Becca, a most unlikely Valentine. It was the shopkeeper in Capel Street from whom we bought most of our linens and carpets. He has presented me with bills countless times, as have all the Shops, but this time he came in Person, to threaten that I Must pay, or face the Law. I owe him an enormous sum, nearly a hundred Pounds, which I am noe more able to Pay, than to Fly. I cannot belieeve what a Fool I have been, to find myself in such Predicament, but I was able to put him off once more with Smiles and Promises, and when he had gonne I knew I must confess to Mr Swift. (Tho' properly I ought now to style him "Dr Swift," for he has got his Doctor of Divinity now, a fine Title).

I have kept the Tale of our money troubles from him these months since his Retourne, with the result that he thinks me a very capable manager and good housekeeper, but alas all his regard for me in that Respect is gonne now, and I feare I shall never regain it. He was very stern when I told him of our troubles, and the bills, and lectured me a long lecture, which I well deserv'd, on Economy, and the Paying of Debts. And then he promis'd to pay the most Pressing of the Debts for us, and to tutor me in economies so that I might pay off the others, and

Incur no more. And all this while my face Blush'd with my shame, to have him chide me soe, as tho' I were a foolish Child, but indeede it was deserv'd, for so I have behaved.

Tonight we go to dine with Alderman Stoyte and his wife, along with Dr Swift, and Dr Stearne, and Archdeacon Walls and his wife. We are fortunate to have so many good Friends at last here in Dublin, but in the main I find I like the Husbands better than the Wives. I hope this does not make me a shameless sort of Woman, but I am almost beginning to agree with Dr Swift about Women in general, for I find their conversation very dull, and they seem so quick to Judge me, as the Men are nott. Dr Swift has little respect for any of our Sex, save myself and Becca and a few others, and the times he praises me most are the times, he saies, when I behave least Womanish.

I would not be sorry if the Rev. Mr Tisdall were at tonight's party: he is always so merry and witty, and I like his Company greatly. When Dr Swift first retourn'd I could see Mr Tisdall watching when we were Together, to perceive if there was a Lover's affection between the Doctor and myself, but now, I believe he has concluded we are only Friends, and I wonder what he makes of that conclusion, or what I would wish him to make of it?

LARACOR
NOVEMBER 29, 1702

We have come to Trim at Dr Swift's invitation, and are staying at the home of M^r and Mrs Wesley, one of the first families in the district.. They are members of Dr Swift's parish here at Laracor. When Dr Swift retourn'd this autumn from his latest trip into England he made at once for Laracor, for he has not dwell'd there since becoming its Vicar.

It is a pleasant little country town, not above a day's ride from Dublin, and only a mile or so from Trim where Dr Swift lodges with a Mrs Mulaly and her husband, for there is no vicarage attached to the church. There are only about a score of Church of Ireland people here, or fewer, for the common people are all Papists of course, and many of our own people have gone over to the Dissenters, which makes Dr Swift very angry, tho' he hopes to reform them.

Our friend Dr Stearne is the rector here at Trim, and makes us welcome in his home, and we goe about to dinners and cards so that it is just like a little Dublin in miniature, with the addition of some new faces and the absence of some old ones. Dingley misses the city, but I find Laracor and Trim very Agreeable, and should be happy to spend more time here when Dr Swift is in these parts.

I have written much of outings and dinners and cards and debts, but little of my work, and I am hard at work, being Dr Swift's secretary and transcriber, as he saies. Over last winter I helped him with the editing of the last volume of Sir William's letters, it made me sad to think that good old man has been dead nearly four years now. I think often of my Mother's words, that were soe Strange. Could it really be that I am the daughter of Sir William? I have wonder'd since if Liza knew that Gossip, and that accounted for her coldness to me, once she came of age. We gott the letters done at last. I saie done, but I should nott, for the last part of the work was most hastily done after the King dyed and Dr Swift decided he must hurry to London, and took the letters with him to the publisher. Now I am at work on his book, A Tale of a Tub, which he has been working at ever since Moor Park days, and I making a fair copy from all his scribblings as he goes thro and rewrites. I did not us'd to understand it when he talk'd of it long ago, but now that I read it whole it is a splendid defence of the True Faith, against Papists and Dissenters alike, and I hope it will be widely read.

I have been writing at my owne verses lately, but I think they are mighty poor stuff! I will nott showe any to Dr Swift noe matter how he beg me, but perhaps one day when I write something Good, I will let him see it. Becca is the onley one sees my poems, and all is wonderful to her, but she knowes little of poetry. Lately Mr Tisdall (whoe saies I must call him William) has shown me some of his writings, which are full of high-flown language but little substance, I tell him, but having criticized his so, I can scarce show him mine, tho' he too pleads with me! The truth is that his poems are quite lovely, but I will nott give him the

*satisfaction of saying soe! If I were to show him Mine, he would say they were
Perfection, better even than Dr Swift's, for Mr Tisdall praises whatever I doe,
but I doe not think this makes him a good Judge of poetry.*

*We are almost out of debt, thanks to living almost like paupers, and doing
next to no entertaining, and receiving gifts from Dr Swift that I wish he did not
have to give us. I am almost too proud to accept them, but I am too proud to be
in debtors' prison, either.*

LARACOR
APRIL 15, 1703

*We have beene in a frenzy of planting here, for Dr Swift is determined upon
improving his glebeland whenever he is heere in Laracor, and I have help'd where I
could, for it reminds me of the old days and Sir William's gardens at Moor Park,
that he took so much Trouble, and Care over. I was Touch'd to find Dr Swift
had taken Sir William's old coppy of Lawson's "A New Orchard Garden"
that I so often us'd to read to Sir William out of, and now it is our guide for the
beautifying of Laracor.*

*We have been planting willows all along the river, and Dr Swift is to have a
vicarage at last; they have begunne building him one. Becca and I came out last
month and are staying with the Wesleys, as we usually doe, but with the straits we
are in for money it pains me to think of our house in William Street lying vacant
while we still pay the rent on it. I am growne so fond of Laracor, I would like to
find a house or cottage here to let, and then we could let William Street go, and
take another lodging when at last we retourn'd to Dublin. Mr Wesley saies the
Percivalls have a cottage on their land, verry close to the church, and I have
determin'd to go down, and look at it, if Becca be Agreeable.*

*There is another Visitor here from Dublin, which gives Becca fresh matter to
jest about. For she has ceas'd to rail at me about marrying Dr Swift, now she sees
we will never be anything but the perfectest Friends, and now she has changed her*

tune, to Sweet William, that is, Mr *Tisdall. He follow'd us this time, to Trim, after all his complaints of us leaving Dublin, and now makes part of our society heere while he staies in D*^{r} *Stearne's house, D*^{r} *Stearne being away. D*^{r} *Swift saies (in jest) that William has but a verry poore, feeble wit, to which I saie that mine must be the Same, for he amuses me Greatly.*

But all this is nonsense. I think I once dream'd of keeping a Journal to some Serious Purpose, but cannot for my Life think what it might have Beene.

DUBLIN
1723

Twenty-two—who would not be two-and-twenty again, given the chance? Folk talk foolishly of going back to childhood, or being sixteen again, but Esther knows better. If she could recapture one moment of the past, she would be twenty-two again, young and pretty, mistress of her own fate and alive to every possibility life offered, having yet closed no gates and burned no bridges.

It was her first taste of independence, and it truly seemed in those days as if anything might happen, as if her life might go in any direction. Now, leaning her cheek wearily against her hand, Esther feels the loss of that hope, that sense of a wide horizon stretching before her. And yet, in truth, no matter how many possible futures were hers at twenty-two, she could not have chosen more than one. Any choice, good or bad, would have meant a narrowing, a closing of doors.

The choices she made—were they good or bad? Was there another door she might have gone through, one that could have changed everything? She cannot know for certain, nor can she return to those days and live them again, choosing another path.

She can only catch the flavour of those years by leafing through these pages, where careless laughter lurks behind every word. But the answer she seeks is not there, among those Laracor willows of her second girlhood—unless, of course, that is precisely where it is.

LARACOR
1703

Esther sat on a wooden bench, looking up at the undersides of leaves against the brilliant August sky. The edges of each leaf were outlined sharp in the sunshine and their greens were translucent, shimmering with the gold light above. She was tired. Mrs. Percival had sent down a maid, Maggie, to help with the work, but even so there was a good deal for Esther and Becca to do, until at last Becca had laid a hand on her cheek and said, "You look all pale, Hetty—go and sit down before you have a headache. Maggie and I can finish in here."

She had just closed her eyes to rest them when she heard footsteps and a voice. "Come now, Miss Esther, dozing in the sun? Surely you've more to do than that on your moving day."

"Have you come to help shift boxes and scrub cupboards?" she asked, without opening her eyes, and was rewarded by a slight pause. She opened her eyes. "As I thought," she said, "only come to gawk, and watch others work. Well, it will please you to know that Becca and Mrs. Percival's girl are doing the work of three women, for Becca decided I was brewing a headache and must sit down to rest."

Dr. Swift's jovial smile turned to a frown at once, and taking both her hands in his he pulled her up from her comfortable seat. "Come then, that will never do. You must not start taking headaches again, or your eyes will grow weak, and I will lose my faithful copyist. 'Tis a silly poppet, to sit in the hot sun when her head is aching—come, walk, walk! What do I always tell you? Exercise will make you strong. Walk by the river with me, and we will see how our willows do."

Esther sighed as she picked up her skirts and followed him down the lane, but he was right, of course—sitting in the sun, comfortable as it might have been, would not do her half the good that a brisk walk would. And a walk with Dr. Swift would certainly be brisk. He had probably walked five miles that morning already. She was only fortunate he hadn't suggested another shooting lesson with the pistol he had bought her, insisting two maiden ladies needed such a thing in the house for protection.

Whether it was the bright sunshine, the country air, or Dr. Swift's conversation, Esther soon did feel much better. They walked past the church and Dr. Swift's vicarage, which was almost ready to be moved into. There was a tiny figure up on the roof of the church, and another working on the new wall. During the weeks when he was in Laracor, Dr. Swift never seemed to stop putting his energy and his money into finding ways to improve the humble church and its grounds.

The vicarage made Esther think of her own cottage again— her head felt fine now, and she was sorry to have left Becca with so much of the work. How lovely to have a cottage all their own—though Becca preferred a town house, and Esther had had to promise many times over that they would return to Dublin in the fall and not settle permanently in what Becca called "the back of beyond."

But at the cottage, where Esther and Swift returned presently, Becca was so full of being mistress of the house that she seemed to have forgotten her resentment of country living, and looked around the plain, well-scrubbed main room with all the satisfaction Esther felt. A cartload of their belongings had arrived on Saturday from Dublin, the rest having been packed away and stored with the Wallses, and though it had taken all weekend to unpack things and put them to rights, the cottage now looked like home. A humbler, simpler home than a Dublin house, as befitted a country cottage, but it was clean and bright and every surface had been polished till it shone.

"I sent young Maggie home," Dingley said, surveying her work with satisfaction, "and no sooner had she gone than another girl came from Mrs. Percival, her kitchen maid, Jane, with a dinner Mrs. Percival sent down for us. Cold roast goose and mutton—there's enough for the doctor to join us for dinner."

"Then the doctor accepts with gratitude," said Swift, sitting down on one of the straight-backed wooden chairs, "for the products of Mrs. Percival's kitchen are never to be sneered at."

Dingley handed a parcel of papers to Esther. "Our mail came as well, to Mrs. Percival's, so she sent it down with dinner. Nothing for me and all for you, as usual."

"That is only because I *write* letters, and people tire of seeing their correspondence vanish into the mists, Becca," said Esther, going through her letters. "One from Mama, in London, which will be full of news of her ladyship and all the family—we'll read that after supper—and two from Dublin, one from Mrs. Walls and one from Mr. Tisdall."

"Ah, a missive from Sweet William!" said Swift. Esther shot Becca a murderous glance: why had she ever been fool enough to use that nickname in front of the doctor, who lived on raillery? "Come now, Miss Esther, you must open your love letter first, or do you wish to save it to read all alone? Tell us, is he coming again to Trim? 'Tis odd he finds the place so congenial all of a sudden."

Esther would have given anything to lose the power of blushing, for she knew what satisfaction it gave her tormentors. She opened Mr. Tisdall's letter, scanned it quickly, and laid it aside in the middle of the table. "Anyone may read it; there's nothing in it of the sort of folly you two talk of."

"Nothing in it of pining or dying for love?" said Dingley.

Swift began to sing. "*'Twas in the merry month of July, with all the flowers so handsome—Sweet William on his deathbed lay, for the love of Esther Johnson …*"

"Hold your peace!" Esther cried, which only made the other two laugh the harder.

"I only hope he has written you no poetry, for if it is made of the same stuff as his essays, the letter will be so heavy you will hardly be able to carry it to your bedroom."

"Stop mocking his writing—you do it all the time, and to his face too. 'Tis cruel—he preaches a very pretty sermon. What more should a clergyman need?"

"What more, indeed? That is what I always tell him. Why should he feel the need to prove himself a writer as well?"

If Dr. Swift could not see the reason for that, he was missing it on purpose, for nothing could be clearer to Esther than that poor William, a very nice and talented young man, always felt the need to measure up to the great Dr. Swift, who was only a few years older but already had such renown as a writer and was so well known among poets and politicians in England as well as in Ireland. *Why*, exactly, he felt he had to measure himself against Swift was another question.

William himself arrived a fortnight later and was present on the very first occasion that Esther and Becca entertained friends at the cottage. Along with the two ladies, Dr. Swift, and Mr. Tisdall were Mr. and Mrs. Wesley, Joe Beaumont the merchant from Trim with his wife, Dr. Stearne, and Mr. and Mrs. Percival. The evening was lively, with several games of piquet, which people in Trim seemed to prefer over the game of ombre they always played in Dublin. When the card games were over, Dr. Swift was reckoned to have lost the most money—eight shillings—and as a penalty, William Tisdall suggested, he would have to recite some of his poetry.

Swift stood up in front of the fireplace in fine style, one hand in the pocket of his waistcoat, and cleared his throat while Dingley took a nice big pinch of snuff and the others all settled themselves to listen. Then he began to recite, "The Petition of Mrs. Frances Harris."

Esther, who had heard the poem before, shifted uncomfortably as the rest of the company roared with laughter. It was quite the funniest and most interesting thing he had ever written, Esther thought—he had captured so perfectly the fussy, wheedling voice of the poor lady-in-waiting whose few shillings were stolen. Yet it made her uneasy. The poem had been written in the Berkeley household, and the imaginary Frances was lady's maid to Lady Betty Berkeley, that glowing, vivacious girl a few years younger than Esther herself, who was such a great friend to Dr. Swift. Esther had once been introduced to Lady Betty, and the brief encounter had made Esther feel terribly aware of her own awkward status, her lack of social position. She could not quite forget that if she, Esther, were ever to be part of the Berkeley household, it would be exactly in Frances's position, poor Frances who dreamed of marrying his lordship's chaplain—and who, Dr. Swift had assured them, was purely a fiction, for no lady's maid in the Berkeley house cherished such an ambition! Yes, she was a fiction, yet Esther felt … not exactly as if Mr. Swift were mocking herself and Becca and her mother, but mocking women like them, perhaps.

Still it was a merry evening, full of laughter and jests, and when the guests left Esther and Becca walked partway up the road with them. William Tisdall took both Esther's hands in his and said how good it was to see her again, and looked as if he might have lingered, but for Dr. Stearne, who was clearly eager to get on into Trim. So William said good-night, and Dr. Swift stayed on to talk and walk Esther and Becca safely back to their cottage door. "With all this entertainment, Esther," was his parting comment, "I shan't chide you for not having my papers finished, but I will be quite stern tomorrow, and expect a copy ready for the printer."

"Don't expect too much, for I plan to sleep till noon!" she called back, but all the same she stopped a minute to lift the lid of her desk and look at the final draft of *A Tale of a Tub*, all spread out for her to continue work tomorrow. In a sudden rush of happiness she turned around and said, "Becca, I do believe I have everything in life I have ever wanted!"

"Have you?" said Becca, already settled back in her chair. "You're easier pleased than I am, then. I want a proper house in town, and a dog, and another pinch of snuff left in this box, for Joe Beaumont emptied it on me. Why are you so content of a sudden?"

Esther stood still by the desk, her fingers resting on the papers. "I used to dream of this—having a cottage or a house of my own, and friends to come and go, and work to keep me busy—and now I seem to have it all."

"Did you never dream of a man?" Becca raised her eyebrows—gingery like her hair—though she did not look up from the swift motion of her needle. She stabbed it in and out, in and out as she added, "Most women do, or so I'm told."

"Of course—I mean, I dreamed of being in love, and all that, but that was just fantasy. When I thought of a real life for myself, I thought of something like this. Do you remember how devoted Lady Giffard was to Sir William, keeping his house and helping him with his work? When I thought of a man I thought of someone like that—a brother, someone I could be a help to. I almost feel I have that with Dr. Swift—now that there's none of your silly talk of marriage to spoil it all."

"Spoiling, is that it? You'll think of marriage sometime—I'll swear you've thought of it plenty already and just won't say. If not with Dr. Swift, then with Sweet William. You're not natural, a girl of twenty-two, if you don't think of it."

"And what of you? You used to talk a good deal about this young man and that one, back at Moor Park," Esther challenged, sitting down across from her friend. The room had grown very dim in the candlelight and the glow from the dying fire. "Do you want to be married?"

"Me?" Becca snorted. She seemed almost shocked. "What would I want with a man, and what would a man want with me? No, you were right the first time, my girl." Now she did look up, her brown eyes taking in the simple room lit by the turf fire. "We've got all we want, all we need, right here in this room." Becca's eyes fixed on Esther, and there was such warmth there, such contentment, that all at once Esther felt uncertain and questioned her own contentment. Was this really what she wanted—*all* she wanted, ever?

Ah, well. She was twenty-two, and there was time ahead for more than one kind of life, she was sure. Romance might still beckon. She thought of William saying good-night, his hands on hers, his smile, the way he looked when she came into a room. But he had spoken no words of love. She pushed Mr. Tisdall firmly to the back of her mind.

He refused to stay there. All through the summer and early fall, Esther stayed in Laracor, visiting Dublin for no more than a week at a time. But in October Becca put her foot down and said they must go back to the city before the cottage got cold and drafty, so they paid their last week's rent to the Percivals, packed up their things, and went to Dublin. There they stayed with Archdeacon Walls and his wife while they looked for new lodgings.

Becca had gotten very chummy with Dorothy Walls, whom Dr. Swift called "Gossip Doll," but Esther never felt entirely comfortable around her. She had not forgotten that first apprais-ing glance in the church, and though she would not have held a grudge that long against anyone, she could never quite be at ease because she felt as if Mrs. Walls's eyebrows had never quite come down. Whenever Esther was in her company and talking with a man—usually Dr. Swift or Mr. Tisdall—she would catch Mrs. Walls darting glances at her that seemed to say Esther Johnson was a dangerous, wanton woman who had to be closely watched. Perhaps she was even afraid Esther might tempt her husband—a hilarious possibility, since many of her private chats with Swift and Tisdall concerned a wager among the three of them as to which would ever be able to coax a smile from the sombre archdeacon.

So Esther was not eager to outstay their welcome in the Wallses' home, and was by no means sorry when William Tisdall said one day, "Do you know where I've just moved into?"

"No, have you moved at last?"

"Yes, and you'll laugh, for I've moved into your old house in William Street."

"Have you? I'd heard it was for let again, but I was saving it till we'd looked at all the other places we'd heard of, for I never was very fond of that house."

"But the best part is, there's another place, much nicer, not far from it on William Street, that's also for rent. If it suits you, you might move back into your old neighbourhood, and we might be neighbours."

"But if it is much nicer, as you say, it will be much more expensive, and I'm sure we can't afford that."

"Not so! For it's farther out the street, where there has been even less building, and consequently the rents are cheaper."

Esther tried to picture a house "farther out" William Street than their old one had been, and thought that Becca wouldn't like that at all—she was always worrying about robbers and other imaginary dangers—but Mr. Tisdall was very insistent about their seeing it, and both ladies had to admit it was a very comfortable house for the money. And so the whole process of moving, unpacking, hiring servants, and turning the place into a home began again. In the midst of it, Dr. Swift left for another long trip to England, laden down with messages for their family and friends and lists of things he was to buy and bring back for them.

"Make sure you get spectacles for Hetty," Dingley chided as they said goodbye to him. "Her eyes are fair worn out looking over those manuscripts of yours."

Swift fixed Esther with a keen glance. "Have your eyes been troubling you again, poppet? I would not give you my copying to do if I thought it would hurt your poor little eyes and head."

"No, of course not. Pay no mind to Becca—she loves to fuss over me." Esther brushed off his concern, then added, "But if you want to bring me spectacles, 'twould be no harm, for I could always stand to have things made a little larger."

In truth, her eyes and her headaches and her breathing troubles had all been bothering her a great deal lately, especially since returning to Dublin, but she would not risk telling Swift how badly her eyes hurt. If she lost her work as his secretary, she would have no idea how to fill her days.

Outside of her working hours, there was nothing too difficult about life in Dublin that winter. Becca fussed and worried over the housekeeping while Esther tried valiantly to make sure the bills got paid. A servant crisis arose when the maid, Kitty, turned out to be pregnant by the manservant, John, and both had to be let go. Esther insisted on giving them both their dismissal and a stern lecture, while Dingley insisted on making them a small present of money for the wedding and baby. Then of course a new maid had to be hired, "And a boy instead of a manservant," Esther decided. "He can work as well, and cheaper, and there's less of that kind of bother." So a quiet Jane and a timid Billy joined the household as day servants, in company with the faithful Mrs. Sally, who had returned to their employ.

Christmas was a merry time with much visiting, and on Twelfth Night Esther and Becca invited as many friends as the little house would hold. Mrs. Sally outdid herself putting on a great spread, and after the supper everyone played charades, and there was music and even a little dancing. Esther had not had the opportunity to dance much since arriving in Ireland; whirling about the crowded floor, bumping into friends and laughing at those who did not know the steps, and coming back to meet a smiling William and join hands with him at the top of the line, made for a pleasant evening indeed.

When the dance was done everyone retired to their seats, coughing and clapping, and William leaned over Esther. "You must be hot, after such a turn—can I bring you a glass of wine?" She nodded, though she had intended to drink and eat as sparingly as possible, knowing how much this gala evening was costing her—even with the help of a generous Christmas gift of money from Dr. Swift. William returned with a glass of wine and a cake on a plate for her. Becca had made the cakes herself, not trusting them to Mrs. Sally's hand, and despite worrying about shortages Esther could not resist having one.

"Share it with me, Will," she insisted, and he broke off a little less than half for himself.

On the other side of her, Mrs. Walls said something that sounded as if it had the word *piss* in it: Esther caught her breath with laughter and felt the cake catch in her throat. She coughed, but nothing came up; she gasped for air. William noticed her plight at once and thumped her firmly on the back. After another round of coughing, the crumb of cake flew out into her napkin. By now, of course, everyone was watching with great concern as Esther took a swallow of her wine and waved her hand to let them know she was recovered. "Don't worry, I'm quite all right," she assured her friends, putting on the accent of the native Irish. "Ye'll all be glad to know you've only to hear me coughin', not follow me coffin!"

"Well put!" William said, laughing and obviously relieved. "Mrs. Johnson, I do confess that in spite of all our contests, you have won forever in the department of puns."

"That was not such an outstandingly clever pun, was it?" said Mrs. Walls, eyeing Mr. Tisdall closely with a crooked little smile.

"No, but our hostess's gallantry in making a pun with her very first breath on recovering puts her in the very highest class of punsters."

"I agree wholeheartedly, for the bun caught the pun in her throat, and did battle, but the pun was triumphant, and the bun both banished and pun-ished," said Dillon Ashe, a new friend who, Esther had confided to William a few weeks before, deserved to be admitted to the "inner circle" of their company because of his quick-witted humour.

"I don't think much of puns myself," said Archdeacon Walls.

"No, you hardly think of them at all, do you?" said Esther with equal gravity, which drew another laugh from William Tisdall.

That was the real pleasure in being with Will, she decided—rather than trying always to improve her, he seemed to want her to be just as she was. He had his flaws, including the fact that he was ever urging her to read his essays and comment upon them, but his lighthearted gaiety, so at odds with the sombre tones of his writing, made it easy to overlook his faults. "And it doesn't hurt that he's an easy sight for the eyes," Becca pointed out when she and Esther discussed Tisdall and other men of their acquaintance.

"*You* ought to marry him, then, as you think he's so good-looking," said Esther.

"A bit young for me, I'm afraid. I need someone with a few lines on his brow."

"Take one without; you'll soon put them there."

"Go to, I have a letter to finish writing. See, you can't say I never write letters—I'm finishing one to Dr. Swift now," Becca announced.

"All full of shopping lists. He'll come back from London more loaded down than a cart horse."

"It's not just shopping, I'm telling him all our doings, about your choking, and the wicked jest you made in church last week, and all the foolish things you and Mr. Tisdall have done, together and separately."

"You goose. Let me see it before you mail it."

Swift wrote often: his letters were full of London gossip about ordinary people they all knew and great people they had heard of, and there was plenty of mockery and jesting in them. William came in one day as Esther was at the desk in the sitting room, rereading a letter of Swift's that Becca had read out to her the night before when her eyes were bad. She wanted to begin a reply, and was scanning his page to remind herself of what she'd wanted to say, when she heard William's voice behind her. "And what course of reading entrances Mrs. Johnson so?"

She looked up, laying down the paper. "Nothing, only a letter from Dr. Swift."

"Ah! That reminds me, I had a letter of him very lately. He writes about politics, and how things in town are so contentious that the very cats in the streets are divided into Whig and Tory camps and quarrel all night long."

"That sounds like something he would say!"

William Tisdall's laughing face grew suddenly serious. "He is always here with us, is he not?"

Esther hesitated. "Yes, I suppose, in our thoughts—as absent friends always are."

"He is in your thoughts a great deal."

"Of course—just as he is in yours, and Becca's—his being such a good friend to us all."

"Not exactly in yours as he is in ours."

"I don't know what you mean, Mr. Tisdall."

"I thought I had got you used to calling me William."

"I don't know what you mean about Dr. Swift, William."

William, who had been standing, sat down uninvited and stared at the floor rather than at Esther. His hands twisted together in his lap. "Forgive me, Esther, for any … any sort of presumption at all, but as we are such good friends, I felt … I have often wondered, whether there is anything warmer than friendship between Dr. Swift and yourself. Any … any thought of love, or of marriage?"

The room was very quiet. The enormity of the question, and of the fact that William Tisdall was asking it, felt himself entitled to ask it and in need of an answer, gave her pause. If she were to be truthful, what could she say? That she had come to Ireland on the expectation of marrying Jonathan Swift, not because of anything he had said but because all her friends and family had told her it would be so? That she had once got herself accustomed to that idea and quite liked it? That no one's approval and esteem mattered to her as much as Swift's? That she could not imagine her life without his friendship and guidance? That she was now sure Swift did not want to marry her, and felt relieved, because she was tumbling headfirst into love with William Tisdall?

The truth, of course, would not do. Instead she said, "Dr. Swift has been my friend from childhood, as you know. Because he was my tutor, I have always admired and looked up to him. He has never talked of marrying me, and I do not think of him in that way. He has been my friend and guide—I believe I think of him as something like an elder brother, if I have to find a name for it."

William smiled. It was not a smile that tried to hide his thoughts, and even at the best of times he was a man—so unlike Swift—whose every thought could be read on his face. Now he beamed at Esther, and she knew he was finally ready to speak.

"I am glad to hear you say that, Esther, for I have wanted to say something to you for a long time, but I feared … well, what I have to say would have been most wrong, if there were any such understanding between you and Dr. Swift. But now that I know your feelings for him, I can keep silent no longer. We have been great friends, and I have come to admire you deeply and, yes, to love you. I would be very proud to make you my wife. Could you ever consider such a thing?"

Esther looked away from him. She could not bear the thought of his frightened, hopeful face, so dear and kind, while her own heart was knocking in her chest and her cheeks were flushing. *Yes! Yes!* she thought, but did not say it—this was not a romance tale, this was a proposal of marriage, life's most serious business. She stood up and crossed the room, swallowing down her eager agreement, took handfuls of her petticoat in each fist in a gesture she had not used since childhood. She looked out the window at the bare muddy street and tried to frame an answer. The first thing she thought of to say sounded petty and prosaic, but she said it anyway.

"William, you know I have no great fortune, and my family is very humble. Perhaps more than humble"—she had not meant to tell him this, but she was driven to go on—"for I must tell you that back in Surrey, where I grew up, there were rumours that Sir William Temple was not only our family's benefactor but my natural father. So in many eyes there is scandal attached to my birth. I can bring you nothing of what you ought to expect in a wife—no money or great family connections. I am afraid you would … that you wish to marry me because of your fondness for me, and our friendship, and that later you might regret it when you wish to rise in the world and find that I am holding you back."

"You, Esther? Hold me back?" He strode across the room and stood behind her, laying a hand on her shoulder with a gentle pressure that made her want desperately to turn in to his arms. "I said I was proud to ask you to marry me, and proud I am. There is nothing in your family or your fortune that could sway my choice—only you yourself, the loveliest, cleverest, sweetest girl in Dublin. Rise in the world? Why, if you were my wife, I should mount up on wings as eagles!"

She turned to him then, with a wavering half smile; whatever happened from here, it was worth it all just to have heard those words. But marriage was a sober prospect. "I must think about it, William. I need time—and properly, you ought to write to my mother and ask her."

"I know—I have been very rash, coming to you directly like this. If you had family here in Ireland, I should have spoken to them, but—"

"But my position being what it is, you did not know what was best," she finished for him. "You correspond with Dr. Swift, and he knows my mother well and is in contact with her. Perhaps he might advise you—if you do not mind speaking to him of this."

"Oh no," William said, almost laughing in his relief. "I would not have liked to do so when I thought he might be my rival. But when you have assured me that he stands in the role of an elder brother, I think he is the very person to speak to your mother on my behalf. I dare tell you he has written a dozen things about you in his letters, mocking me for my devotion to you, for he knows my feelings quite well, so I do not think this will come as any surprise to him."

"William—remember that I have not said yes. Whatever Dr. Swift advises, whatever my mother says, the choice is mine to make, and you must remember ... how very fond I am of you. Whatever choice I make. Will you remember that?"

He grabbed her hand and pressed it hard. "I shall—I always shall. Think on it, Esther."

Of course, she thought of nothing else for a month, though William did not raise the subject again. She caught his gaze steady on her sometimes when they were in company; he took care to be alone with her and Becca less than he had before, and never alone with Esther only. She wished she had a ready answer to give him—any answer, either answer—but it was not as simple as that.

She loved him. Probably she had loved him since the gallery crashed into the pit in the Smock-Alley Theatre, though only now would she say to herself, *I am in love*. She wanted to be with him, to touch him and be touched by him, to feel his lips against hers. She had been kissed once, by a handsome young soldier when she was sixteen; now she was twenty-three and ready to be kissed again, by this handsome, witty man who adored her.

And he would be a good husband—a clergyman, respectable, bright, and with a solid future. It would not be a foolish marriage for her—it would be a very good match indeed. He could take care of her. Passion and reason seemed, for once, to be walking hand in hand.

And yet. She hesitated. She would be a wife, a clergyman's wife like Dorothy Walls and many another she knew. She would keep a house and likely have children. She would do as her husband wished; his work would be her work; his friends would be her friends. Folk said the fires of passion died in marriage. Would she be happy, in that life, being that woman?

For a fortnight she did not tell even Becca. She kept the proposal to herself, turning it over and over in her head, just as she had done four years ago when everyone had told her she was expected to marry Jonathan Swift. But this was different—this was a real proposal, a man who truly wanted to marry her, had asked her outright. When at last she was sick of her own thoughts, she finally told her dearest friend about the question.

They were in Esther's bedchamber, Esther sitting before the mirror and Becca standing behind her, brushing out her hair. Becca dropped the hairbrush when Esther told her the news. Esther, watching her friend's reflected face in the mirror, saw a moment of shock and an expression she couldn't read cross Becca's usually placid features. It was replaced at once by a broad smile, then Becca picked up the hairbrush and lightly smacked Esther's arm with the back of it.

"There, haven't I said?" she demanded. "Haven't I always said he had intentions? You wicked baggage, waiting all this time to tell me! A fortnight ago, did you say? And you not given him an answer yet?! Poor man must be in torment. Why are you keeping him waiting?"

"For the simplest of reasons, Becca—I don't know the answer. I haven't made up my mind whether to marry him."

"Made up your mind? What's to make up, I'd like to know? Hetty, I've heard of a woman being too choosy, but you beat them all. What more could you hope for? He's young and handsome, a clergyman with a good career ahead of him, and he's besotted with you—that's plain."

All this was true. "He's not so very young," Esther protested lamely. "He's past thirty."

"Humph—and that's the end of life, is it?" Dingley pulled the brush through Esther's hair with quick, vigorous strokes. "A man doesn't know his arse from his elbow before he's thirty. At any rate, Mr. Tisdall's young for his age. He looks like a boy still—and acts it too, some ways."

"And he probably always will," Esther said, before she had time to think whether she was complimenting or insulting him. "He is sweet, and kind, and handsome," she conceded. "I could not ask for a better man, if I wished to marry."

"It's my experience that every woman wishes to marry, when the right man asks her," said Becca.

"Not always! Silly women, perhaps, who don't think of what marriage means. I've never wanted ... well, my mother and Lady Giffard both used to say I ought not to marry, that my health would never stand up to it. To bearing children, and all."

"Perhaps not to bearing children," Becca said, nodding slowly. Then she broke into laughter. "But I think you'd be plenty strong enough to live through the 'and all' part of it!"

"Hush, Becca! What do maids like us know of such things? I've never even seen a grown man naked, only little boys—and I know no more of what happens in a married couple's bedchamber than gossip and filthy talk I've heard. Who knows what it might really be like?"

"Ah, I've heard everything—that it's the bliss of heaven and that it's the torment of hell. If you ask me, I'd say it had everything to do with who was in the bed with you!"

"As for that ..." Esther did not finish the thought aloud. But as for that, she knew she wanted to be in no man's bed but Will Tisdall's.

Becca was nodding as though she read Esther's every thought. "So, where is your trouble? Are you waiting to be swept madly off your feet by love, like in some foolish romance?"

"You're the reader of romances, not I." But that was the worst of it—she *did* feel swept away, swept off her feet, she who was so proud of standing on her own feet, of charting her own course.

"And think of having a husband who could take care of you—he'll do well, our Mr. Tisdall," Becca rambled on, laying down the hairbrush and sitting on the edge of Esther's bed to take off her own shoes and stockings. "No more money worries, no more debts—"

"That *would* be nice. What will you do if I marry, Becca?"

There was a silence. Becca bent down to cover it, hauling down her stockings, and when she looked up she said, "That's not a thing for you to be worrying about, Hetty. You marry to please yourself, not your friends. I might go back to England—"

"No—don't. I couldn't bear it if you went away. You could live with me, if Will—if my husband pleased. If I were to marry."

"No new couple wants an old maid under their roof. Now, how long do you intend to keep Sweet William waiting for his answer?"

"I told him he must write my mother and ask her leave, but I suppose I could give an answer sooner if I wished."

"Write your mother! That will slow him down—as he doesn't know her, he may be afraid to approach her," Becca pointed out.

"Well, I told him to write Dr. Swift and have him speak to Mother."

Becca straightened up slowly and looked full at Esther again. "Oho, so *that's* the game you're playing, is it?"

"I don't know what you mean."

"You do, very well. Esther Johnson, I'm telling you now, Will Tisdall is a good man, and it's wrong of you to use him to make another man jealous." She was in deadly earnest, and Esther suddenly felt cold.

"What are you saying, Becca? That I—"

"That you want Dr. Swift to know of this proposal so he'll be goaded into making one of his own!"

"I never thought of such a thing! How dare you say it!"

"It's him you've always wanted to marry—now you think he'll make his move if he thinks he has a rival."

"I would *never,* never think of anything so wicked, nor use either William or Dr. Swift so! And I do *not* wish to marry Jonathan Swift!!"

"Fine. Please yourself," said Becca. She picked up her shoes and stockings and left the room.

Esther sat alone, staring at her reflection. She had told the truth—such a thought had never entered her mind. But she could see how it might appear that way—not only to Becca but to either of the men concerned. She had wondered how Swift would respond to the news of Tisdall's proposal. What a tangled, twisted web she had woven by suggesting William write that letter.

She was angry with Becca for three days, and they barely spoke at all; after that they made up, as their enforced closeness could tolerate no longer estrangement. They still talked of whether Esther ought to marry Mr. Tisdall, but Swift's name did not enter the conversation again. Tisdall himself left Dublin to visit his family in Carrickfergus. Esther concluded that with both Mr. Tisdall and Dr. Swift away, Dublin was a dull town indeed. She lay awake half one night trying to decide which of them she would bring back, if she could return only one, and came to no satisfactory conclusion. But Mr. Tisdall returned first; one day at the end of April she and Becca returned home from the shops to find that he had called in their absence.

Esther was quiet all through dinner that day, though Becca naturally wanted to talk of William's return and press Esther into revealing her decision. When dinner was done and Becca set about her afternoon's work, Esther went downstairs again and pulled on her cloak. Better not to delay.

She walked through the brisk spring afternoon up the rutted road to the house where William lodged. Though she tried not to rehearse speeches in her mind, it was inevitable that she play over the conversation about to take place. She had thought it through and through and still was not entirely sure if her answer was the right one. But she was ready to give it nonetheless.

William came to the door and took her hands. "The fairest face in Dublin!" he cried. "How I have missed you."

"As I have missed you, William," she assured him.

When they were seated in his sitting room, he took a long look at her, as if enjoying the sight of her again. "You don't know how glad I am to hear you say you missed me, Esther. Do I dare to hope that means you have an answer for me?"

She looked away from him, out the window, then decided that was too easy, and since this would not be easy for him she must not make it simple for herself. Love and longing wove a silken web about her as soon as she looked in his eyes—but she had to be strong and break through it.

"I have, William, but I must tell you it's not the one you've wanted to hear. I wish it could be—I've thought it through a thousand times—and I hope we shall always be the best of friends. The reason is nothing to do with you, dear William. It's simply that … I don't wish to be married. I don't think I ever have wished it, really, and I don't believe I ever will marry."

She had once thought that if love came, she would be carried away, unable to say no. But she had proved stronger than she thought—or love, perhaps, was weaker than poets made it out to be.

"I am not made for marriage, William—I value my independence too much, I think, and as my health has never been good, I greatly fear childbirth. I have no special inclination to be a mother, and I do not think I would make you a very good wife. I am sorry, because I am most fond of you—but it simply cannot be."

He looked stricken, as she had known he would, and some shameful part of her was glad it was so, proud that he cared so much, though her better self felt pity for his pain amid the ache of her own loss. Then William's face changed a little, and he reached into his waistcoat pocket and brought out a folded piece of paper.

"You sound very decided. I suppose no pleas or tears of mine will change your mind."

"Please, William—do not do that. Even if you could change my mind, would you urge me into a marriage I know I will not be happy making? Please believe me, it is not you. I would give this same answer to any man."

"*Any* man?" There was a knife in his voice, and he leaned forward and handed her the paper. She took it but did not unfold it, looking her question at him.

"You may think I show you this to change your mind— perhaps I do. If you are hanging on to hopes of a different proposal from a different suitor, perhaps this letter will tell you how long to wait." His tone had grown cold, and her hands shook as she took the paper from him, knowing he wanted to use the letter to wound her in some way. Well, she deserved that. She knew the too-familiar handwriting as soon as the page was open, but she was in no hurry to read. There turned out to be so many things one did not really wish to know.

"I did as you asked," William said, "I wrote to Dr. Swift asking him to speak to your mother for me. I burned his first letter—it made me angry. It said little about you yourself, but it seemed to advise me against marrying, and talked of how an early and unwise marriage might stand in the way of a young man's career.

I thought … well, I suppose that the suspicion I had voiced to you arose again; I thought that even if there were no understanding between yourself and Dr. Swift, that he might have … intentions, and not spoken of them to you. I wrote, saying as much, asking him if he discouraged me because he wanted to marry you himself. I told him his letter was unfriendly and unkind. And he wrote me this in reply."

She scanned the page, curiosity winning over her other confused emotions. *You think I obstructed your insinuations to please my own, and that my intentions were the same with yours … I think I have said to you before that if my fortunes and humour served me to think of that state, I should certainly, among all persons on earth, make your choice; because I never saw that person whose conversation I entirely valued but hers; this was the utmost I ever gave way to.*

Esther took a deep breath: she would be thinking of these words for a long time. It was, then, as she had long suspected: Jonathan Swift did not want to marry, but he found no shame in saying that if he did, it would be no one but her. He "entirely valued" her conversation, above anyone else's. She did not look up at William.

And secondly, I must assure you sincerely, that this regard of mine never once entered into my head to be an impediment to you … Just as it had never entered her head to try to make Swift jealous by telling him of William's proposal—but how very many things might be in one's head without one ever knowing they had entered there! He went on to repeat his caution about William's career, and that he had wondered whether William were rich enough to support her, but that if that were no longer a concern, then he had no objection to the match and had already spoken to Esther's mother on William's behalf. *Nor shall any consideration of my own misfortune of losing so good a friend and companion as her, prevail on me ... since it is held so necessary and convenient a thing for ladies to marry; and that time takes off from the lustre of virgins in all other eyes but mine.*

There was more; he said several more kind things about Esther's humour, wit, judgement, and conversation, remarking that he had never met any lady better possessed of those qualities. Indeed, it would make a fine character to recommend her to a prospective employer—or a prospective husband. She looked up finally.

"What do you make of that?" he said.

She paused, collecting thoughts and words. "It seems he encouraged you and had no objections to the match. He said he had spoken to my mother for you. Is that not what you wanted?"

"I read the letter myself, Esther, I know what it says. I wanted to know what you thought of it."

"I am ... very flattered, naturally."

"Has he answered my question, as to whether he has any interest in you himself?"

"I think he answered it very fairly."

"I think he answered it in a manner designed to confound and confuse me. Has he written of this to you?"

"No—he writes often, but always joint letters to Becca and me, never of anything personal. He always speaks well of you in his letters, just as he tells you here that he does." William still looked at her with a gaze so reminiscent of Dingley's departed lapdog that she stood up and flung the letter into his lap. "What I do not see is why it matters so much! I never intended to take Dr. Swift's opinion into account when you asked me the question—why is it so important to you? Are you so bent on winning his friendship that you will not marry without his permission? Or is it that you think of me as his property and will not take me without consent?"

The room seemed hot and close; Esther could bear to look at William no longer. She moved toward the door as he rose to stop her. "I know not what you intended that letter to do, William— to make me give up my imaginary hopes of marrying Dr. Swift and wed you instead? Do you think I would ever have considered a proposal I thought second best? I told you the truth: I want to marry neither you nor him, nor any other man. Good day, Mr. Tisdall. I am going now."

She turned; her hand was on the doorknob—then she felt him grip her shoulder so hard that it hurt. She swung back to face him, and it was almost as if William Tisdall had disappeared and a different man stood in his place. The man before her bore little trace of the genial, cultured young cleric who had courted her with patience and wit all year. His eyes seared her with pain and passion, and his voice was quiet but hard.

"Esther, Esther, do not leave. I love you, Esther—so much I cannot breathe without you. Can you not love me?" She could hear his breath, suddenly heavy, between his words. His hand had not loosened its grip on her shoulder.

Her throat knotted: she could say nothing. She could feel her heart beating against the green holland of her sensible gown. She had not imagined Will could want her—need her— so much. Could anyone want another person like this? He looked as if he were drowning, fighting for air. "Say you will marry me, Esther. Do you love me? I love you, and all the rest"— he brushed the air to indicate Swift's letter, her words, all the world about them—"all else is folly. I care for none of it. Only you, my Esther."

His other hand was on her arm, again gripping too tightly; then he pulled her to him. Always before he had been a model of propriety: she had never imagined an advance or caress from Mr. Tisdall that was not entirely appropriate for a clergyman to give an unmarried young woman. Now she could feel her bosom pressing against his chest; he pulled her head up toward his and his mouth covered hers with hard kisses that tasted like blood and spices. A huge wave towered over her, threatening to crash: as warmth spread through her limbs, she knew that in a moment she would be overwhelmed, her tiny self carried out to sea by a force so powerful that she could no more resist it than fly.

Anger and fear saved her: she pushed her hands against William's chest and forced him away. He gasped and stumbled back a step; she pulled her cloak tight around her.

It was not William she was afraid of: he plainly had no intent to hurt her. It was that flood she feared, that great tide that had almost borne her away. But the danger was past now: she was safe alone on the shore. And William, a few feet away on the worn oriental rug, looked so distant that he might have been on the opposite shore, with all the sea between them.

"If your intention was to change my mind, Mr. Tisdall, you will not do so by those means," she said, "nor by any means, for as I said—"

"Forgive me." He spoke barely above a whisper. "I had no intentions at all—I could not help what I did. I did not mean to offend you."

"I think it best if I say good-day," said Esther. William did not reply. How was it possible to feel fear and anger, desire and affection, pity and contempt, all for the same person? Was this tangle of emotions what people meant when they spoke of love? Esther had no idea, so she turned to go, out of that cramped and oppressive house into the darkening Dublin afternoon.

She walked away briskly, rage fuelling her steps even as her head pounded and her breath tightened in her chest. Instead of heading straight home, she went across the fields. Her mind would not stop replaying the visit that now seemed to be divided in two parts. The conversation during which she had told William she could not marry him and he showed her Dr. Swift's letter seemed to belong to an entirely different world from those last moments in the hall, from William's kiss and his desperate plea for love. The first was a world she knew and could control, a safe and ordered place where unpleasant things sometimes happened but could be dealt with. The second was a landscape of dream, or perhaps nightmare, and she tried hard to push it to the back of her mind.

After half an hour's stumbling across rutted, muddy trails she had reached a street full of houses, a safe and familiar landscape, and began to puzzle over why she was so angry at William and Dr. Swift. Both of them seemed somehow to assume she was a piece of property to be bargained away—but was not a woman just that, in a marriage arrangement?

She thought suddenly of the duchess of Somerset, Elizabeth Percy, so beautiful and passionate that even at fourteen a man was willing to commit murder for her. Esther as a girl had never understood why the duchess had not run away with her lover, why she had stayed in dull old England to be married to one dull old husband after another. She thought differently now of Elizabeth Percy, lady of Petworth, friend of Queen Anne, as powerful in England today as any woman could be. Mistress of her fate. Her lover was a tale from the past. Elizabeth Percy's choice no longer seemed so unlikely.

Despite the quarrel, the anger, the sharp pain beneath her breastbone, Esther felt an odd buoyancy. William had done better than he knew in showing her that letter. She sorted through the remembered words again, wondering which of them had convinced her that her choice was right. Not the fact that Swift had said he would marry her if he married anyone. Nor was it Swift's prediction that he would lose "so good a friend and companion" as her, if she married—though that thought chilled her, made her realize how little freedom a married woman would have. She would much rather not lose that intimate friendship with Swift that only a single woman could enjoy. But what had truly vindicated her—the phrase was burned on her brain—was his contemptuous dismissal: the match should go ahead, *since it is held so necessary and convenient a thing for ladies to marry.*

As she turned back into William Street, the shadows lay across the road like long black furrows where she might lose her footing and fall. *Necessary and convenient*—yes, that was what it came down to Passion was a fever, a dream, a momentary madness best forgotten, and everyone said it did not last but burned out quickly. She had to remember that. Marriage was the cure for love's fever; marriage was a necessary and convenient business arrangement. She walked down the dark and deserted street to her own house, passing William's without a glance up at his window.

"Necessary and convenient," she said aloud to her reflection in the window when she reached her own house. No, she would do nothing, certainly not barter her freedom and independence, only because marriage was considered necessary and convenient. Necessity and convenience be damned!

She opened the door and walked in, looking around the front hall of the house where she and Rebecca Dingley were joint mistresses, with no master. *Time takes off from the lustre of virgins in all other eyes but mine.* That was a prize to carry with her: beauty would not last, nor would passion, but the esteem of a true friend would last forever.

The servant girl, Jane, scurried into the hall. "Good evening, ma'am," she said. "Mrs. Sally was wanting to know, would you be wanting your supper, ma'am, for Mrs. Dingley's had hers early and gone off to bed. She said her feet was tired and she must put them up."

Becca might not be asleep yet, only resting or reading, and for a moment Esther considered knocking on her door as she passed—but no, not tonight. She had thought she would discuss with Becca the whole tale of her visit to William, but now that she had come and found Becca gone to bed, she realized there was something of a reprieve in that. She went up instead to her own bedroom, accompanied by Jane with a warming pan. The little servant girl turned back the covers and lit the fire in the grate, then asked, "D'you need me for anything else, ma'am?"

"No, Jane, I shall be fine. You run along and tell Mrs. Sally I won't need any supper tonight. If she doesn't need you for anything else, get home, for it's growing dark out."

The girl curtsyed and backed out of the room, leaving Esther to undress, let down her hair, and brush it out. She lit a candle and took out her journal, leafing through the pages of the past as if reluctant to commit this day to paper, but at last she turned to a clean page and dipped her pen, scratching out a few paragraphs that did not, she thought, half touch the surface of the day's emotions.

That done, she put away pen and ink and paper and went to her bed, glancing at her nightstand for something to read. There was a new book of poetry Dr. Swift had sent over from England, which he would be certain to quiz her on when he returned, but although the poems looked interesting enough, she did not relish educating herself for his approval tonight. She took up her prayer book instead, thinking her turbulent mind might be calmed by devotion, and was reading the order for Compline when a noise at the window, louder than wind or rain, disturbed her thoughts.

She paused, listened, heard nothing, and read again. *"From all ill dreams defend our eyes / From nightly fears and fantasies—"*

Bang! It was unmistakable this time; someone or something was at the window. Up here, on the third storey? She thought of the dark empty stretch of William Street and the fields beyond and all the warnings of her friends, who had said she and Dingley were mad to live so far out of town.

A scraping as if someone was trying to open the window. The curtains were closed, but the noise from beyond was clear. "Who's there?" Esther cried out. Silence. Would the intruder go away, knowing he had been heard—or would he take comfort from the fact that only a lone woman had cried out?

A moment passed. Then the scraping again, and a sound of something hitting the glass. Esther froze. The pistol Dr. Swift had given them was in the house—how they had laughed at his foolish fretting when he bought it!

She went to the door. There was no noise from Dingley's room, and no light from the floor below her. If Mrs. Sally was still at work, it would be downstairs in the kitchens. Were Jane and Billy still there? What did it matter—a houseful of women and one thirteen-year-old boy?

A tinkle of shattered glass brought her to her senses. They were going to break through the window—she heard rough male voices outside now, so there must be more than one man—break in, steal, and no doubt murder. She went back through her bedroom into her dressing room and took the pistol from the drawer where it lay. Her hand shook. She hurried through the bedroom again—the voices at the window were louder—and stood once again in the hallway.

"Mrs. Johnson, ma'am!" Her heart almost stopped at the voice behind her; whirling around with a hand against her chest she saw Billy, white-faced on the stairs. "Mrs. Sally sent me to tell you, ma'am, she thinks there's robbers outside. She heard something at the dining-room window."

"Go down and tell her … tell her she is right, Billy—there are robbers. But we'll see to them, won't we?" She smiled and nodded, but the boy stood stock-still on the stairs, for he too could now hear the shouting and banging.

Quickly, quickly. The window here at the top of the stairs was in a line with her bedroom window. She went to it, pulled the curtains, flung up the sash, and leaned out, her hands clutching the pistol. She had a hasty image of the man at the next window—a black shape balanced on a ladder, trying to break through—before she aimed and shot into the darkness. If only she had a brace of pistols and could fire a second shot! But before the report died away she heard the scream, saw the dark shape fall from the ladder, the ladder falling too, and she heard cries and running feet below. She pulled her head in quickly. Billy still stood there.

"You shot him," the boy said in awe.

Esther was shaking. "Yes, I did. I shot him," she said, staring at the gun. On the ground outside was a man who could be wounded or … dead.

Becca's door flew open, and Becca herself appeared, wrapped in her brown mantua, her hair in curling pins. "What is it? Mercy, I thought I heard a gun!"

Billy raced downstairs, shouting, "Mrs. Johnson shot a thief!"

"You did what?" said Becca.

Esther laid down the gun carefully on the hall table. She looked at her hand. It still trembled. Only a lone woman—but she had defended her household, shot a man.

They all gathered down in the sitting room, and Becca got out the brandy. Esther told the story over and over, and Billy told it twice as often, exaggerating his mistress's bravery. Mrs. Sally made Billy go outside to look for the man, and when, reluctantly, the boy had gone, he returned with the news that there was nothing and no one out there. "So either he managed to drag himself off, or his friends came back and got him," said Becca with satisfaction. "I hope you killed him, Hetty."

"I rather think I might have," said Esther, sipping her brandy.

"We'll send for someone tomorrow to repair the window in your chamber," Becca decided, "and I'll send a message to the Stoytes, if you like, Hetty, saying we can't have them for dinner."

Esther collected her scattered wits. "Whyever not?" she demanded. "They won't be dining in my chamber, so what odds to them if the window is broken?"

"But your nerves—the shock to your nerves—"

"My nerves are perfectly fine. And do you think I would miss an opportunity to tell this story before an audience?"

They all laughed then, and Esther said that Jane and Billy must not venture home tonight, with robbers about, but that Mrs. Sally must make them a bed in the kitchen, and that she herself would lie in Mrs. Dingley's chamber. Both mistresses embraced the servants, and each other, several times before saying good-night at last, and Esther went upstairs and got in bed beside Becca, who made her tell all over again how she'd shot the robber.

Esther relaxed into the warmth of Becca's feather mattress—Becca had ever liked softer mattresses than Esther did—and the gentleness of her friend's hands as Becca rubbed her back with goose grease, bringing balm to her tense muscles. She felt like a heroine—she felt loved and cherished—and she slipped into sleep without ever remembering to tell Becca the tale of Mr. Tisdall.

LARACOR
JUNE 24, 1706

We have just come from witnessing the Reverend Tisdall's marriage to Mrs Eleanor Morgan of County Sligo. The wedding was held in Carrickfergus. The bride wore cream satin and lace of Irish manufacture (the Irish are great lace makers—Becca has bought some for our table), and the groom looked as happy as a man could. They have been engag'd nearly a year now, and my Friendship with Mr Tisdall is as Amiable as ever it was, befor he sought mye hand over two years ago. For some time there was Strain betweene us, but now we are perfect Friends, and I was glad to see him marry'd.

I doe believe Becca, and maybe even Dr Swift, were of some Apprehension that I might feel a lingering Regret over having refus'd him, that might make its appearance on the occasion of his wedding day. But I feel noe such thing, and can see easily that Mrs Morgan, who is a quiet, pleasant Creature, is soe well fitted to make him a Wife, as I should never have beene. Surely it is true what they saye, that Passion is a fire that dies quickly if none tends it, for I cannot recall at all what I once felt for Mr Tisdall, and his Love, which was surely greater than Mine, is now forgotten too. I hope I shall be friends with her, and that we may visit them often.

Immediately after the wedding we remov'd here to Laracor, and here we intend to spend the rest of the Summer, tho' Becca will no doubt find Excuses for several visits to towne, yett I have nott her Affinity for City life and am well content here at the cottage. After all the deliberations of the past Months, we have firmly decided ourselves to let the house in William Street go and retourne to it noe more this winter. Dingley has never been easy there, since the attempt at robbery, and tho' we have continued to rent that house each winter out of Habit, this spring we found a far better, in Mary Street near Ormonde Quay, which is in a much more settled Area of the city, and there we shall make our home when autumne brings us back to Dublin againe.

But all is not Play, for Dr Swift is hard at work on a pamphlet about the English treatement of Ireland, as compar'd with the favour they have showne to the Rebellious Scots. This I have read and copy'd for him, and truly I am coming to much admire his fervent defence of the Irish cause and hope it finds him ready hearers in London. England must do more for the Irish, I have become convinc'd of that after five yeares' Residency here, sometimes it seemes to me the English are bent on ruining this Country. Dr Swift has not beene back to England this two years, and seemes to think that his Career in politics is all done, for he is no favourite of Queen Anne and the present Administration, yett no matter how he talks of his quiet retirement in Laracor, I can see that the Yearning to be part of a greater world is by noe means dead in him, and that were the opportunity to Present itself, he would take his place at once, upon that Larger stage. Then he might be lost to his Friends here, but we could scarce regret it, for the good it would bring.

DUBLIN
NOVEMBER 30, 1706

I have been so Ill, since retourning to this City, that I could well have wish'd myself back at Laracor, tho' both Becca and Dr Swift have assured me that the Cottage would be no fitt Habbitation in the fall months, and that the cold there would weaken my poore Condition even more.

I wish above all that I might be in better health, for now mye spirits are reviving (I doe not shrink from admitting, in this Private place, that at times they have *beene so Low that I cared nott whether I liv'd or dyed), and with the revival of my spirits I wish I might know a Revival of health too, that I might visit againe, and read, and write. I have seene no one but Becca and the servants all this longe while, save a few evening visits from Dr Swift when I felt well enough to sit up in the drawing room, and sundry calls from Mrs Walls, whose Company I have come to value more than I did Formerly, tho' it might be from want of any Other.*

But even sitting up to write this tires me, and my eyes and head Ache againe, and soone Becca will find what I am doing, and come in and scold me for the strain on my ey's. She is so good to me: she reads all my letters, and reads aloud to me in the evenings, that I have hardly tir'd my eyes at all, and now they burn, so I must putt aside my pen. Becca talks of going to take the waters at Templeogue or Wexford, and if it would doe me any Bennefitt, I would be most eager to try it.

DUBLIN
FEBRUARY 25, 1707

I have nott written in heere since Twelfth Night, and with good cause, for in all that Time, today is the first day I have felt myself able to sit up at my desk, and hold my Pen. Our feeble Attempts to keep a Christmas of sorts weary'd me so that I was full three weeks in bed after that.

At last I begin to feel mye strength retourning, and can sitt up all day, and see well enough to read and write letters. Were it not for Becca's kind care I know nott what might have become of me, and I knowe I am truly becoming Well again when I start to Fret at her constant Fussing. She would chide me now, if she sawe me write in heere, and saye I was straining my poor Ey's.

Dr Swift saies I will be better when fair weather comes, and I may goe out walking and riding, for as usuall he thinks Ecksersise the cure to ev'ry Ill but admits that there is little to be done in that way in Dublin in winter. Tho' he has a new Fancy now, that when the weather does nott permit him to Walk or Ride,

he runs up and down the Steps in his house, which he saies gives him as good
Effect as walking out-of-doors, save that he misses the fresh Aire!

I am in no hurry to try his Cure! But I doe wish for summer, and a return
to Laracor. I long for the Breezes there, and our little Cottage, tho' Becca saies if
we goe this summer, we must hire a maid to live in, for she will not suffer me to
do any housework at all in mye Condition. Mye mother writes that she would
have me retourne to England, to stay at Sheen with her and Lady Giffard and
recover mye strength. Becca would like that well, and we might travel with
Dr Swift, whoe is talking againe of a journey to England. Last summer Jack Temple
invited him to visit Moor Park, but he reply'd he would not, and could not afford
the journey. But now his affaires are in better order and he plans to travel, not
to Moor Park (for in truth he has little love for Jack or Desire to visit him) but to
London. Alas, I cannot saie so much for Dingley and me, that we are in such
good straits, for mye Illnesse has strain'd our poore budget much, and we could
in no way afford a trip to England.

That the thought of visiting Home might be so near, yet nott to be, does not
Trouble me as I once thought it might, for I believe I have truly begunne to think
Ireland my home, and look forward to a summer at Laracor as much as ever I
might to one at Sheen.

DUBLIN
1723

A harsh cough tears across Esther's chest, leaving a trail like flame behind it. One of the candles sputters and dies. She relights it from the other candle; her hand shakes a little as she does.

It is hard not to curse this body, not to rail against the years of illness, against her present condition as a near-invalid. Blessed with good looks and a sharp wit and ambition and kind friends—what could she not have done, if she had only had good health as well! There were women, she knew, who chafed at the usual restrictions of a woman's lot, women of letters who published books under their own names. She had met a few such in Swift's company, and had always found them faintly ridiculous. For a moment she wondered if what she felt was envy. If she had had health and strength, might she have been more than the secretary and friend of a great man?

Too late, now, to wonder that. The candles are burning down: time slips away. She has not many years left even to be a secretary, she thinks. *What I have made of my life is all I have.* For once this thought gives her no pleasure. She thinks again of Swift, of his ravenous lust for power, fame, influence. He, too, is ever aware of the shortness of days, of time slipping through his grasp. But he is a man, and has his health, and his feet are firmly planted upon that upward path. Hers slip and slide beneath her: she scrabbles to hold on to what little she has.

And what is that? Half a night of reading has given her nothing more than sore eyes and a headache. On the journal page in front of her she contemplates a return to England, to Sheen and Moor Park. Returning like a ghost to haunt the scenes of her own girlhood—perhaps it was a mistake. Yet here she is again, doing through the written word what she once sailed across the Irish Sea to do: revisit the past, see if it holds any answers for the present.

ENGLAND
1707–1708

"Well, Becca Dingley has survived two sea voyages in her lifetime and hopes never to make another," announced Esther as she took a cup of coffee from Lady Giffard's parlour maid, "so when I return to Ireland, I shall either have to leave behind my dearest friend, which is quite impossible, or fashion for her wings of wax and feather so that, Icarus-like, she may soar across the Irish Sea. You will have to be careful of the sun, Becca, for it does no good to the complexion or to the elevation."

"Are you so resolved upon returning, then?" said Lady Giffard, shaking her head a little at the torrent of words.

"Goodness! Hardly landed in England, and talking of going away again! Have time to be settled, girls, before you need to talk of leaving," said Bridget. "Was the crossing so very bad, Becca?"

Becca sighed and took a long drink of her coffee. "When I walked into this room I thought the floor still swayed a little, but if I sit long enough I'll no doubt get my land legs back again." She stroked the white fur of Pug, her latest lapdog. "And this poor little scoundrel was miserable enough too—no wonder there are no ships' dogs, for they aren't made for seafaring."

"I tried to tell you it was folly to bring him."

"You have no feeling. If I had a child, would you have had me leave it behind?"

"If you had a child, I am sure Lady Giffard would not consider you virtuous enough to keep house for her nephew and his children," said Esther. "It would be a scandal! Better you keep your little seasick dog."

"You shall spend a few days here at Sheen before you remove to Moor Park," said Lady Giffard, "so that you will be rested from the rigours of travel. And now, dear Hetty and Dingley, you must tell us every word of your adventures in Ireland, for six years' worth of letters cannot begin to make up six minutes' worth of conversation."

Lady Giffard had aged; her strong-boned face looked like an old linen sheet many times folded and ironed. *What might you have expected?* Esther chided herself, as she knew Becca would when, later, she would share that observation aloud. Six years had passed, and Martha Giffard had not been a young woman when they left. But Esther had never seen her as old. Lady Giffard had always moved and spoken with such decisive energy and certainty that she seemed ageless. One could no more imagine her ancient and feeble in a bath chair than one could picture her a passionate young girl with long, unbound hair. She was forever locked into the confident complacence of middle age.

Now, though she was by no means feeble, Esther saw her with different eyes. The lines in her face were more deeply etched, the tendons in her thin neck more apt to strain, and the hand that held her cup was thinner and tremulous. As Becca chattered about people and events in Dublin, Esther looked, almost reluctantly, at her mother to see if the same change had touched Bridget. Yes, she too was older: there was more grey in the faded hair that had once flamed red, and her figure, unlike her mistress's, which grew thinner and more taut with age, had become more rounded and sagging. Her role in the household had changed too; she was no longer the housekeeper but had moved into Becca's old role as Lady Giffard's companion.

Esther glanced at Becca, realizing that her mother and Lady Giffard were also looking for changes, for the traces of time. Becca appeared to her eyes no different than she had when they first went to Ireland. But then, Esther was accustomed to the daily sight of her. One did not notice differences in one's constant companions, only in those one had been separated from. Least noticed of all were changes in oneself. She had left England at twenty and returned at twenty-six. Girlhood was certainly behind her now, both for good and for ill. She was a woman now, mistress in her own house, and she felt the alteration in herself as she spoke with her mother, with Lady Giffard.

She would have enjoyed seeing Liza—Mrs. Temple, as she certainly would have called her—once again, to consider what six years had brought to the child bride, but Liza was on the Continent still, and only a recent portrait of her above the mantel in the Little Parlour greeted them when they arrived at Moor Park a few days later. Lady Giffard's nephew and his children had not yet arrived, "and I am glad of that," Esther told Becca as they sat together on the terrace on their first afternoon.

"I know," Becca agreed. "'Twill take me a day or so to get used to the idea of managing a household this size, and for a widower and four youngsters. Quite a change from our Dublin digs!"

"Yes, there is that," Esther said, "but what I thought of was just coming back here, after so long—I wanted a little time for us to have it just to ourselves." She could see the green sweep of the gardens before her where Pug now played as so many of his predecessors had: the Diana fountain in the foreground, the carefully tended trees and flowers Sir William had loved so, the silver ribbon of canal beyond the wilderness. She had not realized how accurately and indelibly this vista had been imprinted behind her eyes, the backdrop for all she saw and did in Ireland and elsewhere.

Their lives were quiet during the months they stayed at Moor Park; the little social life they had was among old neighbours in Farnham, one of whom was Esther's sister, Anne. Six years had altered Anne more than anyone, Esther thought, sitting awkwardly in her sister's tiny parlour. Anne's gold hair had faded to the colour of dishwater; her figure, rather than thickening with the birth of four children, had grown thin and brittle, and her narrow face looked pinched and discontented.

"Must be a grand life, over in Ireland, with your own house and all," Anne said. She was sewing—mending actually, working her way through a great basket of children's clothes. Esther, who rarely did needlework now that her eyes were so bad, was stitching a cushion cover because she could not sit empty-handed in Anne's house.

"We love Ireland, but we haven't our own house there—we rent rooms in Dublin in the winter, and a cottage in Laracor in summer," Esther explained, choosing her words with care.

"Rented rooms? Nice ones, though, I'm sure," Anne said, looking around at the hard wooden settee Esther sat on, the wooden table with its coarse cotton cloth, the shelves that held her second-hand plate and her cooking pots.

"Nice enough for our needs—we live very simply." Esther could feel her mouth becoming primmer and more ladylike, as Anne pushed her further and further into the role of Lady Bountiful. She was still using the royal *we* although Becca was not by her side; after two visits to Anne's house Becca felt her duty done, there being no ties of blood to bind her to more regular calls.

"I'm sure you've got used to being your own mistress there."

"Just as you are here," countered Esther.

"Mistress! If you can call it that—one maid, no manservant, a houseful of squalling brats, and a roof barely over our heads. Joseph must get a better position—we simply can't go on—but alas, we've no friends in high places to help him to anything." Shrieks rose from outside the window as the squalling brats chased one another around outside: the littlest brat was asleep in a basket by the fire.

"Cannot Lady Giffard help you at all? Surely Mama has some influence—"

It was the wrong thing to say. "Influence! The only influence Mama ever had with the Temple clan was with the old fellow, and it's died with him. Anyway, that influence was all used long ago, for one person's benefit, as you well know."

Finally, words were spoken instead of chafing under the surface. Esther wondered how long her sister had wanted to say that.

"Anne, I'm sorry, but you must know I didn't wish Sir William to leave me money. And it's not such a great fortune as you imagine, for an unmarried woman who has to keep herself—"

"Keep herself! That's not what I hear!" Anne took a sip of her coffee.

"What do you mean?"

Anne shook her head, set down her cup, and picked up her sewing. "Never mind—we're not entirely at the ends of the earth, even here in Farnham, you know. And at any rate, if Sir William remembered you and not I, there's good reason for that, and no one would have expected him to do different."

Esther had laid aside her needlework when her eyes began to sting; now she picked it up again and poked the needle through the fabric at random, making odd jagged stitches that followed no pattern. "You believe it too, then?"

"Believe what?"

"That Sir William was my father."

Anne raised her eyebrows as if it were perfectly proper to allude to the subject in any number of oblique ways but indecent to say the words aloud. "That's what I've heard *said*," she replied, "but who's to know, except himself and our mother—and you, I suppose."

"I know only what Mama told me, and she told me nothing. But you took it for truth?"

"Nothing makes any sense otherwise," said Anne.

Esther waited for her to say more, but when Anne did not, Esther nodded slowly. From Anne's perspective, what else could account for such inequity? The question that would torment Esther to her grave was settled for Anne in the only way that she could begin to erase their mother's monstrous unfairness. Even for her own peace of mind, Esther could not meddle with that.

"I don't really know very much about Sir William, for all I grew up in his house," she said at last. "Until he died, and Mama told me that gossip said he was my father, I always thought he and Lady Temple were devoted to each other—I'd never have thought him to have taken a mistress, either Mama or any other woman." She thought of the old bundle of faded letters, a memory from which the guilt had long drained away while the poignancy remained.

Anne snorted. "You always had your head under the ground, up there at Moor Park," she said. "Perhaps everyone up there worshipped the old fellow and wouldn't say a word against him, but it wasn't that way all around, let me tell you. He had mistresses enough, and bastards too—you needn't think you and Mama were anything special. What of your great friend Mr. Swift? You don't think Sir William took him in because of his handsome face, do you?"

"You mean—are you saying …?" Esther had dropped her composure completely; Anne's words had tilted the universe too sharply for her to hold on to equanimity.

"Yes, that your precious Mr. Swift is supposed to be another of old Temple's by-blows—now you can't say you'd never heard that, can you? A good laugh it'd make if he ever does marry you after stringing you along all these years—if he turned out to be your own brother!"

Cold and then hot rushed over Esther in quick succession.

Jonathan Swift—her brother? With huge effort she shut out the roaring sound in her ears and drew herself up in her chair.

"I hardly know what to make of all your ancient gossip, Anne," she said, "but your recent news is certainly faulty. There is no question of my marrying Dr. Swift. We are great friends, and I should be proud to count him as a relation if it were possible to do so without slandering my mother, or the memory of good Sir William. And now, I really must be going. I have more to do than listen to idle talk."

When she was outside, on the step of her sister's house, alone at last, she looked down the rutted main street of Farnham. The crowded houses, the people, the sweep of land up to the castle were sights as familiar to her as her own hands, yet suddenly everything seemed unbearably sharp and clearly focused. She had to move away from the house—to begin walking down the street, for Anne was sure to be watching, cherishing her little moment of triumph.

Esther did not visit Anne's house any more during her stay at Moor Park. But in one of her letters to Dr. Swift she mentioned the poverty of her sister and family and asked whether he might be able to speak to anyone about getting Anne's husband a better position—some minor government office, perhaps?

Slipped in among the gossip of London society and the complexities of politics that filled his frequent letters came the news that Swift had been able to obtain a position in the Salt Office for Joseph Filby. Anne came up to Moor Park before Esther and Becca left, and sat stiffly in the Little Parlour sipping coffee with the two of them as she said her stilted thanks for Esther's intervention. The whole visit was awkward in the extreme, and gave Esther pleasure.

⁂

When Lady Giffard's nephew told Esther late in the winter that he would be moving his family to the Continent, Esther and Becca began to pack up their belongings. "Now we can write to Dr. Swift that we are free to visit him in London before we return to Ireland," Esther said. "I should like a stay in London, if only for the sake of the shops."

Becca picked up her needlework. She looked down at it without speaking, her lips pursed and her forehead creased with a frown. "Is that the way of it, then—that we go back to Ireland when our work is done here?" she said at last. "We never have discussed it."

Esther felt a pang of remorse. She took the reins so readily; she seldom even bothered to think what Becca might like, as though only Esther's will mattered in their joint household. But though Becca's tongue could be sharp, she rarely complained about Esther's decisions. "I spoke as a matter of course, without thinking," Esther said quickly. "Of course we must decide. *Do* we wish to go back to Ireland?"

The fire was dying, but they had to call for a manservant to build it up again before their discussion was finished that night, for the question of returning to Ireland was no simple one. They could as easily stay on here in England, Becca pointed out: Lady Giffard might have a place for one or both of them in her household, or they could share lodgings together, in the country or in London, just as they had in Dublin. Money would be an even greater concern in England than in Ireland, for living was costlier. But it would not be impossible for them to live in England, if that was what they agreed on.

"It is what you truly want, is it not?" Esther asked her friend after two hours of wrangling over the advantages and disadvantages. She had not seen before that Becca really preferred England.

"I've been quite happy in Ireland," Becca said. "But what family I have are all here, and—well, when all's said and done, it's my own country. It feels right to me, in a way Ireland never quite does, d'you see?"

"Yes," Esther said slowly, "I see that it seems that way to you. But you know that I feel differently. I feel—I know not why—as if Ireland truly *is* my home. Yet I would not force you to return there, if you really don't wish it."

She remembered herself, a child, sitting in this very parlour, telling Jonathan Swift that when she was grown she wished to travel all around the world. For the first time she faced the possibility that her life might not contain such adventures—might never extend beyond the boundaries of Ireland and England

"You know, Becca," she tried softly, "we are great friends, but there is no law that says we must always live together. If you were sure you wished to remain in England, and I wanted to return to Ireland, we might each do as we wished …"

Becca's eyes widened and her mouth hung ajar. Esther felt as if something had clutched her chest—it was clear at once that in Becca's mind, they could never be separated, and she felt relief and disappointment at the same time. How reassuring to be so loved, to know that she need never be alone—yet how confining!

"Oh no, Hetty, I couldn't do that," Becca said, her words tumbling out in a rush. "Couldn't leave you to go back to Ireland on your own. A young girl like you living alone in Dublin? That would never do. No, if you have your heart set on Ireland, Ireland it shall be for both of us."

⁂

At the beginning of March, Esther and Becca went up to London with Lady Giffard and Bridget to spend some time at

Lady Giffard's house there. Stepping down from the carriage into the brisk air, Esther was engulfed at once by the sounds and smells of London and overcome by a wave of fondness for the great, stinking city that had grown no less enchanting since she had first seen it at seventeen.

She was determined to make the most of her stay in London despite the ill health that plagued her as soon as they settled there. Though the city brought out the worst in her constitution, it sustained her spirit, so she doggedly ignored blinding headaches and a wheezy chest to venture out day after day and night after night in company with Becca, her mother, or Lady Giffard, and of course Dr. Swift. He was at their doorstep the day after they arrived, kissing everyone's hand and scattering puns in all directions. Esther pressed his hand and looked him over thoroughly. He had a new wig, finer than his old one; his chin had receded a little more and his eyes seemed more pronounced; he was better dressed than he ever was in Dublin. Yet he was the surest and most familiar friend of all, and the city was a warmer place with him here.

Swift was staying with his friend Sir Andrew Fountaine—"Stand well back, lest you be sprayed by the droplets of his wit," he told Esther when she came to visit—and was caught up not only in the political intrigues that had brought him to London but also in the silliest literary practical joke imaginable, which gave him huge delight. It concerned a man by the name of Mr. Partridge, an almanac maker who took great pride in his ability to predict the future: the sort of man for whom Swift had nothing but contempt. Writing under the pen name of Isaac Bickerstaff, Swift had concocted a prediction of his own: that Partridge would die on April Fools' Day. The war of printed words between the imaginary Bickerstaff and the all-too-real Partridge was the talk of literary London, and Esther was quickly drawn back into her old role as Swift's secretary, copying out manuscripts for him and listening with approval while he read aloud to her, Becca, and Bridget, and sometimes her ladyship too, the latest installments in the hoax.

She studied him covertly in those moments: here in London, Swift the politician, the poet, the critic positively glowed in a way that Swift the vicar of Laracor had never done. He often dropped comments about "our lovely gardens back in dear Laracor," and commented how splendid it would be to see his fruit trees in blossom now that spring was coming, "away from all this dirt and stink of London," but Esther was not fooled for a minute. Yes, there was something of the gardener, the countryman in him; he had a certain peaceful contentment when he was back in Laracor among the willows, just as he had had long ago in the gardens of Moor Park—but that was never more than second best for him. She had long sensed it; now, together with him in the great city for the first time, she could see it.

He sparkled in the city, in the midst of great men and great dealings; here was his rightful place. He had always felt it to be so and chafed with longing for a place in the wider world; seeing him here, she had to agree that his assessment of himself had been right. He probably did not even notice that he was rubbing his hands with glee as he described a meeting at the coffee house with Mr. Addison and Mr. Steele, publishers of *The Spectator,* and of course he could not see the gleam in his eye or the flush in his cheek when he talked of his latest visit to court, or the intrigues of Queen Anne's ministers, or the latest theory of who Mr. Bickerstaff really was. His tales of his daily doings were entertaining and his visits were a highlight for the ladies, but Esther felt a tiny sense of loss as she saw more clearly than ever that he would never truly be contented in Ireland after this. London was within his grasp, and he would not draw back his hand for all the willow trees in Laracor.

When Lady Giffard and Bridget returned to Sheen, Esther and Becca stayed on for a few weeks more in the city. They had decided to go back to Dublin at the end of April, and Esther could see that Becca was eager to drink in a few last days of London, for she remained convinced that she would never see her native land again. It was a pity she felt that way—but Esther had offered her the choice of parting ways, and Becca had chosen not to stay in England alone, so Esther could harden her heart to her friend's wistfulness.

Becca was not such a success at being hard-hearted, though, and she worried every day about what London was doing to Esther's health. "Put down that book!" she commanded in the evening. "Your eyes are nearly ruined anyway, and peering through this city smoke and fog does them no good. Look how red they are"—she thrust a looking glass into Esther's hand—"you'll be blind before you're thirty if you keep on this way. Have you a headache?"

"Hardly at all," Esther lied.

"Hmmph," said Becca, with a knowing nod of her faded curls.

In fact, she had suffered all day from a headache so severe that she had been unable to leave her room or open the blinds, and her breathing was bad too, but she had rallied for dinner because Dr. Swift was coming and she would not let him see how ill she was, lest he cancel the trip he had planned for them on the next day. They were going to Greenwich, to see the observatory and the new palace there, and to picnic along the river, if the warm weather held.

By some good fortune, she felt a little better in the morning, and was able to convince Becca that she had no trace of a headache and her eyes were fine, so that both ladies were dressed and ready to go when Swift arrived to collect them. They were walking down to the river to catch a boat to Greenwich.

"Ah, what lovely breaths of spring are in the air!" Swift said, drawing a deep lungful as they stepped into the street. "Cherry blossoms, fresh grass, a hint of dogs' shit, a trace of stale vomit in the alleyway beside a tavern—"

"Oh, do stop! 'Tis a beautiful morning and well you know it!" Esther protested. She felt her spirits soar giddily as Swift continued to catalogue the horrors of the city. He was laughing too, rising to ever greater heights of grotesquerie over her protests, while Becca clucked her tongue and hurried on ahead of them.

"I'm working on a poem about morning in the city," said Swift, taking Esther's hand and tucking it under his arm. "There now, Bec has Pug tucked under her arm and I have you under mine—everyone to his own pet. What was I saying?"

"Your poem—I can scarcely imagine what your pen would do with such a topic as a city morning. No rose-red sunrises, I imagine?"

"I've only a few lines done—*Now hardly here and there a Hackney-Coach / Appearing, show'd the ruddy Morn's approach*— shall we hail one, by the by? Or do you feel up to walking down to the river? Yes? Shall I ask Bec—no, she's bound to choose the coach, and then we shan't have our way. Where was I?"

"The ruddy morn," Esther said with a laugh, "as close to rose red as we're likely to get."

"Oh yes—it goes on, *Now Betty from her Master's Bed had flown / And softly stole to discompose her own* …"

"Dr. Swift!" Esther exclaimed, in half-pretended horror. "Becca, have you heard this latest outrage from our grave and reverend churchman?"

Becca turned back, and Esther repeated the line for her benefit. Becca clucked her tongue. "You oughtn't to say such things," she scolded, shaking a finger at Swift.

"What, am I to be condemned because I dare to imply that there are houses in this city where the master of the house sleeps with the chambermaid? Was such a thing ever heard of in London!"

"Of course it's heard of, of course it happens, but it should not be spoken of. Especially not by a man of God," said Esther.

The rebuke silenced him for a half minute; he looked sideways at Esther as if evaluating how serious she was. She was hardly sure herself. She loved the sparkle of his wit and understood him well enough to know why he had to drag out the unpleasant side of life that most people preferred to ignore—but she did feel that there were things that ought not to be written about, especially for a man who had chosen a career as a clergyman.

"I suppose you'll not like my poem about a rain shower either," he said, eyes downcast but still shining.

"I can scarce wait to hear it."

"'Tis not written yet either—only a line about a sewer: *Sweepings from Butchers Stalls, Dung, Guts and Blood / Dead Cats and Turnip-Tops come tumbling down the Flood*. It isn't much, I'll grant, but I believe there's enough poetry in those two lines to build an entire ode around."

"Enough!" said Esther, clapping her hands over her ears.

Was it because he was beside her that she saw the filth in the gutters, the pox scars on the face of the girl selling flowers, the floating garbage on the waters of the Thames? Yet superimposed on all this was the image of a beautiful spring morning that no amount of dirt or decay could obliterate. When they were seated on the boat, Esther tilted back her head so her face was washed with sunshine, and breathed deeply. It was still cool, but the air was definitely growing more spring-like, as greening buds on the trees along the riverbank attested. And she felt so well today—her deep breath had not even cost her a cough, and her head hardly ached at all.

Swift was eager to show them the Observatory, where they spent the better part of the morning examining the instruments and listening to Reverend Flamsteed talk about his work. Natural science interested Esther but little and Becca not at all, but Swift, though he mocked scientists, was curious about everything, and so the best of the morning was gone before they ever got to view the Queen's House with its fabulous painted ceilings.

That tour finished, they sat on a bench in the park, almost in the shadow of the Naval Hospital, to eat cold chicken and pies. "The old royal palace sat on this very spot," Swift lectured as they ate, "but Sir Christopher Wren has just finished this new building. Note its splendid design—"

"Seems awful fancy for a seamen's hospital," sniffed Dingley. "You'd think it was still a palace from the outside."

"Why, do you think England's ailing sailors deserve less than the best?" Esther asked with a smile, slipping a bit of chicken to Pug, who was begging.

"Why not ask a seaman?" Swift suggested. "If I am not mistaken, here comes one of that brotherhood himself."

"Dear me—what *shall* we do with a drunken sailor?" said Esther. "Becca, are you still fond of naval men?"

The old man weaving toward them had long since lost his crisp military bearing and costume, though his coat retained a hint of gold braid and his wig was caught back in an untidy queue. Whether his unsteady gait was due to drink or injury was hard to tell, even after he accepted Swift's invitation to join them and sat down on the bench across from them.

His name, he told them, was Lemuel Harding, "and when you hear tell of sailing the Seven Seas, my friends, think of that name—think of Lemuel Harding—for I'm a man who's sailed all seven, and a few more besides." He leaned forward, rubbing weathered hands together. "Have you heard tell of islands in the Pacific where men feast on other men's flesh? 'Tis no legend, 'tis truth, I assure you, for I've seen it with my own eyes, and damned near ended up in the cooking pot myself. Now there's a tale—"

"And another behind it, and another still," Esther whispered to Becca. "Shall we take Pug for a walk?"

Swift barely saw them leave: far from simply feigning interest in Captain Harding, he seemed genuinely intrigued with the old man's tall tales, though Esther doubted he believed any of them. She and Becca headed for the trees and soon came in sight of deer grazing. Unfortunately, Pug saw them too and took off in yelping pursuit, and his mistress expended a fair bit of energy in trying to lure him back again. The deer, with their long graceful legs, were in little danger from their tiny pursuer, and Pug's barks shrilled to a fever pitch of such frustration that both women laughed to see him.

An hour passed before they headed back toward the garden where they had picnicked, and when they got there they found Captain Lemuel Harding gone and Dr. Swift walking toward them. Becca left Pug in Esther's care while she went to find a privy, and Swift and Esther continued walking down to the riverbank.

The air had warmed considerably and was filled with the tang of green growing things. A pale blue sky arched over the silver thread of the Thames, and around them the beautiful buildings, crowned by the Observatory on its hill, looked as if they had grown in the setting. As they neared the river, they could see boats of all kinds plying its waters and hear the ring of voices carrying clear across the Thames.

"So, you heard all Captain Lemuel's tales, did you?" Esther asked.

"Indeed I did."

"And believed perhaps a tenth of what you heard?"

"A tenth? Call it a hundredth!"

"Do you not think there are strange things to see on foreign shores?"

"Far stranger than we shall ever guess. But what I find far stranger is the wisdom and folly of human beings. I despise most of mankind, yet I will stop to listen to anyone talk. I never cease to be amazed at my own species, even when I am disgusted by them."

"There is where we differ," Esther said. "I enjoy listening to anyone I consider wise and sensible, but when I think someone is boasting or lying or doesn't know what he's talking of, I lose all interest." She paused a moment. "I think that is what makes you a poet—a really great one, not a mere dabbler, as I am."

"Do you think so?" he said, keeping his voice light but turning so eagerly that she almost laughed. For all his cynicism, he was such a child, so delighted by praise—she thought for a moment of Pug nipping at the heels of the fleet deer.

After a pause, Swift, looking out at the river, said, "Dearest Esther, what would I do without your eyes through which to see the world? Or myself? We have known each other so long that you are like a second self to me, a voice chiming in my head. I always hear myself asking, 'What would Esther think of this?' or 'How would Esther speak to that person?'"

She had no reply. He was the very same to her, but she some-times felt that inner voice to be a burden, for it carried the weight of authority. She glanced away, at two boys poling a raft down the river. Then, unbidden, words came to her lips that were quite different from anything she had expected to say.

"I heard something when I was in Farnham. From my sister ..."

"Yes?" He seemed puzzled by the change in subject.

"A piece of gossip. Old gossip. But first I have to tell you of another piece of gossip—one I'm sure you are familiar with. Perhaps you have heard both of them. Perhaps you even know the truth of it." Words tumbled over themselves, as eager as Pug to get free at long last. For so many years she had resisted speaking of this to him. But he had lived in the same house, been older and wiser than she. "My mother told me when Sir William died that many people said he was my father. I had never heard that before—but I heard plenty of it after, once he left me my legacy. And she did not tell me the rights of it, what was true." She saw he was nodding slowly; of course he had heard all this long ago. "And now I hear—my sister says it is common talk that you, too, are a child of Sir William. Do you know anything of this?"

He glanced up the hill and she followed his gaze to where Becca, well within sight but out of earshot, was engaged in conversation with a well-dressed couple. He took his time replying.

"I have heard both those rumours, over the years," he said at last, "and the truth is, Esther, that I know no more than you do of what the truth is. Sir William certainly said nothing to me of these things—would you expect it?"

"If he was your father, you might have expected him to own you," she said. "Or me."

"I would have thought he was that kind of man. Yet he owned nothing. One might say, I suppose, that he took good care of us both, if it is true."

"Better care of me than of you," she said. "You always felt he never gave you the help you needed to start your career."

It was Swift's turn to look out at the river. When he turned back to her, he had that sharp gaze again, as if really seeing her for the first time in years. "I think it unlikely in my case, and possible but by no means certain in yours," he said. "But I have no evidence for either conclusion. What do *you* think is true? What do you want to be true?"

She had asked herself the first question thousands of times but had given little thought to the second. "I don't want it to be true," she said after a moment. "I don't want to think of Sir William as that sort of man, nor to think that of my mother. I suppose I ought to be proud of my fine parentage—but I was never ashamed when I thought my father was a common sailor and tradesman. But the strangest part of it all is that if both stories were true, you would be my half-brother."

He smiled, and touched her cheek with one finger. "Indeed," he said. "I have thought of that. Another, likelier, tale says Sir William's father, old Sir John, was really my father, which would make us uncle and niece. Is that any more to your liking?"

"I don't know. Uncle Jonathan. Brother Jonathan." She, too, smiled. "It would be a fine answer for all those who still seem to expect us to be married."

"Do folk expect that still?" He began to pace along the riverbank while Esther remained standing still, a fixed point around which he circled restlessly. "No woman would be getting a bargain in having me as a husband—and I am not sure there is anyone, man or woman, whose company I could tolerate day after day in close quarters. Yours might come closest. Did that fool Will Tisdall ever tell you what I replied to him when he wrote years ago, asking my permission to marry you?"

"I did not need your permission. I hope you know that. And yes, he did more than tell me—he showed me the letter."

Swift raised his eyebrows but did not stop walking. "So you know, then, that I wrote that if I were ever inclined to marry, it could only be to you."

"I assume you intended it as a compliment to me, so I took it as such."

At the same moment they both glanced up on the hill: Becca was still deep in conversation, but Pug had wriggled away and was racing down toward them, barking a series of high-pitched yelps. Esther scooped the dog up when it reached her skirts and smoothed its white hair.

"A great many people, Esther, both here and in Ireland, have asked me these past eight years what my intentions toward you were. *Have* I wronged you, my friend? Would you … do you wish to marry me?"

She choked on a wild burst of laughter. "What is that—a proposal or a question?"

"A question, I suppose. But if the answer were yes, a proposal might follow. If it was your wish."

There. She had it. Ten years after Sir William's death, ten years after everyone had assumed they would be married, Jonathan Swift had finally proposed to her. After a fashion.

A boat passed on the river; she could hear a woman's laughter, a child's cry. "I have never been overly fond of the idea of marriage either," she said after a long silence. "I wish we truly were brother and sister, or uncle and niece! Then there would be no questions; then we might be together whenever and wherever we chose, and not a word of gossip. *That* would be the best thing."

"But it cannot be. I would not brand myself a bastard, and my mother a whore—would you?"

"Of course not."

"Then what's to be done, Esther? Shall I tell you what I want? I want things to go on as they were before, but I want to know that I will never lose you to another man. That is hardly a fair thing to ask, is it?"

"Hardly. Yet I can almost feel safe in promising it. The older I get, the less appeal marriage has for me—and, of course, the less likely I am to be asked."

"I think men will think you are lovely when you are fifty, Esther. But I, too, feel no desire to ever marry, so perhaps with those assurances we can carry on our friendship." He took her hand with a smile so merry that she could not tell how much of what he said was mockery and how much was in earnest. "Should we make a pact? A vow never to marry, and to be friends always?"

"Friends always, yes. But not a vow never to marry." She drew her hand away. "Let us be content with assurances but make no vows."

"Very well. Ah, I see Bec has disentangled herself from her new acquaintances and is returning to us. No more talk of serious things, then, but only of puns and folly."

"Buns and holly? What a strange topic of discussion to introduce!" said Esther loudly, as Dingley approached. "Becca, Jonathan has been giving me his views on buns and holly—have you any idea why?"

DUBLIN
SEPTEMBER 27, 1709

We are back in our lodgings on Capel Street, near Ormonde Quay, after gadding about like a pair of ladies in fine style. It seems hard to beleeve that a year ago we were yett in England. After all the journeys we have made in Ireland this summer, I am more sure than ever that I will have no Regretts if Ireland is to be mye home till I dye. Such a lovely land as it is! We have been of course to Laracor, visited twice with the Ashe brothers at Finglas, and have just now come from a long stay at Wood Park with Charles Ford, or Don Carlos as we call him. I have not writt much heere of him, but he is the merriest man ever was; he us'd to be a friend of Jonathan's and is still, but now is just as much a friend of ours. And staying with him at Wood Park was the pleasantest part of our summer, for I was much tyr'd after my latest illnesse, and Laracor did not restore me as much as usually it does, for there were soe many people there, and so much visitting, that I gott no rest.

Jonathan staied on in England long after we retourn'd to Dublin, and he has now pitched here in Ireland, but for how long, who can say? While he was there he publish'd the final volume of Sir William's Memoirs, and tho' I am gladd to see it bound betweene covers, it makes me sad too, for he and Lady Giffard quarrel'd so over his publishing of it (Jonathan saies she tho't it should be left unpublished till all her friends were dead, for that it casts some of them in an unflattering Light!) that I feare they may never be friends againe. They were never the best of Friends, and both are soe stubborn I am sure there is no hope of a Reconciliation. I looke at the cover of that booke now, and have such Memories, of myselfe and Jonathan in the olde study at Moor Park, he correcting Sir William's work and I transcribing his, and the Selfe I was then seems soe young, so far away, I can scarce imagine that I once was She. How time has turned! And the book itself, lying in front of me, and the quarrel it spawn'd, all make that world of Moor Park seem soe much a part of the past, a past I can never retourne to, much as Eden must have look'd to Adam and Eve. Is Lady Giffard, then, the angel with the flaming sword? I must tell that to Jonathan; he would like that Comparison! He has as fond memories of the old days at Moor Park as I doe, but I think we have both seen it for the Last Time.

Mr Addison has gone back to England. I doe not see that I have writt much of him in heere, since I have made time to take up my Pen onley a few times this summer, but he has been much a part of our lives since coming over as Secretary to Lord Wharton. Jonathan has soe filled mye mind with what a Great Man Mr Addison is, and how great a Wryter and all, that I was half paralyz'd with fear when first we mett, but after half an hour's talk I realized he is nothing to Feare; he is a very well read and wise man, but his mind, I dare say, is not one whit greater than Jonathan's (tho' I would not say soe much to the Poor Dear Foolish Rogue, as Becca and I have taken to calling Jonathan, lest it would puff him up even more than he already is!). And Addison is a kindly man, easy to speak to, even to one of such lowly station as myselfe. Now when we read the Spectator, which usually Becca reads to me for my eyes are so poore, I shall imagine his owne voice speaking and enjoy it so much the more.

In all it has beene a most pleasant summer, onley very tiring, and I could wish for Nothing, just for Better Health, that I might enjoy everything more.

DUBLIN
MAY 1710

"Nothing but trouble today, ma'am; young Jane isn't here again," said Mrs. Sally as Esther entered the kitchen, shopping list in hand.

"Not here again! Wasn't it only last week she disappeared for a day because her mother was supposed to have been sick?" Esther sighed. The latest Jane was a red-haired, freckle-faced Irish girl of about fourteen who had been with them less than three months and had seemed to be working out well. Now she had begun to shirk. That would never do, but Esther dreaded the search for a new housemaid, though most of the trouble of dealing with staff fell to Becca.

"Yes, ma'am, she said yesterday her mother was still sick," Mrs. Sally said, vigorously rolling out pie dough on the wooden-topped table. "The next youngest girl's only ten, there are two boys between, but they're not much help with the babies. Poor child was worried sick yesterday about what was going on at home, so I'm hardly surprised she's not here today—but that's no excuse, of course."

"Of course ..." said Esther. She wondered would it be better if the maid lived in. "Babies? How many children are there in the family?"

"Oh, eight or ten, I believe. That's usual with the Irish. Jane's the eldest." Mrs. Sally was born and bred in Ireland but, being of English family, was in a separate class from "the Irish." Jane's family were native Irish, papists, and poor. All the housemaids had been—girls of a better class were far more expensive. But Jane had the makings of a good servant.

"Well, if she's not in tomorrow, we'll have to begin looking for someone new," said Esther.

Mrs. Sally nodded, but there was a worried look about her eyes, and Esther heard her whisper, "Poor child," under her breath as she turned back to her stew.

In the middle of writing her letters, later in the morning, the thought of Jane came unbidden back to Esther's mind. Eight or ten children under fourteen! She thought of the families in the tenant cottages back at Moor Park. Had any of them had so many children? She heard conversations all the time among her friends about the poverty of the native Irish and the terrible conditions that prevailed among the poor of Dublin. She had always vaguely assumed that the Irish lived much like the tenant farmers had back home—the little cottages she passed in Laracor did not look very different from such cottages back in England, yet Dr. Swift waxed eloquent about the "appalling poverty" and "squalour" of the poor in Ireland. She had never walked through the parts of Dublin where the poor lived.

Suddenly she felt sorry for poor Jane and her own high-handed decision to dismiss the girl if she missed another day. Putting down her pen, Esther looked at her own hands. She had never been poor, but she had been a servant and had once assumed that such would be her lot all through life. Kind fortune—or an accident of birth—had made her mistress instead.

Esther got up, tidied away the papers on her desk, and went to get her cloak. Becca had gone out to do some marketing, and anyway Esther was not sure she wanted company on what might turn out to be a fool's errand. She was already embarrassed about having to reveal her intentions to Mrs. Sally, but there was no way around that.

"Where does she live?" Sally repeated, cocking her head to one side to think. "I'm sure she's said … wait now, 'twill come to me … ah, Garden Lane, that's the place. Surely you don't want to go down there, ma'am? It's very rough. Perhaps you might get Rob to go with you? He's likelier to know the way, at any rate."

"Yes—that might be a good idea," Esther said. "And—ah, a basket? Would you make up a basket of food, things I might bring for her mother and the little ones? Whatever you think would help … I'll go talk to Rob."

Rob, the manservant, was Irish too, and Esther caught a flicker in his green eyes when she explained that she wanted to visit Jane's family. "No, ma'am," he said, covering it at once with deference, "no, you won't want to be going there, ma'am. It's dreadful rough and dirty. You wouldn't like it at all."

"I am not going for pleasure," said Esther, drawing herself up with dignity, "I am going to see what good I can do for that poor family. I do not expect it to be like a visit to the archbishop."

But what had she expected, she wondered half an hour later as she followed Rob, basket on his arm, into Garden Lane? The pleasant name was entirely out of keeping with this squalid street where not a blade of grass flourished, where no flower had ever ventured. The narrow, rutted track was hardly a path, much less a road, and crowded on either side were ramshackle houses with uncurtained, unshuttered windows and gaping doorways. She had not known such places existed in the city. Dirty barefoot children clad only in shifts played all over the place. She was ashamed of her first thought, which was that if she had known Jane came from a home so filthy, she would never have hired her to work in the house. The girl probably had lice, at the very least.

"Hold on now, ma'am—I'll find the place for you," Rob said, and stepped over to a group of half-grown boys throwing stones at a wall. In his absence a half-dozen children—Esther could not tell boys from girls—swarmed upon her, hands outstretched.

"Penny, ma'am? Spare a penny?" Bright eyes peered from under tangled hair and dirty faces—a mixture of hope and cunning. Esther dug into her bag for pennies and distributed a coin to each child.

Rob, after a short conversation with the boys, returned, scattering children before him like chickens. He shouted something after them in the Irish tongue, and Esther looked at him quizzically. "Only tellin' them to be off while luck was with them," he said. "They'll not get such good fortune here another day. This way, ma'am." He led her to a doorway that looked exactly like all the others in this row of crumbling hovels. Esther's steps faltered. What was she thinking of? What madness had brought her here, and what did she think she was going to do inside this wretched place? Out of the corner of her eye she saw what might have been amusement pass across Rob's features; that made her angry enough to lift her shoulders and go on.

Rob pushed open the door of the house, and Esther stepped into a pool of blackness. While she was still blinking she heard him ask something of a person she could not see in a tongue she could not understand. A response came, and Rob led her up a flight of stairs. She could feel her lungs tightening already in the fetid air, and climbing three sets of stairs did nothing to ease her breathing.

The room at the top of the house was as dark as the one below. Esther could hear human sounds but could see no people, no signs of life whatsoever, in the pitch-dark interior. From a corner came a baby's wail, then a second, higher-pitched scream from what must have been another baby.

"Who's there?" cried a woman's voice.

"Ma'am—Mrs. Johnson! What are you … I'm sorry, ma'am, I'll be in to work tomorrow, I swear to God." A scrambling on the floor at her feet changed, as Esther's eyes adjusted, to a small wild-haired figure hurrying to its feet. Only from the words did she recognize her quiet, dutiful little serving girl, Jane.

"Fiona, who is it? Why is she here?" Fiona—that was Jane's real name, Fiona O'Dea or O'Shea. Rob must have known the name to be able to ask the way to the house.

In the dim light filtering in through the open door and the many cracks in walls and ceiling, Esther was now able to see shapes, figures, objects around the room. Jane—Esther could not think of her as anything else—stood in the middle of the bare wooden floor wearing a torn shift. A child of about three or four cuddled in her arms, its head against her shoulder. The wailing cries came from a basket in the far corner of the room where a baby or perhaps two must have been placed to an uneasy rest. In the centre of the room was a tangle of bedding and the shape of a woman who had to be the sick mother. She struggled to raise herself up on one elbow.

Rob had stepped back into the doorway. Esther moved forward toward Jane and patted the girl's shoulder awkwardly, brushing the curls of the child nestled there. "Hello, Jane. I came to see how you are, how your mother is. To see if I can ... help, in anyway." While the girl stood drop-jawed, Esther peered beyond her to the mother. "You must be Jane's—ah, Fiona's—mother? I am Mrs. Johnson, her mistress. We heard that you were ill and wanted to come help."

"Help." Jane had latched on to the word and repeated it incredulously. "I don't know, ma'am, there's nothing ... Mama's sick, you see, but she'll get well ... it's only since the baby—"

"A little childbed fever," came a weak voice from beyond the fire. "You'll know how it is, ma'am. The midwife's been and says if I keep quiet, I should be fine in a few days ..."

Esther, of course, did not know how it was. She lifted her basket. "I brought some food."

"Food?" Jane's eyes brightened; she set the child down on his feet. "Jamie, go sing out to Katie and Sean and them, tell them to come in. And make sure they don't bring none of their crowd with them—only ours!" She shoved Jamie toward the door and turned back to Esther with an expression far brighter than her earlier blank face. "It's very kind of you I'm sure, ma'am," she said. Her tone clearly indicated that further conversation would be an unwelcome delay. *Get that basket open,* her hungry eyes said.

Esther looked about for a table; finding none, she went to the single bench against the wall and opened the basket, lifting out cold chicken and pies, bread and cake, herring and cold cooked potatoes. It was such a little basket—it hurt her to see how Jane's eyes widened as though a feast were laid before her. The younger children crowded about, but Jane made them all sit down in a circle and picked out the best of everything and brought it, in handfuls, over to her mother. There did not seem to be a plate in the house.

Other children crowded in at the door: Jane surveyed the group with a wary eye and sent two of them on their way. The others, apparently her siblings, were allowed to remain. The food suddenly seemed very little to Esther as she watched the children devour it, but she knew it was likely more than they had had at one time in their lives.

With Jane directing everything so efficiently Esther felt super-fluous: she looked at the mother lying on the floor and began to edge her way toward her. One of the girls had brought her a baby, and the child was now greedily sucking at its mother's breast, while the woman ate a slice of pie with her free hand.

"We're ever so grateful to you, ma'am—sure we're grateful anyway that Fiona's got such a good place, and I hope she's a good girl for you, and minds herself, does she?" The woman's voice seemed to have grown stronger as she ate, and Esther, wanting to feel a little more as if she was having a conversation rather than delivering an address, crouched uncomfortably down near the floor. It would have been easier to kneel, but she was too aware of the dirt gathering on the hem of her skirt and could not bear the thought of any closer contact with the floor.

"Have you seen … I mean, is there anyone … anyone to help you?" Just in time Esther realized the futility of asking about a doctor. What physician would come here, to treat these penniless people?

"My sister says I should call the midwife back, but she won't set foot through the doorway without pay," the woman said, and Esther almost laughed with the relief of it. The midwife! Of course! There was someone who would tend to the needs of a poor woman with childbed fever—there was always a local midwife. And it was a simple matter of finding her and paying her. There was, after all, *something* Esther could do. She felt the huge weight of her helplessness lift a little.

Mrs. O'Dea—for that, Esther finally learned, was the family name—made no effort to dissuade Esther when she offered to pay the midwife. Rob trailed along tolerantly, still looking amused, as Jane led Esther to the midwife's house—a ground-floor apartment in a similarly dilapidated house—and waited while Esther negotiated with the shrewd older woman. Satisfied at last that Jane's mother would receive some treatment, Esther finally allowed Rob to lead her back home.

She felt pleased with herself for her afternoon's work and could scarcely wait to tell Becca, who would be as eager as she to do more for the family. They could make up a proper box of food and have Rob bring it down tomorrow—but could he be trusted? A tiny smile played about his eyes. She ignored it as long as she could. It was beneath her dignity to quarrel with her own servant, but—

At last she burst out, "You find this all very funny, don't you?"

Immediately the mask of servile deference slipped back over his face. "What d'you mean, ma'am?" he asked innocently. He did everything but tug his forelock.

"I know you were mocking me—the fine lady there in that street, that house."

"I'm sure I don't know what you're talking about, ma'am." This time he allowed a note to creep into his voice, just that edge of mockery, a hint of an unseen smile.

"Very well then, Robin. No more need be said about it."

"No more indeed, ma'am." He was silent a moment, walking a deferential half step behind her. Then he said very softly, "If you could just have seen yourself lifting up your skirts to keep 'em out of the shite!"

"What?"

"Beg pardon, ma'am." Before he dropped his eyes he met hers for just a brief second, a testing look, as if each wondered how far the other could be trusted. Could he have had some way of knowing that years ago in her English girlhood, a footman might not have been considered a bad match for the housekeeper's daughter? He could not have known where she came from, yet for a moment he had spoken almost as to an equal. *Am I so common, still?* Esther wondered. *Do I betray myself?* Or was it something about the boy himself—some pride that sprang up through servitude like grass through paving stones?

Whatever it was, she could not keep back a smile. "Yes, you are right, I was … put off. I suppose I did not give much thought to how the poor in Dublin lived. I have heard people talk about the plight of the poor and given my opinion—but it is something else to see it first hand."

"And now that you've seen it, you think you'll be able to cure it all, do you, with a box of food and a few pennies for the midwife?" They were walking again, and he was looking away so that his gaze might not be taken to be too bold, but his words certainly were. Yet again she felt compelled to answer, drawn into this conversation with the only native Irishman with whom she had ever exchanged more than a few words.

"Of course not!" But he had scored a point: she had been caught up in her image of herself as the gracious, generous lady of the manor. "Do you think your mistress such a fool, Rob? I know the problem is far greater than I can solve."

"I'd never say you were a fool, ma'am. But you're feeling grand about your little visit today, aren't you? Rich folk, English folk, feel good if they can toss a few coppers to the Irish now and again"

"But whether I feel good—self-satisfied—or not, the O'Deas have food in their bellies. Can you deny that? Or should I stop bringing them food until I can find a more high-minded motive?"

He raised his eyebrows and gave a nod that almost looked as if it should have a wink attached, as if acknowledging that this time it was she who had scored a point. "They wouldn't argue with you, ma'am."

"But you would?"

"Ah, I'm just a cussed fool—that's what me brother says. Don't mind me."

"Yet you have a point," she admitted, as they turned into Capel Street—how broad and clean it looked now. *I'm not rich,* she had been going to say when he spoke of rich English people, but how foolish a claim that was after what she had seen today.

Rob nodded again, a perfectly proper servant-to-lady nod this time, touched his cap, and opened the door for her. The cocky young Irishman who had challenged her was submerged behind the manservant; she wondered if she would ever see him again.

What was not gone was her lingering horror at what she had seen. After dinner she sat in the parlour with Becca and Mrs. Sally, who had been invited to join them, and told them about the visit. Becca, never one to waste time deliberating about motives, had laid aside her latest embroidery and begun at once to sew dresses for the two babies at Jane's house. Mrs. Sally, who was also sewing, was more inclined to talk.

"Terrible, terrible all over the Liberty, ma'am," she said. "Why you wouldn't know, living here in St. Mary's, what it's like down in St. Nicholas Within. Twenty and thirty people to a house, more in some. And they throw their piss—ah, their chamberpots and all, straight out the windows into the yard behind their houses. Did you notice the stink, ma'am? That's what it is. If they'd convert from their papist beliefs, at least a few of their children might get a decent education and better themselves, but will they convert? No, they'll cling to Rome, for all the good it does them. But that's the evil of it, ma'am, the hold it has over them."

"Yes, of course." She had not thought of things in this light before—she knew, of course, that papists were banned from education and from most careers. With no proper churches of their own to go to and even their priests outlawed, how could their religion be so important to them, to make them give up all hope of rising in the world?

"Well, papists or not, they're not animals and shouldn't live like it," said Becca with surprising firmness. She scratched Pug's ears; he was curled up in her lap all among the sewing. "Indeed, there's plenty of animals, including this one, lives much better than those poor folk, don't you, Pug? It's a sin is what it is, especially for the poor children."

The dog whimpered and pushed his flat face into Becca's palm as she murmured soft endearments. Esther had a sudden flash of vision: Becca there, cossetting her dog, sewing a dress for a poor infant she had never seen—it ought to be her own baby on her lap, a dress for her own child she was sewing. Or by now grandchild, for Becca was in her forties. She would have taken that scrawny, crying baby in her arms today in spite of the dirt. Even a well-fed, clean infant, like the plump little treasure the nurse had brought out to view on their last visit to Mrs. Walls, was not very interesting to Esther. But Becca had taken the baby on her lap and exclaimed over it endlessly.

Does she think life has cheated her? Esther wondered. Long ago at Moor Park Becca had set her cap for handsome footmen and been disappointed, yet since they had come to Dublin Esther had never heard her mention her own marriage prospects. She seemed well settled in the life they shared and never spoke of regrets. *How little we know even our dearest friends,* thought Esther.

She told none of them about her conversation with Rob, for everyone—herself included, in most moods—would have agreed that he ought to be severely chastised, perhaps whipped, for such insolence. But she retold the rest of the story of her visit to Garden Lane to Dr. Swift later that evening when he came around to call, and the hint of a smile she saw on his face reminded her very much of the young manservant.

"So, Mrs. Johnson now proposes to throw the entire weight of her considerable energies into the cause of Dublin's poor, does she? I am afraid you will find that something of a bottomless pit, my dear. Pearls before swine, if you recall the parable."

"I don't, I'm afraid—don't recall the parable, that is. And I don't believe I can solve all the troubles of the poor by taking them baskets of food, if that's what you are accusing me of. It is simply that … I suppose I have had my eyes opened today. I have heard enough talk about the poor of Ireland, but I had no idea it was like this."

"More degraded than you can ever imagine," said Swift. He sat back in the most comfortable armchair, his legs stretched out on a footstool, carelessly displaying the fact that he still had a very fine leg, although he was somewhat stouter than in his younger years. Esther sat across from him on the other side of the fire, and Becca and her dog were back by the window, catching the last of the daylight for her sewing. "But do not waste too much pity on these wretches, my dear poppet, for so much of it is their own doing!"

"That is what Mrs. Sally said," Esther admitted. "Because they are papists, and will not change, thus they cannot better themselves."

"Yes, that is a good part of it," Swift admitted. "But I doubt many of them would have the brains to rise any higher in the world if they were given the opportunity. What they do have is good strong backs, which they will not bend to the labour they are suited for. Lazy! My dear ladies, if you knew how many of these beggars and layabouts in Dublin's streets—no doubt the very men who robbed your house in William Street years ago—are hardy peasants from the country, well able to work, but happier to come to the city and beg, and live in filth and idleness."

"But it was women and children I saw today," Esther insisted. "Even if the woman's husband is lazy or thieving, should she and the children be made to suffer?"

"One hates to see the innocent suffer. Especially one so kind-hearted as you, dear poppet—or you, dear Dingley. No, of course we must offer our charity to the helpless—but that does little to change my opinion that most of the wretches in Dublin should be whipped back out into the country!"

Despite his harsh views, Dr. Swift was, as Esther had known he would be, most useful in helping her find avenues for her charity. But over the next few months, as she and Becca threw themselves into sewing blankets for the workhouse and making up baskets of food for the poor, he cautioned her to take care.

"I only think that you ought not to give so much that you leave yourself in need," he told her one evening as she sat folding a stack of small flaxen pinafores. "I mean not only mere money—I am thinking also of your strength, your health. You know you are not well—and sewing tires your eyes; you have ever said that."

Esther blinked—her eyes were sore, these days. "It is true, it does. But so does copying your papers, or writing my own poems—everything that is interesting, that gives any purpose to my life, robs me of strength in some way!" She was surprised at the urgency with which the words poured out; they were followed by a volley of coughs like exclamation points. Swift's brow wrinkled, but she caught her breath and went on. "I know I shall never be really strong—indeed, I'm nearing thirty now and I imagine I shall get less and less strong—but I *cannot* wrap myself up in a shawl and declare myself an invalid. I *must* live— even at the cost of ill health. Even at the cost, if need be, of fore- shortening my life." She had never said that aloud before; she searched his eyes for a response and saw that it troubled him. Well, good. It troubled her too, but it was the truth.

Swift was silent; he stared at her for a long time before speak- ing. Becca, who had been well out of their conversation in her chair by the window, came over and put a hand on Esther's shoulder; even Pug nuzzled his wet nose into her hand. But it was Swift who finally broke the silence. "You are quite, quite right, my dear. You must live, whatever it costs. We all must. And you are the bravest of us all, for we hardly see what it costs you daily. It is only that we who love you"—his glance swept briefly up to include Becca—"hate to see you suffer, and want the best for you. So go on living, go on doing your work and giving to the poor, but do, please, try to take better care of yourself. For we want you around a long, long time to brighten our lives."

The tears, which she had successfully checked, threatened to well up again, but dear Becca saved the moment with a practical suggestion. "You see, Esther, it's as I've been saying—you really ought to go take the waters at Wexford. Everyone I've talked to says it has done them the world of good."

"Take the waters? An excellent plan," said Swift briskly. They were all glad to have a plan to pull them back from the brink of emotion. "It is only a shame you cannot go back to England, to Bath. But I have heard good things about Wexford—enough so that I would certainly be glad to help with the cost of a visit there."

Esther brushed her eyes fiercely with the back of her hand. "Wexford? What folly? Templeogue is so much nearer. Why should we not go there?" Dingley and Swift both laughed, relieved to see her practical nature reassert itself.

"Very well then, Templeogue," said Dingley. "When you go off to London again, Dr. Swift, we shall take a journey of our own."

Becca began preparing at once. "'Tis folly, really," Esther said one night, as Becca sat frantically sewing a new petticoat for the trip. "They bring the water up in bottles to Dublin every day; people have it delivered to their homes. Why should we go down there for it?"

"Now, Hetty, you know full well that the waters are more potent when drunk at the source, and if I cannot persuade you to go to Wexford and bathe, you must at least get best value for the water at Templeogue." She squinted at her handiwork. "Curse this quilting! My eyes are nearly as bad as yours with staring at it."

Esther laughed. "And all this torment because a letter from England tells you that ladies there are wearing their petticoats quilted now. What care you whether English ladies, or Irish ones, for that matter, are wearing quilted petticoats? Why is it worth so much labour?"

Becca looked up with a smile. "I cannot be like you, Hetty, so unconcerned about fashion. I'm not so young or so pretty as you, so maybe that's why I have to make the effort to look good. I don't know when you became so careless of clothing anyway. When you were a girl you cared enough about finery."

"I did, didn't I?" Esther let her mind roam back, touching lightly on the picture of a fourteen-year-old girl in ecstasy over a new flounced petticoat. "I hardly know when or how I ceased caring so much."

"I don't know when, but I know how," Becca replied. "It's because you believe all the rubbish you hear Dr. Swift say about modesty and simplicity in women. Bah! The man's problem is, he simply doesn't *like* women—the more like men they are, the better, in his eyes."

"Becca! What a foolish thing to say. Dr. Swift not like women? Why, he has a great many women friends!"

"Oh, of course—he likes *you* fine, and he tolerates me, and a few others as well. But women as women—he's not fond of them. The highest compliment he can pay a woman is to say she's almost as good as a man."

That left Esther silent for a moment, for it was true that Swift had more than once congratulated her on having "a quite manly grasp" of history, or literature, or philosophy. But she shook her head. "You're speaking folly, Becca. Dr. Swift is a wise man, and what he counts as folly in women, I count the same—if to be concerned with nothing but gossip and fashion is womanly behaviour, then I do not strive to be womanly!"

Becca clucked her tongue. "Suit yourself," she said, deftly pushing her needle through the quilted layers of her petticoat. "I don't mind a few frills and flounces, or a little gossip if it comes to that, but then, I've never claimed to be wise, have I? Now, Miss Simplicity, tell me what you've packed to take to Templeogue, and I'll unpack it all and do it properly for you."

TEMPLEOGUE
SEPTEMBER 12, 1710

I sitt here wryting my familiar book in unfamiliar Surroundings: the common-parlour of the Guest House here, before a fire at a round table, with dark drawing in outside. Becca and I have just come up from our afternoon walk down to the Pump House; we take the waters here morning and afternoone, as the Doctor recommends.

The Physician heere at Templeogue is a very young man, so Young indeede I do not knowe that I dare trust my Health to him, but he is very kind, and learned, and has written a treatise on the healing Properties of the waters here. He listen'd with the greatest concern to all my woes and miseries and swears that drinking the waters will do me the world of Good.

We have beene here a week now, and with us came Mrs Stoyte, who had likewise a mind to take the waters. We made a merry threesome on our journey down, and since then we have often beene join'd in Company of an evening by Lady Eustace, who staies here also at the Guest House. I had heard her Name before now in Dublin but never met her: she is a most Agreeable lady and very good at whisk also, so that we have four to play and make up a table in the evenings. Onley Becca will not let me sit playing, or talking, very late, nor reading at all, and I can only suppose what Punishment she would mete out if she saw me writing now! For she has become most Strict in insisting I obey all the Physician's orders, and spare my health.

She reads all our letters, and answers them with my suggestions, and reads aloud to me from whatever I choose in the evenings. I cannot beare to hear her read Poetry, though, for she has no feeling for it and the words fall from her lips like potato parings from the Cook's chopping board—and so, thud, onto the floor! Now that is a pretty turn of phrase, I should tell it to Jonathan in a letter, but how would I doe that if Becca writes the letter for me? Ah well, I shall not spare her feelings; she shall be a sacrifice to my Witt! (Indeede, she may not even think it an Insult, for she has as much use for Poetry as I have for her reading of it.)

Jonathan writes to us always, every day it seemes, telling us of all the doings in London, and all manner of foolishness besides. No one would make sense of his letters if they read them, for they are all full of our little language, where he talks to Becca and me, but me especially, as though I were a child, and all our pett names: he has taken to writing "ppt" in place of my name, for poppet, you see, and we call him Podefar, or pdfr, for Poore Deare Foolish Rogue. And a great deal other such foolery, that his fine friends in London who think him such a great Wryter and so wise a man would laugh if they could see.

WOOD PARK
JULY 24, 1711

How refreshing it is to be here! On every visitt I think Wood Park must be my favourite place in all the world, for here Everything is to our Liking, and there is no work to be done, only strolling and riding on these beautiful Grounds, and visiting with amiable Friends, and reading good Books. How it reminds me of Moor Park, and my childhood, and Becca saies the same, that it reminds her of Moor Park too.

Moor Park, that I may never see againe. All has chang'd there, all mye family and old Friends either chang'd or Gone. Mye mother has Marry'd Mr Mose, that was Sir William's Steward. The past is a country to which we can never Retourne.

I recall longe yeares ago, when I first began to keep a Journal, that I kept it, as I suppose every Impressionable young girl does, to the Improvement of my Mind and Character. I doe not think I have troubled much about such things in Recent *yeares. I have try'd to read good Books and sharpen my Mind with good Conversation, but I have thought little about my Character, supposing, I assume, that now that I am growne it is all settled, like my Face and Figure, and as little likely to Change.*

But now I see that this is nott soe, that I can still change, or at least that I must, for a chance remarke in conversation has open'd my eyes to behold my own Character as in a glass, and I find I doe not much like the Reflection.

I should tell this tale properly, start to finish, instead of jumping about like a trout just pull'd from the stream (See how Rustic my Metaphors have become since coming to Wood Park? I must put that one into a letter for Jonathan. But back to my Businesse). Yesterday there dined here half a dozen friends of Don Carlos', most of them well known to us and friends of ours as well, and a merry Party we made, save for one man, Whom I will nott name here, for I have harm'd him enough, I think.

I did nott like this fellow, for he was Boastful, and Stupid with it (as I find many boastful people are, as though the lesse they have to boast of the more they must brag). He went on about his exploits on the Continent, and air'd his views on politics and religion, all of which were ignorant, and when anyone else try'd a comment or opinion that differ'd he put them down most Rudely. Indeede, he dared tell me, when I ventured an Opinion, that Women could not hope to understand such Dealings—and this on the subject of the poor of Dublin, about which I think I knowe as much as any man. Indeede I wish'd Jonathan there, to Swiftly put the man in his place, but it was left to me to doe that, and I wish I had done it better.

Later in the evening it Came out that this man's son, a lad of about fifteen, had drown'd in an Accident a little under a Yeare ago, and when he spoke some-what Sadly of this event, someone else in the company try'd to cheere him, saying, "Do not weep for your son, for you know he is in Heaven." I was across the room, and lean'd over to Don Carlos and Becca and a handful of others, and saied in a low voice, "Nay, that is the very reason he weeps, for his son is in Heaven and he knowes he will never see him there!"

Don Carlos burst out in a great guffaw, and Becca clucked her tongue and shook her head, and all the others laughed, so that the party at the other side of the room, gather'd about this man, did not heare my Jest but heard our laughter, and the man look'd most vexed, that we should be laughing just as he talk'd of his son's death. And there was some clamour, that we should tell the whole company what had beene said, but I refused, but I know Don Carlos was soe much amused by my comment that before the Night was over everyone had Heard it whisper'd, save perhaps the man at whom it was directed, and I am nott sure even He was spared.

And Don Carlos would nott stop talking of it and repeating it, and saying what a Wit was Mrs Johnson, to putt this fool so in his place, with such an Apt word. And I basked in his praise, and thought no more of it till bedtime, when Becca saied, as if by the merest chance, "Poor man, to lose a son so young. How he must have suffered, and his poore wife!"

And all at once I saw, as if lightning flash'd across the sky and Illuminated the roome, what I am, and what Becca is. For I am ever laughing at her (both to her face and in Secret) for being a fool, and slow-witted, while Every man praises me for being so Quick-witted and Clever. And I saw that while I had only chafed at this man's folly and rudeness, Becca had felt his sorrow as a fellow man, and shared it. To put it most simply, I saw that she is good and I—I am silly, and sharp-tongued, and cruel.

This is only the latest of so many Thoughtlesse remarkes I have made, I dare not think. I am forever railing at Becca, and she beares it well, yet I think that some of my Sayings must hurt her, for she is tender-hearted. I doe the same with all my Friends, trusting they will understand and Value me for my Witt. And I make the most casual Judgements of other Men and Women, without knowledge or thought, such as I told Jonathan in a letter when he spoke of his new friends, the Vanhomrighs, and I wrote back that they were of no consequence and no one in Dublin thought well of them. I doe nott even knowe the family, except by Reputation, yett how readily I slander!

I rode a long time alone this morning, thinking about this, and resolv'd that I must doe better. I am a Christian, I spend myselfe on goode works, yett it comes

to me that there is something in the Scriptures to the effect that, without true
Charity (which, I interpret to meane, is Love of one's fellow man), all our gifts
to the poore are worthless. I ought to knowe the passage. I read soe widely yet I do
nott knowe the Scriptures as I ought, though I sometimes reade my prayer book. I
must get a Bible for myselfe and read the Gospels through. I think I neede more of
the Charity and Humility of Our Lord, for I see now that I am (tho' none of
us like to admit it in ourselves) a Sinner.

I confide these thoughts onley here in my Journal, for the Men of my
acquaintance, men like Don Carlos or even that poor foolish rogue Jonathan
(clergyman tho' he be) would think it silly in me to scruple over such a thing.
And somehow I doe not want to bare my soul to Becca on this, for it is her
Goodnesse that show'd me my own Thoughtlessnesse, and I feel ashamed to tell
her soe. Perhaps if I truly had more of the virtue of Humility, I would not
mind at all.

DUBLIN
1723

Esther lifted that page with a wry smile and read the last line
aloud: "*Perhaps if I truly had more of the virtue of Humility …*"
She glanced back at the date—1711. She had been thirty that
year. How old, how wise one felt at thirty! And looking back
now, from two-and-forty, how young that Esther seemed, that
woman who glimpsed her own vanity and shallowness for the
first time and truly thought that diligent effort would improve
her character. Would she someday be an old lady, looking back
on the forty-two-year-old Esther and wondering at her callow-
ness? *Or shall I live so long?* she mused.

So much of the twelve years since had been spent in prayer, in
reading, in journal writing, trying to make herself a better,

kinder person—and to what end? She was still sharp-tongued, still liked to think herself a wit, was still quick to criticize.

The page she held in her hand was, she thought, a turning point in the journal in some ways. Along with her attempt to reform herself, it marked the beginning of greater self-knowledge and the first stirrings of spiritual hunger. And, on quite another note, it marked the first time the name Vanhomrigh had appeared in her journal.

That was the beginning, the first thread in this tangled sorry tapestry she now held before her, the latest thread being the letter she had received tonight. A letter signed with her own first name and that same surname: Vanhomrigh.

It was frighteningly easy to throw open the packing case of emotions that travelled with that name, to rummage through them and try them on like old clothes. Yet was she neglecting something, forgetting something important? She turned back to the journal, to the words: *I see now that I am a Sinner.*

She was reluctant to turn the pages after that, to read on into the quest those words had prompted. But she was here to examine the past, and she could not close her eyes to painful memories. Why should the memory of the Laracor church, and the days before and after her visit there, be painful? It was like reading about falling in love with Will Tisdall—a romance almost forgotten, a promise unfulfilled. One more story of Esther turning her back, choosing to think rather than to feel.

She looked down at the journal again, reading what she had written on a summer day in 1712, and was drawn back into the little church at Laracor as forcefully as if a hand had reached out from the page and pulled her in.

LARACOR
1712

It had rained all day. Esther and Becca had gone to church in the morning and to dinner with Mr. and Mrs. Percival. Back at their cottage, Rob had put a fire in, which took some of the chill out of the air. Becca settled beside the fire with some letters and a lap desk, but Esther paced around the small room, staring at the windows, clicking her fingers on the window frames. Becca had read Jonathan's latest letter from London aloud, but Esther did not want to answer it just now. She wanted to be outdoors, she supposed, to ride or walk. She wanted to be back at Wood Park, though it was she who had suggested coming down to Laracor. She wanted it still to be summer—she had always found the onset of autumn brought on attacks of spleen.

She tried to read. She had brought a number of odd books from Wood Park with her, for Don Carlos had a large and eclectic library. Jonathan had, at her request, sent her a Bible from London, and she had taken some religious writings from Don Carlos's shelves. She wanted to be quite serious in her quest to become a better person, but it was slow work and she was forever getting drawn down interesting byways. Lately she had been reading about saints and mystics: the *Revelations* of Juliana of Norwich and the *Dialogue* of St. Catherine of Siena made fascinating reading but did not seem to contribute in any very direct way to making Esther Johnson a more charitable, less vain woman.

Esther pulled her cloak from a nail by the door so hard that she heard the hood tear. Becca looked up. "You're not going—"

"Out in this rain, yes I am. I can't stay inside, Becca, I shall go mad." She laced her boots with strong quick pulls and listened to the rain on the window instead of to Becca's litany of all the reasons she should not go out and all the precautions to take if she did.

The morning's downpour had softened to a fine misty rain through which late-afternoon sunlight could almost be seen. Esther walked past the rows of willows Jonathan Swift had planted and tended so lovingly on his glebeland. He had not seen them for two years now—who knew if he would ever walk under them again? He was destined to be more than vicar of Laracor now—that was clear from his London letters. The new curate gave a very dull sermon. Esther's mind had wandered all through the morning's service.

Now she was alone in front of the church, its grey stone gleaming with rain. Esther's cloak was shining too, and her skirt was soggy below the hem of her cloak. She opened the church door and went inside.

She hung her wet cloak on a hook to dry and sat down in a back pew. It was cool but not cold, and the rain was a distant whisper outside. She took up a prayer book and traced patterns on the cover with her fingers but did not open it to read. In this dim, filtered light her eyes would never stand the strain. She opened it with her mind instead, rolling over inside her head the phrases stored there. Once on a Laracor Sunday no one had come to church but Jonathan Swift and Roger the clerk, and Swift had stood up to say, "Dearly beloved Roger, the Scripture moveth us in sundry places …

"… *in sundry places,* to acknowledge and confess our manifold sins and wickedness … We have followed too much the devices and desires of our own hearts … We have left undone those things which we ought to have done; And we have done those things which we ought not to have done; And there is no health in us."

She had said the Morning Prayer that morning, as so many mornings in her life, surrounded by the tiny congregation, with the dull curate she did not like droning on in the pulpit. She said it again now, and it leaped to life inside her: the heavy stone of guilt that had been lodged in her stomach since Wood Park, since she first looked hard at her own evil nature, would not go away no matter how many times she read the service or perused the lives of saints. And there was no health in her.

Esther looked at the altar: she did not know that she was kneeling, nor that she was weeping, nor could she have explained why she was doing these things. The words of the prayer book rolled on in her head, a mighty tide that could not be turned back, churning over her thoughts and words and explanations, reducing them to foam on the wave. Laracor's church had no choir, no fine singers, yet all around her now she heard the *Te Deum*:

> *We praise thee, O God: we acknowledge thee to be the Lord.*
> *All the earth doth worship thee: the Father everlasting.*
> *To thee all Angels cry aloud: the Heavens, and all the Powers*
>   *therein.*
> *To thee Cherubim and Seraphim: continually do cry,*
> *Holy, Holy, Holy: Lord God of Sabaoth;*
> *Heaven and earth are full of the Majesty: of thy glory.*

She had come in a fit of petty spleen and been moved through penitence to sorrow, yet words of praise were now resounding in her head, and she knew with utter certainty that she was not alone in the small bare church. All angels, cherubim and seraphim, crowded into the pews around her; she could hear their voices; she was one of them. She shed spleen and melancholy and ill health as simply as she had shed her wet cloak, and she was Esther she had been made to be, alive and joyous and glorious in the Presence of her Maker.

For there was a Presence in the room, beyond the hosts of angels she could almost see. A shaft of light touched the altar, and from some faraway corner of her mind came the thought that the rain had ceased outside and the glow of sunset was coming through the windows. But no Irish sunset could cast a light as intense and golden as that which now lit the altar: Esther put away sensible explanations and surrendered to the Presence in the room, which was Love.

How long she sat there she did not afterwards know, or try to guess. Everything was very real: the singing, chanting voices; the Light; the one Voice speaking words she knew she would not remember, the love and peace completely enfolding her.

When she was again aware of time, and the church surrounding her, and her own body, Esther found that she was no longer in her pew but kneeling on the stone floor before the altar, her hands raised above her head, repeating aloud the words "Holy, holy, holy." If she had been asked that morning what she thought of someone who adopted such an attitude at prayer she would have thought it odd and shameful, yet at this moment it felt the most natural thing in the world. She rose from her knees, knowing the moment for that kind of worship had passed, yet in no way ashamed to have found herself there. Indeed, she could not imagine feeling anything but joy if any of her friends or acquaintances had walked in at that moment and found her before the altar.

She left the church; it was time to go and to return to the world, yet as she put on her cloak she felt the reluctance the drunkard must feel when sober morning breaks; she only wondered how soon it might be before she could come here alone again, seek the Presence, be lost in the moment again.

Outside, night had fallen, but the rain had not stopped. As she walked home in the mist, she no longer felt it as drizzly and gloomy but cool and refreshing.

Esther thought that when she got to the cottage she would tell Becca at once what had happened. She could not imagine what words she might use, but neither could she imagine hiding it. Indeed, she must tell everyone—did others know this joy, this buoyant certainty? She remembered the books of saints and mystics she had been reading. How strange their experiences had seemed to her before, how perfectly natural now! The words God had spoken to Julian of Norwich drummed in her head like the rain: "All shall be well, and all shall be well, and all manner of thing shall be well." She knew it, too.

As she turned on to the main road she wondered what the clergymen of her acquaintance would think. Had any of them who preached God every Sunday in the pulpit stood in the presence of God and felt his touch? Would they think her mad? Dr. Stearne, Archdeacon Walls, William Tisdall, Dr. Swift—Jonathan. She thought then of Jonathan and his scathing contempt for all manner of excess, including religious ecstasy. She had often heartily agreed with him when he held forth on the madness of would-be mystics.

Now her steps faltered a little, and she stopped in the road. "I must never tell him," she said aloud, and with the words she felt a little colder, as if some of the Divine Presence had lingered around her like a shawl and now had slipped off her shoulders. But no, this thing she had to keep from Swift at all costs. She could not expose herself, or God, to his mockery.

A thought troubled the corner of her mind: he was a learned man, as they all were; did they not know more of God than she did?

If Dr. Swift and all his colleagues would assert that God did not reveal himself in maddening moments of ecstasy in empty churches, might not they be right and she wrong? *But I was there,* she reminded herself, and walked a little faster, for it really was cold now. Perhaps it was not wise to spend so much time reading about visionaries and mystics. She was, after all, a practical woman.

The cottage lay ahead of her—now she was at the door, now turning its knob, now inside. She was vividly aware of the solid feel of the doorknob in her hand, the screech of the hinges, the dim candlelight within and the smell of the peat fire. *These things are real,* she thought—*so terribly real.*

"Lord, Hetty, where did you go? I was about to send Rob out after you. I thought you were lost for sure."

Esther stood in the room, the small, bare, real room, and said, "I ... oh, I went for a walk, up to the church, and I went inside and sat for a bit and forgot the time. I was in the church, so ... I wasn't out in the wet. Don't worry—everything is all right." And there was enough of the Presence left inside her that those four words, at least, were true.

LARACOR
1716

"Jane! Fetch my whip, and my hat and gloves."

"Yes, ma'am, right away, ma'am." The girl nodded and scurried away.

"And tell me if Rob is there with my horse!" Esther called down the corridor.

"Yes, ma'am," the little voice came drifting back. This new Jane was a country girl from right here in Trim, but Esther hoped she could win the girl's mother's consent to bring her back to Dublin in the fall. Their faithful, reliable little Jane of many years—the same one whose squalid flat in Garden Lane Esther had visited long ago—had finally left them to marry a nice young fellow apprenticed to a butcher, and in the year and a half since there had been two unsuccessful Dublin Janes.

On coming out to the country this spring, Becca had hired a new girl, very young and timid, "but those are the best kind," Esther said, "for they're most docile and easiest to train. And we may have a few years out of her before she takes off to get married." Mrs. Sally was still with them; their manservant Rob had stayed with the household too, so they had that much stability, at any rate.

Jane arrived back bearing hat and whip, almost the perfect maidservant save for being a little out of breath. "Mrs. Dingley says to tell you, ma'am, that the dean has arrived and is waiting for you outside."

"Thank you, Jane. Please send him word I shall be down directly—as soon as I have my *gloves*," she added, with a gentle stress on the last word that made the child's eyes widen.

She bobbed a half curtsy and murmured, "Sorry, ma'am," as she scurried off to find the missing accessories.

Esther tied her hat ribbon below her chin and surveyed her image in the glass with a critical eye. She had but lately celebrated her thirty-fifth birthday and felt that middle age was wearing well on her. Yes, she was a little stouter than she had once been; there was certainly more grey in her dark hair, but with the severe-looking spectacles laid aside for her ride, her eyes still looked bright and pretty in a round, unlined face. Her riding dress was cut simply and severely, for reasons of economy as well as because it became her that way. She turned away, satisfied.

Outside she found Jonathan Swift, dean of St. Patrick's Cathedral, standing between his horse and her own. "Bec importuned me to come in and have coffee, but I knew if I should, we would never ride today," he said. "So I told her to hold her coffee till the ride was done, and I dismissed your groom that I might have the pleasure of serving you myself," he said, holding out his cupped hands to help her into the stirrup.

"Thank you most kindly, sir," she replied. She found it a little awkward, though, stepping into his hand; she was so used to Rob performing this service. She took her seat and accepted Daisy's reins from Jonathan. He had arrived only the day before from Dublin; she and Becca had been down here over a fortnight, so it seemed a long time since they had seen him. In Dublin they were forever in and out of one another's lodgings. "What gossip have I missed from being out here in the country?"

As Jonathan brought her up to date on the doings of their Dublin circle, they rode down the lane past Esther's cottage, past the church and vicarage, and up the road toward Trim. "Shall we ride as far as the castle?" Jonathan asked.

"Which castle—mine or King John's?" Esther asked, laughing. She felt well today—she had awoken without a headache, her breathing was clear, and the fatigue that so often dogged her had melted away when she mounted her horse. She felt like a young girl again, ready to ride all the way to Dublin if her companion should so choose. Certainly she was ready for a ride to Trim.

"I meant King John's castle ... the other one, I believe, is still called Talbot's, unless you have been doing business deals on the sly and are now entitled to call it Poppet's Castle, you sly rogue."

"No, 'tis still Talbot's, but I should be glad to see it become Queen Esther's Castle. I have been talking to Mr. Blakely, and I think he is likely to sell."

On a gentle rise in the town of Trim, looking down on the great crumbling bulk of the medieval castle, was a neat three-storey stone house called Talbot's Castle, also known as St. Mary's Abbey. Esther had long admired the house, though it was in poor repair. She loved the prospect of the sloping green gardens down to the river, King John's great castle in the distance, the Yellow Steeple standing proud against the horizon. And she wanted to own something—one piece of land, one pile of stones—something that would be hers alone, before she died. She had grown up a servant and lived in rented rooms since she was twenty, and the thought of having a house all her own was alluring. She had set her heart on owning Talbot's Castle, though both Becca and Jonathan told her she could not afford it.

But Jonathan was looking not at Talbot's Castle but at King John's, spread out in the valley before them. "Strange to think of all the kings and great men who called this place their own—and now it crumbles into dust, just as they do," he said. They had reined in near the Yellow Steeple; it had been a long ride and the horses were winded.

"*Sic transit gloria mundi*," Esther quoted softly.

"Yes—yes, indeed. I should know it of all people—I, a church-man. That reflection is intended to lift our thoughts above mortal things and turn them to the heavenly, is it not?"

"I believe so."

"And yet, Esther—how I longed for that *gloria mundi*! Long for it still, if the truth be told."

"Would be in England pursuing it still, had the government not fallen," Esther ventured.

He turned to look at her. "Yes, I admit it—I would. Ireland will always be a poor second to me. Dean of St. Patrick's Cathedral—it was an English living I wanted, not an Irish one, where I could ever be at the heart of affairs. In the court of our new German king of England."

"Do not judge him too harshly for that—King William was a Dutchman, you remember."

"With an English wife."

"Yes." Esther remembered her childhood glimpses of that plump, gentle girl—she seemed so young now, in memory—Queen Mary. And now her poor sister, Queen Anne, dead after all her years of sickness and suffering, and all her poor babies—eighteen of them, some said!—stillborn or dead in infancy. "What a double tragedy that was," she said aloud, as though Jonathan had overheard her thoughts and could pick up their train. "A tragedy for a mother to lose so many children and never bring one to adulthood …"

"And a tragedy for a queen to produce not a single heir to her throne. The first queen to reign as sole sovereign since Elizabeth—and Elizabeth, too, had to call on a foreign cousin to take the throne after her."

"But not for the same reason. Elizabeth was the Virgin Queen, Anne just a singularly unfortunate one."

"Unfortunate in her choice of friends as well," said Swift sharply. He would have risen a great deal higher in Court circles had he not fallen afoul of the powerful duchess of Shrewsbury, Queen Anne's closest friend—and a woman Esther had often told him would make a formidable enemy. She still remembered the beautiful red-headed countess a little fondly from her long-ago visit to Petworth, though Swift spoke as though his mouth filled with bile every time her name came into the conversation. He was not really interested in the misfortunes of queens, only insofar as they touched on his own misfortune. And even his own seemed to be receding a little—mercifully, for Esther had heard all she wanted about Oxford and Bolingbroke and the fall of the Tory government—as he got accustomed to living again in Ireland and to his new duties as dean.

"Well, shall we mount up and ride on?" Jonathan suggested. "We must allow Madam Poppet time to make herself presentable for this evening's card party."

"Oh, indeed!" Esther said with a laugh. "I spend hours at my toilette, as you well know. Exceeded only by Becca."

"Dear Bec—still believing that powders and paint can succeed where nature has failed her. Ah well, we are all vain in our own ways, I suppose."

"And your vanity? Where would that be?" Esther ventured, as they rode again past the castle.

"In my intellect, in my skill as a writer—I truly still believe I was made for a greater role than life has yet given me. Is not Podefar a foolish rogue indeed, poppet?" He lapsed into the "little language" again, talking as though to a child, though his words were those of a man grown middle-aged and weary. "Does you not laugh at Podefar, you and dear Dingley, saucy wenches, when you is all alone and the curtains drawn? Such a man, such a foolish man. Dean of St. Patrick's, yet thinks himself made for so much more!"

Esther said nothing. Years ago she had given up trying to cajole him out of dark moods. The moods came, they went again, without her aid or permission. He wanted her to assure him that he was, in fact, capable of greatness, and though she believed that was true with every fibre of her being, she did not always want to tell him so.

What she wanted to say instead was quite impossible. She wanted to say, *So, Miss Vanhomrigh is in Ireland, I see?* But by some twisted unspoken agreement, while they gossipped endlessly about everyone of their mutual acquaintance, the name of Hester Vanhomrigh was never mentioned between them.

It had not taken long for Esther to realize, during the long years Jonathan had spent away in England, that there was something odd in the fact that he had seemed to spend so much time with a family named Vanhomrigh—a middle-aged widow who had come over from Ireland with her grown children—yet wrote so little about them in his letters. And then gossip began; their friends in Dublin began to make comments about "young Miss Hessy" and speculate as to "whether Dr. Swift really intends to marry the Vanhomrigh girl."

She remembered vividly the first such comment she had heard; she was at the Stoytes' home visiting, and Mrs. Stoyte's sister Catherine was Esther's partner at ombre. Esther was surveying her cards for the next move when Alderman Stoyte said, "So, does anyone know if there's truth in this rumour about Dr. Swift, eh? Going to marry Mrs. Vanhomrigh's older daughter, I hear?"

There had been a little embarrassed silence broken by the clinking of coffee cups, and Catherine caught Esther's eye; at the same moment Esther saw Becca look up from her needle-work with a half-anxious glance. Then the moment passed with Mrs. Stoyte saying heartily, "I don't believe half the gossip I hear from London; can you ever really imagine Jonathan Swift married?"

"And to a girl half his age?" someone else put in. "What is her fortune, does anyone know?"

"Half his age—why, yes, that I can imagine," Esther had said smoothly, laying down her cards. "He does so enjoy being looked up to, does he not?" She prayed silently that her remark would sound friendly and just the slightest bit cutting. She would not for a moment have let one of them see that she was stung by this news—as much by the fact of having to hear it from others as by the news itself. Surely if it were true, and they were such friends as she imagined—surely he would have told her!

But all that had been three years ago, and Swift had got out of London without the encumbrance of a wife, though gossip continued to swirl about the name of Vanhomrigh, especially now that Hester and her sister had returned to Dublin.

Esther said nothing about Miss Vanhomrigh now, nor did she tell Jonathan he was a great man and a great writer. Instead she began to relate a funny story Charles Ford had told her, and before long they were making plans for another visit to Ford's home at Wood Park, while the road from Trim to Laracor sped away beneath their horses' hooves.

And so it would have remained, Esther thought afterwards, Hessy Vanhomrigh's name unspoken between them, if Swift had not reined in his horse at the bridge and sat looking moodily down into the rushing waters. He held out a hand to her and she took it, having brought her horse alongside his. "I enjoyed this ride—you made me smile again. And again I must say thank you, dear, dear poppet. Life would be a tawdry proposition indeed, were it not for you. You are all the light in my life, dearest friend, do you know that?"

He looked so serious, and so sad and sincere—why then did a wicked little demon whisper in her ear and spring to her lips? "You are too kind, Jonathan. I am glad you enjoyed our ride, but you know you have many other consolations in life besides our friendship."

He sighed heavily. "Politics, writing, work—all of them are burdens, not consolations."

"Other friends," she suggested.

"Yes, friends, but most of them are merely sparring partners to exchange wits and words with. Only a true friend, an old friend, can touch the heart, can truly share my thoughts."

"An old friend? Might not a new friend do the same? 'Tis not impossible you might find a new friend to fill that role—and to be so much more than a friend. That would be a consolation indeed, now, would it not? A wife instead of a friend to warm your lonely hours?"

The change that came over his face was shattering—she knew at once she should not have spoken, should have bitten her tongue in half rather than speaking those words. The fog of gentle, affectionate melancholy cleared from his eyes at once, chased away by alarm and anger. "What do you mean?" It was a wholly different voice from the one that had spoken before.

She shuddered; she almost backed down before him. She could have blushed and stammered a reply, said that she was only repeating idle gossip—that was what he would expect from his dear little poppet. Instead she gathered what courage she had and said, "Dublin gossip links your name with that of Miss Vanhomrigh. They say you intend to marry her."

A long pause. "Do you believe it?"

"I do not know what to believe. I hope that if you contemplated such a step, you would tell your dearest and oldest friend before half the town knew."

He turned away and dug his heels into his horse's sides. Horse and rider cantered across the bridge, not looking back, and Esther kept her horse still and watched them ride. He often walked away from a quarrel—not from a verbal battle over literature or politics, but from anything that touched the heart. Rarely was anyone foolish enough to engage him in such a quarrel.

A little way down the road he stopped but did not turn back. She understood—he had made his concession by stopping; hers must be to ride ahead and join him. As of course she did. When he finally met her eyes he was still frowning.

"Would you care if I married?"

"If you married Miss Vanhomrigh?"

"If I married ... anyone at all."

"Of course I would care. I would—our friendship would change. We talked of all this, long ago."

"Yes—on the banks of the Thames." She had thought he might have forgotten that day at Greenwich. "I asked if you wanted to marry me."

Not the same thing, she noted, as *I asked you to marry me.* A subtle difference, but a vital one. "And I said no."

"What *do* you want?"

A fair question. He was looking at her squarely now, the gauntlet having been thrown down. She swept her eyes away from his face and around the green hills; it was too little time to compose such an important answer. "Little enough," she said at last, "just what I have now. Except for better health, which no one but God can grant me, I would ask for nothing different from the life I have now. Only for it to remain the same."

"And if I were to marry, things would change?"

"Of course they would."

"As they would for me, if you were to marry."

"That is hardly likely."

"As likely as my marriage, don't you think? A woman of thirty-five, still attractive, with a modest enough fortune but a vast store of wit, intelligence, and good sense—and a great many male friends. Do you think I do not hear gossip? Do Dublin tongues not wag whenever you go up to Wood Park with Charles Ford, or off to visit many another friend?"

Esther actually burst out in a peal of laughter. "Don Carlos! Is he suspected of designs on me? I should have said no more confirmed bachelor existed in all Ireland, save perhaps—"

"Exactly. Save, perhaps, the dean of St. Patrick's. I *am* a confirmed bachelor, and you a happy spinster, and why should that ever change? Of course I fear that another Willie Tisdall will come along—someone a bit more dashing than that insolent young puppy with the smelly feet—and take you from me. I suppose you have the same fears, for we are comfortable in our routine, you and I. But you know there is only one way in all the world for either of us to be quite sure the other will never marry."

"And what is that?"

"What I suggested seven years ago … to marry each other."

Esther looked down at her gloved hands holding her horse's reins. Two proposals from this man—she could hardly complain, even if they were more in the nature of challenges than of proposals.

"I have said before I do not think either of us would be well suited to marriage, especially with each other," she said quietly.

"Marriage as the world knows it, conventional marriage, no, of course not! I could not bear such a relationship—I was not made for it, nor were you. But what if … what if this were a different sort of marriage?"

Swift's eyes were gleaming; he looked almost excited, as though he were proposing some daring adventure. Despite herself Esther was drawn into it. "What do you mean—what sort?"

"A secret marriage, a vow between you and me—we would go on living as we do, continue our friendship—but know that we were bound together with a tie that could not be severed.

We would have all that we have now, but be forever rid of the fear that we might lose each other. Do you not see, Esther? It is the perfect solution—for us!"

All the passion and excitement that had been missing from his earlier suggestions of marriage were present now; his cheek was flushed and his words tumbled over one another. This stout middle-aged churchman in a neat powdered wig looked as hectic as a lad in love—in love, Esther saw clearly, not with her but with his own idea, this unconventional marriage so outside the bounds of society. She was both attracted and repulsed by his excitement.

"Certainly it seems the perfect solution to you," she replied. "I would take a good deal more convincing. A secret marriage, Jonathan—a marriage in name only—are you mad? What could either of us gain from that, save sorrow and frustration?"

"Why? Why should we be sorry, why frustrated? We know what we desire and this is the way to achieve it. Unless"—he frowned—"unless you do not relish giving up your freedom. Perhaps you really *do* desire a conventional marriage—if the right man were to appear?"

"I cannot say, Jonathan, the idea is too strange. You had better never have spoken of it. Let it be forgotten, and I will forget all the gossip I have heard." A band of pain was tightening around her forehead, drawing in further and further, making her eyes sting with its force. For a moment the landscape in front of her shimmered, and a wave of nausea coursed over her.

"I will not forget," said Swift stubbornly.

"Come, let us ride back," Esther said. "I have a headache, I must lie down. And Bec is waiting for you to drink her coffee."

"I'll drink no coffee today."

"As you please."

They said little on the ride back; he left her at the cottage door and called Rob to put away the horse. Esther went inside and lay down, and missed her card party that evening at the Wesleys'. She said nothing to Becca of Jonathan's strange proposal. For a week she did not even write of it in her journal. Then she wrote it all out, dismissing it as madness. He did not mention it again.

A month later she was back in Dublin, coming out of a milliner's shop with Mrs. Stoyte and Catherine, into a crowded market street. "Look who is across the way," said Catherine, nudging Esther.

Esther scanned the street but saw no familiar face. "Who?"

"Why, Miss Vanhomrigh—do you not see her?"

"How could I? I have never met her: I don't even know what she looks like."

Esther did not miss the surprised glance that passed between her two friends. Yes, of course it was odd that Dean Swift's two closest women friends had never met. But Miss Vanhomrigh did not socialize with the dean's other friends; she kept much to herself in her house at Celbridge. Esther followed Catherine's nod and picked out the young lady—so very young!—across the street. She was dressed quite simply in a grey and white gown of good cut and good cloth. She looked no more than twenty-four, and her dark hair was piled above a small, pretty face. She walked with a younger girl who was not nearly so pretty: "Her sister, Mary," Mrs. Stoyte said. "The sickly one."

Esther had been feeling well for several days, yet she was a little faint suddenly as they walked out into the Dublin sunshine. Surely she was not—could *not* be—jealous of this girl? Yet the thought that Jonathan might marry her was unbearable. How selfish, how temperamental am I! thought Esther—not to want the man for myself but to want no other woman to have him either!

"Of course it is all foolish gossip about her and Dean Swift," Catherine said decidedly as they continued on their way. "There is no question of a love affair, I am sure."

"*Are* you so sure?" said Mrs. Stoyte. "You have not read the poem, have you?"

"The poem? What poem is this?"

"Why, the poem Dean Swift wrote about her. It hasn't been published, but it is circulating everywhere in Dublin unofficially—surely *you* have seen it, Mrs. Johnson? *Cadenus and Vanessa?*"

Esther managed to shake her head. To her knowledge she had seen, critiqued, and hand copied every poem Jonathan Swift had written for twenty years. If he had written a poem about Miss Vanhomrigh it was no accident that Esther had not read it. *Cadenus*—an anagram of course, one of his favourite word games, for the letters could be rearranged to spell Decanus, the Latin for dean. And *Vanessa*? His choice, no doubt, of a classical name for the lovely Miss Hessy.

"Has anyone a copy of this masterpiece?" she managed to ask.

"Oh, several people. I'm sure Mr. Ford has one, as he is such a great friend of them both."

"I shall have to ask him to let me see it," Esther said.

She penned a short letter to Charles Ford the next day. She worded it discreetly, but she knew that it was very likely Don Carlos would mention her request to Swift unless she specially asked him to keep it secret. She did not ask.

A few days later Don Carlos's letter came, with the lines folded up inside them. He was tactful enough to make no special comment about them beyond saying "Here is the poem you asked for by our mutual friend." Of course Becca would see the letter, and of course she asked about the poem.

"Ah, so we're to see the famous *Cadenus and Vanessa* at last, are we?" she said when Esther explained.

"You knew of it?"

"All Dublin knows of it. I've only been waiting for a chance to read it."

"You must have known I had never heard of it, much less read it."

"Ah, Hetty, do you take me for a fool?" Becca looked up from the chair where she sat with the day's post in her lap. She pushed a sprig of fading hair up under her cap and narrowed her eyes. "Everyone takes Becca Dingley for a fool, but I'll turn out to be the wise woman yet, you'll see. I'm wise enough not to raise the question of Dean Swift and Miss Vanhomrigh to you. I've no wish to see you fly into a fury insisting you don't care at all."

Esther managed a wry smile in response. She had imagined reading the poem alone in her chamber at night, where her reactions, if any, could be kept private. But now she handed it across to Becca. "You read it, then. Let us both hear it at the same time."

"You know I'm no good to read poetry—you've said yourself. You'd far better read it for both of us."

"My eyes are tired, and reading Don Carlos's letter has strained them."

Becca lifted her eyebrows and took the poem. She scanned the folded pages. "'Tis shocking long," she said.

"We have all afternoon," said Esther.

"*The Shepherds and the Nymphs were seen, Pleading before the Cyprian Queen*—who's that?"

"Aphrodite. Venus. Goddess of love. Do go on, Becca."

"*The Council for the Fair began, Accusing that false Creature, Man. The Brief with weighty Crimes was charg'd, On which the Pleader much enlarg'd*—I'm all muddled already, Hetty—who is accusing whom?"

"Venus's council is accusing man—human beings, I suppose—and I can't tell you of what because you haven't got there yet. Please, Becca, do just read it and I'll explain it all afterwards."

"You'll have to," said Becca.

Apparently the Nymphs and Shepherds were accusing men and women of having completely lost the ability to love truly; they had given themselves up to money-grubbing and the coarser passions. "As usual, he puts all the blame on the women," Becca said. "*But Women now feel no such Fire, and only know the gross Desire; Their Passions move in lower Spheres ...*"

The poem went on for some time in this vein, until Esther began to wonder if it would ever turn out to have anything to do with Miss Vanhomrigh and the dean of St. Patrick's. It was a good hundred lines into the thing before Venus, deeply disturbed that her kingdom of Love was no longer honoured on earth, chose an innocent human girl-child and endowed her with every grace, beauty, and virtue. "This is Miss Vanhomrigh, of course," Esther said when Becca paused for breath after "*The Child with native Beauty shone.*"

"It is?"

"Of course it is. She is Vanessa, you see?"

Becca read on: "*Vanessa be the Name, By which thou shalt be known to Fame: Vanessa, by the Gods enroll'd: Her name on Earth—shall not be told.* So you think that's Miss Vanhomrigh?"

The poem went on—it really was intolerably long—as Venus tricked the goddess of wisdom into giving Vanessa brains as well as beauty: "*Seeds long unknown to Womankind,*

For manly Bosoms chiefly fit, the Seeds of Knowledge, Judgement, Wit—"

"I wonder why it is that whenever Dean Swift wants to praise a woman he tells her she's as clever as a man?" Esther interrupted.

"I've told you that before," said Becca.

Poor Vanessa was not the toast of the social scene that Venus had planned her to be, for her good sense and wisdom lifted her above her peers. Both the men and ladies found her as dull as she found them, for their gossip and dalliances and their obsession with fashion held no appeal for her. Esther recalled receiving, when she was Miss Vanhomrigh's age, dozens of lectures from Jonathan on the folly of fashion, the idleness of gossip. Even today he often praised her for dressing simply and plainly. Was the young Miss Hessy as simple, sober, and unworldly as the poem made her out to be, or was Swift writing her as he wished her to be? Or had he, in fact, made her over in his image of the ideal woman—*and did he make me that way, too?* Esther suddenly wondered.

"Cadenus" finally made his appearance in the poem, nimbly dodging the darts Cupid shot at him to make him fall in love. Vanessa was not so lucky; she was shot fair and square and fell in love with her elderly tutor. *"Vanessa, not in Years a Score, Dreams of a Gown of forty-four,"* read Becca. "So he's saying she fell in love with him."

"Apparently so."

The poem was almost comic now that Swift had turned from eulogizing Vanessa to lampooning himself: *"Declin'd in Health, advanc'd in Years."* The mere idea that a young girl could be in love with such an old man became a joke, as incomprehensible to the reader as it was to poor old Cadenus, who simply took a fatherly pride in the girl's accomplishment. Just as he had once done with little Hetty Johnson—but Esther, thank whatever gods and goddesses blessed her, had not been fool enough to fall in love with him.

For that was clearly the message of the poem—Vanessa was a fool, a wise and beautiful and virtuous fool but a fool nonetheless, for trying to ignite the passion of a man who was dead to passion. "She might have been flattered by the first part of it," Esther said, "but the rest must have made her furious. If it's circulating all through Dublin, I wonder she still speaks to him."

"Ah, but it goes on," said Becca. She had read the bit where Vanessa argued with Cadenus, explaining that she had every right to love him. "*It was an unforseen event, Things took a Turn he never meant.* You see, she's starting to convince him."

Indeed, Cadenus was flattered by Vanessa's declaration of love, and though he still pronounced himself incapable of feeling the passion of love, "*Friendship in its greatest Height, A constant, rational Delight … Which gently warms, but cannot burn; He gladly offers in return.*"

In other words, Esther thought, he was offering Hester Vanhomrigh the very same thing he had offered Esther herself these many years—friendship and respect in the place of love and marriage. It had sufficed for her: why should she be jealous that he offered it to another young woman? Surely there was room in a man's life for more than one close friend?

But the poem rushed on; Vanessa undertook now to be Cadenus's tutor in the arts of love. Surely she would fail—but then Becca, who was getting a bit hoarse, read:

> "*But what Success Vanessa met,*
> *Is to the world a Secret yet:*
> *Whether the Nymph, to please her Swain,*

Talks in a high Romantick Strain;
Or whether he at last descends
To love with less Seraphick Ends;
Or, to compound the Business, whether
They temper Love and Books together
Must never to Mankind be told,
Nor shall the conscious Muse unfold."

"Hah!" said Becca. "That's very coy of him."

"You're understanding it well enough now," said Esther.

"Clear enough for anyone to see—he's not going to say whether they ever fell in love."

"I should think the mere fact that he leaves it a possibility tells us that it certainly did happen."

"If that's so," countered Becca, "why hasn't he married her?"

"Stop asking questions," said Esther.

There was a denouement, of course, with Venus concluding it was not women but men who were the greater fools—for not all falling at Vanessa's feet, apparently. And that was that.

"Well!" said Becca, at last laying aside the sheets. "You said you'd explain it all to me—now tell me what you think?"

Esther stood up and straightened the folds of her gown around her petticoat. "I think I will go lie down," she said. "I feel a headache coming on."

CLOGHER
1716

She had hoped for a sunny day, but the sky was overcast, though the air was very hot and still. Esther put aside the blue ferrandine gown she had intended to wear and took from her trunk the poplin, which was lighter. She held it up against herself and looked down—yes, it would do well; she could still wear the quilted petticoat underneath. She moved about the unfamiliar room—they were staying with St. George Ashe—looking to see where her maid had put her underclothes and combs.

Becca knocked lightly at the door. "Do you need help dressing?"

"Yes, please," said Esther. She had been going to call for Jane, but it was nice to have Becca here instead, fidgeting with her straps and hooks, touching her bare back and shoulders with the practised hand of an old friend.

"I'll put your hair up for you, too," said Becca.

"Thank you," said Esther, knowing it was no small offer. They had talked till three of the clock this morning, after Esther had finally told Becca what she was going to do today. Becca had argued, scolded, even wept a little. But Esther was firm.

"This is what we have decided to do, Becca, and I've told you my reasons. It may be unconventional, but it makes perfect sense, so I don't see why you are so against it."

"Perfect sense!" Becca had said, dabbing her cheeks with a handkerchief. "I knew you'd marry someday, Hetty. Indeed, anyone as pretty and good as you—'twould be madness to think you'd live with me forever, two old maids getting old together. I'd be happy for you, if I thought you were making a good match. But this! Where's the romance in this?"

"Romance? Becca, be serious. How many people do you know who have truly married for romance—for love?"

"Very well," said Becca, leaning forward and poking the air with a finger, "but *they* have prospects. They have a fortune, a home, children, a husband who will support them and a place in society. I'll grant those are just as good reasons to marry—but you'll have none of those. A secret marriage, indeed! What folly!"

"'Tis not folly, Becca—I've explained it to you again and again." As she had done to herself, Esther thought—until it finally did seem to make sense. "I don't wish to be married and have a fortune and a place in society. I certainly don't want children, or a man underfoot day and night. Jonathan and I have simply decided that if we quietly marry each other, we can be assured that neither of us will ever marry anyone else, and everything can go on just as it always has. No one need ever know. I wouldn't even have told you if I hadn't wanted you to be my witness."

"Well, I wish you hadn't," Becca had said. "If it's to be a secret, I'd sooner be kept in the dark."

Yet here was Becca now, fastening Esther's mantle around her shoulders as tenderly as if she were a real bridesmaid and Esther a true bride, leading her by the hand out into the garden. As they reached the doorway Esther turned back and took Becca's hand. "At least, Bec, at least nothing will change. For you and me, I mean. We'll be just as we were before."

Becca said nothing but tightened her fingers around Esther's for a moment before Esther pulled her hand free and went outside into the grey-white day.

Jonathan Swift and St. George Ashe were waiting under a tree. From the look on Bishop Ashe's face, his conversation with Swift had gone little better than Esther's with Becca. His approval was rather more crucial to the scheme, since he was going to marry them. He took Esther's hand and looked as if he were about to try to persuade her to abandon the whole idea. He was a dear friend—Esther had often suspected he might admire her, might even have asked to marry her himself if she had any fortune. Clearly he was wishing today he was not party to this secret.

"Dr. Swift has told me, Mrs. Johnson, what you have planned. I cannot say it is usual, but I do not think there is anything in the wedding vows to prohibit what you are doing—only I must ask, are you both quite sure you wish this? To be married, in this secret fashion?"

His glance included Jonathan, so Esther looked at him as well, and felt surer. Jonathan looked grave but nodded at her, and she at him. They had talked all this over so many times, till both were convinced it was the right thing, the best thing to do. Esther had not, of course, said to him in so many words, I want to marry you so I may be sure you never marry Miss Vanhomrigh, but it was certainly true that reading *Cadenus and Vanessa* had changed her mind. The old, comfortable order she had enjoyed for all her sixteen years in Ireland was not stable or unchangeable, after all—the irrational fires of love and passion might yet sweep through and destroy everything. The marriage ceremony was a stone wall, a boundary, a protection.

"Come then, let us be wed!" said Jonathan, in a heartier voice than she had expected, and took her arm. She felt none of a bride's passions, which made her glad, for was not this an escape, a defence against passion? Instead she felt comfortable, and secure, holding the arm of this friend who was dearer than a brother. She moved with him to face Bishop Ashe and motioned to Becca to join them.

Becca had been a little away from them, in the flower gardens, and when she turned Esther saw that she had a handful of flowers she had cut, a little bridal bouquet, which she pushed into Esther's hands and which quite unexpectedly brought tears to Esther's eyes. So she was damp-eyed after all, as a bride should be, while she clearly and firmly repeated the vows. And it was true, there was nothing in those vows to prohibit what they were doing, for she surely intended to love and honour and obey Jonathan Swift, as she always had, and would willingly forsake any other and keep herself only to him, since he promised the same.

When it was over, the sky threatened rain, and they went inside and ate cold goose and pease porridge. Esther and Jonathan talked of a poem he was writing for the earl of Oxford, who was imprisoned in the Tower of London; they drew St. George Ashe into the conversation, while Becca sat and stared at the fire and said nothing at all. And when dinner was over, Esther retired to her bedroom along with Becca and read for a while and wrote in her journal. At last she blew out her candle and lay down in the big bed next to Becca, who was already snoring softly. Becca flung out an arm in her sleep and it rested across Esther's stomach. Esther stayed briefly still and then wriggled out from beneath Becca's arm, which was heavy. She closed her eyes and tried to fall asleep on her marriage night.

LARACOR
1716

Esther sat alone in her chamber at the back of the cottage, reading an essay of Mr. Addison's by candlelight. Her eyes burned, but she was not ready for sleep. Something stirred behind her—a noise in the doorway.

Jonathan stood there, rain on his coat, his hat in his hand. She gasped and reached for the mantua she had flung on the bed; she pulled it around her shoulders.

"What ... how did you get in?"

He smiled. "Bec let me in—she was flustered, but she can hardly deny me now, can she?"

Esther stood up. "Jonathan, this is … unexpected." She had been going to say *preposterous.* "What do you want?" She was keenly aware that her hair was down and she was wearing her nightdress. She never received any morning visitors, and since she was a child no one but Becca and the servants had seen her without her toilette complete.

He took a step into the room. "Must I have a reason to come to my wife's bedchamber?"

She stared at him. There was no denying the literal truth of his words, but it was not a right she had ever expected him to claim. The silence grew. Finally she said, "Does this mean you come as a husband?"

"That is what I am, your husband, I believe. If that ceremony in Ashe's garden meant anything."

Words. Words. The strange hurried scene in the bishop's garden, embarrassing even to remember now, had been nothing but words. A form, they had agreed. Nothing to do with husbands and wives and suddenly appearing in the bedchamber of an old friend who had always maintained the strictest decorum.

She felt very cold; she glanced toward the window but knew already that it was closed. She pulled the mantua a little tighter.

"It is no true marriage, Esther. Not in the eyes of the church, not in the eyes of God. A marriage is not a marriage until it is consummated. In the marriage bed."

"You don't mean this, Jonathan. This was never what we agreed."

He took another step closer. She saw that he swayed slightly, as a drunk man might. But he was no drunkard, and his words were as sharp and clear as always. Something else had robbed the steadiness from his steps and clouded his eyes. Fear, perhaps? A mirror of her own fear?

"But I thought about it, Esther. I thought all through our wedding night and all the days since, and finally tonight I had the courage to come to you. It is right, Esther. It is what we ought to do."

He reached a hand out, so tentatively that she might have been a coiled snake, and touched the hair lying on her shoulder. She saw how his hand trembled and realized there was no need to fear he would force her against her will. She had not even known she feared that until the fear left her.

"What we *ought* to do?" she echoed. "What about what we want to do?"

"We wanted to be married. To be bound to each other forever, even if we could not live together. The other is just a ceremony— this will make us one."

His stilted, rehearsed words, the incongruity of his being here, caused a sudden wild shift in Esther's mood, and she had to choke back laughter. He was still fondling her hair awkwardly, and she had a mad urge to do the same to him, to reach out and touch his wig, take it off. How bizarre to be talking of going to bed with a man when she had never even seen him without his wig! No—once or twice long ago, when they were both young, she had seen his brown hair tied back. No doubt it was as grey as the powdered wig now.

"Jonathan, are you sure this is what you want? Because I am not sure at all. Do you not remember that one of my great reasons for not wanting to be married—in the normal sense—is that I do not wish to run the risk of bearing children?"

He shook his head. "No, there is no risk—there are ways, Esther, ways of dealing with these things. Not foolproof, to be sure, but only this once …"

"Oh, so this is to be once only, is that it? You don't propose to turn up in my bedchamber night after night?"

"Do not laugh at me, Esther, I am in earnest. Put all the rest aside—all the reasons why you did not wish to marry, why I did not wish to marry. I do love you. I meant that much by our marriage— I love you and I never wish to lose your friendship. And coming together as man and wife will make our union complete."

"This was never what we intended, Jonathan." At least, she amended silently, it was never what *I* intended. Perhaps he had wanted this all along. She could not deny that the idea was flattering. And they were legally married. It would be no sin. Did she really want to go to her grave a virgin, wondering forever about the act of love and why all the poets sang of it? "But if you think it right, very well then." She smiled. "You are the dean of St. Patrick's and I your parishioner. I would not question your judgement."

At last he smiled too, a genuine smile of humour and not the strained odd smile that had been on his face when he came in. His hand moved from playing with her hair to cupping her shoulder; he drew her closer. His face came nearer and nearer and she realized he was going to begin by kissing her.

Esther had not been kissed in a very long time; Will Tisdall had burned his last, desperate kisses into her memory almost fifteen years ago. Before that there had been only a brash young soldier in a London ballroom—and she hated to think how long ago that had been. But she still remembered the softness, the sudden heat, and found that she was anticipating it again.

Only she could not help noticing that Jonathan's breath was a little foul and wondering if her own was too; his lips pressed against hers but did not move, and his teeth were huge and seemed to be crowding into her own mouth. Without the slightest trace of passion or ardour the physical act of kissing was acutely embarrassing. His hands—they were both on her shoulders now—travelled down her back to her waist and drew her closer against his stout belly. She closed her eyes and pretended to be seventeen again, pretended the man kissing her was a handsome stranger. It was no use. He remained stubbornly her oldest and dearest friend, as clumsy and awkward as she.

Then he was fumbling with the buttons on her nightdress and touching her bare chest, though not yet her breast—perhaps he was working up the courage. A flood of affection washed over her—nothing as strong as love or passion but a warmth, a kindness for this man without whom she could not imagine her life. Perhaps foul breath and jutting teeth and middle-aged girth did not matter so much, after all; perhaps she could lose herself in this experience and give herself up to his touch. She began to feel a little bit warmer. His fingers strayed onto her breast, and she no longer wanted to shrink back, though she was still keenly aware of his every move and she realized with a little shock that his other hand was at the buttons of his breeches.

Things seemed to have been moving very quickly, but now everything had slowed, as if they were moving underwater. Jonathan's fingers were still making circles on her breast, edging no closer to the nipple, and his mouth was still on hers, and she was still trying to hang on to her feelings of warmth and fondness for him—and all this seemed to be going on endlessly, without progressing any further. Quite suddenly he pulled his hand away from her, took her by the shoulders, and thrust her back a step or two.

When she looked at his face she saw, just for a moment, that it was averted and that it bore a look of pure disgust—not mere embarrassment as she had felt a moment before, but real disgust like a man who had just stepped barefoot in a chamberpot. She no longer felt warm; she was much colder than before, frozen in place. At once a mask covered his face, an apologetic one. "Forgive me, Esther. This was a bad idea, a terribly stupid idea—can you forgive me, forget I ever came here tonight?" He was buttoning up his breeches again, as quickly as he could.

"Forget this? Forget that you … you coerced me into playing the part of your wife and then put me aside? What are you, a madman? What is *wrong* with you?"

"That is exactly what I would like to know, Esther. What is wrong with me? I cannot—I would like to be as other men, but it seems I cannot. A man must be—well, I will not be indelicate, but a man must be ready to perform this act, and I cannot, it seems."

"I know what a man needs—do you take me for a fool just because I am a virgin? I can listen, I can read, I know what men and women do in bed. And I know any man can do what he must if the woman is the least bit attractive, or even if he imagines her to be so."

Jonathan was backing out of the room as he spoke. "That isn't so, Esther, you must not think this is anything to do with you. I am … I am not like other men. That is all I can say. I thought it might be different."

"Do you mean to tell me you have never bedded any woman?"

She watched him sharply and saw that he hesitated, but that might mean any one of a number of things. That he was lying, or that he was ashamed of the truth. Shame—it hung in the room like a bad smell. "No, never. No woman."

"Never? I thought every boy did it with a whore or a scullery maid."

He looked hurt, as though she had taunted him—and perhaps she had. "Not I, Esther. No whores, no scullery maids for me. I thought, only this once—I thought, as I told you, that this would make ours a real marriage. Not a public one, perhaps, but a true one."

"Our *marriage*—it is what it is. A promise, a mistake, call it what you will, but nothing we do now will make it into anything else. We have done our deed and we will live with it all our lives. Now I think you ought to go." She was amazed to find herself trembling with rage, barely able to keep her voice low. "Do not come to my bedchamber again, Dean Swift."

He paused a moment, then bowed. "I assure you, I will not trespass on your privacy again, Mrs. Johnson."

Esther listened to his steps, out through the common room, out the door. She counted seventeen footsteps before the door closed.

She blew out the candle and sat with her head in her hands. The headache she had been holding at bay for three days beat in on her with blinding force, arrows of white lightning shooting through her skull. Her chest tightened and she struggled for breath. She was angry—but that was only the top layer, the safest one. If Becca had come knocking at her door then, Esther would have raged that she wanted to be left alone—but Becca did not come.

She hurried across to Becca's little room, barely pausing to knock, and sat on her friend's bed. Becca was sitting up, reading by candlelight too. She put a hand on Esther's shoulder.

"He's gone, then."

"Yes, he has gone."

"Did he … is it … are you all right?"

Esther laughed through the pain in her throat. In only three tries Becca had found a safe question to ask. "I am all right," she announced, and began to sob.

She wanted to sit up, to hold herself together, but Becca's touch on her shoulder turned to a caress and she melted under the gentleness of that touch. She lay face down on the bed and let sobs shake her body, shutting out thoughts and questions, allowing only feeling. She felt Becca shift on the bed and then both hands were on her back, on her shoulders, massaging out all the tension and pain. Warm comforting words flowed past her ears, words whose content was less important than their presence, their kindly assurance.

"I don't know what I'd do without you, Becca, truly I don't," she said when her sobs had dwindled to tears.

"I could tear him limb from limb, I could indeed—I hate to see him hurt you," Becca said with unaccustomed fierceness. Esther laughed.

"There'll be no tearing up the dean, Becca—and he hasn't hurt me. He made a foolish mistake—we both did."

"'Twas that, all right," Becca said, meaning the marriage. Was it a mistake? Esther was no longer sure. Nor was she sure Jonathan hadn't hurt her. Something other than hurt was there—shame, she thought again. But it would be even more shaming to share that with Becca.

The fingers of pain wrapped themselves tighter around her head, and the pillows swam in front of her eyes. "My head hurts," she murmured, laying it down so Becca could move her plump fingers through Esther's hair, coaxing the pain away. She was growing warm again, warm enough to sleep under her friend's kindly touch.

"You stay here tonight," Becca said, but Esther was almost asleep already.

DUBLIN
1718

"Very nice penmanship, Jenny. Finish these lines up, now, and then go to Mrs. Dingley—she has work for you to do." Esther patted the girl's shoulder lightly as she moved away from the desk.

Esther and Becca were launched on their new project—the education of Jenny O'Dea. One of their previous Janes, Fiona O'Dea of Garden Lane, had come to Esther's door a few months earlier, weeping because her mother was dead, her brothers and sisters scattered, and her littlest sister, seven-year-old Jenny, consigned to the workhouse. Esther had taken Fiona to the workhouse to release the little girl, hoping to find a kind foster family to raise her, since Fiona and her young husband were unable to give her a home.

After years of doing charity work among Dublin's poor, Esther had heard many tales of the horrors of the workhouse, but nothing prepared her for the reality—the filth, the squalling untended infants, the drunken nurses who paid no attention to the dirty children at their feet. She brought Jenny to her own home that same night, and the little girl worked her way into the household so quickly that there was soon no talk of finding another home for her. Becca was fond of the child and pointed out that she could be trained for a good place in service. "Why, Esther, who'd know better than me and you how to train a lady's maid?"

The little girl had a warm and cheerful nature once she realized she was safe and cared for—though Mrs. Sally reported she had night terrors that made Esther wonder if the horrors of the workhouse would ever leave her memory. She took most of her meals in the kitchen with Mrs. Sally, Jane, and Rob, though sometimes, if no company was about, she shared a meal with Becca and Esther. She was Sally's charge throughout the morning, learning kitchen tasks or shadowing Jane while she cleaned the house. In the afternoon Esther tutored her in reading and writing, or Becca taught her sewing and needlework. On the evenings when they stayed at home and there was no company, Jenny sat with Becca and Esther by the fire, doing her needlework and, often as not, falling asleep on the settee as she had that first night.

"It does make a difference, a child in the house," Esther said, watching Jenny's swift flight down the stairs to deliver a message to Mrs. Sally.

"It makes all the difference in the world," Becca said firmly. "I don't know what we did before she came."

"Are my two old spinsters enjoying motherhood?" said Dean Swift, who had his feet stretched out before their fire that afternoon.

"You're one to talk," said Esther. She did not even shoot him a glance now, when he called her a spinster or himself a bachelor—so completely had two years swallowed up the memory of their marriage ceremony. After a little awkwardness at first, they had fallen quickly back into their usual pattern of friendship, a mixture of familiarity and distance to which only they knew the proportions. Just one thing had changed—in the old days, they had rarely been alone together, but now Swift went to almost awkward lengths to be sure they were never without the chaperonage of Becca or some other third party. Whether he feared Dublin's sharp-tongued gossip more now that they really did have a secret to hide, or whether he simply did not want to risk a private conversation, Esther didn't know.

"You fancy yourself a tutor now, and expect to find a little pearl of a scholar inside that unlikely red-headed oyster, do you?" said Swift, glancing at the books Esther had laid out for Jenny.

"Not at all, you mocker. But look at this—she writes a nice hand, a fair copy of mine," Esther said, passing him a sheet on which Jenny had reproduced a dozen sentences in Esther's handwriting. "Of course she hasn't the makings of a scholar, but she's picked up her letters and simple words quickly, and I think she will learn to read quite well."

"That's one up for you and one down for Gossip Doll, then," said Swift.

"Why, what did Dot Walls have to say about it?" Becca asked.

Esther glanced at the door to see if Jenny had returned; she was never sure how much the child understood of the adult conversation she overheard. "She said I would be driven mad trying to teach the simplest things to an Irish child, for none of them were any better than idiots when it came to learning to read and write English, and I'd be better leaving her to Sally to train as a scullery maid. She said it was impossible for an Irish street urchin to learn anything."

"Ah, so you have the pleasure of vindicating your beloved Irish while proving your not-so-beloved Mrs. Walls in the wrong," said Swift.

"Pleasure?" Esther stopped the retort that sprang to her tongue and paused to think. What *was* her pleasure in taking in this fosterling and training her for a better position than she was born to? "I suppose I have a weakness for playing the gracious lady," she admitted. "I've been accused of it often enough. And 'tis not just vanity—I truly do enjoy helping someone, making another person happy. And, yes, I suppose it is a pleasure to be a tutor—to have some hand in shaping a young mind. You'd know about that yourself."

"Indeed I would. Though only one of my attempts has proven an undisputed masterpiece," he replied with a little mock bow.

"Thank you for your flattery—I have nothing to complain of in my education."

Jenny was running up the stairs—Esther could hear her steps slowing to a more ladylike pace as she came down the hall. She came into the room as demurely as any foster mother could have wished, brushed by Becca's skirts and earned a pat on the cheek, and went to her desk to resume her copying.

"I believe I've found a buyer for your house," Swift said.

"You have? Who is it?"

"A Mr. Harris. He's been up to look at it, and I think I can get 250 pounds out of him for it. Which puts the lie to your suspicion that I was making you a kindly gift."

"Yes—I suppose." Esther sighed and looked down at her needlework. It was a relief to know the house would sell, a relief to know Swift's price had been fair and not simply generous. But she couldn't help feeling sad whenever she thought of Talbot's Castle in Trim. She had dreamed of that house so long, and been so exhilarated when, a year ago, she had purchased it for sixty pounds. A house of her own, at long last! She had spent the whole summer and fall hiring workmen to repair and rebuild, paint and plaster. Her image of what the house might be had run so far ahead of her resources, both physical and financial, that after six months of home ownership her pockets were drained and she was ill with exhaustion from constant trips up to Trim to oversee the work.

She had bought her dream house too late, she realized, not only because she no longer had the strength for such an endeavour, but because they now spent little time in Laracor and Trim. With Swift's deanery here in Dublin, there was no real reason for them to go there anymore, and their circle of country friends grew smaller and more remote. During those winter months while she lay sick in bed, Esther fought against the knowledge that she would have to let the house go. She would never own anything; she would die in rented rooms. It was not an easy thing to accept. But she was a sensible woman, she reminded herself. When Swift offered two hundred pounds for the house, she had to accept. "It's in much better shape than when you bought it," he said, when she weakly protested the price. "I'll find a buyer and make money on it." And so, it appeared, he had. But she really did not want to discuss it.

Swift excused himself a few minutes later; he would call for them later that evening, as they were all invited to Donnybrook for dinner and cards with the Stoytes. Esther went over to the desk to inspect Jenny's work. "You've done very well here; watch those letter *O*'s now, the loops need to be nice and round, like a row of rings. Go on downstairs now, and Mrs. Sally will give you your dinner. Send Jane up to us; Mrs. Dingley and I have to get dressed for our dinner party."

Jenny went to the door, then turned back, the urge to speak written plainly on her face. Finally she darted over to Becca, tugged her arm, and whispered in her ear.

Becca smiled. "We'll have to ask Mrs. Johnson, will we? Jenny says you promised she could watch next time you dressed for dinner—she says she'll have to see ladies getting dressed if she's going to be a lady's maid."

"Of course we ought not to neglect that part of your education," said Esther to Jenny. It was funny—Becca doted on the child and Sally adored her, yet her deepest hero worship was clearly reserved for Esther herself. "You may come up with Jane and watch me get dressed, and perhaps you can hold the pins while Mrs. Dingley fixes my hair. And you can help Mrs. Dingley get into her hoop, since the silly woman insists on the latest fashion, no matter how awkward or uncomfortable. Can you do that?"

"Oh yes, ma'am," said Jenny.

"Don't scoff, Hetty," Becca said, reaching for Jenny's hand. "You'll be ordering a hoop for your own petticoat by Christmas. There's no extra virtue in being three months late to adopt every style, you know. Come along, child."

DUBLIN
1721

"Look, there's Dr. Steevens's hospital. Isn't it coming along well?" said Esther, pointing to the imposing new building. She used walks with Jenny as opportunities to educate the child, and in this case Jenny's curiosity was rewarding: she stared up at the hospital and even craned her neck to look back at it once they were past.

"What are you so interested in?"

"Trying to see the pig lady," Jenny said.

"The what?"

"Sure you must have heard of the pig lady, Mrs. Johnson. It's Miss Steevens, the doctor's sister. A beggar woman put a curse on her mother, and when she was born she had the face of a pig. Everyone knows it."

Esther sighed. "That is gossip and superstition, Jenny. Miss Steevens does not have the face of a pig."

"Everyone says she does."

"What everyone says is not necessarily true."

"She wears a veil when she goes out visiting."

"A great many ladies wear veils, and they do not all have the faces of pigs. You will have to give up repeating gossip, you know, if you are to get a good position someday. Ladies don't like their servants to gossip."

"Yes, ma'am."

"And remember not to answer back when you're corrected by your elders."

"Yes, ma'am. Sorry, ma'am. Can we go down to the river, ma'am?"

"I suppose so—it's not far out of our way." Together they walked through the noisy, crowded streets to the Liffey. It wasn't a beautiful river—it certainly didn't smell very nice—but both Esther and Jenny liked to stand on the bridge and watch grey-green water flowing beneath them, laden with small boats that bumped and jostled one another to the yells of their drivers.

"I like living by the river," Jenny said.

"Why?"

"Because it goes somewhere. I want to go somewhere."

"Do you want to come to Wexford with Mrs. Dingley and me when we go next month?" They were off for another jaunt to the spa; Dingley's faith in the waters was greater than Esther's, perhaps because Esther's need was so much greater. She wished drinking from mineral springs would soothe the ache in her head or let her breathe freely, just for a day. What she really needed was the Fountain of Youth, which was not known to be located in Wexford.

"Yes, thank you, I'd like that very much," Jenny said, though it was obvious she had had her mind on broader horizons. After a moment she said, "Do you think I might ever go to England, Mrs. Johnson?"

Esther wrapped her cloak a little more tightly around her; the March wind off the water was hardly spring-like. "Come, let's go home—'tis cold out here. Yes, Jenny, I think you might well get to England, if you get a good place with a lady who enjoys travelling."

Jenny walked a little ahead, her sturdily booted feet skipping just slightly over the ruts and puddles in the road—not enough to earn a rebuke for running but enough to communicate that the prospect of travel excited her. It was impossible not to make comparisons, Esther thought—at the same age she had dreamed of going to France, and then across Europe and around the world, if she could find a way. The picture was so laden with memory—the bright little girl in the big house, raised above her natural station and aiming even higher. Esther knew she herself was probably as austere and forbidding in Jenny's eyes as Martha Giffard had seemed to little Hetty. Of course in this Dublin scene, the child was a penniless street orphan and the great lady was mistress only of a small rented townhouse: everything was brought down a notch on the social scale, as it were. But that had been true of her life from the moment she had set foot on Irish soil: it was hard to remember sometimes that she had lived in a house as grand as Moor Park. Even the homes of her richest Irish friends did not approach its remembered splendours.

That thought, though, brought satisfaction instead of disappointment, for when she opened the door of her house in Mary Street and followed Jenny inside, she was well satisfied with what she saw. Better to be mistress of a narrow three-storey townhouse than a servant in the greatest mansion in Ireland or England.

Her letters waited on the table in the hall; among many notes from friends were tradesmen's bills and the other burdens that went along with being her own mistress. One was a legal document and concerned some trouble she'd lately had with the manservant, Rob; he had got into a fight with three Englishmen one night when drunk. To everyone's surprise, including her own, Esther had not only decided to keep him on but had advanced the money for his hefty fine—out of his wages, of course. She had not been able to explain adequately to Becca why she sympathized with a drunken servant, but Becca voted always on the side of mercy and was happy to agree. The business was all done with now, save the paperwork; Esther scanned the letters and put them in her bag for later reading.

"You go sit down in the parlour, ma'am, and I'll just go down to the kitchen and bring you up a nice cup of coffee," Jenny said, taking Esther's cloak and cap from her, along with their parcels. Her serious solicitousness made Esther smile; Becca had taught Jenny something of her own concern for Esther's fragile health. She was not about to protest. After walking through Dublin's streets for an hour, she found the prospect of sitting with her feet up, sipping a cup of coffee, was quite welcome.

Becca was not in the parlour: no doubt she was down in the kitchen, harrying Mrs. Sally and Jane over the preparations for tonight. It was really quite a small party, but in their little house it would seem a crowd—the Stoytes, the Wallses, the Sheridans, Dr. Delany, Swift of course, and a few other friends—all coming around for dinner and the evening, to celebrate Esther's birthday. Her fortieth birthday.

Jenny reappeared, a coffee cup in one hand and the morning's letters in the other. "I've got to go downstairs, ma'am. Mrs. Dingley wants me to help, but she'll be up in a little bit, she says, to see if you need anything else."

Esther laughed. "You may tell Mrs. Dingley I'm not an invalid—not just at the moment, anyway—and the fact that it's my birthday doesn't entitle me to sit and be waited on all day. I'll be down myself to see if anything needs doing." Though she very much hoped it didn't; in fact she was exhausted and would have loved to be waited on.

Alone with her letters, she looked through them—not much of interest, save a note in Jonathan Swift's familiar hand. She flipped it open, then closed again. *Stella's Birthday, 1721.* Should she wait for Becca to come up so they could read it and laugh together, or should she read it first alone? His birthday poems were invariably flattering—indeed, the whole fact of having a poem written in one's honour was flattering in and of itself. When the first one had arrived on her birthday two years ago, she had pointed out that he'd been promising to write her a poem for almost thirty years and it was about time he paid. He had even remembered the name he had promised to give her so long ago—Stella. A star.

When she had opened that first poem, two years ago, Becca had been quick to criticize. "*Stella this day is thirty-four,*" she'd read. "Well! I like that! He knows perfectly well you're thirty-eight."

"He may not—he has a dreadful memory for dates," Esther had said. Then she'd smiled. "I think he did remember, though—see the next line? *We won't dispute a year or more.*"

"A year or four, more like it. And what about this: *Stella, be not troubled, although thy size and years have doubled, since first I saw thee at sixteen, the brightest virgin of the green*? Sixteen? You were nothing but a child when he first saw you, not much bigger than our Jenny is now!"

"My size has *certainly* not doubled since I was sixteen!" Esther protested.

"It has since you were eight."

"Becca, it's convention, it's poetry—the bit about being sixteen, I mean. It wouldn't sound poetic to say you'd first met a girl when she was a child of eight—it's not romantic. But really—my size has *not* doubled!"

That was his style—gentle mockery combined with sincere praise, but certainly no attempt to spare her feelings about growing old. He knew how women felt about things like wrinkles and grey hair—apparently he simply thought Esther, or Stella anyway, far above such concerns.

If only he knew! Esther resisted the impulse to look in the mirror; she knew exactly where the strands of grey were mingled in her dark hair and the precise location of every line around her eyes and on her neck. Was any woman, truly, ever beyond such concerns? And what about men? Did they hate getting old, looking old? They certainly never admitted it.

And now she had missed her chance to read this year's poem alone, for Becca was here, eager to know what was in her letters. "Another birthday poem, then?" she said. "I hope he got your age right this time!"

"I hope he did not," said Esther, and indeed he hadn't. This year she was credited with being thirty-six, and her face was *An angel's face, a little crack'd.* "He compares me to an inn," Esther reported, scanning the lines.

"An inn? And he's supposed to be a great poet? How are you like an inn, pray, Hetty?"

Esther was laughing herself by this time; she couldn't help it. "Apparently I'm like a good old inn that all the men still like to stop at because it's comfortable, even though newer inns are opening up all around. Those would be the beautiful young women, I suppose—oh, this is clever. *Nay, though the treacherous rascal Thomas, Hangs a new Angel two doors from us.* That's a poke at Dr. Sheridan and his new wife."

"Hmm. Some angel, she is!" sniffed Becca, who did not like Elizabeth Sheridan. To be fair, not many people liked the wife that silly, affable Thomas had chosen for himself: she was young and pretty in a hard, brassy kind of way, and she was certainly rich—but those were the end of her assets. She was so ill bred that it was difficult to tolerate her company, even for the sake of such a good friend as Tom Sheridan.

"Oh and look at this!" Becca always scanned Dean Swift's poetry with a keen eye for allusions to people she knew. "*Then who can think we'll quit the place, When Doll hangs out a newer face.* Dot Walls will eat him for supper—she thinks no one's noticed she's been laying the paint on an inch thick since *she* turned forty. And who's this *Cloe*?"

Esther sighed and snatched the poem back. "*Cloe* isn't anyone—it's just a name, a name they use in poetry for pretty young girls. And why should Mrs. Walls ever know what the dean wrote in my birthday poem, pray tell?"

"Because he'll read it tonight—of course he will. He'll get no wine until he reads."

"He's bought the wine himself, so I don't see how you can deny him."

"Hush, you. And get you up to bed, Hetty. 'Tis only four hours till everyone starts coming. You were out marketing this morning and you'll be up till all hours tonight: you'll never stand the strain if you don't rest. Go on, now, no arguments!" Becca made shooing motions with her hands, as if chasing a crowd of hens into their coop, but she laid a hand for the barest moment on Esther's cheek as she passed. No more words were needed.

I should be like Becca; she's the one who has found the Fountain of Youth, Esther thought as she settled into her pillow, her birthday poem still in her hands. Becca was … what, fifty-five? She had twice, no, three times Esther's energy, and was seldom sick a day. Jonathan was the same age, and though he was often sick and full of complaints, he still seemed to have boundless energy whenever he was well. While Esther, the youngest of them all, could not survive a morning of marketing and an evening visit with friends unless she took to her bed for the afternoon.

She thought again of Jenny on the bridge this morning, looking out at the grey Liffey and dreaming of the oceans beyond. What had happened to little Hetty's dreams? She had got as far as Ireland, and seen a good bit of that country, but that was all. No France, no far horizons—probably she would never even go back to England again. Money had been a problem, of course—and perhaps it had been a mistake to tie herself so closely to Becca, who hated to cross the water. Most of all, though, her body had betrayed her. Even if she had wealth and a travelling companion, how could she bear a long sea voyage, an unfamiliar climate, bone-jarring coach journeys and nights in strange inns? Just the thought of their journey to Wexford next month made her weary.

She held up the poem only a few inches from her nose, since she had left her spectacles on the table, and scanned the lines again. No, Jonathan was not one to gloss over the realities of growing older; wrinkles and grey hair were only small obstacles for his gigantic wit to leap over. *Then, Cloe, still go on to prate / Of thirty-six, and thirty-eight / Pursue thy trade of scandal picking / Thy hints that Stella is no chicken*. No sops to her poor wounded vanity here!

But he offered her what he always had—honest praise for what he honestly admired in her. *Breeding, humour, wit and sense*. That was what kept Stella surrounded by *crowding swains*, even at her advanced age. And poor Cloe, the beautiful young girl in the poem—Esther could not help attaching Hester Vanhomrigh's face to the name, though Miss Vanhomrigh herself must have been near thirty by now—Cloe was warned that no matter how long she held on to her youthful beauty, *No bloom of youth can ever blind / The cracks and wrinkles of your mind / All men of sense will pass your door / And crowd to Stella's at fourscore.* She remembered the words he had written so long ago: *Time takes off the lustre of virgins in all other eyes but mine.* They had been young when he had written that, but perhaps he had told the truth.

An idea was taking shape, slicing through even her fatigue. She wanted to write something in return, for she had never written a poem for him. She still wrote poetry whenever the fancy struck her; she showed a few of her pieces to Jonathan and a few more to Becca but kept most of them locked in her strong-box with her journal and her letters. A lady did not publish her poetry, but she secretly fancied a few of her poems were almost as good as a man might write—though not as good as Jonathan's, of course. But still, she could write him something like this—another birthday poem, perhaps, that would give her months to work at it. It would be a way to say the things that she could not say in ordinary conversation.

Just having the idea was not enough; words, phrases, rhymes began to crowd into her mind, and at last she turned over his poem and went to the table to get her spectacles, pen, and ink. Returning to bed, she started to scribble:

> *St. Patrick's Dean, your country's pride,*
> *My early and my only guide*

That would be a good start—he wasn't exactly her *only* guide, but he had been her most important mentor and the word *only* fitted nicely in there. Besides, a birthday poem ought to flatter the recipient a little.

When men began to call me fair,
You interposed your timely care;
You early taught me to despise
The ogling of a coxcomb's eyes.

She thought again of Will Tisdall, of his proposal and Swift's letter. Poor Will wasn't a coxcomb, not really—but he *had* thought her fair once. If her poem could flatter Swift, it could flatter herself as well.

She tried a few more lines, crossing out and rewriting in the margin, trying to capture the words that would tell him that if she really was still admired at forty, or even at eighty, she knew whom to thank.

Sad is the fate of female race
With no endowments but a face;
Before the thirtieth year of life,
A maid forlorn, or hated wife,
Stella to you, her tutor owes
That she has ne'er resembled those;
You taught how I might youth prolong
By knowing what was right and wrong;
How from my heart to bring supplies
Of lustre to my fading eyes …

Your lectures could my fancy fix
And I can please at thirty-six.
The sight of Cloe at fifteen
Coquetting, gives me not the spleen;
The idol now of every fool
Till time shall make their passions cool;

Then, tumbling down time's steepy hill,
While Stella holds her station still.

She read the lines over, smiling. There was more she wanted to say—but this was enough, for now, to capture the idea and some of the best lines on paper. She could work at it later. Was she giving him a bit too much credit? Perhaps so. But it was terrible to see those pitiful women—even some of her friends—who used paint and powder and fashion to hang on so desperately to a pretty face because it was all they had ever had. She well remembered preening in front of the glass as a girl at Moor Park—would she ever have had the sense to learn otherwise without Swift's tutelage? Certainly neither Becca nor her own mother had tried to tell her that a woman's mind was more valuable than her face could ever be.

The door creaked, and Esther quickly tried to hide her paper and pen. Too late. "What, reading? You'll pay for it tonight, if you don't rest," Becca said, shaking a finger at her. "And you shouldn't be straining your eyes."

"I was writing a poem," Esther admitted, laying the evidence aside.

"Even worse! I've told you before, if you want to write, let me take it down for you. Your poor eyes …"

"Becca, I can't, not with a poem. I don't mind dictating letters, but when I write poetry I have to have the pen in my own hand—I simply can't do it otherwise. I'm sorry, I know I should be resting, but I wanted to write something for the dean, to thank him for what he said in the birthday poem. It's not done yet—I think I'll wait till his birthday, anyway."

"That's not for another eight months; I don't see why you had to work at it today."

"Because when the words are there, I have to—oh, Becca, never mind. I can't explain."

Becca smiled and picked up the paper. "Can I read it?"

"Certainly—but remember, it's just the beginning. I have a lot more to do, and I'll rewrite some of that—"

"Hush." Becca scanned the page, smiling and even chuckling in a couple of places. "I don't know why the dean is supposed to be the great poet. Your poems are ten times better than his, any day."

"They are not."

"Well, they're certainly easier to understand. Plain talk, that's what I like, none of this business of saying a woman's an inn and an inn's a woman." She read a few more lines and laughed aloud. "So, you're thirty-six in this one too?"

Esther rolled her eyes. "It rhymes so well with *fix*—and *forty* wouldn't have fit the metre at all—"

"And if he's willing to call you thirty-six in his poem, why should you say any different?" Becca stood up, gathering paper, pen, and spectacles and putting them well out of reach on the table. "It's a grand poem, love, but it'll keep. Your poor head won't. Now go to sleep; I'll wake you in plenty of time to dress for dinner."

With the words pinned safely to paper, Esther felt more relaxed; weariness washed over her and she let her eyelids fall over her stinging eyes. It was so good to just rest ... to have someone else to worry about all the chores and business ... just to sleep ...

When Becca woke her, three hours later, Esther felt as if she were swimming up to the surface from the bottom of a deep, thick sea. Her head still pounded with pain and she groped for the cup of physick in Becca's hand, hoping it would dull the ache a little. If only she could stay here, just stay in bed—but it was her birthday, and all their friends were coming. She laid down the cup, took Becca's hand, and got slowly to her feet.

When her toilette was complete she dressed in her best green gown—a few years old, but Becca had done some alterations to make it more fashionable, and the petticoat beneath was one of the new hooped ones. She had finally given in to the craze for hoops, though this was a much smaller one than most ladies were wearing. It was a cursed style, heavy and awkward, but even the most virtuous, witty, and wise of women had to bow to fashion at some point or look a complete fool.

Becca had gone downstairs to welcome their guests; Jenny and Jane would both be serving tonight, and they were no doubt down in the kitchen receiving their orders from Mrs. Sally. Esther waited alone upstairs, listening to the faraway sounds of ladies and gentlemen arriving, laying aside their cloaks, chattering. Twelve to dinner—it would have bankrupted them if Jonathan had not insisted, as he always did, on paying for the meal as a birthday gift. They must have all been down there now—it was time for the guest of honour to make an entrance.

Her spirits were lifting already as she set foot on the stairs; she loved company. The very occasions that put the most strain on her weary body were the best balm for her spirit. The curls and pins Becca had put in her hair made her headache worse; half a dozen different perfumes crowding the air would make her lungs tighten so she had to fight for every breath; shimmering darts of pale light danced through her vision and made the faces swim before her, but despite it all she would not have missed this gathering. Their faces were upturned to her as she came down into the hallway: dear Jonathan, and sweet Catherine and her sister, foolish Tom and kind Dr. Delany.

She could not eat much at dinner, but the talk was excellent and she threw herself into that. Over dessert Becca persuaded Jonathan to recite Esther's birthday poem; he rose and did so, from memory, and everyone applauded. Then the women went up to the parlour while the men drank their port.

A card table was already set up for ombre; Esther took her seat there along with Mrs. Stoyte, Mrs. Walls, and Becca. Catherine, who did not care as much for cards as the others, sat down at the spinet and began to play.

Esther was grateful for ombre: she would have found this part of the evening dull otherwise, for she found the company of women alone rather trying. She joined the game with enthusiasm, hoping to win a few shillings before the men came up.

"You must be flattered, Mrs. Johnson, by that splendid poem the dean wrote for you," Mrs. Stoyte said as the cards were dealt.

"Yes, well, he was very kind," said Esther. It was hard to know how else to respond.

"He is certainly kinder to you than he is to most women," Mrs. Walls said. "Have you all read *The Progress of Beauty*? What a shocking description!"

A few of the ladies laughed: Dean Swift's poem about the young woman putting on her artificial beauty before appearing in public was certainly amusing—though hardly flattering to their sex. "But surely he means a woman of a certain type," Mrs. Stoyte said, "the sort of empty-headed young girl who only cares for fashion and admiration. Doesn't his poem about Mrs. Johnson make it quite clear that he admires women of intelligence and virtue?"

"Of course, as every sensible man should," Catherine agreed.

"Then there must be a great many senseless ones," said Becca with a sniff, taking a hearty snort from her snuffbox.

"But of course the dean has written good things about women before this," said Dot Walls, gazing at the cards in her hand with an expression so mild that it would have been hard to say whether she intended malice. "I know it hasn't been published, but surely everyone has read *Cadenus and Vanessa*. I'm sure the subject of *that* poem must be a woman of more than common virtues—to inspire such a great poem."

The song Catherine was playing ended just at that moment; Becca cleared her throat and laid down a card; Mrs. Stoyte jiggled her coffee cup in its saucer. Into the little well of silence Esther said, "I hardly know about that; the dean has already proven he can write well on any subject—even that of a broomstick!"

"How true!" said Mrs. Stoyte amid a swell of laughter—they had all read his broomstick poem—and the moment was saved. Esther looked up to meet Gossip Doll's eyes, but the latter looked down at her cards again. It was with no small relief Esther heard the men coming up the stairs a moment later.

The women's game ended with Esther seven shillings richer, and she and Mrs. Walls got up to allow Alderman Stoyte and Dean Swift to join the game. She always liked to go on playing once she'd won a little money, but it was her birthday party and she ought to mingle among her guests. She was feeling better than she had before dinner—not exactly well, but well enough to pretend she felt well.

An hour later she sat beside the fire talking to Tom Sheridan, Patrick Delany, Charles Ford, and Dillon Ashe, who had all drawn their chairs up around her. They had been talking about the poetry of Alexander Pope, but somehow the conversation had degenerated into nonsense and word games by the time Swift pulled up another chair to join them.

"May I join the crowding swains?" he asked Esther, and she smiled but did not blush, as he had probably wished her to. *See at her levee crowding swains, Whom Stella freely entertains,* he'd written in the birthday poem, and here they were. Four confirmed bachelors and one newly married man whose wife was absent, all laughing at Mrs. Johnson's jests.

"You ought to have heard her, Swift—she makes worse puns even than you do," wheezed Dr. Delany, who was still wiping away tears of laughter.

"Forgive me, I have sinned and must do pun-ance," Esther said, just for the fun of seeing him choke up again.

"Ah yes, pun-ance. Are you truly pun-itant, Mrs. Johnson?" Dr. Delany's bright eyes shone behind his spectacles.

"Indeed, sir, and I need a sympathetic clergyman to set my feet back on the path of grace. Have you a pun-ance in mind for me, Doctor?"

"Oh, indeed, I must give this some thought. Your punishment must involve sacrifice, forfeit, and loss—therefore I counsel you to be my partner in a game of cards against Dean Swift and Mrs. Dingley, for then you will surely suffer all three!"

Everyone laughed; Swift slapped his knee and said, "You've hit her soundly there, Delany, for nothing will make Mrs. Johnson suffer as much as to pair her with a poor card player!"

Esther stood up and swept a deep curtsy before Dr. Delany, holding out her hand. "The dean slanders you, Doctor, I am sure. Let us prove him wrong."

The doctor took her hand and led her over to the card table, where he proceeded to prove himself every bit as bad a player as he was rumoured to have been. Despite Esther's best effort they lost eight shillings to the dean and Becca.

"It seems my tribute to you was right, after all," Swift said as they finished the game. "*Stella freely entertains,* and puts her guests to small expense, and gets little for what she gives—so much so that she has finished this evening poorer than she started it!"

"Not at all, she is still seven shillings to the good, for I insist on paying the whole debt," said Dr. Delany, fishing through his pocket for eight shillings to give Swift. "Do not protest, Mrs. Johnson, you know quite well you would never have lost with a better partner, and I owe far more than eight shillings for the pleasure of your company this evening. And strangely, though my pocket is lighter, I think I am much richer than when I came in here tonight." He took her hand again and kissed it with a bow, and Esther returned him a smile without missing the sharp glance Swift gave her.

She remembered Swift's raised eyebrows when he had commented, a few days before, "Dr. Delany is certainly an ardent admirer of yours. I can scarcely get your name past my lips in conversation before he has attacked me with battalions of praise."

Becca stood behind her, saying farewell to their guests. "That man worships the ground you tread," she said in Esther's ear as Delany, last to leave, made his exit.

Esther started: she wondered, once in a while, if she and Becca had lived together so long that they actually could hear echoes of each other's thoughts. "Nonsense," she replied automatically.

"Have it your way, but 'tis not nonsense. I'd be a rich woman if I had a shilling for every time I heard someone say that Dr. Delany is head over ears in love with Mrs. Johnson but won't say a word out of respect for Dean Swift."

Esther turned. *That* really was news—were their friends actually talking about her affairs so freely? "You must be mistaken," she said. "Or rather, everyone who says such things must be." But she saw him again, a short, trim figure in a green waistcoat and an immaculate white wig, bending to kiss her hand, his eyes fixed on hers. All her friends laughed at her jests, told her she was witty, enjoyed her conversation—but did he laugh and enjoy just a little more? He was a kind, handsome, gentle-spirited man, and very clever—a few years younger than she, but it did not seem a great gap. So many years had passed since the possibility of a new romance had arisen that she felt a blush spreading across her cheeks, down her neck, and into the facings of her gown. Becca, watching her, gave a half smile and turned briskly away, picking up a candle as she started for the stairs.

"What a pity you've shut the door on all that," she said. "'Twould be easy enough to let him know you were interested and available—if only you were."

Esther stood alone in the hallway, listening to the creak and swish of Becca's hooped petticoat disappearing up the stairs, astounded at herself. For just a moment she had forgotten—completely forgotten—that five years ago she had gone through a marriage ceremony and was in fact the legal wife of Dean Swift. That embarrassing little ritual, hidden away among unmentioned memories, had been designed to shield her against exactly this moment. "All I want is for things to remain as they are," she heard her own voice telling Jonathan Swift, and so they had sealed it with a vow. Had she been an utter fool to think she might never wish for change?

She went slowly upstairs and got ready for bed. Jenny had brought the warming pan up to her bed and waited to help her out of her gown. The child was wide-eyed, as she always was after a party, from the splendours she had seen—a few middle-aged clerics and their wives, dressed in Dublin's best imitation of cheap London fashion, eating a passable dinner, playing cards and gossipping. Jenny was as awe filled as if she had visited court; remembering Garden Lane and the workhouse, Esther understood. Jenny would be a good little maid and probably would get a place in a nice house; she would see many such dinner parties, and perhaps someday she would accompany her mistress on a trip across the water to England and think every childhood dream had come true. It was not a bad accomplishment, to have lifted a child out of poverty to a place where she could, at least, have such dreams.

Esther read the order for Compline from the prayer book and then a passage from the Gospel of Luke. She no longer indulged herself by reading the works of mystics, and she did not go to pray alone in empty churches. But she tried to read the Scripture regularly, which she found comforting, though tonight she would sooner have forgotten her devotions and gone to sleep. She turned instead to a favourite passage, the tale of the woman with the issue of blood. Twelve years of suffering, of physicians who could not heal—and then, all in a moment, cured when her fingers grasped the hem of the Lord's garment in the crowd. How Esther envied the woman—so keenly that she could almost feel the touch of that homespun cloak in her hand. She closed the book and turned her thoughts toward prayer.

But even after her prayers were done, she lay awake a long time, thinking of Jenny's dreams and her own dreams, and of birthdays. She wanted to get up and go to Becca's room or to have Becca come into hers, for a few moments' talk and laughter that would erase the sting of malice in Becca's last comments. Becca had always been against the marriage to Jonathan; she had assured Esther it would bring her grief and now she seemed almost glad it was. *Was* it bringing grief? No, that was too strong a word. Esther was not, after all, in love with Dr. Delany, and she would take great care to make sure she did not fall in love with him. A moment's regret, perhaps, like the regret she had felt earlier that day looking out at the Liffey and knowing she would never see France, or what she had felt when she sold Talbot's Castle.

"You've shut that door," Becca had said, but if she listened closely, she could hear doors closing all around: that was the way of life. You could not walk down one corridor without leaving others, and Esther, calling up Becca's image to argue with instead of going down the hall to her friend's chamber, said, "I've closed a few doors, too, by living with you all my life—everyone has to make choices."

She was forty years old, and her life had been made by her choices. They had won her a life of comfort, friends, and work, and she was not displeased. Her headache had slipped far enough into the background for her to fall asleep, and she closed her eyes at last, drifting down to dreams.

Part Three

DUBLIN

1723–1728

DUBLIN
1723

Wax candles burned on the table in Esther's room. She sat alone, wearing her nightdress and her spectacles. Her day's work—a pile of poems she was transcribing for Jonathan, and a poem of her own she was trying to finish—was pushed to the edge of the table. She no longer tried to read or write late in the day, much less at night: candlelight was too hard on her eyes. But she was reading after dark now. All night she had spent searching the pages of her old journals, reading her own story as one might count back through the rows of needle-work, looking for the missed stitch that had thrown off the whole pattern.

Now she laid aside the last journal and picked up the letter again. This letter had had been dropped through her door by some passing hand, carried up to her room by Jane, unsealed and opened like Pandora's box to wreak its havoc on Esther's peace-ful, ordered world. She had scanned it four times, the cold stone in her heart growing hotter each time. She read it once more, wondering if the other woman's words would sound different now that she had read so many of her own.

My dear Mrs Johnson,

You will forgive my writing to you, whome I have never seen but whose virtues I have heard so highly prays'd. I think you must be a veritable Saint among Women, nott subject to the weaknesses and faylings all the rest of us are prey to, most commonly, the weakenesse of Love.

I think you knowe well what mutual Friend has spoken so highly of you, for I cannot imagine you doe not know his regard for you. Dean Swift speakes of you as his Oldest and Dearest Friend, and more like a Sister to him than even his Natural sister.

What you have heard of me, I doe not know, for unlike you I do nott know in what regard our Friend holds me; his Conduct to me has beene so uneven, these many yeares of our Acquaintance.

Forgive me, I write in haste and confusion, my mind is nott clear, I am much distress'd. I feele Death is near, I cannot beare the burden of my loathed life much Longer, but I have businesse I must attend to before I can lett go the Threads of my Existence.

The Dean said once to me that he ever feared the tattle of this nasty town, and a Nasty towne it is for gossip too, for I have heard such stories I dare not repeat. But I have heard a thousand times that you and Dean Swift are lovers, or that you are secretly marry'd, that you are truly his wife but that you will not own it in public, or that he will not, or I knowe nott what. These tales distress me, they bring me grief, and I must know the Truth of the matter.

To me Dean Swift has never represented you as anything other than what I say'd already, his Oldest and Dearest companion, but never as a Lover. That role, he once assur'd

*me, was reserv'd for Me alone, though in other moods he has
told me he cannot love any woman. But I knowe he loved
me, though he has Cast me Off now, and the token of our
love is that most common love token of all—a child.*

*The child is seven years old now, may God forgive me,
and he is the son of myself and Dean Swift, which I can
sweare true for I have neither known nor loved any other
Man in all my existence, as I truly love Him, mye Heart's
only Desire.*

*Our child is foster'd with an Irish family and has their
name, M'Loghlin, his Christian name is Bryan, and the
Dean will never acknowledge him, says his Career would
be ruin'd if he did. I have pay'd the M'Loghlins for the
child's keep and visited him. I doe not suppose I have been
the Mother I ought to have beene to him, but now that life
is slipping from me I want to Commend him to the Care
of one whom I knowe is kind and charitable, and as an
old friend of the Dean's, will care for that which is His,
though he will not own it. I beg you, Mrs Johnson, if you
are the woman that Dean Swift and reputation have
painted you to bee, please see to this child, that he is cared
for after my death. I consider nothing else but that
Cadenus, my one true love, might shed one Tear for me
when I am Gone.*

> *Farewell,*
> *Hester Vanhomrigh*

Esther crumpled the letter automatically as she came to the
signature, then unfolded and smoothed it again. This was reflex
by now: she had done the same thing after each reading till the
page was as creased and crossed as a crone's face.

So many emotions sparred inside her—but one she hung on to, one that kept out the clamour of the others, was contempt. The overblown phrases, the shrill edge of hysteria behind the words, the image of a woman so obviously in love with her own tragedy—it made Esther want to spit. She pictured the pretty dark-haired girl she had seen in the street seven years ago—was she even then carrying Jonathan's child?—pictured her in a dark room, writing by candlelight as Esther was reading by it, the dim light turning the hollows under her eyes to a grotesque mask of melancholy as she wept, shouted, poured all her tawdry emotions onto this piece of paper for a complete stranger to read. Rumour had it that Miss Vanhomrigh was very ill and had become almost a recluse in her house at Celbridge. Nastier rumour said she had taken to drink.

The tattle of this nasty town. Yes, that was Dublin, all right, and that was Swift, ever wary of talk. Rumour said Esther Johnson and Dean Swift were lovers, were even, perhaps, secretly married. Rumour had such an odd way of being right and wrong at once.

Esther's vision blurred; pain lanced through her head from temple to temple. Around her, the house was utterly silent. Becca had gone out earlier in the evening, visiting the Wallses, and come home to bed, not guessing that Esther was still awake. The maid had returned home for the night; Mrs. Sally was abed downstairs, as were Rob and Kevin. Kevin, Rob's nephew, was their second foster child; his parents had died of plague a year ago, and Esther and Becca had offered at once to take the little boy into their home. He was learning a manservant's work from Rob and was a cheerful presence in the house, compensating a little for the loss of Jenny. Jenny had gone to stay with her sister Fiona, who was having yet another baby; when she turned thirteen she was going into service with Esther's friend Lady Eustace.

There had been no question of Esther's going out with Becca tonight. Esther had been ill for five weeks, leaving her bed for only a few hours a day this past week. Becca would have been furious to come home and find her out of bed, reading. Esther finished smoothing the letter beneath her hands and began to read it a fifth time.

The words had ceased to have any meaning; they had become dark marks on white paper, nothing more. Esther put her head in her hands. She was ashamed of everything she had ever done or thought: ashamed that Dublin gossips spoke of her; ashamed that she had done the very thing they charged her with, married a man who could never, would never, love her; ashamed that somehow, in some way, she had allowed herself to love him. For this had to be love, no matter how she had tricked it out in the name of friendship or sisterhood all these years. Why else was she furious when she saw herself named as his oldest friend, a sister to him—if that was all she'd wanted to be? Why was she horrified and betrayed to learn he had lain with this pathetic Vanhomrigh woman, that he had got a child on her?

Her breath wheezed into her lungs and came out in a tearing, rasping cough—the same cough that had pinned her to her bed all these weeks. The spasms tore at her chest. Every bone, every joint ached, whether she was coughing or not. Even between illnesses, she was never really well anymore.

She saw now that she had loved him, she must have, a love twisted and denied but love nonetheless—and that it had been founded, from the very beginning, on a lie. Everything he had ever told her was a lie. She had built her life—her pleasant, proper, orderly life—on lies, lies, lies. If Jonathan Swift stood in front of her right now, and she had in her hand the pistol she had shot the robber with so many long years ago, she knew with certainty she could steady her hand long enough to shoot him through the heart.

She looked not at the paper but at her hands lying on top of it: they were thin, the fingers brittle, covered in skin that had begun to wear and wrinkle like old parchment. Was it only two years ago she had turned forty and moaned about growing older? She was ten, no, twenty years older now than she had been then, when she had hosted her party and played the flirt with Dr. Delany and half a dozen other men. In the past two years she had spent as many days in her bed as out of it. Her hair was iron-grey now; there was no trace of black. She was so gaunt that the gowns she had worn then hung off her like those shapeless sacque dresses from France that were all the fashion these days. She glanced in the mirror, and away. How quickly, quickly it had happened.

Between her fingers, the words peered out. *I am much distress'd ... I feel Death is near.* A woman writing alone, by candlelight. She hated and pitied Hester Vanhomrigh, but how much they had in common. The other Hester, her shadow self.

Trembling, her knees shaking beneath her, she turned away from the letter and back to the pile of journals and paper she had pulled from her strongbox. Earlier, when she had taken it out, driven by her need to search the past, the pile of paper had seemed huge. Now that she had read through it all, she saw it was actually very little. For one who had played with and dealt in words all her life, she had not so very many of them to leave behind. Yet here among them, here in her past, had to be the answer to how she had gone so terribly wrong, how she had let herself love the man she had been so sure she did not love.

She had to stop using the word *love*. It had no meaning, it was an empty vessel into which anyone could pour whatever liquid she wished. There was a precise word for what she had built her life on, for this bond she shared with the man who had lied about everything. But all her frantic search through the past had not revealed the word to her.

Grey dawn crept into the room. Esther sat shivering, turning pages, though she could scarcely make out the words. Tears streamed from her eyes: whether from emotion, or from blinding pain, she could no longer tell. In the last hours she had travelled from Moor Park to Ireland, back and back again, from Laracor to Dublin, from youth to middle age, to the doorstep of old age. And she knew nothing more than she had known before.

A light tap came at the door; Becca appeared with coffee at about this hour every morning. Esther tried to say "Come in," but no sound emerged from her dry throat. A moment later, the door edged open a few inches. Becca looked first at the bed, then, startled to see it empty, turned to the table where Esther sat.

"Hetty! What are you about? You should not be up so early!" Then, when Esther did not answer, she approached, saw the wreckage of papers. "What is this? What have you been doing? My dear, you're shaking. Get you back to bed!" She set down the coffee atop a precarious pile of letters and wrapped a shawl around Esther's shoulders. And Esther, too exhausted to protest, let herself be chided and bundled back into bed.

She drifted into an uneasy sleep, plagued by dreams. She thought perhaps Becca came again to check on her, or to sit beside her for a while, but she could not be sure. After what seemed a long time, when the light lay differently across the room, she woke up a little more clear-headed. Jane was at the door. "Mrs. Johnson, ma'am, Dean Swift is downstairs, and Mrs. Dingley is gone out to the market. I'll tell him you're not well, shall I?"

"Yes—no, Jane, no. Tell him ... tell him to wait."

"Are you ... sure, ma'am?" Jane no doubt had strict orders from Becca not to let Esther out of bed; it was hard on the poor girl when her mistresses were at cross purposes.

"I'm ... quite sure, Jane. Tell him I shall be down."

"Do you need help to dress, ma'am?"

"No thank you, no help." She did need help, she realized, as she heard Jane's light footsteps going down the stairs. Her fingers shook and a cough bent her double as she took off her night-dress. She couldn't lace her stays on her own, or put on a hoop. Well, hoops and stays be damned. She found an old petticoat and a gown to go over it, and awkwardly pushed a few pins through her hair. None of this mattered. The letter mattered—she had to find it—it was here, somewhere, under everything, underneath her whole life ... Hester Vanhomrigh's pitiful little letter.

Swift was pacing in the front parlour. He looked startled when he saw her; she had never before appeared looking dishevelled, even when ill.

"Poor poppet, you ought not to have come down! Jane said you were not well—this could have waited." He waved the sheaf of papers in his hand. "'Tis only a new batch of poems and another bit of foolishness about Brobdingnag—I've half a mind to give that tale up altogether, as I am so full of ideas but I cannot think what to do with them, how to piece them all together. I thought if you read it, you might be able to suggest—but no, you should not be working over my papers now anyway, straining your poor little eyes."

She stood still in the middle of the room, staring at him, hearing the endearments fall so readily from his lips, wondering what, if anything, they meant to him. Then she handed him Miss Vanhomrigh's letter.

"I came down to show you this," she said, putting all the strength she had into making her voice clear and steady. "It arrived at my door yesterday evening."

He unfolded it, frowning a little, but when he saw the handwriting he recoiled as if a scorpion had sprung out of the paper. He looked sharply up at her.

"Where—how—who—"

"I told you, it was delivered to my door. Read it."

Shaking his head, he did so, and his frown deepened with every line till his expression, so often dark with anger and indignation, turned more bitter than she had ever seen it. She knew she was not the target of his anger, but even so it frightened her.

"This—how *dare* the trollop write such things to you! I'll have the bitch flogged for daring to write this—I'll—"

"Has she written lies?" Esther asked through his sputtering.

Swift himself did not lie well; her question caught him in the middle of his rage, and he looked blankly at her. She felt another twinge of pity for her rival, who had spent so much love on a man who treated her with such contempt.

"Is it true?" she asked again.

"True? True? She writes out of a fevered, obsessed, drunken mind, Esther. She doesn't know what's true and what's not. She imagines herself in love with me, always has, for years now, and I—"

"Then it's a lie. You never loved her, never lay with her, she never bore you a child. There is no child." Esther kept her arms wrapped around herself, tightly around her own waist as though to hold herself together.

Swift said nothing, shaking his head. Their eyes locked and held until finally he was the one to drop his gaze. "She is right about that. There is a child."

"Your child. Yours and hers."

"Yes."

"You lay with her." *As you could not—would not—with me,* she reminded herself.

Swift said nothing.

"You lied to me when you said you had never known another woman. You lied when you said she meant nothing to you. You lied when you said you had never wished to marry anyone but me. You broke the vows we made, to take no other and keep true only to each other. You lied, lied about *everything*." Only on the last word did her voice quaver a little, the last syllable breaking a little shrilly. It was enough to pierce his silence, to send words tumbling out one after another in desperate pleading.

"Esther, please, listen to me, it was not as you think. She was— yes, I lied about some things. How could I tell you, my dearest, my only true friend, that I was in love with another woman? Yes, I was in love with her—love of the kind all of us dream of in our youth—a madness, a fire in the blood, something dark and dangerous and—Don't wish for love, Esther; it is a terrible thing, it will destroy you. It has destroyed her, nearly destroyed me. If not for you—if not for you, I would be destroyed too. You are all my sanity, all I have clung to. You are my rock; you saved me. She was ... a temptress, a succubus, a—"

He was babbling; she had to stop this. "You married me to protect yourself from her."

"No, no, I married you because—Esther, I was a fool, a fool to do what I did. And when I told you I could not—that I was not as a normal man should be with a woman, that was truth. Even with her, even when I loved her, she urged me into her bed but I could not—"

"You got a child on her."

"Yes—poor child, worse luck for him, for all of us! I lay with her, a few poor times—God, how it shames me to tell you this, Esther—but even when I wrote that poem for her, when I imagined myself in love with her, I never was ... in love with her body. I do not know how ... why, men are so in love with women's bodies, I—I cannot understand it. I never wanted—"

"I have heard enough of this," Esther said, suddenly feeling as though she was far away, out of this room, speaking across a great distance. "Go away, Dean Swift. I have nothing more to say to you."

"Esther, no, please—you mustn't let this poor, twisted woman—her bitterness—it must not ruin everything—"

"Miss Vanhomrigh has ruined nothing for me—nothing of any value. I am not angry at her. Good day."

He stood for a moment as if he was about to make another plea, then said harshly, "You are being a fool, Esther," and turned to go. Before he reached the door, he addressed her again. "I must tell you one thing—I have never dishonoured my vows. After you and I were ... wed ... I never—"

Esther walked into the rear parlour, slowly, her back to him. She stood at the window, looking out at nothing, until his words ran out and she heard him go downstairs. A moment later, the door closed, not quite heavily enough to be a slam but enough so that, she imagined, the pictures in the downstairs hallway stirred a little.

Esther went to the settee and sank down on it, her legs buckling underneath her. She was going to be sick and did not have enough strength left even to call Jane for a basin. Shaking, she retched, soiling her old gown, the settee, the carpet. Even afterwards she could not move. She sat, cold and still as stone, her head in her hands.

A long time later, she heard Becca's voice, and a man's. *Go away, Jonathan Swift,* she told him in her mind. But Becca, yes, she wanted to see Becca. Needed her. Her voice, and the man's, came closer and closer. "Hetty, you'll never guess who I met at the market, and who insisted on following me home—Hetty, are you all right?"

A rustle of skirts, and Becca was beside her, kneeling, putting soft hands around her face, murmuring. The man was kneeling too: to her aching eyes he was a blur of wig, waistcoat and breeches, but she vaguely registered that he was shorter and slighter than Swift—someone else, then, someone she ought to know. Becca's hands felt cool, so cool on her face. They were lifting her off the settee, up the stairs to her bed. This man, whoever he was, ought not to see her bedchamber. But she could not think of the words to explain that to Becca.

She drank something; time passed. The world grew no clearer. She still felt cold, distant, immobile. She could not see clearly, but she could hear Becca's voice. "She needs to be away from here, out in the country—perhaps then she will recover. We had a letter—Charles Ford sent us a letter just today, inviting us to Wood Park. I thought we might go in a fortnight or so—"

"He would welcome you now, or any day. I can arrange for a carriage—"

"Oh, dear Dr. Delany, would you? It wouldn't take me long to pack our belongings—"

"Send a message to Ford. We must get Mrs. Johnson out to the country—the rest will do her a world of good. She is getting no better here."

"I fancy she is worse. I thought she was recovering, until today—"

Their voices layered over each other, blending like threads in a tapestry until the individual stitches were invisible and only a bright-coloured blur of compassion and concern surrounded Esther as she closed her eyes and drifted again into sleep.

WOOD PARK
MAY 15, 1723

Today finds me sitting up at the table in my room here, wrapped in a dozen blankets, writing with a hand that trembles so I can barely see the lines before me. It is the first time I have sat up since I came here, three weeks since. I have beene in such ill health they have had Dr Grattan to see me, and he declar'd he despaired of saving me. Yet my Life has been preserved a little longer, for whatever Purpose I know nott, and now the Doctor saies I am recovering.

Outside my window the sun shines down on the beauties of Wood Park, its gardens and its hills, the loveliest place in Ireland, I think. Sometimes, these past weeks, I thought I would die here, and I reckoned it not a bad Place to die, nor in a bad way, surrounded by so many dear Friends. Don Carlos has offer'd me every kindesse, Becca has scarce left my side, Doctor Delany has visited three times, and a score of other friends have sent letters almost daily, which Becca dutifully reads out to me. All but one friend, who never Writes or Visits. I wonder shall I ever see him again.

Nobody, save Becca, to whome I have told nearly all the Story, nobody knowes what happened betweene the Dean and myselfe, yett no one speakes his name to me. His absence does not leave such a Gap as I might have suppos'd—it is as though, until he had gone, I did not fully notice how many other Friends and Supporters I have. Yett I long to heare his voice, his laughter, that is so Familiar to me these many years. I suppose I have been a fool for Love after all, tho' I have sought so Diligently not to be caught in Cupid's snares.

But not such a fool as She who shares my name. A Name we may share, but not a fate. I am the stronger. I am sure of that. It is almost all I am sure of now.

No—having come so near Death, I must lift mye thoughts higher. I am sure of God and Heaven, and ought to place my faith more in Him and less in weak earthly friends, and in my owne Strength. For have I nott been showne the frailty of both? I must pray more, meditate on what is good and Holy. No good can come of the things of this world.

I am very tired, I can write no more. The words dance on the page before me.

WOOD PARK
MAY 25, 1723

I read over this last that I have writ here, and laugh—for I have the strength to laugh now. How readily I turn to God when all else—health, strength, love, friendship—seems to have deserted me, and how quickly I forget my resolutions once I feel well againe! How He must shake His head at foolish Esther Johnson. But I no longer think him as Harsh, as once I did. I beleeve now He is as Longsuffering as the Scripture says, and a good thing for his Poore child Esther, for I am sure I try His patience very greatly!

My illnesse has crawl'd away againe, like an ill-mannered cur that will not leave me quite alone, but will slink away to the shadows till his next chance to attack. I am no longer keeping to my bed, but can manage being up all day with only a short rest in the afternoone, provided I sleep well at night, which I doe, most nights.

I know that I am not "well" as I once would have thought it—I shall never againe know the rude health of youth, but count myself well when I have only a few aches and paines, when I can carry on Conversation despite the pain in my Head, when I can—

"Come, Mrs. Johnson, you will strain your eyes!"

Esther started, and made a vague motion as if to push away her paper, to deny she had been writing. Her host, Charles Ford, stood in the doorway, his long shadow reaching almost to the edge of her writing table. He was dressed for riding—a surprise, since until this summer she had not known him to be very fond of riding. "This will never do," he went on, striding over to her. "Your prescription is complete rest, tempered with a little mild exercise on a warm, sunny day. Also pleasant company and good conversation. All of which will be amply supplied if you come for a ride with me."

She rose from the table, smiling in spite of the pain that shot from her knees up her back. A ride would be a terrible jolt to her sore joints—but so exhilarating for her spirit, so refreshing to lungs that had breathed little but sickroom air for almost three months. "You are a most conceited physician, Dr. Don Carlos."

"Have you even known any other kind?" he said. "I brook no refusals from my patients—you have a quarter hour to dress, then meet me on the terrace."

"A quarter hour to put on my riding costume! 'Tis no trouble to know you're a bachelor. I shall meet you in a half-hour, no less."

"Women!" Ford rolled his eyes, turned and left.

"Becca, come help me dress—Don Carlos is taking me riding," Esther called down the passage between their rooms. Her thoughts skipped away from Becca's automatic flood of protests and worries and back to their friend Don Carlos. He had been more than generous, taking her, Becca, and their servants into his home at Wood Park for as long as Esther might need to recover—and longer, he assured her. There was to be no question of returning to Dublin until she had fully recovered and enjoyed a pleasant visit afterwards.

Even her recuperation, after those first few hazy weeks, had had much of the pleasant visit about it. Ford was the most affable of companions—a generous-spirited, sanguine man who used his riches to surround himself with all that was pleasant—a lovely house, good servants, fine wines, good food, brilliant men, beautiful women. Well, to be fair, some of the women were brilliant as well—Esther thought of the would-be poetess, Mrs. Barber, who had visited a fortnight ago. Esther did not particularly like Mrs. Barber's bold, self-assured manner and thought the idea of a woman publishing her poems was ridiculous, but she had to scramble to keep pace with Mrs. Barber's intelligence as she had never had to do with any other woman. She had been glad to have her illness as an excuse for slow wits.

When she joined Ford on the terrace, he offered his arm and led her down to the stables. Ford was no great horseman, but his stables, like everything else at Wood Park, were excellent. Esther chose a gentle grey mare over the more spirited horse she had ridden on previous visits. Ford rode a black gelding. Mounted, he cut a finer figure than he did on foot: his short stature was less noticeable than his gorgeous clothes and impeccable white wig. His features were strong; ruddy skin, brown eyes and dark brows suggested dark hair beneath his wig. On the black horse, his cloak blowing behind him in the wind, he looked almost like the "Don Carlos" that Esther and Swift had christened him in jest long ago.

"It's grand to see you looking so well; you had us very frightened," he said as they rode away from his stables into the rolling emerald hills surrounding Wood Park. Summer would soon be here; Esther had no memory of this year's spring.

"You ought to know by now that I always recover," she said lightly. "I've been so often at Death's door that I have a spot worn on his front step, but he will not let me in."

"Nor any of us, I suppose, till our hour comes. But who knows when that will be?" He kept his horse reined to a slow walk, to keep pace with hers. "I visited yesterday with a lady who is sitting on that same doorstep, but I think for her the door will swing open. It is no surprise, for she is at the knocker, begging to be let in."

"Poor soul! Who is she?" Esther knew Ford had been away visiting for a couple of days but did not know where.

"Hester Vanhomrigh," said Ford, looking down the valley toward the cottages of his tenant farmers.

Charles Ford was a lighthearted cynic, but he was no fool. Everyone in Dublin knew that Dean Swift's two closest women friends were no friends of each other. Ford had not mentioned Miss Vanhomrigh by accident.

Esther tried to think of something polite to say. "Is she really so very ill?"

"I do not think she will recover."

"You sound sad."

"I am. She is my friend."

Esther's back bothered her already from sitting on the mare, yet her heels itched to dig into the horse's sides, to urge her into a canter. "Is she such a fascinating companion? I would not have thought so, from what I have heard of her."

Ford cast her a sideways glance as they passed under the overhanging branches of a row of elms. "Do not waste your venom on poor Hessy. She is a sick, miserable, unhappy creature whose only comfort these days comes from a wine bottle."

So it was true that she was a drunkard. Esther sniffed. It was unfortunate when a man turned to drink; in a woman it was disgusting. "Venus must not be so proud of her Vanessa now."

Ford was riding a little ahead, but she could guess the

expression on his face from the way he lifted his shoulders. "Pardon me," Esther said. "I am always resolving to be more charitable and less critical, but I find it no easier the older I get."

Charles Ford slowed his horse again to wait for her at the other side of a small bridge. "No, I have never agreed with the common belief that virtue accompanies old age. I have too many disagreeable old relatives, I suppose."

Esther said nothing: there were questions she would have liked to ask about Miss Vanhomrigh, but she could not think of a way to phrase them without some loss to her own dignity. It was Ford who broke the silence. "She is more like you than you guess."

"Like me?"

"When she met Dean Swift, she was a bright, pretty young girl, just as you were at Sir William Temple's house long ago. He took on the role of tutor with her, as he did with you. But in your case it ripened into a true friendship, perhaps the best friendship between man and woman I have ever seen. With her it became … something else."

"Love," said Esther.

"Whatever you choose to mean by that much-abused word, yes. On her side first, but eventually on his too, it became true, devoted, passionate love. Poor devils."

The bleating of goats—or could they be children?—came faintly from a tiny, tumbledown cottage at the roadside. A woman walked to the cottage from a well, her back bent almost double under the weight of two great buckets of water. "You are very cynical about love."

"Have you ever fallen in love, Mrs. Johnson? A grand, all-consuming passion?"

She remembered Will Tisdall's mouth on hers, her hands pushing him away. She remembered the same hands, the same night, holding a pistol. Shooting a man. She was what she had chosen to be—a woman alone. "No—I have not," she replied. "I dreamed of romance when I was a girl—but that sort of love never came to me."

"Count yourself lucky. I fell in love once—many years ago."

"How did it end?"

"The way true, devoted, passionate love always does—horribly. Badly. With everyone hurt. And that, you see, is what has happened to Dean Swift and Miss Vanhomrigh. Long ago, he fell out of love, as one person always will in time. And then the other person is sealed in a self-made tomb forever—something poor Hessy Vanhomrigh has handled with even less grace than most of us do."

Over there, in the field, must have been the farm woman's husband—a wizened creature digging in the dirt. No doubt they worried little about true, passionate love. Perhaps they were the wiser. Esther did not inform Charles Ford that there were many kinds of love, not only the love that burned up in a sudden, all-consuming blaze but a love that grew slowly, like a harmless garden plant, and thickened and lengthened and strengthened with the years until it wrapped around you tight enough to choke. He was right—it always ended badly.

"From all I hear, she has certainly made a fool of herself."

"As I said, she is to be pitied. Surely you can find it in a heart as large as yours to pity her."

Esther couldn't, in fact. Perhaps her heart was not as large as her friends assumed it was.

"You are right, of course. I do pity her," she lied. A donkey brayed behind a stone wall.

"She sent me a letter," said Esther after a pause.

"Oh?"

"Yes." She would not tell him more than this; the existence of Bryan M'Loghlin was not her secret to reveal, whether or not Ford knew it already.

"I don't mean to pry, but did you show it to Swift?"

"I gave it to him, yes."

"Ah. That explains the letter."

"What do you mean?"

Ford reined in his horse. "Are you tiring? We can turn back if you like."

"Yes, please. It's the first time I've ridden in months."

They returned along the road they had come. "Hessy told me something about a letter—she said that Swift came to Celbridge, stormed into the house, threw a letter onto the table in front of her and stormed out. I asked what was in the letter, but she wouldn't say. She hasn't heard a word from him since."

"Neither have I," Esther pointed out.

"Then I am more—or less—fortunate than both of you. Only today a letter came from him. He plans to leave Dublin, leave this part of the country altogether, and go on a grand tour of Ireland. Already he boasts of how many miles he will ride each day."

"He always has believed exercise is the cure for everything."

"Even wounded hearts and wounded pride, apparently. At any rate, he asked in his letter whether I had any news of you. He didn't even know you were staying here." They rode in silence for several minutes, then Ford said, "What should I tell him?"

"Why, the truth, of course. I have no reason to hide from Dean Swift the fact that I am staying at Wood Park."

"And that you have been very ill, but are out of danger now?"

"And that I am keeping well, and do not know when I will return to Dublin since I have such a congenial host here, and

I am receiving visits from friends all the time, and riding, and resting my eyes. Tell him all that, if you wish—it's no matter to me."

"What if he asks would you receive a visit from another friend? If he wishes to come here, when he returns from his tour?"

Esther sighed. Her backside was hurting now; and so was her back, her neck and her shoulders. She shrugged. "I would not turn him away if he came." She had been angry once, but she had not the energy left for it now. They had been friends all her life. If he wanted to come back and try to salvage that friendship, so be it. She would not fight him any longer—nor would she trust him. Then she thought of something, "Will he not stay, if Miss Vanhomrigh is really dying? Have you written to tell him that?"

Ford frowned. "I am writing tonight, and I will tell him. I promised her I would. She wants him to go to her. What I did not tell her is that I am quite sure he will not go."

Hours later, Esther sat playing piquet with Don Carlos in the Green Parlour. At the next table Becca played with Dr. Delany, who was visiting again. Out in the garden, Esther's foster child Kevin was playing with the housekeeper's son. Their shrieks— apparently they were trying to incarcerate a frog they had captured—drifted up through the summer evening air.

When her game ended., Esther walked to the patio doors and looked out. She could see glimpses of the lads playing in the long shadows, in and out among the willows. They were wrestling now. Kevin was a fine strong boy; Rob said he had the makings of a good worker, and he loved and understood horses as no boy his age she had ever seen. They would find a good place for him in a few years. *I've done this much at any rate,* she thought, for during her last illness she had fallen into the habit of tallying up her accomplishments, trying between the fever dreams to decide if her life had been worthwhile. *I've taken two children, Jenny and Kevin, poor Irish children who might otherwise have starved, and given them a good home and good training so they can be useful adults.* And she had enjoyed it. She had never really wanted children of her own, but her fosterlings had awakened something warm in her, something she was glad to have had the chance to feel.

Becca and Dr. Delany were deep in their game, which Becca was winning; Ford stood at the other window, gazing at Esther as she gazed at the children. "Is it true, what you told me the other day?" she said in a low voice. "About Miss Vanhomrigh being close to death?"

"It is truer now than when I told you."

"Will you see her again?"

"I plan to go there tomorrow, or the next day."

"I want you to take a letter for me."

"A letter to Miss Vanhomrigh?" Esther had the impression Ford was struggling to keep from raising his eyebrows.

"Yes. A letter to Miss Vanhomrigh."

September came before Jonathan Swift visited Wood Park. Esther and Becca were still staying there, though Becca was beginning to make noises about being back in Dublin before the cold weather began. Esther saw the sense in that, but she was loath to leave the comforts of Ford's estate. They left Wood Park from time to time only to spend a few days at the homes of friends with other pleasant country houses; it reminded Esther of Moor Park and her youth. She had once been glad enough to leave those comforts to be mistress of her own home, however simple; now she wondered if she was reaching a different time in her life, when being mistress of a rented townhouse had lost its allure and she wanted again to be cared for in someone else's manor. Certainly the prospect of going back to Dublin to look for another house to rent had little appeal.

Swift did not write to say he was coming: he simply appeared one morning, on horseback, with only his manservant Jack for company. Esther was sitting in her room, writing a letter to Lady Eustace, when Jane came in with her breakfast on a tray. "There's a wonderful clatter downstairs, ma'am," she said as she laid the tray before Esther.

"Is there?" Esther said, adjusting her spectacles on her nose and wondering was it possible to get lenses that were strong enough to make the words come clear without being so strong as to make her headaches worse. She never encouraged her servants to gossip, but Jane stayed, obviously eager to tell more.

"It's the dean, ma'am, the dean of St. Patrick's."

Esther glanced up. "What of the dean, Jane?"

"He's here, ma'am. Just arrived a half-hour ago. His man Jack was just down in the kitchen getting Cook to make him some breakfast."

Jane's use of the English language made it difficult to be sure whether Swift or Jack was the recipient of the breakfast—perhaps both—but that was immaterial. Esther put her own breakfast tray aside except for her coffee. She took a long drink. Jane was still hovering.

"Thank you, Jane—you may go now." Jane bobbed a curtsy and went to the door, disappointed. Despite the many years that separated Esther from life below stairs at Moor Park, she had no difficulty remembering how avidly servants gossiped about every detail of life above stairs. What were her own servants, the

Wood Park people, and Jack expecting? How much did they know, and what did they speculate, about the relationship between Dean Swift and Mrs. Johnson?

Esther set down her cup and took off her spectacles. Jonathan would not expect to see her this early in the morning, but still she wanted to dress. She wanted to feel ready. In truth she was as ignorant as the servants were of what to expect from her old friend's arrival.

Their meeting, at dinner in the hall that afternoon, was an anticlimax. Both were very polite, as was Charles Ford. Only Becca seemed oddly strained, and barely spoke to Swift. He filled most of the conversation with tales of his travels around Ireland, the things he had seen and the people he had met. There were no uncomfortable references to Miss Vanhomrigh or to the reason for his sudden departure. He did allude to Esther's removal to Wood Park, asking if she was quite better of her illness. He was quick-witted and opinionated and talkative, with both Esther and Ford doing their best to keep up with his repartee—in fact, it seemed as if nothing had changed at all. The Wood Park servants, who glided silently in and out bringing trays of food upstairs and empty dishes and gossip down, were no doubt disappointed to have little to report.

But when they rose to leave the hall, Swift caught Esther's arm lightly at the elbow. "Don Carlos tells me you are well enough to ride again," he said softly.

"I have ridden with him nearly every day this summer," she said, without looking up. "I think we may make a horseman of him yet."

"Then ride with me, this afternoon."

Becca's loud voice cut across Swift's low one. "'Tis terrible cold out these days, with autumn coming on. You should take care, Hetty, you may catch a chill. Perhaps you'd best stay inside."

What on earth was making Bec so contrary, Esther wondered. "I will be fine, Becca—you needn't worry." She did not expect to enjoy this ride greatly, but a private conversation with Swift, however painful, was preferable to leaving things unsaid. It might be better to ignore their quarrel, but there was one thing she had to tell him, and that privately.

"Don Carlos, you'll go along and make sure Hetty doesn't strain herself?" Becca said. Esther shot him a pleading looking— surely he would be a little more sensitive than Becca, and have the wit to understand that she needed to talk to Swift alone.

He only smiled. "I am sure the dean will take excellent care of Mrs. Johnson; I have business to attend to. We'll meet again for cards this evening?"

Becca looked as though her next offer would be to come along herself, which since she never sat a horse except under absolute duress would be the ultimate sacrifice, but instead she lifted her chin and followed Ford out of the room without another word.

"I think Bec has come to dislike me," said Swift.

"Nonsense, she only worries about me."

They talked of inconsequential things again on the way to the stables, and once they were mounted, the conversation continued in the same vein, till Esther began to wonder if it would be left up to her to turn the talk to painful and difficult channels. But quite out of the blue, Swift said, "Did Ford tell you Hester Vanhomrigh had died?"

"I knew she was dead—a month ago, now."

Swift eyed her with a careful sidelong glance. "There are folk who blame me for her death. Do people really die of broken hearts, Esther?"

"Fools may."

"But you would not."

"No, I intend to die of something a bit more substantial. If my heart breaks, it will mend itself, given time."

"So was Miss Vanhomrigh a fool?"

"That is not for me to say. I'll speak no ill of the dead."

Swift blew out a gusty sigh. "I was the fool, Esther, to fall into that sort of violent love that robs one of reason. What else do we have, if not reason? Without it we are no better than animals—a good deal worse, in fact." He patted his horse's mane. "Violent love—all violent passions—are the enemies of reason, and the enemies of our better nature. I always believed it, but I forgot it for a little time, and made myself very unhappy, and poor Hessy desperately unhappy—and, perhaps worst of all, I made you unhappy. I swear I did not intend that."

Esther said nothing. She knew he wanted absolution, but she was not sure she could, or would, grant it. They rode in silence for a few minutes.

"I hope you can forgive me," Swift said, "and that we can be friends, as before."

"Nothing can be as before," Esther said. "But of course we will be friends. You are my oldest friend. We have shared too much to turn our backs on each other. I would be happy for all this business to be forgotten and never spoken of again—but there is someone who makes that impossible."

Swift wrinkled his brow. He honestly did not know what she meant. "Of whom do you speak?"

"A child, Jonathan, a boy. He goes by the name Bryan M'Loghlin, but that is not his true name, is it? His mother is dead now, his father will not acknowledge him, his foster family are Irish, and no fit people to raise him. What is to become of him?"

"That is not your concern, Esther! I know—in her madness, Hessy wrote to you and told you of him, but you are not to—do not trouble yourself, I pray! I will continue to pay for his keep with the M'Loghlins—they are good people, Irish to be sure, but Protestants and shopkeepers, not peasants—he is well enough off with them."

Esther felt the rage in her bones and fought to quell it before she spoke. "He is a *child*, Jonathan, not a horse or a dog—your child! How can you speak so carelessly? The M'Loghlins don't want the burden of his care anymore, and even if they did, are they the people to educate and train the son of the dean of St. Patrick's? That is who he is, whether you acknowledge him or not!"

Swift's eyes were blazing: where a few moments before he had been all contrition, all eager for reconciliation, now he was furious. "What gives you the right—"

"I have the right to talk of Bryan because I am his legal guardian."

Swift pulled his horse up short in its tracks and stared at her. "You are what?"

"I wrote to Miss Vanhomrigh before she died and agreed to do as she asked me—to care for her son. I am now his foster mother. He remains with the M'Loghlins, where he is happy enough for the time being, but he is seven years old and ought to be in school. Tom Sheridan has offered to take him in his school, but I think he would be better off at the cathedral school. He can board there: the M'Loghlins will still be happy to have him for visits, but I think I will have him come to me for some of his holiday time, for the boy needs an influence that he cannot get either in a boarding school or in an Irish household."

In thirty-five years of acquaintance she had very seldom had the pleasure of seeing Jonathan Swift speechless—few of his friends had—but she tasted that pleasure now, and enjoyed it. "So you see," she went on, "things cannot go on exactly as before.

I will have your son in my care, another of my foster children, like Kevin or Jenny. He will receive a different class of education than they have, because he is a different class of child, but the world will know him as another of my charity cases."

"Esther why … why are you doing this mad thing? Are you trying to shame me or yourself?"

"I have my reasons, but I assure you that shaming either of us was not among them." Not entirely true—she had no desire to shame him publicly, but she wanted to see him condemned by his own conscience. "Why should I shame myself? Everyone knows I have a reputation for charity work."

"Have you *seen* Bryan M'Loghlin?"

Then she knew what he meant. She had seen the boy, had gone into Dublin to visit him at his foster home. And the first glimpse she caught of the stocky, fair boy with the huge blue eyes erased any lingering doubt she had had about Hester Vanhomrigh's story. She nodded slowly.

"So you know that there will never be doubt in anyone's mind that he is my son—certainly not if he's being fostered by a friend of mine. And if you are his foster mother, what will people assume? Not that his mother was Hester Vanhomrigh, that is certain."

The tattle of this nasty town … Anger surged in her again. "You mean people would think he was *my* son? I wouldn't give a damn for anyone who would think such a thing of me!"

"Esther, I know your virtue is unassailable, but to the tongue of a gossip—"

"Virtue? Do you think I care if people believe I've borne a child by you? Half Dublin—even half our friends—believe we're lovers anyway, and I've lived with that for twenty years. That's no shame to me! Most of them think we're secretly married, so that's no assault to my virtue—though a great laugh to them, if they only knew the truth of it. But would anyone ever believe me capable of bearing a child out of my own body and hiding him away in secret, denying he was mine? Perhaps you could do that—it may be different for a father than a mother. Perhaps your precious Vanessa could do that—I don't think she had room in her heart for more than one love. But I could never, would never, do that if he were my own child—indeed, I cannot do it, even though he is not. If Dublin gossips want to say that Bryan is my child, let them—I won't let that deny him the upbringing, the care, the love he deserves."

They were still, their horses unmoving near the little bridge where she had gone for her first ride months before with Charles Ford and he had told her Hester Vanhomrigh was dying. Esther's grey mare tossed her head and stomped a hoof impatiently. Swift seemed still to be groping for words. There was a little tinge of cold in the air—Becca had been right about that much.

"That was what I needed to tell you, Jonathan," she finished. "I know it makes a difference to whether we can be friends again. I hope we can—as I said, I should hate to lose your friendship. But my mind is made up, and now you must make up yours. I'm getting cold; I must ride back to Wood Park."

She eased the mare into a gentle trot and headed back to the house, not looking to see if he followed.

They played ombre that night in the parlour, and Swift was genial and pleasant to Esther. Once the game was over and Ford had gone to fetch a servant and Becca had taken out her needle-work, he laid his hand over Esther's and said quietly, "You are doing the right thing, my dear. Forgive me." And no more was said.

❧

When they all retired that evening, Esther went down the passage to Becca's room, as she often did before bed. Becca had remained quiet and formal toward Swift all day; it was not like her, for usually she was the butt of his jokes and made him the butt of hers. Esther tapped on her door and Becca let her in. "Brush out my hair for me, Becca," she asked, and sat down on the edge of her friend's bed.

Becca pulled the pins from Esther's hair as she had done so many nights, going way back to when the hair was shining black with not a hint of grey in it. She drew the brush gently through again and again till it ran smoothly, but she did not talk and laugh as she usually did.

"Is something wrong, Becca? You've been in the oddest mood all day."

"Hmph," said Becca. "I should think you'd know what's wrong."

"But I don't, or why would I ask? Tell me."

"I don't see any need—you're obviously happy enough, now he's back. Ought to see your face light up when he came into that dining hall. Haven't seen that look on you since we came to Wood Park."

"You mean Jonathan? Of course I was glad to see him again." Esther was puzzled. Becca knew the whole tale, or most of it; she knew how hurt Esther had been by Swift's betrayal, and Esther would have thought she'd been glad to see the quarrel mended. "We talked it all over, Becca. It's all right between us now. We're friends again."

"Friends! Is that what you call it? You've been a fool for that man all your life, Hetty, and now you're an old fool."

The word *fool*—the word she herself had so often used to describe Hester Vanhomrigh—stung. Esther pulled away from the hairbrush. "How can you say that, Becca?"

"I can say it because it's true! You listen to his stories, copy out his poems, laugh at his jests, act like the sun rises and sets on him, and he's not worthy to wipe his boots on you! And that's just what he does, too—wipes the mud off his boots on you, treats you lower than a servant. Can you not see how little he makes of you, and how much you make of him?"

"That is not true!"

"It is and I'm sick of seeing it. I thought he was gone for good this time, and I was glad. I can't bear to watch him hurt you, to make little of you after all you've done for him. Now you're going to take his bastard into your home and make a martyr of yourself for that child, and drag your reputation through the dirt again—because you know what they'll say, Hetty, you know they'll think the child is yours—and ruin your sweet eyes copying out a hundred more useless poems— and all for what? For a man who'll never treat you as you deserve. It sickens me!"

Becca turned her eyes away from the hairbrush she was slap- ping into her palm, and up to Esther, and everything made sense. A strange, distressing sense, for it was plain to see in those haunted angry old eyes. Love—what Ford would have called true, devoted love and Swift would have called violent love—that passion that unseated reason and put another human being on the heart's throne. The kind of love that had destroyed Hester Vanhomrigh and might have destroyed Esther Johnson if she had let it—a love inseparable from its twin, jealousy.

Esther stumbled out of Becca's room and closed the door behind her.

In her own room she sat at her table, waiting for Becca to come, knowing she would not. How could this be? To love another woman like that—it was unnatural, grotesque. Becca was a simple, wholesome, ordinary woman. She could not be in love with Esther.

Love, love—throw away the useless word, try to find another. Becca was devoted to Esther, worshipped her, cared too much for her. In bitter honesty Esther had to admit a kind of truth to everything Becca had said about herself and Swift—he had never cared enough, never valued her as much as she had him. And all unnoticed, all these years, she was playing the other side of the same game with Becca. Taking her old friend for granted, accepting her comfort and care, never giving back even a tenth of the love she was given.

She had no idea what to do with this painful knowledge. She would not speak of it. Even to imagine such a conversation was impossible. Poor, poor Becca! No, even her pity had to be stilled, for she could not let Becca imagine she might ever respond in kind. She touched her hair and thought of Becca's hands and the steady, soothing motion of the hairbrush. All those nights … all that devotion. She would miss Becca's touch terribly.

She would have to distance herself from Becca—she could not encourage this unnatural, twisted passion. And she would have to—

She would finish her poem. She had been writing it for ages, writing and crossing out and crumpling and burning, trying to find words honest enough to say what she'd felt the night she got Hester Vanhomrigh's letter. It was hard to admit she loved anyone enough to be jealous over him. But now, for a moment, she saw the world through Becca's eyes, through the eyes of someone else who loved and was not loved in return. Hester, too, must have seen the world through those same eyes. And any woman, anyone who had loved like that, could finish this poem.

She took out her latest draft, crossing out and rewriting as she read. She had been trying to make a sonnet out of it, but now she saw that it was not meant to be a sonnet. Trying to stretch it out to fourteen lines just inflated it: all she had to say was said, neatly and completely, in ten short lines of verse.

Jealousy

0 shield me from his rage, celestial pow'rs,
This tyrant, that imbitters all my hours :
Ah, Love, you've poorly play'd the hero's part,
You conquerd, but you can't defend my heart.
When first I bent beneath your gentle reign
I thought this monster banish'd from your train:
But you would raise him, to support your throne
And now he claims your empire for his own.
Or tell me tyrants, have you both agreed
That where one reigns, the other shall succeed?

DUBLIN
1724

"Oh, Bryan, not daydreaming again, are you? Surely you have finished those lines of Virgil by now!"

The small figure at the writing table started, turned from the window to his paper, and hastily picked up a pen. Esther moved behind him to see only the first of the ten lines she had set translated—and two mistakes in that. She sighed. Bryan turned round blue eyes up at her.

"'Tis too hard," he said.

She bit her lips down over the reply that at eight years old she had been doing twenty lines of the same stuff. No need to compare him with herself—just look at the other boys in the cathedral school! She no longer even dreamed of his being at the top of his class—but might he not fall somewhere in the middle? She said none of this, but disappointment was plain enough on her face, and Bryan's fell in response.

"I'm sorry," he said. "I will try harder."

She reached out and slipped an arm around his shoulders; she had never been able to touch any other human being so simply and impulsively. "It's all right," she said, though of course it wasn't.

She felt a small rush of pleasure when the boy's shoulders sagged and relaxed into her touch. Once he would have stiffened and squirmed away. She enjoyed the solid feel of his small body under her arm. "Do your best, Bryan—that's all anyone can ask of you."

If only that were true. Since she had begun to know Bryan M'Loghlin, she had been glad, rather than angry, that Swift had never acknowledged him as a son. If the world knew—if his schoolmasters knew—even if he knew he was the son of the great Jonathan Swift, poet, dean of St. Patrick's, how heavy would be the burden of expectations on those little round shoulders. And he was so unsuited to bear that burden. Esther could see it; Becca could see it; Swift himself could see it. They were the only three who knew his parentage, and all three of them were surprised at how ordinary, how plodding his mind was. Esther privately blamed the boy's mother, who could certainly have done more for him had she chosen. Growing up in an Irish shopkeeper's household could hardly have been stimulating. The wonder was, she often reminded herself, that he could attempt Greek and Latin at all.

"That's enough Lily for now," she added, remembering that when she was a child Swift had taken her for walks through the rolling gardens of Moor Park when she grew impatient with her studies. "Do you want to go out in the garden?"

"No." Bryan shook his head.

Esther was about to ask why, but she knew the answer. Kevin was down there, splitting firewood. When she first brought Bryan to their home—another house in Mary Street, much smaller than the one they had rented there before—she had thought he and Kevin would be playmates. Both fosterlings were about the same age, and although Kevin was being trained for service and Bryan would be going to school, she imagined they would be friends. It hadn't worked that way. Perhaps it would have, if Bryan had been a different sort of boy. "Young Kevin's just doing what any young lad would do," Becca said. "It's that other one who's queer—won't stand up to him, won't play, won't fight, just sits off in a corner and sulks and sneers. I don't blame young Kevin—I don't like the look on his face myself."

Small wonder, that. The look on his face was a copy of his father's, stamped onto a child's unlined skin. Becca had precious little use for Swift these days, and none at all for his bastard son. Despite her motherly instincts, she had never warmed to Bryan. Neither had Mrs. Sally or Rob. Swift himself kept his distance from the boy—Bryan knew him as the man who had sometimes come with his mother to visit when he lived at the M'Loghlins, but had no idea Swift was his father. If the boy had been brighter, showed some promise, Swift might have taken an interest. As it was, only Esther had warmed to him. Even the dog, Tiger, growled and snapped when Bryan came near.

"What about a walk, then?" she asked, and was rewarded by the sudden brightening of the dull little face.

"I'd like that, ma'am," he said, jumping up to get a cloak.

Esther got to her feet slowly. She deserved some reward for making that offer. A walk took a good deal out of her these days. But for the boy ... "Bring my cloak too, please, Bryan," she called.

A fierce volley of yipping barks from somewhere in the house warned her Bryan had crossed paths with Tiger. She sighed. Bryan had been part of their household for over a year now—since her return from Wood Park the previous autumn. Of course he was not there all the time; he boarded at the cathedral school and during his holidays usually spent a few days with the M'Loghlins, though those visits were growing shorter. He seemed to have no very close tie to the couple who had raised him. Poor boy. Everyone in his life either actively disliked him or simply didn't care much for him.

Everyone but Esther. She smiled when he came into the room with her cloak; he was trying so hard to keep it from trailing the ground that a little frown of concentration appeared on his brow. She wished, as she helped him into his cloak, that she was his real mother, that she could smooth away that frown with a kiss to his forehead. She had never thought any such thing about a child before. He slipped his hand into hers as they went down into the hall, and her heart lifted. She had been fond of Jenny and enjoyed Kevin's liveliness, but caresses and gestures of affection had been Becca's province, not hers. Her pleasure in her other foster children had been more a teacher's pleasure than a mother's; she had been proud of what she was making of them, what they were going to make of themselves someday.

She wasn't making anything much of Bryan—sometimes she despaired of him—but for the first time she understood how a mother could love her own child even when he failed dismally, even when other folk found him uninspiring and even unpleasant. She had no words for it, but she watched his small feet in their sturdy boots plodding through the mud of Mary Street and she was happy in spite of the aches in her bones and the dizzying dance of lights at the edge of her vision.

Three gulls rose into the sky, shrieking their hoarse calls. "Going down to the river to look for garbage," said Bryan. "Fish guts. Dirty things."

Perhaps he has a little of his father in him, after all, Esther thought, and wished she had someone to share the joke with.

Like the gulls, she and Bryan headed toward the Liffey, and across it. "Where are we going?" asked Bryan, who was used to Esther's walks having a purpose.

Esther hesitated. What she wanted was to go to the deanery and see Swift. He had been ill for three weeks, and she had visited almost daily, bringing jars of homemade soup from Mrs. Sally's kitchen and books to read aloud to him as he lay on his settee. He had had a bad bout with his dizziness but was getting better now, and she had missed seeing him yesterday. She knew he relied on her visits when he was sick, but she seldom took Bryan to the deanery—it made Swift uncomfortable—and what patience he had with the boy was likely to be even less when he was recuperating. Yet it was toward St. Patrick's that her footsteps were tending.

"You're not taking me back to school, are you?" said Bryan, when he saw the bulk of the cathedral in the distance. His thin voice was animated by a note of fear that made Esther wonder just how awful school was for him. Was it the masters, or the other boys, who made it such an unwelcome destination? She had heard horror stories from almost every man of her acquaintance about school days—it was one thing she was glad she had been spared.

"We are going to visit Dean Swift," she said, the decision made.

"Oh," said Bryan, kicking a stone in the road. His tone implied that a visit to the dean was only marginally better than school.

Esther started to chatter, pointing out interesting buildings and people along the way, to silence her own thoughts. Whenever she saw Jonathan and Bryan together—or even thought of them together—it was hard to escape sadness. Father and son. If only things had been different.

She expected Swift's housekeeper, Mrs. Brent, to open the door at the deanery, but it was his manservant who answered. "Ah, your friend's been here and gone an hour ago," he told Esther as he ushered them in. "Her and Mrs. Brent are gone off to the markets."

"Thank you, Jack. Will you tell the dean that Mrs. Johnson is here, and has Bryan with her?" She hadn't known Becca was coming to the deanery today, though it made sense that if she came without Esther, she would be going to visit the house-keeper, Mrs. Brent, rather than Swift. Becca had got very friendly with Mrs. Brent, but she remained cool to Swift. He still made jokes at her expense and had even written a few silly poems for her, but she scarcely thawed in her attitude to him. At the same time, Becca and Esther went their separate ways much more than they had once done. It wasn't unusual for one to set off in the morning without the other knowing where she was going.

The dean's servant reappeared. "He says to come on up, ma'am—he's in the study."

"How is he today?" she asked, following him up the stairs.

"Oh, he's better today, ma'am, better than he's been in weeks. He's been scribblin' all morning, and you should see him, he's that pleased with himself—" Jack's cheery commentary on his master's mood stopped abruptly as he swung the study door open for them.

Swift was at his writing table, surrounded by the usual clutter of books and papers. His fingers were ink stained and his wig was askew, but Jack was right: he looked better than he had in ages. His face, when he turned it to Esther from his writing, glowed with such energy and happiness that even the presence of Bryan, shrinking behind Esther's skirts, seemed not to perturb him.

"Sit down, Bryan—there's a good lad. Now Esther, you *must* read what I've been writing. You remember the sketches I wrote a few years ago about those fantastic lands—the land of the little people, and the land of the giants—and I could never decide what to do with them?"

"I do remember, but I had not heard you speak of them in so long that I thought you had put them aside," said Esther, arranging her skirts around her in the chair nearest the fire.

"I had, indeed. But the ideas still plagued me—so much so that they were even in my fever dreams. But even some of the dream matter may find its way into this tale—for it is a tale so strange, so foreign, that perhaps it will seem like a fever dream. You must read it, Esther, you must read what I have written now!"

"Very well!" She took the handful of papers from him, laughing at his eagerness. Across the room, Bryan sat by the window, staring down into the cathedral grounds. She pitied little boys at moments like this: a young girl surrounded by the dull chatter of adults would at least have her needlework to occupy her. "Has Becca been here this afternoon?" she asked as she looked down at ten pages of closely written text.

"Has she! Yes indeed, I heard her voice, and Brent's, gossiping away down in my kitchen, then Brent poked her head in to say they were off to the shops. I've written them a poem. Do you want to hear it?"

My Father had a small Estate in Nottinghamshire; I was the Third of five Sons, the manuscript began. *He sent me to Emanuel-College in Cambridge, at Fourteen Years old* ... "A poem? In addition to all this prose?" said Esther.

"It was not very taxing," said Swift, turning his chair from his desk, planting both hands on his knees. "It's more of a song, actually." And he began to sing in his tuneless voice, to the tune of "Ye Commons and Ye Peers."

> *Dingley and Brent*
> *Wherever they went*
> *Ne'er minded a word that was spoken;*
> *Whatever was said,*
> *They ne'er troubled their head*
> *But laughed at their own silly joking*
>
> *You tell a good jest*
> *And please all the rest*
> *Comes Dingley, and asks you, "What was it?"*
> *And curious to know,*
> *Away she will go*
> *To seek an old rag in a closet.*

A small explosive chuckle lit the room; Bryan, his face still to the window, had clearly enjoyed the bit of doggerel. Dingley's slowness to catch a joke was legendary, as was her habit of coming in on the tail end of conversations and begging to have everything explained.

"Very amusing, but apparently not the best work you have done today," she said, looking back at the manuscript. *I was bound Apprentice to Mr. James Bates, an eminent Surgeon in London, with whom I continued four Years; and my Father now and then sending me small Sums of Money, I laid them out in learning Navigation, and other Parts of the Mathematicks, useful to those who intend to travel, as I always believed it would be some time or other my Fortune to do.* "Jonathan, what *is* this exactly? I'll confess I was expecting a poem or an essay, but this is something … quite different."

"Quite different, indeed!" Swift only laughed. "Read on, read on!"

"It sounds as if it's going to be an adventure tale … ships and the sea," she said. Out of the corner of her eye she saw Bryan turn from the window toward her, his interest perhaps caught by the mention of sea voyages.

"An adventure tale, a fantastic tale, a moral tale, a tale that will set the whole world on its ear!" Swift laughed. He was so clearly pleased with himself—a state he was always in when beginning to write a new piece, though his mood throughout the process of creation might range from ecstasy to despair within a day. She had never seen him quite so exhilarated, though.

"It looks most exciting," she said, scanning the next few pages.

"Take it home, read it, and make a fair copy for me—if you think your poor little eyes can stand the strain. How have they been?"

"Better," she lied. "I can make you a copy; it may take a few days."

"By then I'll have another chapter done. It flows out of my pen, Esther—it writes itself!"

They talked awhile longer before they heard voices downstairs—Becca and Mrs. Brent returning from their shopping. "Come, Bryan," said Esther, reaching for his hand as she rose, "we'll go tell Mrs. Dingley that we're here, and walk home with her. Say goodbye to Dean Swift."

"Goodbye, Dean Swift," the boy echoed.

On the way back to Mary Street, Becca, laden down with parcels, chattered about what she had seen and done at the shops. "And we saw Mrs. Walls there with Mrs. Worrall—Lord, she is growing fat, isn't she? Mrs. Worrall, I mean. Not that I'm one to talk—and they hardly spoke half a dozen words to us, can you imagine? And—"

"Can you blame them?" Esther blurted.

"Why, whatever do you mean?"

"Don't be a fool, Becca! What *can* our friends think, when they see you out in the streets with Nelly Brent, thick as a pair of thieves?" She had not meant to say any of this, but the words came tumbling off her tongue as easily as Jonathan's story flowed from his pen. "What would they say if they saw you out with Mrs. Sally, linked arm in arm like sisters? It's the same thing, you know— Mrs. Brent *is* the dean's housekeeper. Everyone knows her."

Becca's step quickened; she gave a quick tug on Bryan's waist-coat as he wandered too far out into the street and almost under the hooves of an oncoming horse. "I don't see what it matters— she's my friend, and we have a good deal of fun together."

"If you don't see, there's no point talking to you about it." They walked on for another street before Becca's placid silence drove Esther to add, "It's just that you might be a bit more careful of appearances—one has one's position in society to think of."

Becca drew a long, gusty sigh. "I had that to think of when I was twenty, and thirty, and forty—now I'm nearly sixty and I don't care tuppence for my position in society. Your trouble, Hetty, is that you've never got over thinking of yourself as the housekeeper's daughter, wondering if you're going to be allowed to sit at the second table for dinner in the hall."

These days Esther could never tell what her reaction to Becca was going to be; she had been angry, and thought she would go on being so, but something in Becca's tone made her laugh instead and say, "You goose!" as they turned into their own street.

But it did not stop her brooding on Becca's friendship with Mrs. Brent. It did lower her in the eyes their friends—and, though she hated to admit it, Becca was right. Esther *did* worry about her place in Dublin society—despite her wide circle of friends, she could never feel that she and Becca were quite legitimate, quite accepted as members of their class. Without Swift's friendship, surely they would have sunk back a notch or two and been working as companions to some elderly lady—the role Esther's own mother and Swift's sister, Jane, still filled for the indefatigable Martha Giffard.

But it was no good taking Becca to task any more over her friendship with Mrs. Brent. She seemed to have made up her mind that she was old enough now not to care what folk thought of her, and to do exactly as she pleased.

The next day, Esther set about the task of copying the first chapter of Swift's new text. As she read beyond the opening paragraphs she had already skimmed, she was quickly drawn into the tale of Lemuel Gulliver and his fantastic adventures. How often she and Jonathan had laughed at those intrepid world travellers who seemed to compete with one another to see who could tell the most outlandish tale! This one, surely, topped them all. She understood, as she sat at her desk before the window in the brightest light the house had to offer, why Jonathan had been so excited. A story like this would free his gigantic imagination to roam at will—and give him scope to touch on every subject that intrigued or enraged him.

When dinner was over and Becca had bundled up her needle-work and sat down before the fire in the parlour, Esther said, "Dean Swift has started a new story—would you like me to read it aloud?"

Becca clicked her tongue as she wetted the end of her thread to pass it through the needle's eye. "Still ruining your eyes on his scribblings? Is it funny? If 'tis worth reading at all, let me read it, and spare your eyes."

"No—my eyes are really quite well lately, I'll wear my specta-cles and sit right beside the lamp," Esther protested. She wanted it to be her voice that brought these sparkling words to life; Becca, who read all their letters aloud as well as the *Tatler,* the *Spectator, Pue's Observances* and the *Dublin Gazette,* would make a tale of South Sea adventure sound as dull as a marketing list.

"Jane!" she called to the maid. "See if Bryan has gone to bed yet—if he hasn't, tell him to come down; he may enjoy this story too." It struck her that it might be an entertaining story for children, though surely that had hardly been Swift's intent.

When Bryan was settled on the footstool and Becca was well into her work, Esther began to read the first chapter aloud. Reading by dim light did make her eyes sting, and the words danced a little on the page, but it was worth it to hear the story come alive, to see how intently both her hearers listened. Especially Bryan—she had tried reading aloud to him so often before, but neither poetry nor mythology nor the Bible had captured his attention. He was riveted to the story of Gulliver's misadventures among the Lilliputians.

Partway through, Gulliver, surrounded and tied down by the tiny people of Lilliput, needed to relieve himself *"with making*

Water; which I very plentifully did, to the great Astonishment of the People, who conjecturing by my Motions what I was going to do, immediately opened to the right and left on that Side, to avoid the Torrent which fell with such Noice and Violence from me." Becca snorted and Bryan laughed aloud at the vivid picture—that vast, terrifying stream of piss—and Esther heard a muffled chuckle from just outside the room. She leaned forward to see Jane and Mrs. Sally sitting on the stairs. "Come in, Jane, come in, Sally," she said. "You've heard this much, so you might as well hear the rest of it."

A day later she overheard Mrs. Sally relating the whole tale to Rob and Kevin down in the kitchen. The same afternoon, Swift arrived with another bundle of paper. "Chapter two," he announced, looking over her copy of chapter one with pleasure. "How much nicer it always looks when you have it all copied out," he said.

"You must be pleased with it; usually you look cross when you read over anything you've written."

"Not this; this does give me pleasure."

She announced to the whole household—Becca, Bryan, Mrs. Sally, Jane, Rob, and Kevin—that she would read the next chapter of Dean Swift's book aloud after supper. It did not take long for this to become a custom: every few days Swift would arrive with a new chapter, Esther would copy it in the afternoon, and in the evening everyone gathered in the parlour to hear her read. By the fourth chapter, Swift found out about it and began attending as well, laughing aloud at his own wit.

Gulliver had joined the household like an unseen lodger. Esther's eyes and head ached more than ever from the extra reading and writing, yet she was never disappointed when a new chapter arrived. Becca, who hadn't had a good word to say about

Swift in ages, now joked with him about his hero's misadventures and declared she had never heard such an entertaining tale. And one afternoon Esther passed by the open dining room window and heard boyish voices in the yard.

"Let's play at being Gulliver and the Lilliputians," said Bryan.

"All right!" Kevin replied, but after a moment added, "How can we? One of us can't be that huge, or that tiny."

"No, I'll show you—you be Gulliver and lie down, see, and I'll make my fingers to be the Lilliput people, and they'll walk on your hand."

"And play hide-and-seek in my hair—don't forget that!" Squeals of laughter drifted up to the window; she leaned out a little to see Kevin lying on the ground with Bryan kneeling beside him. "Out of the way, I might have to piss!" Kevin warned.

"No, we won't do that part—the ladies would scold us if they knew," said Bryan. "Anyway, get up. It's my turn to be Gulliver now."

"It's not. We never said we were having turns."

"But I want to be Gulliver!" Bryan's voice rose in a whine.

"You can't be; you're littler than me." Both boys were on their feet now, squared off against each other.

"I'm taller—a good half inch taller."

"Yes, but you're scrawny, you puny thing—I could lift *you* up on my hand like Gulliver did."

"No you couldn't!"

Esther shut the window. At least Gulliver had given them a moment's peace and amity.

All through the long months, while Swift perfected his final draft and Esther copied it out, she continued reading instalments aloud to her household in the evenings. Bryan was not always there; he went back to school and Esther was glad, for he surely would have got bored, as Kevin did, with some of the long tedious bits in book three. Miniature people and giants made books one and two entertaining enough even for a child, but in book three, Gulliver travelled to a strange world called Laputa, which gave Swift a chance to satirize virtually every political, scientific, religious, and artistic development that had ever annoyed him. Esther wondered how much Rob and Mrs. Sally got from these readings; surely the servants could not follow Swift's lofty mental gymnastics. Jane generally fell asleep while Esther was reading.

Finally they—and Swift—reached book four, where Gulliver landed among a race of intelligent, cultured, rational horses called the Houyhnhnms. They were obviously meant as a paragon, an ideal of everything humankind ought to be, and when Gulliver described his own world, humanity came off very poorly in comparison.

Then, in chapter nine, it was revealed that the savage, filthy, smelly creatures called Yahoos, which the Houyhnhnms kept as a kind of unsuccessful domesticated animal, were actually Gulliver's own species—human beings. The antics of the Yahoos drew a little laughter from the assembled audience, but Esther could see none of them were quite comfortable being classed among the Yahoos.

At last they reached the next-to-last chapter. Esther was reading that night to an audience of Becca, Sally, and Rob—Bryan and Kevin were already abed, and Jane gone to her own house. This was the chapter in which Gulliver was returned to his family in what ought to have been a joyous reunion. But it was fatally marred by his realization that his own people were

Yahoos, and were now revolting to him, after his time among the Houyhnhnms; he preferred the company of his horses.

> As soon as I entered the House, my Wife took me in her Arms, and kissed me, at which, having not been used to the Touch of that odious Animal for so many Years, I fell in a Swoon for almost an Hour. At the time I am writing it is Five Years since my last Return to England: During the first Year I could not endure my Wife or Children in my Presence, the very Smell of them was intolerable, much less could I suffer them to eat in the same Room. To this Hour they dare not presume to touch my Bread, or drink out of the same Cup, neither was I ever able to let one of them take me by the Hand.

Becca sniffed as Esther finished the chapter. "Well, he always was dreadfully fond of horses."

"Who was?" said Esther.

"The dean," said Becca, stabbing her work with her needle.

"He isn't writing about himself, Becca, but about Gulliver."

Becca rolled her eyes. "Well, it's shocking all the same, for any man to say that about his wife and children, his own flesh, who he ought to love. Only a man who never had wife or children could write such a thing."

Mrs. Sally spoke from her corner. "No doubt that's the very reason he never had them."

"Whatever do you mean, Sally?" said Esther. "It's not as though Dean Swift actually went on Gulliver's voyages himself, you know. The whole thing is a fairy tale."

"Begging pardon, Mrs. Johnson, I'm not a learned woman like you and I don't know much about books, but I'm sure a man only writes what he thinks and feels. The man that wrote that did not think very well of his fellow human beings, you may be sure."

Esther sighed. She knew it had been a mistake to read this in front of the staff. "Sally, you know what a generous and charitable man the dean is—how could you say he does not love his fellow man?"

Mrs. Sally looked down at her apron. "I'm sure you know best, ma'am," she said.

But Becca's tongue was not so easily stilled. "He may give folk money, but that don't mean he approves of them, Hetty. Sure, isn't he forever criticizing and complaining and pointing out the worst in people—specially women?"

Esther put down the sheets of paper she had copied with such care. The light was fading and her eyes stung. She took off her spectacles and laid them on top of the paper. "The point of the story is not about what Dean Swift feels toward human beings but about what we *are*, we human beings. We are fond of saying that man is a rational animal, but it would be truer to say he is an animal capable of reason. When man—or woman—chooses not to use his reason, but lives by his animal passions, he is no better than a Yahoo. And that is all too often the case. That is all Dean Swift is saying." She was proud of her summation and looked quickly at her audience, hoping she had edified them as much as was possible. Mrs. Sally was still looking into her lap; Rob met her eyes, but his expression was unreadable. He did not look humbly edified, however.

And Becca shook her head. "The dean could have got a trained parrot to say his words for him, at a good deal less expense."

"What?"

"You heard me. You're doing nothing but repeating his words and his thoughts, and if you ask me, they're not worth repeating.

There's something wrong with any man that could write that—he's clean mad, if you ask me."

"Well, I did not ask you," said Esther, standing. Becca was the one going mad—to call Esther a trained parrot and the dean of St. Patrick's a madman, in front of servants! "I am going up to bed," she said. "There is one more chapter to copy tomorrow, but it is dull, dry stuff that has little to do with the story, so I shall not read it."

"Does it say anything about his wife?" Becca shot back, standing up and collecting her needlework in her bag.

Esther paused. "Yes," she said, "it says that at the end of five years Gulliver was able to allow his wife to sit at the table with him—as long as she sat at the far end."

Rob burst out in a huge guffaw, which he tried belatedly to cover with his hand. Then he held out his arm to Mrs. Sally. "Come, Mrs. Sal, we'll off down to the kitchen to clear away supper—if I can stand the stink of you, that is. Goodnight, m'ladies." He sketched a bow that had a trace of mockery, and then led the cook out of the room.

Esther lay awake that night, turning both the chapter and the conversation over in her mind. Swift's point, his barbed contrast between Houyhnhnms and Yahoos, was so succinct and so … so right. She thought, as Swift surely must have when writing it, of Hester Vanhomrigh, growing from a beautiful cultured girl to a mad, obsessed, drunken woman because she allowed passion—love—to rule her life, and poor Bryan, the product of that passion, who thought with his stomach and his fists and could not learn Latin. She felt an unaccustomed pity for dead Hester when she thought of the laughable scene where a deluded female Yahoo attempted to mate with Gulliver.

One had only to contrast Esther's own life—a careful and well-planned life, an orderly life based on sensible choices—to that of poor Hester Vanhomrigh to see that Swift was right in his indictment of human passion. Yet Becca's remark about the trained parrot lodged in her brain—as did the image of the returning traveller turning away in disgust from the embracing arms of his wife and children.

Esther copied the last chapter the following day and brought the pages to Swift in the evening. She knew he had been eager to hear her critique of book four. When she laid it on his desk, he looked at her closely and said, "You do not like it."

Esther was quiet, considering the pages. They were carefully copied in her own handwriting—a neater, clearer version of Swift's own, as if her whole life's work had been to sweep through his thoughts and tidy them, polish them to present before the public. He had never asked whether the words she so painstakingly copied reflected her thoughts also. To offer such opinions was not a scribe's place, not a woman's place.

"I—it makes me uncomfortable," she said at last.

Swift beamed; he almost laughed. "Then I have done all I hoped for! If my writing troubles people, if it makes readers uneasy, then my work is done." He pulled out the last page, dipped his pen, and signed his name at the end with a flourish. Then he held it away a little and frowned before giving it back. "You'll have to copy that page again; I mean to publish it anonymously, of course. But I'll keep this autograph to remind myself that Jonathan Swift has at last written his book—the book he was born to write." As she rose to take her leave, he added, "Thank you for your work, Esther—you have done wonderfully, as always. I could do nothing without you. After all, this last book will surely displease you less than it will most other readers—for you are the most nearly a Houyhnhnm of any woman I know."

"Good evening, Jonathan," she said, omitting the thanks. He rose to help her with her cloak, but she fastened it herself and was gone down the stairs.

Walking home through the grey streets of Dublin, she looked at the river of humanity all around—as wide and fast and smelly as the Liffey itself—and saw the people as Swift saw them: the braying, greedy, hungry, angry Yahoos who lived with their bellies and hearts and loins. And the wealthy and well-dressed English in their carriages were just as surely Yahoos, though better-groomed ones, as were the dirty and ignorant poor on the streets. They knew what reason was but did not live by its dictates: perhaps they were more to be despised.

So Swift saw the world, and so Esther, year after year and season after season, had trained herself to see it too; yet she saw with a double vision. It was as if Swift had given her spectacles that she had worn faithfully all her life, but when they slipped she saw the eyes of the servant girl who was pregnant and left to beg in a doorway, the burning pride of the boy who fought and was beaten, the aching loneliness of the silly woman who prattled of cards and gowns all day.

And now she turned the corner into Ormonde Street, to a house where lived Becca, a plain, sensible spinster who loved too much and was silly with money and cried too easily, and a servant named Rob who was born with some other name and perhaps other dreams and desires that only flashed through when he was drunk or angry, and a confused, belligerent little boy who was the son of a passionate, bitterly unhappy woman. They were flawed and irrational and sometimes actually evil; they were human, they were Yahoos, and she loved them. Which likely simply meant that she was a Yahoo too, for all she had been passing as a Houyhnhnm all these years.

Becca was in the parlour writing a letter, a blanket folded over her knees and a dog curled on the blanket. She looked up as Esther came in. "Did you deliver those papers?"

Esther nodded. She had thought that of late she and Becca were losing track of each other; Becca often went out, and Esther had no idea where she was going or what she was doing. Esther had assumed the reverse was true but now realized it was not.

"Did you tell him we didn't like book four?" Becca asked.

Esther dropped her cloak across a chair and laid her bags on the floor before lowering herself slowly onto the settee. "No, I didn't." She picked up Becca's needlework and looked at it vaguely—how long had it been since she had worked a stitch? Would she even remember how? "The truth is, Becca, there's no good talking to him. I've been talking and listening to Jonathan Swift since I was eight years old, and I've nothing new to say now. Perhaps everything has been said, and we should just be silent now till we die."

"My, you're in a fine mood today," said Becca, and then was silent till dinner.

QUILCA AND DUBLIN
1726–1728

The carriage swayed back and forth in a steady rhythm that was almost soothing—until it jarred violently to one side, and Esther was thrown against the wall. Becca's hand was on her arm at once, steadying her; Esther pulled away. When she looked up, Becca had turned and was staring out the carriage window as if the approach to Quilca were the most interesting vista in Ireland. Esther sighcd. Once, Becca's touch had been a commonplace in her life. In recent years awkward moments like this seemed to crop up every time Becca offered a soft word or a caress. When Esther was feeling stronger, she sometimes worried about it and wondered if things could be put right. Just now she hadn't the energy to care.

"Here we are, then," Reverend Worrall announced a quarter of an hour later, as the carriage came to à halt. He opened the door for the ladies—Esther, Becca, and his wife, Mary—and began helping them down.

Mrs. Worrall rolled her eyes. "You can tell by his tone 'tis his first visit to Quilca—how eagerly he anticipates it!"

"That's right," Becca said. "He'll be singing a different tune before long, when the fireplace in his bedroom begins to smoke and the roof starts leaking."

"Now now, my friends—is this the greeting I get when I bring you all to my humble home?" scolded Tom Sheridan, who was bouncing down the drive, rubbing his hands and grinning. "I had enough of that last year with Dean Swift—I thought with him safely off the scene, my other guests might be less critical of the lodgings."

"Don't mind the ladies at all, Dr. Sheridan. We're more than grateful for your hospitality," said Reverend Worrall. "Reach down that case, would you, Rob—there's a good lad. Now, can you carry Mrs. Johnson's trunk as well, or will you come back for that?"

As the servants bundled their baggage toward the house, Esther stood apart from her friends and their jests. Her legs trembled beneath her; she wondered if she would be able to walk into the house. The cheerful, laughing voices swirled around her.

She looked up at the great bulk of Quilca, elegant but decaying, like an old lady tricked out in her best dress. *Not unlike me,* Esther thought, but did not share the jest with the others.

Then Tom Sheridan was at her side, offering his arm, which she leaned on heavily. "And how is our invalid? Come now, we have your room all ready, and I assure you 'tis not the one with the smoking fireplace or the one with the leak in the roof. And I've had the shutters repaired. You shall be as comfortable as if you were at Wood Park."

She had been at Wood Park for a while, and before that they had been staying in the deanery in Dublin while Swift was in England. She and Becca had not kept their own lodgings for nearly two years—they and their small household stayed with one friend after another, in Dublin and in the country. Last year they had spent six months—all the spring and summer—here at Quilca, when she had been in better health and had enjoyed riding every day, and entertaining a stream of visitors, and teasing Tom about the poor repair of his house. Now she was back at Quilca as an invalid.

As if to underscore the point, her knees buckled under her as they reached the broad steps. She slipped from Tom's grasp, but Patrick Delany—dear Patrick—was waiting for them on the steps and he rushed forward to gather her in his arms. And so she was carried into Quilca just like one of the trunks, only rather more tenderly, she thought, for Dr. Delany bore her over the threshold like a bridegroom. *He would have liked that,* she thought—she had known for a long time that he was very fond of her. *What a pity I didn't meet him when I was younger ... a sensible, kindly man ... we might have been married, perhaps had children.* No, she had never wanted children, had she? What odd thoughts she had these days! Anyway she had had too much trouble because of love, because of people falling in love. Thank goodness Dr. Delany was a sensible man. No tears and weeping for him, no dying for love—he simply carried her, firmly and confidently, up the great curving staircase with half its railings missing or broken, down the damp-smelling gallery and into the Blue Chamber where she was to stay. Jane had gone ahead of them and turned down her bedclothes and put a warming pan between the sheets, even though it was a fine April day.

She told everyone she would come down for dinner, but in the end she felt too ill, and Jane brought it up on a tray. "Mrs. Dingley says she's coming up, ma'am, to see if you've eaten. She says you must drink the soup anyway—Mrs. Sally made it, not Dr. Sheridan's cook—and she expects to see the bowl empty when she comes."

Esther managed a smile. All her friends scolded her about how little she ate, but when she sat up at dinner and took four bites out of a meat pie she felt she had accomplished wonders. The food sat in her stomach like a stone, and she suffered indigestion for hours afterwards. Mrs. Sally's soup would go down a little more easily, but even then she could never think of drinking a whole bowl. Jonathan was forever scolding her to eat more; Becca was just as bad, but they could not understand what a trial it was to eat at all.

She drank a few spoonfuls of soup and then slept; when she awoke it was not Becca beside her bed but Mary Worrall. "How are you feeling, my dear?"

Esther shook her head; she could find no words. "Never mind," said Mary, clearing away the tray of untouched food. "A few days in the country will have you feeling well again."

All her friends put a touching faith in country air, bundling her off to Quilca or to Wood Park as soon as her coughing fits overcame her and she took to her bed. She did enjoy being in the country, but the trouble was that once she got there she had to act a good deal better than she felt for at least a few weeks, to justify all the trouble everyone had taken to get her there.

This time she couldn't manage it. Each morning she awoke full of good intentions: this day she would get up, walk a little, play cards, go down to dinner. But the hours slipped by, and she drifted in and out of sleep and coughed up flecks of blood, and when she did swing her legs over the edge of the bed, they would not bear her weight. When Tom Sheridan came to sit by her one afternoon he said in his usual jaunty tone, "Now, Mrs. Johnson, do you wish to lie abed all day again today? There's talk of taking a picnic in the wilderness, and since nothing could be gloomier than dining in my hall, I'm highly in favour—but I wish you might join us."

Esther pulled in a deep lungful of breath; it seemed to take a long time. "I'm sorry, dear Tom, I can't. I want to be outdoors, to be with you all—but I can't."

His merriness dropped like a mask; he reached for her hand. "Poor dear girl, do forgive me. You've nothing to be sorry for. I keep thinking of last summer—how we rode and played and read out Dean Swift's book as you copied his final draft for him. I suppose I'm wishing it could all be like that again. When he writes to me, I know that's the picture he has in his mind—none of us have dared tell him how ill you are. I suppose we haven't dared tell ourselves, even. We must stop pretending, stop urging you to do things you cannot, and simply let you rest and get well."

Rest. That sounded wonderful, though she was less sure about the getting well part. He had to say that of course—he couldn't very well say, We must just let you rest until you die. Though that sounded appealing too. "I wish I could go out," she said.

"Could you sit up for a little? I can have a comfortable chair—a settee, even—moved out onto the balcony outside this room, and you could be carried out there. I'll sit with you awhile, and we'll gossip about the others, and they'll never know."

So Rob came, and moved a settee outside and carried Esther herself out to it. Rob lifted her even more gently than Dr. Delany had, because he had carried her about so much these last few years and knew just where and how she ached. He set her down and arranged her pillows and touched his cap when she said, "Thank you so much, Rob." Then Tom Sheridan sat by her side in the spring sunshine and gossiped, as he had promised, about all their friends. She didn't have to talk much, just listen and smile, and enjoy the sun on her face. She hoped Becca, who disapproved of fresh air for invalids, would not come up. But she wouldn't. Becca seldom intruded on Esther's privacy, these days. Esther knew she ought to be relieved.

"My wife writes that she is coming next week," he said, "so we will all have to suspend our frolics, and I will have to give up flirting with Mrs. Worrall and act very sober and sensible till Elizabeth tires of the country and heads back to town—about two days, I should think."

Esther managed a chuckle at that. Nobody liked Tom's wife, including Tom himself. He would never have got back his family's estate at Quilca if he had not married the girl whose family bought it, and dilapidated as it was, Tom loved Quilca. But apart from Quilca, the marriage had brought him nothing but trouble. They lived mostly apart.

"Poor Tom, you are not very happily wed, are you?" she said suddenly. It was a very blunt question, but she didn't feel embarrassed about it.

He shook his head. "Is anyone? I see very few happily married couples. I think you were wise, Mrs. Johnson, to avoid the married state."

"But I didn't, not entirely." The words surprised even her, this time. She knew her sudden willingness to speak plainly had something to do with her illness, with her fear that she might not have many more afternoons to sit in the sunshine with a friend, but she had not planned to be this frank. Tom was in the act of passing her coffee to her: she saw his fingers freeze around the cup for a moment.

"I beg your pardon? I didn't know you had ever been married."

"I was married in 1716, in the bishop's garden at Clogher, by St. George Ashe, poor man. Did you know him, before he died? A good man—he didn't want to perform that ceremony." She stopped, out of breath; a cough ripped across her chest. "Becca was the only witness, and she didn't want to be there either. Only one witness … I don't think that was legal, was it? And for … other reasons, I don't know if it was really a marriage. You wouldn't call it a marriage, would you? I have never thought of myself as a married woman."

Tom's brow wrinkled; his eyes darted about nervously. *He thinks I'm in a fever, that I'm raving,* she realized. Perhaps she was. But what a relief, to speak the truth after ten years' silence!

"Are you saying … Do you mean you and—"

"Dean Swift? Yes, of course. We were married—it was a great secret, of course. We never wanted to live as man and wife. It was only …" *What* exactly was it? She searched for words, and fell silent.

"And he has never owned it? What a fool!" Sheridan had shot straight from incredulity to indignation without pause for reflection. "When he might have had a woman like you, by his side all these years—"

"No, that was not … It wasn't meant to be that way," she protested, but Tom was working himself up to a fever pitch now. He was a great romantic, in his own silly way, and now that all the years of rumours he'd heard about Mrs. Johnson and Dean Swift were confirmed, he was ready to mount his white charger and ride into the lists as her champion. How she had been wronged! Surely if she pressed him, Dean Swift would acknowledge her before the world—did he not owe her this much? And on he went, till Esther felt quite sorry for telling him.

He'll have himself believing I'm dying of a broken heart next, she thought, *instead of consumption and rotten lungs and a lifetime of complaints. Which is what I am dying of.* And then that thought, *I am dying,* struck her so with its simplicity and clarity that she stopped listening to Tom altogether, or thinking about the old, foolish secret she had told him.

But she didn't die. Summer at Quilca came, and Esther felt not much better, but she made an effort to sit in the sunshine every day for a while. Don Carlos came for a visit and brought a wheeled chair for her, and wheeled her about the terrace in it. When he left, Patrick Delany took over the task of pushing her chair. August was a brilliant, gleaming month, and one day Tom Sheridan wheeled her down to the spot in the garden where she had spent so many hours the summer before—the spot they had taken to calling "Stella's Bower." They all called her Stella in jest now, the name Swift used in his poems for her. She had not sat in her bower in almost a year; it was pleasant to be there again under the boughs of cherry, though the blossoms were gone.

"Have you had a letter from our friend the dean lately?" he asked.

"Several; Becca has been reading them to me. Have you?"

"Yes, I wrote him when you were at your worst, and told him how ill you were. He is much distressed—I have seen other letters, ones he has written to Worrall and to other friends, Jim Stoppard, Charles Ford. See what he wrote here?"

The familiar handwriting danced on the page before her tired eyes; she had done hardly any reading this summer, though others often read to her. Swift had written expecting that the next news he heard would be of her death: he worried that even as he wrote "the fairest Soul in the World hath left its Body." She smiled.

"The dean is always given to flights of affection when he thinks he may lose me," she said. "We are very old friends."

"More than that, Mrs. Johnson, surely more than that! He loves you so—can you not see it? Why else would he write this? Surely, now that you are feeling better again, surely when he comes back to Ireland he will do the honourable thing at last? How could he refuse you, after what he has written here?"

"Dear Tom—" No, it was pointless to try to explain. He had got it in his head that she was pining away with love for Swift, that she would never be happy till he acknowledged her as his wife, and the truth was simply too different, too complicated, to explain. She had long since given up trying to explain it to herself or even thinking about the whole business of the marriage. It was a mistake to have confided in Tom, but if he wanted to weave a garment of romantic fantasies, she could hardly stop him. "Has he any news about the book?" she asked, hoping to divert him.

"Ah yes, the book! It looks as though it will be published in London, by Mr. Motte, under the title *Gulliver's Travels*. What a flurry it will create in London when it gets into the booksellers' stalls!"

"I imagine it will!" Esther closed her eyes and thought again of last summer, when the drafts and copies of Swift's story had filled a good part of every day, and they had sat by the hour discussing his corrections and additions. She was amazed she'd had the energy—even remembering it now exhausted her.

Swift himself came back the following month—back in triumph from London, for once in his long career. "I am so glad to see you," he said when he came up to her chamber. She was sitting up in a chair and had intended to come down into the hall to welcome him, but was too tired.

"And I to see you," she said. "Congratulations—about the book. It is a wonderful book, and I am very happy for you. When will it be printed?"

"Before Christmas, they tell me. But, darling poppet, saucy little rogue, all the books in the world would have been small comfort if we had lost you. They wrote me that you were so ill!" He pulled her to her feet and put an arm round her waist; she felt his little start of surprise at realizing how thin she was.

"I was ill—very ill. I feel a little better now. And where is my gold watch?" He had written when she was at her very sickest—when no one expected her to recover—to tell her he had bought her a gold watch in London. Now he pulled it from his waistcoat pocket and led her to the window, his arm still about her waist, as he set and wound it for her.

"And where is Bec? Where's my other naughty slut?" he called out a moment later, and Esther looked up to see Tom Sheridan in the doorway, hesitating to interrupt what he no doubt thought was a tender lovers' reunion.

"I've not seen her all day," Esther admitted. Becca still oversaw every detail of Esther's care yet avoided spending much time with her. Now that Swift was back, she would no doubt be less in evidence than ever.

They were back in Dublin for Christmas, staying with Lady Eustace. In the short winter afternoons, Esther took to her bed for a few hours—that way she was strong enough to get up for dinner. When it came time to dress for dinner, Jenny would come to her room to comb out her hair and help her into her clothes. Esther was proud of Jenny. The thin, frightened child she had pulled from the horrors of the Dublin workhouse was now a polished young girl who gloried in being Lady Eustace's personal maid and was looking forward to making her first visit to England with her mistress. "Are you sure Lady Eustace doesn't need you this evening, Jenny?" she asked the first time the girl came to help her dress.

"No, ma'am, she's got Fanny helping her. She told me, ma'am, Lady Eustace told me that as long as you was here, I was to help you, any afternoon you felt like coming down to dinner. And I'm glad she did, ma'am, for 'tis a pleasure for me, truly it is, to do any little thing for you. Anything at all, Mrs. Johnson, ma'am." Jenny had a deft hand with a comb and pins, and she was able to arrange Esther's thin, dry hair into an acceptable coiffure. After dinner, she might come up to brush out Esther's hair and get her ready for bed. Otherwise, Esther called for her own maid, Jane, or shifted for herself. She no longer went to Becca's chamber to have her hair brushed. She missed that long, slow intimacy at day's end, the pull of the brush through her hair while they unravelled all the day's events, but it was for the best.

Lady Eustace put on a grand Christmas dinner, roast goose stuffed with boiled eggs and sweet apples, hares cooled in port wine, stuffed with chopped herbs and cinnamon, beef and chicken pasties. Esther picked at a few mouthfuls of goose and tasted the pasties. Under the currents of talk and laughter she saw people glancing at her plate—Jonathan, Becca, Patrick Delany, Lady Eustace—all looking to see how much she had eaten. Even to please them she could not force down more than a few bites. She was not coughing as much these days, but her head pounded and she had trouble breathing whenever she was in company.

The same party—all Esther's best friends—assembled at the deanery for New Year's with Dean Swift. He made them all exchange names and write a poem for the person whose name they drew. Esther got Tom Sheridan's name: it was a shame, since he deserved a really good poem, and she could manage only four lines. She got Jonathan to read them out for her: she wasn't up to reading aloud. Dr. Delany had written a very nice poem for her, four or five verses and really quite sweet as well as funny, but once she had smiled and said how lovely it was, she shut her eyes and let the voices drift by her. Swift, Sheridan, and Delany were challenging one another to a battle of riddles, but she couldn't follow them—the jests were flying by so quickly. Becca bent over her chair. "Do you want to go home early?" she said softly, and Esther nodded, relieved.

Bryan was with them for the holidays. At eleven he was even more awkward and silent than he had been when younger; he was comfortable with no one but Esther. He sat in her room for hours in the afternoon; he made attempts at reading to her, but his reading was so halting and slow that they were both relieved when he stopped. Swift had spoken to her about Bryan. "John Walls tells me there's little point in his continuing beyond this year," he said. As far as their old friend Archdeacon Walls, the master of St. Patrick's school, knew, Bryan M'Loghlin was Mrs. Johnson's foster child, an Irish bastard with an English father. That was the fiction commonly put forward to explain his being given an education. Dublin gossip had its own explanation, of course, and looking now at the boy sitting slumped in her armchair, playing with a carved spinning top, Esther wished gossip were right. If she were Bryan's mother instead of his benefactor, she could ... Well, what could she do? Make him cleverer, happier, more at ease with himself? She could do none of those things; she could not even live to see him grow up.

"What can be done for him?" she had asked Swift when he told her the schoolmaster's verdict.

"He will have to be bound apprentice to a trade, of course. It is the best he can look for." As always, Swift spoke as if he knew no more about the boy's parentage than Archdeacon Walls did.

She would have to leave Bryan a legacy so that he would be cared for if ... if she wasn't able to care for him herself. She had to make a will. Everyone hinted at it, though no one would say so. She had little to leave—something for Bryan, and something for her mother and sister back in England. She hadn't seen them these twenty years, but family was family, and poor Anne had had nineteen children, though only twelve or thirteen were alive, she thought. And charity. She would leave the rest to someone who would do some good—not the workhouse, she thought with a shudder. Perhaps Dr. Steevens's hospital. She had always approved of that, and Swift was a trustee on the board. Her thoughts drifted again; she was half asleep when Jenny tapped on the door. "Please, ma'am, 'tis time to get ready if you're going out to Donnybrook."

It was Twelfth Night, and they were invited to Donnybrook to celebrate with the Stoytes. Esther was too weary, really, to go, but she knew how disappointed they would all be if she stayed at home. For her friends, she really had to make the effort. She shuffled up to a sitting position and reached out a hand. Jenny stepped forward to help her, but Bryan got there first, steadying her hand and pulling a little too hard as she got to her feet.

At Donnybrook there was music and even dancing after dinner, though all the guests protested that they were too old, that dancing was only for the young. Esther watched as Tom Sheridan coaxed Becca out of her seat and made her take her place opposite him in the line. Catherine was at the spinet; the music began and the couples started moving through the set. Jonathan sat beside Esther, his hand on the arm of her chair. "What a splendid party," he said.

"It has been a lovely Christmas-tide," she said. "Everyone has been so kind."

"We all wanted to make it happy for you," he said. Then, after a tiny pause, he added, "Because you have been so ill all year, and you deserve some good cheer."

"Yes," Esther said. *And because you all think it will be my last.* She did not say this aloud, though. She did not want to make him lie.

❧

"Happy Birthday!" cried Becca, coming into her room with the morning post.

Her birthday. She was forty-six today, and it was one of those mornings when she felt twice that. Three months had passed since the Christmas festivities. She had felt weak and tired then—now she would gladly have gone back to Christmas-tide. At least then she had not felt really ill, had not been coughing as much, had been able to get out of bed a few hours every day. Now she was back to where she had been last summer—and with her increasing illness, her spirits ebbed, till she felt quite melancholy and spleenatick.

"Have we any letters?" she asked.

"*You* have a bundle of them, all birthday greetings from friends. Here's some silly nonsense from Tom Sheridan—I can't read that till I've got my spectacles on. Oh, and a note from Dr. Delany"— Becca liked Delany, and smiled warmly over his epistle—"I'll read that one later, and of course the dean has not forgotten you." She pursed her lips and frowned. "Another birthday poem, no doubt. I wonder what dreadful comparison he's come up with this time?"

"Can't be worse … than the year he likened me to—" Esther stopped to cough.

"To an old bottle of wine dug up out of the cellar? I should think not! He's not spared himself this time, anyway. Two—no, three—letters from him. Will I read those first?"

"No—Dr. Delany's first. I need good wishes … more than wit."

When Dr. Delany's kindly letter was read, and Sheridan's funny verses, and a few other letters from friends, Becca started on the first of Swift's offerings. "What nonsense is this! *The high and mighty prince EGROEGO born to the most puissant empire of the East, unto STELLA, the most resplendent glory of the Western hemisphere, sendeth health and happiness …*"

"The prince of Lilliput," Esther said, smiling. "You remember— from his book?"

"Of course I remember!" It would have been hard to forget *Gulliver's Travels* even if they had not lived with the manuscript for years: all Dublin was talking of it, and Dublin talk was only a faint echo of the clamour in London. For once, Swift's reputation had caught up with and even outpaced his ambitions. Even Becca admitted liking it, "though I still don't like all that about the Yahoos. 'Tis disgusting, if you ask me." Though nobody had, at any point, asked her.

She read on through the Lilliputian letter, a plea for "Stella" to find Gulliver and bring him back to Lilliput, and an invitation to accompany him "because as we hear you are not so well as we could wish." In Lilliput, the prince assured her, *"by the salubrity of our finer air and diet, you will soon recover your health and stomach."* She and Becca were both laughing when the letter was done.

The next was a poem: "A Receipt to Restore Stella's Youth." "This is all about cows!" Becca said after the first dozen lines or so.

It hurt to laugh, but Esther couldn't help it. "You said yourself"—she coughed—"that nothing could be worse than being compared to an old bottle of wine!"

> *Why, Stella, should you knit your brow*
> *If I compare you to the cow?*
> *'Tis just the case: for you have fasted*
> *So long till all your flesh is wasted*
> *And must against the warmer days*
> *Be sent to Quilca down to graze*
> *Where mirth, and exercise, and air*
> *Will soon your appetite repair.*

"Well, there's sense in that as well as the other one, for all they're more than half nonsense," Becca said. "Dr. Sheridan wants us to come back down to Quilca, and though I'm not so very fond of the country at this time of year, I agree with the dean—it would do you good."

You needn't come with me, Esther was about to say. But she couldn't. So much of what had been between her and Becca—the long years of friendship, the perfect trust—was marred. But that final break—going their separate ways—Esther found she could not propose that. Not now.

Not now. She wondered if Jonathan and Becca and Tom and all her other friends still truly believed that fresh air and good food would make her well again. Could they be so blind? She and Becca had taken advantage of Lady Eustace's kindness for a long time now: did she have the strength for another journey to Quilca? Or perhaps she would write Charles Ford and see if they might go to Wood Park—it was so much more comfortable.

"There's still another poem from the dean," Becca was saying.

"That will be the birthday poem." He had even written a birthday poem for Becca this year, which had made her a little less antagonistic toward him since it contained quite a lot of nice lines about her beloved dog, Tiger, as well as a few kind ones about herself:

> *Then, who says care will kill a cat?*
> *Rebecca shows they're out in that*
> *For she, though overrun with care*
> *Continues healthy, fat, and fair.*

Now Becca unfolded the third paper with a gusty sigh and read,

This day, whate'er the fates decree,
Shall still be kept with joy by me:
This day then, let us not be told,
That you are sick, and I grown old—

"Becca?"

"Yes?"

"Leave that one … for me to read."

"Now, you know your poor eyes can't—"

"No, Bec, I can manage this. Fetch my spectacles, and you go write to Tom, and thank him for his poem, and tell him we'd like to come to Quilca. Do, please."

When Becca was gone and her spectacles laid on the quilt, Esther picked up the poem again. *From not the gravest of divines, / Accept for once some serious lines.* He had not written her many serious lines over the years, but these were serious enough, and they answered her question. For all his talk of country air and good food and grazing cows, Jonathan knew the truth as well as she did. And here in her birthday poem, if nowhere else, he could admit it.

Although we now can form no more
Long schemes of life, as heretofore:
Yet you, while time is running fast
Can look with joy on what is past …
Say Stella, feel you no content
Reflecting on a life well spent?
Your skilful hand employed to save
Despairing wretches from the grave;
And then supporting with your store
Those whom you dragged from death before …

Truly, she couldn't think of anyone she had actually dragged from the grave—well, perhaps poor little Jenny, years ago; surely she would have died if she'd been left in the workhouse. But she didn't mind him exaggerating her virtues, or praising

> Your generous boldness to defend
> An innocent and absent friend
> That courage which can make you just
> To merit humbled in the dust.

And on it went, praising the life she had lived.

> O then, whatever heaven intends,
> Take pity on your pitying friends
> Nor let your ills affect your mind,
> To fancy they can be unkind.
> Me, surely me, you ought to spare
> Who gladly would your sufferings share
> Or give my scrap of life for you
> And think it far beneath your due
> You, to whose care so oft I owe
> That I'm alive to tell you so.

Had she let her ills affect her mind? Was she underestimating how much her friends loved and cared? No—it was they who didn't understand, who didn't see what an effort it was for her to be kind and cheerful to them, when she felt so much pain. She found she was crying—not because of Swift's kind words, which were sweet and thoughtful enough, but because here, at last, he had dropped the pretense and admitted what they both knew. Like the merry Twelfth Night celebration, like the New Year's party and the Christmas feast, this was an ending. He did not expect to write her any more birthday poems.

⁂

Summertime at Quilca, again. This summer she seldom got outside her chamber at all, nor did she make the effort to come down to dinner. Becca came up with trays for her—soups and jellies, invalids' food—and spooned into her mouth whatever Esther would allow. She could seldom keep it down. Mary Worrall was at Quilca with them this summer; she gave orders to the servants and bustled about the sickroom, but it was Becca who sat beside Esther and wiped her face with cool water after she vomited, Becca who cut off her hair when she complained that her head ached because her hair was so heavy, and the pins drove into her scalp. One afternoon she opened her eyes to see Becca by the window, patiently stitching away. How many pieces of needlework must she have produced over the years? All ladies did a great deal of fancywork, but Becca's output was prodigious. This chamber now contained all the furnishings she and Becca had left from their own household, and nearly every object— chairs, cushions, firescreens, pincushions—was covered with Becca's neat stitching. *She has stitched my life together,* thought Esther. There was something—not that, but something sensible—that she had to say to Becca, but when she opened her mouth to speak, she coughed instead, a great tearing cough, and Becca came over to wipe her lips, and she found she hadn't breath enough left to speak. And she couldn't remember what it was, anyway.

So many good friends were there—the Worralls, Dr. Delany, Becca, and of course Tom Sheridan. And letters came every day from other friends—from their Dublin circle, and from Charles

Ford and Swift, who were both back in England again. One night
when she was feeling well, everyone in the house gathered up in
her room and Tom read some verses he had written about her
illness, funny yet sad, and they decided to send them off to Swift.
They headed it, "The Humble Petition of Stella's Friends" and all
signed it. She understood that they wanted him to come back, to
be at her deathbed. She wasn't sure if that was what she wanted,
but he did not come. His letters said he was sick too, far away in
London.

Her servants were still with her, Mrs. Sally still elbowing her
way through Sheridan's kitchen staff—no better than savages, she
said—to make soup and cream and jelly for her. Rob came up to
light her fire once the evenings began to get cooler. She saw with
surprise that his hair was turning grey. He must have been close
to her own age—he had worked for her twenty years. His nephew
Kevin was working here in the stables at Quilca—another foster
child she might feel easy about. "Thank you kindly, Rob," she said
each night as he left her room. Once, when she was almost asleep,
she saw him pause in the doorway and look back at her.

Some days her mind was clearer than others. One day when
the weather was cooler and her head did not ache too much, she
asked Sheridan to write for a lawyer to come. "You wish to make
your will?" Tom said, and she nodded.

The lawyer came from Dublin the next day. There was so little,
really, to leave, and she had decided long ago how it should all be
spent. Family, and charity. And she must leave something for
Bryan. "Write that I want to leave twenty-five pounds to Bryan
M'Loghlin," she told the lawyer. "Put down that he is a child who
lives with me, whom I keep on charity. And that I leave him
twenty-five pounds to bind him out apprentice, as my executors
think fit."

"*Twenty-five* pounds, madam?" the lawyer said, his pencil-thin eyebrows lifting a little. "That is very generous for a charity child—one can apprentice a boy in Dublin for less than five pounds. Are you quite sure?"

Bryan's face hovered before her momentarily: he was still at school, but that could not go on for long. She wanted to see him again but didn't know if she would. He had so little—no mother except herself, no father who would help or acknowledge him, no name, no skill or wit or talent to help him rise above his unfortunate lot. And now she would have to leave him. "Twenty-five pounds," she repeated.

Instructions about her monument, a few other bequests. The few furnishings remaining, her books, plate, and a little jewellery—all that could be sold. Becca would have her own share of the household things—they had decided that long ago—and surely she would not want to bother with all Esther's belongings. But what of her strongbox, with her letters and her journal? What would Becca do with that? There was money in there too, in gold. Best not to leave money to Becca—she was so foolish about it. Jonathan would see she was cared for—Esther decided on twenty guineas and the gold watch and chain for Becca. A little gift of remembrance, no more. Let her play with her dogs and do her needlework and not worry about money or papers. Poor Tiger had died, but Becca had a new puppy. She remembered a puppy Becca once had—was it at Moor Park?—with a bright orange ribbon around its neck. Yes, in those days they had all decked their dogs out in orange ribbons, for the king, William of Orange. Who was king now? Some German man, she thought. The lawyer cleared his throat gently.

"To Jonathan Swift, dean of St. Patrick's, I wish to leave my strongbox with all my papers and the money it contains." He would understand about the money—use it to help Becca, or Bryan, as they should need it.

"The will is complete—it wants but your signature, ma'am," said the lawyer, passing her the paper.

The pen trembled in her hands. She wrote "Esther Johnson," and then, underneath it, she paused a moment before writing "Spinster." One didn't necessarily need to state one's marital status on a will, though people often did. But it was her last testament, her last written word. Jonathan would no doubt see it, and read it, as would many others. She underlined the word boldly, for all the gossips who'd chattered about her secret marriage all these years, and for the few who knew the truth. Esther Johnson had lived and died a maid, and it would say so in her will, in her own hand. She took pleasure in writing it.

She handed the will back to the lawyer. She almost never held a pen these days, perhaps never would again. Earlier in the year she had tried to take up her journal again, but she wrote only prayers in it—everything else seemed a waste of her failing strength. Now she only whispered her prayers. God would understand.

What of Jonathan—would he understand? Her writing was done now, but everything she had written in her life—her poems, her letters, her journal—were left in his keeping, with this will. So many things in there might shock or hurt him. Poor Hester Vanhomrigh, when she died, had left orders for all her correspondence with Swift to be published. How angry he had been! No, Esther would not do that. He could go through it, cross out the passages that might show him in a bad light. But he could keep the rest—her poems, her observations, her life in that heap of paper. She wanted something to last after she was gone—some record that Esther Johnson had been here, had seen the world and lived in it. The birthday poem had been right—she had not lived a bad life. She had made mistakes. She couldn't recall, now, quite what they were.

⚶

The lawyer was gone; the doctor was there. "Are you in much pain, Mrs. Johnson?" If only he knew how much. He gave her draughts of physick, and Becca made her swallow them, but they barely dulled the edge. She nodded, and coughed, bringing up blood and phlegm.

He took another bottle out. "This is stronger. It may help."

It tasted worse than the other, but Becca said, "You must drink it. You must, Hetty, it will help the pain." Becca looked dreadful—her face was all tired and worn. She always looked so calm and placid, but now something was worrying her. To make her happy, Esther drank the physick. It must have helped, because she slept.

⚶

Jonathan was there. She didn't know when he had arrived, but he had been sitting by her bed for what seemed a long time now. "It grows very cold, and this house is so draughty," he was saying, but not to her. "Do you think she can stand to be moved?"

"Where? Back to Dublin?" That was Becca's voice, wasn't it? Why were they speaking so quietly? She wanted to tell them to speak up. "We thought we might go to the deanery again, while you were in London."

"No—not the deanery." His voice was sharp, and with one of those sudden lightning shafts of clarity Esther thought, *No— what a scandal, if Mrs. Johnson were to die in the deanery!* "Perhaps Lady Eustace—"

There was a long ride, in a swaying carriage. Becca sat beside her and held her hand and told her it wouldn't be long now. A lie. But finally she was in another bedchamber. This one was warmer. A fire burned. A boy with fair hair and large pale eyes came to her bedside but would not look her in the face. She reached for his arm, eager to touch him, although she couldn't recall his name. "I came home for Christmas," he said.

Christmas. So it was Christmas again. No feasting, no dancing, no music. Yet it was one more Christmas. That was something.

Morning, and Jonathan Swift was at her bedside. He spoke in a low, steady voice, but no one was answering him. Slowly it dawned on her that he was praying. She had heard him preach a thousand times but never heard him pray outside the pulpit.

"Pity us, the mournful friends of thy distressed servant, who sink under the weight of her present condition, and the fear of losing the most valuable of our friends: restore her to us, O Lord, if it be thy gracious will, or inspire us with constancy and resignation to support ourselves under so heavy an affliction—"

His voice broke for a moment: she reached out toward his hands, knotted on her quilt, and put her own on top of them. I *ought to pray too,* she thought. Not for recovery; she knew by now that was not God's gracious will and she knew that it was not hers either. Having come so far along this road, she could not now go back, retrace her steps and do this all over again in a few more years. She had fought through and won almost all the way—to what? To heaven, of course, though she found it hard to imagine. But there would be rest, and beauty—she pictured heaven a little like Moor Park. Hadn't she been in heaven once? No, that was in the church in Laracor—but heaven had been there, she was sure. She ought to have stayed longer.

No strength left now to compose prayers like this one Jonathan was reciting. She would simply have to trust in God's goodness—she had always believed he was good, and merciful. She remembered one prayer—the shortest she could recall from her reading of Scripture. *God be merciful to me a sinner.* That would have to suffice.

The prayer was over. The door opened and closed: someone had gone out. Becca? She had to see Becca, had to say something to her. But it was Jonathan here now, he alone. Esther tried to wrap her mouth around words. "Thank you—for praying."

He looked surprised to hear her speak; he looked wretched, in fact. "Oh Esther, you are going to leave me, and I cannot bear it. All the rest of my life—"

She shook her head, not sure herself what she meant by it. "I always thought I would go first," he went on. "I never imagined having to live without you—I am so … so very grateful. For everything."

"Yes. So am I." Although there were a great many things in their shared past that she wasn't at all grateful for. But on balance, yes. She thought about that word, *love,* the word with no meaning. She ought to have spent less time puzzling out its meanings, trying to sort and arrange it, being afraid of it, stepping back from the water's edge. She had walked carefully and enjoyed the journey, but perhaps she ought to have got her feet wet more often.

Passionate love, violent love, friendly love, unnatural love— what was the difference? That was what she ought to have told Becca, what she ought to tell Swift now. That it didn't matter. She ought to have just taken it, accepted love without finding a name or place for it. It would not have mattered. She had been loved deeply in her life and she was grateful. That was all.

"The ... our marriage," he said, a word that rang oddly harsh. She wondered what he meant, then remembered. An afternoon in a garden. Everyone had been hot, uncomfortable, furtive. Something to be hidden. Another attempt to find a name for love. "I would be glad to ... I mean, years ago, I should have ... what I mean to say is, I will make it public, if you wish it."

She used to laugh a lot, once, and although she couldn't laugh now, she could feel the urge, the thing inside that made her laugh, swelling up. She lifted her fingers and laid them on his lips. "Too late—too late for all that now." She shook her head again. She had to tell him—it was important—what? About the strongbox? About Bryan? No—something in the box. Her papers. Her poems and journals. But he would understand. He would know how important they were, for words were his life, as they had been hers. He would know what to do. Was there anything else?

"Tell ... tell Becca to come in. I want to see her—alone."

But when Jonathan went out, and a little while later, Becca came in, Esther had no words left. Only, she found, she didn't need any. Not with Becca. Esther slipped into sleep, and out again. They held each other's hands, and the light from the window changed, grew dusky. Then it brightened again, but the glow seemed at a distance. Everything was growing dim, slipping away, but Becca's hand was there, the one warm, real thing. Esther opened her eyes, trying to see her friend's face once more. She could not quite see, but she could feel Becca's hand. How long had she been sitting here—hours or days? And she would not let go, would never let go. Esther tightened her fingers in

Becca's for a moment, and closed her eyes again. Firelight whispered in the corner of the room.

DUBLIN
JANUARY 28–29, 1728

In a dim room of the deanery of St. Patrick's Cathedral, a strongbox lies open on the floor. A flood of papers, envelopes, and bound notebooks spews from it onto the floorboards. One notebook has been lifted from the rest and laid on the desk next to a candle, an inkwell, and a pile of books. It lies open to the first page, headed "Moor Park, Surrey, England, December 28, 1694."

A man sits at the desk, staring at the book, running his hands through thinning grey-brown hair. His periwig hangs over the back of the chair; his waistcoat is unbuttoned and his feet stockinged. His visitors have gone and his servant has been dismissed; he is alone for the night.

He stands up, pacing the small room. He feels caged. He should feel weary, under the burden of his great sorrow, but instead he senses an enormous coiled energy inside, energy that can find no outlet. Each time he passes the window his eyes stray beyond the cathedral, over the rooftops north and west in the direction of Harbour Hill, toward a house he cannot see, though he can picture its every detail—the great hall, the staircase, the second-floor bedroom with the dusty wall hangings and the cloying scent of the sickroom: perfumes layered over piss and vomit. He visited two days ago, and read a prayer of his own composition over the dying woman. He was summoned earlier today but could not bear to go. He kept his usual routine, preaching at the cathedral in the morning, dining with friends, entertaining visitors in his room after supper. In the evening he was briefly interrupted by a servant delivering a note.

He wants to write something about the woman who has just died—an elegy, a tribute. Pulling a fresh piece of paper toward himself, he lays it on top of the notebook page and dips his pen. His hand hesitates a moment. The he begins to write.

This day, being Sunday, January 28, 1727–8, about eight o'clock at night, a servant brought me a note, with an account of the death of the truest, most virtuous and valuable friend that I, or perhaps any other person, was ever blessed with ...

The ink runs dry, and Jonathan Swift sets aside his own paper. He looks again at the journal that is open beneath it. The handwriting there, though not mature, is tidy, so much like his own that friends who receive letters from them both often remark on how alike their hands are. He knows this handwriting as well as his own; he would have said until tonight that he knew the mind of its writer as well as he knew his own mind.

An hour ago, when his guests had gone, a second messenger from Lady Eustace's house had knocked at his door. Swift's manservant answered, and came up to the dean's room bearing a strongbox. "It was Mrs. Johnson's, sir. Her man said she left it to you in her will, and Mrs. Dingley wanted it delivered straight away. They're having the funeral day after tomorrow, sir."

The strongbox is full of papers. Her papers—Esther Johnson's poetry, copies of the letters she wrote bundled with their replies, and volume after volume of bound journals, going back to her girlhood. The page now open on the desk before him is the first page of the first journal.

*Moor Park, Surrey, England, December 28, 1694. I sett my
pen to paper to write this Journal, which I intend to keep for
the Improvement of my Mind ...*

Jonathan Swift is consumed, suddenly, by the urge to find out
what legacy his closest friend has given him. Across town, she lies
dead, and he was not at her side because ... because he would not
have known what to say, or to do, because deathbeds make him
uncomfortable. A strange complaint for a priest, but perhaps he
is not much of a priest. Nor can he go to her funeral—he has
already decided that. She has many friends to mourn her
publicly. He will mourn privately, away from the hundreds of
Dublin eyes that have stared into every corner of their friendship
for twenty-five years. He will write something—yes, his own
version of her story, a tribute to her. Something appropriate.
Something the world can see and remember.

But first, he reads her words, voyaging into the journals, into
the past, into the dark uncharted waters of a woman's mind.

Outside, the first light of dawn sceps over the rooftops of Dublin.
Jonathan Swift closes Esther Johnson's journals at the year 1716.
His hand trembles.

She should never have put such words on paper.

Once before, he suffered because a woman had been indiscreet with the written word. Hessy Vanhomrigh—how she had
hated him before she died—left to her executors copies of all her
correspondence with Swift—her mad, impassioned pleadings,
his affectionate but cautious replies. But he had expected that
kind of venom from Hessy. She was crazed at the end, had been
crazed for years. Love ruined her, as it had a way of doing.

But not Esther Johnson. She was discreet; she was cautious; she was proper. He relied on Esther, his Stella, his guiding star, to spare him all that. As, indeed, she did. Even as he read through this heedless rush of words that forms her journal, he was confident there were some things she would never commit to paper. Things that would hurt both their reputations badly. She would know better.

He was wrong. She has been most indiscreet. His fingers move back over the pages of the journal for 1716 again. The garden at Clogher. The secret vow. The shameful night in the cottage at Laracor. She wrote it all down.

And she left these papers to him. Why?

One thing is certain. This terrible, shaming jumble of passion, pride, and piety will not be her legacy to the world. This is not how Esther Johnson will be remembered. Throughout the night he has alternated between her words and his own, writing his stately and impassive tribute for a few lines before being drawn back into the frightening female tangle of her thoughts and memories. Now he carefully lays his own sheet of paper atop her journal for 1716 and continues to write.

Never was any of her sex born with better gifts of the mind,
or who more improved them by reading and conversation …
I cannot call to mind that I ever once heard her make a
wrong judgment of persons, books, or affairs …

He can neither read nor write more now; the day's duties call him. And yet he finds himself unable to perform them. Another messenger comes from Lady Eustace's house. Mrs. Johnson's funeral is on the morrow. Can he attend? Will he pray, or read? Jonathan Swift sends a reply in the negative. He will not. He cannot. He sends his servant to refuse an invitation to dinner and retires to his room again in midafternoon.

The truth is, he cannot yet bear to go out into a world where she is absent—where her loss is commemorated and mourned—when she waits, alive and enticing, in his room. She is *there,* in the pages that enrage and disturb him. He cannot bear to let her go—not yet.

Night again. A candle burns on Jonathan Swift's desk. There are no more journals, no more letters, no more poems. Esther Johnson has been dead more than twenty-four hours. Her voice is silent.

The dean looks at the pages he has written, his own account of Esther Johnson's life. He adds a single line: *My head aches, and I can write no more.*

He sleeps poorly. The next day he keeps to his bed. Her funeral is at night; he stares out his window to the light in the cathedral. There, now, John Worrall is saying the ancient words over her body.

> *We brought nothing into this world, and it is certain we can carry nothing out. The Lord gave, and the Lord hath taken away; blessed be the Name of the Lord …*

He kindles a fire in the small grate, not calling his servant to tend it but lighting it himself. As the flames flicker to life, he sorts through the papers on his desk, pulling out the pages of his own writing. He moves these, with his paper and ink, down the hall to his bedchamber. A better room in which to finish writing, in due time, the definitive account of Esther Johnson's life. The bedroom window does not face the cathedral. Its desk and floor are not cluttered with the debris of her life. She had never, in life, set foot in this room.

Back in the study the fire is blazing. He sits surrounded by her writing, her words, her womanly weakness. She has given him her whole life in these pages. He knows what he must do.

Page after page, years of pages covered in the tidy handwriting of his old pupil. The handwriting so like his. He crumples the letters, tears the journal pages in handfuls from their bindings. Page after page, he feeds them to the flames till nothing is left but her strongbox, its key, and a hundred and fifty pounds in gold.

Afterword

When I finish reading a piece of historical fiction about a real person, I always turn to the back, hoping desperately that the author has been thoughtful enough to provide an afterword, explaining to me what is historical in the novel and what is fictional. In the case of the story of Esther Johnson, all the major events of her life are historically accurate, as are many of the minor details. Virtually all the characters are real people; we even know that the names of her servants in the final years of her life were Mrs. Sally, Jane, and Rob. The only purely fictional characters of any importance are Esther's first two foster children, Jenny and Kevin. I invented them because we know that she had a reputation for being a charitable woman who was very kind to the poor, and because I wished to set a precedent for her having foster children, to prepare for her taking into her home Bryan M'Loghlin—the one foster child we do know she kept, because he is mentioned in her will.

Naturally, the conversations, thoughts, and feelings of the characters are my own invention, though I have tried never to contradict what actually happened when the truth is known. What makes Esther's story so fascinating for a fiction writer is that there are so many unsolved mysteries. There are questions about both her parentage and Swift's: either or both may have been an illegitimate child of William Temple. There has been a long-standing tradition that Esther Johnson and Jonathan Swift were secretly married in 1716; many scholars think it unlikely that this marriage ever took place, largely because they find it hard to see how either party would have benefited from the secret marriage. Many people believe there was a sudden, though temporary, break in their friendship in 1723, just before Hester Vanhomrigh's death: the story of the letter Swift flung on Miss Vanhomrigh's table is another long-standing piece of the puzzle. But no one knows exactly what was in the letter: the text of the letter from Hester Vanhomrigh to Esther Johnson that appears in this novel is my own invention.

Whether Swift ever actually had sexual relations with either Esther Johnson or Hester Vanhomrigh is another puzzle. And Esther Johnson did have in her household at the time of her death a twelve-year-old foster child named Bryan M'Loghlin, to whom she left the unusually large legacy of twenty-five pounds. Gossip at the time was that he was the illegitimate son of Esther and Swift. He is believed to be the same boy who attended St. Patrick's School and whose similarity to Dean Swift was remarked upon. He lived only a few years after Esther's death.

If I were a historian, I would have to try, as many have before me, to piece through the thousands of pieces of evidence on all these puzzles and decide which is most likely to be true. As a novelist, I only have to decide which makes the best story, and in every case I have chosen an explanation that I think has some chance of being true, but that I mainly chose because it fits the story I am telling, and the Esther I have imagined.

It would be impossible to list all the books I have read in the process of preparing this novel, but I would like to acknowledge my debt to Irving Ehrenpreis's comprehensive three-volume biography of Swift, to Denis Johnson's *In Search of Swift*, and to Sybil LeBrocquoy, from whose books *Cadenus* and *Swift's Most Valuable Friend* I borrowed her conjecture about the parentage of Bryan M'Loghlin. Victoria Glendinning's biography *Jonathan Swift: A Portrait* had not yet been published when I originally wrote this book, but I found it very helpful in preparing the final draft.

All the letters and poems by Swift in the novel are authentic, except for the note and poem fragment addressed to Esther in Part One on pages 51 and 54, which I invented. The one change I have made to known history is that I have Swift writing *Gulliver's Travels* somewhat later than he actually did; evidence suggests the book was well under way by 1721, but since it was not published until 1726 I have felt it would not be too serious a misdemeanour to have him completing his first full draft in 1724, as that suits my plot better!

The two poems I have quoted by Esther Johnson are the only things still extant that she is believed to have written. Her journal is my own creation. We know that many women of the day kept diaries and journals: we know that Esther was a writer of poetry and, like most of her circle, a prolific letter writer. The erratic spelling I have used in her journal was typical for writers of her era, when spelling and capitalization were not standard-ized. Another contemporary usage I have retained is the use of "Mrs." for unmarried adult women, hence "Mrs. Johnson" and "Mrs. Dingley." Those familiar with the period will notice, however, that I have standardized the dates to modern usage rather than reproducing the Old Style/New Style system of dates used in England before 1752—properly, Esther's journal for her fourteenth birthday should be dated March 13, 1694/95, but to avoid confusion I have dated it simply March 13, 1695.

The final scene of the novel is, of course, my own invention. But we do know that Esther left all her papers to Swift, and the fact that nothing of hers has survived except two poems strongly suggests to me that Swift was concerned—for the sake of his reputation, and perhaps hers—to make sure her papers were never seen by anyone but himself.

ACKNOWLEDGMENTS

For starting me on the very long road that ends with the publication of this novel, I am thankful, first, to Dr. Ray Leadbetter who taught eighteenth-century literature at Andrews University, Berrien Springs, Michigan, in 1985, and to my fellow students in that class, particularly Sharon Fleshman. It was there that I first (reluctantly) read Swift and wrote the paper that planted the seed for this book.

I'm very grateful to the members of the Newfoundland Writers' Guild who listened as I workshopped various portions of this novel over the years and who cheered me on throughout both the writing and the publication process. The first chapter, the last chapter, and many pieces in between were first read at Guild workshops between 1996 and 1999, and the response helped keep me going. I won't attempt to single out Guild members by name since so many were so helpful, but outside the Guild another Newfoundland writer who deserves particular thanks is Joan Clark.

Much gratitude to the Nova Scotia Writers' Federation for awarding this manuscript the H. R. Percy Unpublished Novel award back in 2000; without that award I might not have had the courage to look for a publisher.

My wonderful agent, Leona Trainer, deserves my heartfelt gratitude for all her efforts on my behalf. The team at Penguin Group (Canada)—Barbara Berson, Tracy Bordian, and Eliza Marciniak—as well as Jennifer Glossop, Alison Reid, and especially Sue Sinclair, editor extraordinaire, have done so much to make this a better book.

Most of all, thanks are due to my family—my parents, Donald and Joan Morgan; my husband, Jason Cole; and my children, Christopher and Emma Cole—for not just tolerating the many hours I spend writing but for supporting and encouraging me. Without you, it would be impossible.